"Mr. Scott!" Picard said, his tone filled with as much authority as he could muster. "I *order* you to stop!"

"His communications system has shut down, Captain," Data said. "All power is being diverted to the warp drive and the shields. He did not hear your order."

"He didn't *want* to hear it," Riker snapped.

The Klingon ship was bulleting toward the Arhennius corona, once again accelerating despite the fact that it was already far exceeding its design specs. Picard half expected it to fly to pieces at any instant.

"Follow him," Guinan said, coming as close to shouting as he had ever heard her do. "If you ever trusted me, Captain, trust me now!"

Suddenly, the chronometric radiation intensified a hundredfold, setting off a klaxonlike alarm on the bridge, and Picard felt the universe—his *memory* of the universe—begin to shift like windblown desert sand.

With his last rational thought, he barked out the order that sent the *Enterprise* plunging into the Arhennius corona only seconds behind Scott and the Klingon ship. But even as the *Enterprise* shuddered under the strain, new images began to appear on the viewscreen, images beyond the corona they were shooting through at impossible speeds.

Images of a solid phalanx of Borg cubes.

STAR TREK®
ENGINES
OF DESTINY

GENE DeWEESE

Based upon STAR TREK and
STAR TREK: THE NEXT GENERATION®
created by Gene Roddenberry

POCKET BOOKS
New York London Toronto Sydney The Nexus

This book is a work of fiction. Names, characters, places and incidents are products of the author's imagination or are used fictitiously. Any resemblance to actual events or locales or persons, living or dead, is entirely coincidental.

An *Original* Publication of POCKET BOOKS

POCKET BOOKS, a division of Simon & Schuster, Inc.
1230 Avenue of the Americas, New York, NY 10020

STAR TREK is a Registered Trademark of
® Paramount Pictures.

This book is published by Pocket Books, a division of Simon & Schuster, Inc., under exclusive license from Paramount Pictures.

ISBN: 0-671-03702-1

First Pocket Books printing March 2005

10   9   8   7   6   5   4   3   2   1

POCKET and colophon are registered trademarks of Simon & Schuster, Inc.

Cover art by James Wang; Cover design by John Vairo Jr.

Manufactured in the United States of America

For information regarding special discounts for bulk purchases, please contact Simon & Schuster Special Sales at 1-800-456-6798 or business@simonandschuster.com.

In memory of Don Senzig, Jr., 1951–2004

A better friend than I deserved, a twentieth-century Scotty of the computer world, whose miracle-working and generosity kept me going the last twenty years.

Acknowledgments

Thanks to Rick Sternbach for patiently answering several *Trek*kish questions, to Marco Palmieri for resurrecting what had once been lost, and to Keith R.A. DeCandido for some provocative and informative editing.

ONE

En Route to the *Enterprise*-B
2293 Old Earth Date

HER NAME, at this particular juncture, was Guinan, and her silent scream reverberated throughout Time, a despairing echo she could never escape. The transporter's grip had not brought with it the usual momentary numbness. Instead, she could feel her body being torn apart, molecule by molecule, while at the same moment everything that had ever brought joy or comfort to her life was being stolen. Even her memories were being transformed from nostalgic sources of happiness to wellsprings of torment, sadistic reminders of what she had once experienced but would never experience again.

But even at that moment of supreme anguish, there was a fundamental part of her that knew that whatever was happening to her, whether she would ever fully understand it or not, was both right and essential. She didn't know why it was right or what it was essential for. She only knew that it *was*.

And that she had no choice but to endure, as she had endured before and doubtless would again.

It was her gift, this sourceless knowledge.

And it was her curse.

It had been a part of her for as long as she could remember—which was a very long time indeed. For all that time, and possibly more, she had been subject to "feelings," sometimes of foreboding, sometimes simply of a vague wrongness or, less often, a similarly vague rightness. Sometimes they came upon her suddenly, other times with maddening slowness. Sometimes they were urgent, forcing her to blurt out a warning to those around her even though she had little or no idea what it was she might be warning them against. Sometimes they were nagging little itches in her mind, the sort of distraction a human suffers through when she realizes she has forgotten *something* but cannot, no matter how hard she tries, remember what it was.

But the intensity and the steely certainty of the feeling that gripped her now transcended any she had ever experienced before. It transcended even the physical and mental agony that had brought it into being and was, in fact, all that kept her from translating her mental scream of anguish into a blind fury of destruction that would have laid waste to everything and everyone that had the misfortune to be near her. And that would only have added to her grief once she regained control and saw what she had done.

Finally, after an eternity that she somehow knew had lasted only the few seconds it had taken the transporter to "rescue" her, the physical pain faded to a tolerable level.

With glazed eyes, she looked around and saw only bedlam. The *Lakul* was gone, replaced by another starship's crowded sickbay. Her fellow refugees, those that hadn't collapsed to the floor or slumped across the beds, milled about aimlessly, helplessly. She wished she could share with them her certainty of the rightness of what had happened to them. It would be small comfort to anyone other than herself, but it would be something.

Then a solicitous young man in a Starfleet uniform was gently taking her arm and leading her to a biobed, assuring her she was safe and well. For a moment, his uniform caught her eye, and something twitched within her. A new "feeling," she thought resignedly, something that had been there all along but had until now been buried beneath the rubble of her own disintegrating life.

There was something—or some*one*—here on this ship that would—

Would *what?*

She didn't know.

She knew—*felt*—only that there was something of monumental importance about this time and this place, something with tendrils that snaked out, not only through space but through time, and enfolded more worlds than even she had seen.

It was why she was here, why she *had* to be here.

Sudden anger surged through her, an anger not at the captain of this ship for the agony he had subjected her to in his misguided "rescue," nor even at the supremely intelligent yet essentially mindless creatures whose destruction of El-Auria was still like a corrosive acid in her veins.

This anger was directed inward, toward whatever it was within her that was responsible for these "feelings."

But it was a futile anger. To be angry at something that was so intimate a part of herself would be like being angry at her own heart for beating too loudly.

As it had countless times before, the anger passed, leaving in its wake a mixture of bemusement and implacable determination.

Whatever the object of this latest feeling was, she would find it, as she had found countless others.

She had no choice, not as long as she still wished to allow her existences to continue.

Putting everything else out of her mind, she eased herself off the biobed, took one last, sorrowful look at the still-dazed faces of her fellow refugees, and, leaving that part of her life behind her, began her seemingly aimless search through the starship's sterile corridors.

TWO

Glasgow, Scotland
2294 Old Earth Date

CAPTAIN MONTGOMERY Scott, Starfleet Retired, clung to
the engineering station handgrips as the bridge of the
Enterprise-B bucked and lurched, the entire ship shaken
like an eagle in the jaws of an angry tiger.

"Keep her together till I get back," Kirk called over his
shoulder as he once more lunged up the quaking steps toward
the turbolift doors, already shuddering open.

"I always do," Scotty said, his aging eyes riveted on the
wildly fluctuating readouts. But even as the words passed
his lips, he knew they were a lie.

For several agonizing seconds, he continued to glare
helplessly at the increasingly chaotic, increasingly deadly
displays while the turbolift doors closed and blocked off
the last fleeting smile anyone would ever see on Jim Kirk's
face. On the viewscreen, the so-called energy ribbon,
which had already destroyed two ships and now had the

Enterprise in its gravitometric grip, looked like the gate to Hell itself: a spaceborne tornado funnel thousands of kilometers long, twisting and lashing, spewing out jagged arcs of some demented form of nucleonic lightning, destroying everything it touched.

You can't let him die, not again! Scotty's own voice screamed in his mind.

Tearing his eyes from the displays and the viewscreen both, he turned and forced his way through the chaos of the bridge, past the grim-faced Captain Harriman, to the turbolift. The doors scraped open as he lunged through them and rasped out his destination. Seconds later and fifteen decks down, the shaking was so bad it had warped the turbolift itself and he had to pry the doors open before he could stumble out into a corridor filled with acrid smoke. His eyes began to water, his lungs to burn even before he took his first breath.

Squinting into the roiling smoke, he realized without surprise that he was no longer wearing the heavy, ceremonial uniform he had reluctantly donned for the *Enterprise*-B dedication. Somewhere during the jolting turbolift descent, it had changed, unnoticed, to the plain red tunic and boots he had worn as chief engineer on the first *Enterprise* a quarter century ago. At the same time, the burning in his smoke-filled lungs faded and his vision cleared, but even so, he couldn't see more than two or three meters through the smoke.

Feeling years younger and pounds lighter than he had only moments before, he set out at a run, trusting to his memory of the blueprints Starfleet had sent him as a courtesy during the construction of the ship.

Suddenly, without quite knowing how he got there, he was staring up through the smoke at the massive deflector generators, at least twice the size and ten times the power of those on the original *Enterprise*. They just might have the power to do what he needed them to do after all: simulate a photon torpedo detonation powerful enough to disrupt the ribbon's intense gravitometric field long enough to allow the *Enterprise*-B to break free.

If . . .

Jim Kirk, Scotty saw out of the corner of his eye, had gotten there ahead of him. He was already prying loose a bulkhead panel, revealing the glittering circuits that would have to be disconnected and reconnected into a configuration its designers had never intended, had probably never even imagined possible. Like Scotty, Kirk looked the way he had decades before, young and trim and wearing the simple, unostentatious uniform of his first command. His voice, too, was young as he snapped an order to the bridge to de-activate the main deflector, making the circuits safe to touch but making the *Enterprise* completely vulnerable until power was restored.

Without hesitation, Scotty brushed Kirk's hands aside and reached through the opening in the bulkhead. Speed was of the essence, and Scotty saw instantly which connections had to be broken, precisely how the glittering circuits had to be twisted and rerouted, and the most efficient way of reconnecting them in the new configuration. Kirk, no matter how good a captain he had been, was not an engineer. From simulated emergency drills on the old *Enterprise*, he would know what circuits needed to be rerouted. He would even, given time, be able to identify them and make the required changes. But he didn't *know* those circuits the way an engineer—particularly this engineer—knew them. For Jim it would be like navigating through a strange city using a memorized road map, while for Scotty it would be like racing through the back alleys of a city he had lived in all his life.

This time, he vowed, the modifications would be made not only in time to save the *Enterprise* but in time to save Jim Kirk as well.

The deck lurched even more violently beneath his feet as he disconnected the key deflector circuits, but Kirk braced him, keeping him from being thrown backward, away from the open bulkhead panel. Without that instinctive assistance, he would've lost precious seconds.

But then it was over, the circuits reconnected, the new configuration complete. Even before Scotty had slammed the bulkhead panel back in place, Kirk barked an order to the bridge to activate the main deflector.

Then they were both running, lurching back the way they had come short minutes before. Behind them, the deflector generators trembled under the strain of doing what they had never been designed to do.

Even if the turbolift doors could still be pried open, Scotty worried as they ran through the smoke, would the lift itself move? Or had the buffeting by the wildly varying gravity been too much for the structural integrity field, warping the turbolift so far out of shape that it was frozen in place?

But the doors opened, letting them both plunge in. The last thing Scotty saw as the doors closed behind them was the far bulkhead vanishing in a coruscating energy flare. As had happened all those other times, everything not bolted down would be sucked out into space, but *this* time those things did not include Jim Kirk.

This time he and Scotty were both safe within the turbolift, which to Scotty's huge relief lurched unsteadily upward. Grinning, the triumphant engineer watched the indicators as they counted down toward deck one and the bridge.

"We did it, Captain," he said, limp with relief. "We did it."

But Kirk didn't answer.

In fact, there wasn't a sound of any kind. Even the earthquake-like shaking of the *Enterprise*-B had stopped. And Scotty was once more weighted down with age, as if invisible masses of neutronium had been attached to his arms and legs.

His heart pounding, he turned toward his friend, fully expecting to see that Kirk as well had been returned to his rightful age.

Instead—

Scotty gasped, almost choking as the stench of burning flesh engulfed him.

A corpse, its face charred beyond recognition above a still-pristine ceremonial uniform, stared blindly back at him out of blackened eye sockets.

"You didn't keep her together, old friend," the corpse said, its voice like the crackle of flames.

As he always did after the fourth or fifth repetition of the soul-shriveling accusation, Scotty woke up. His heart was pounding even harder than in the nightmare, his bed-clothes icy with evaporating sweat, his throat so tight he could barely breathe.

Shivering, he sat up and grabbed the bottle that had become his constant bedside companion since he'd moved out of his sister's house in Cromarty and into this small cottage on the outskirts of Glasgow. The guilt would never go away, but he could sometimes at least banish the nightmare.

But not tonight, he realized as he lifted the bottle to his lips and was rewarded with only a sour-tasting trickle, then nothing.

Grimacing, he dropped the bottle into the recycler chute and lay back down, his stomach knotted. He was too old for this, far too old.

And too tired.

Even though he wasn't doing anything—except fighting off nightmares—he was exhausted. Constantly.

And there *were* things he could be doing—*should* be doing. Not a week went by that he didn't get another invitation to do an article for some engineering journal or other, and he had a standing invitation to resume being a "design consultant" with Starfleet. There had even been a series of requests for him to "guest lecture" at both Glasgow University, a few short kilometers distant, and at Starfleet Academy, half a world away.

But he couldn't bring himself to do any of that, not anymore, not after the fiasco of the *Enterprise*-B. Knowing what he had done—and what he had *not* done—he would have felt like a complete fraud, hiding behind the façade of competence he no longer deserved.

Even before the *Enterprise*-B—before he'd let nearly four hundred El-Aurian refugees die, before he'd sent Jim Kirk to his death—he hadn't particularly enjoyed any of it. The rosy picture he'd painted for Chekov and the others about his "bonnie retirement" had contained more than a wee bit of face-saving blarney. At best, he had felt "gratified" to know that he was respected for his knowledge and experience, but that was as far as it went. There had been no joy in it, no enthusiasm of the sort that had filled his years with Starfleet.

And he didn't even want to think about the women—widows, mostly—that his sister Clara and her husband Hamish were constantly introducing him to. To them he was "the famous Starfleet officer," not a real person. And not a one of them, no matter how gracious or ingratiating, had a clue as to what he'd really done or why he'd loved it so much. Not that they were all that different from most of the other people he met, men and women alike. Virtually all were well-meaning, as were his family and friends, but more than once he'd found himself considering leaving Earth altogether, going someplace—perhaps even to one of the so-called retirement colonies—where he *wasn't* known, where he wasn't reminded every single day of what he had once been but no longer was.

The Starfleet consultancy and the rest had at least kept him busy in the off hours when the blind dates and his "doting uncle" routine had begun to wear thin, not only with him but with his sister. There were reasons—Starfleet duty tours aside—that he had never had a family. During his long career, even the most domestic of situations had never fully involved him. A small corner of his mind had always remained in its "engineering mode," and that small corner had been likely to surface and take control at any moment. After retirement, matters had only become worse as it gradually sank in that he would never again set foot in a starship's engineering section except as a guest. No such place would ever again be *his*. Never again would he experience the sheer joy, the exultation that exploded in him when an ingenious solution to a seemingly impossible problem popped into his head.

Then came the *Enterprise*-B, the final straw.

Grimacing at the wave of nausea that the memory always brought, he threw back the sheets, got dressed, and set out on his anonymous late-night errand. For a moment, the thought of a lovely bottle of Saurian brandy flitted through his mind, but he quickly dismissed it. It was part of that other life, the life that had ended with the death of Jim Kirk. To make it a part of this one, to use something produced with such care and affection as nothing more than a nightmare repellent, would be degrading, like donning his old Starfleet uniform to go beg on a street corner.

Shuddering at his maudlin train of thought, he looked around the midnight streets and tried to remember where he'd gotten the bottle he'd just emptied.

Scotty almost bumped into the woman as he turned abruptly away from the bar, two bottles of nightmare repellent in the brown paper bag that was still, even in the latter days of the twenty-third century, the concealment of choice for surreptitious drinkers.

Averting his eyes as he tried to slip past her, he noticed only the dark gown that covered her from neck to toe. "Sorry, lass," he mumbled.

"Not your fault," she said. "I was crowding you. I thought you were someone I knew."

He shook his head silently, his eyes still averted. To be recognized was the last thing he wanted.

"No harm done," she said, a shrug in her voice, her hand coming to rest lightly on his forearm. "But I have the feeling you could use a drink. You have a look about you—perhaps a Saurian brandy look? It's been my experience, you can never go wrong with Saurian brandy."

His eyes widened momentarily, then narrowed in a frown as he brought them up to meet hers—and realized with an uneasy start that her oddly regal, chocolate brown face *did* look familiar. He was instantly certain he had seen her—at least glimpsed her—somewhere before, but the circumstances refused to reveal themselves to him.

Was her presence, he wondered irritably, another bit of

well-meaning meddling by his former comrades? It wouldn't surprise him. McCoy had already tracked him down and given him a stern lecture about solitary drinking, among other things. Even Uhura, as lovely and concerned as ever, had checked in from the *Intrepid II* only a few days after McCoy's appearance. Ostensibly she had called to offer belated condolences on Kirk's death and to say how sorry she was she hadn't been able to make it to the memorial.

Her real motives had been quickly obvious, however. As diplomatically as she could, she'd given him a soft-edged version of McCoy's demands that he move on with his life and quit blaming himself for things that weren't his fault. And she had of course gently suggested that the flood of invitations the Academy had deluged him with were still open and would always be.

"In my years at Starfleet Command, I had a lot of friends there," she had said earnestly, "and hardly a week went by that one or the other of them didn't tell me how some engineering student had stumped them with the sort of 'hands-on' question you could answer in your sleep."

Pushing aside thoughts of past meddling by his friends, Scotty returned to the present. Common sense—or what passed for it in his current state—told him to ignore this woman, whether she was someone McCoy had recruited or not. But now that he found himself looking into her solemnly smiling eyes, he felt his resolve faltering. For one thing, she was right about Saurian brandy. His mouth almost watered at the thought of its delicate, smoky savor.

And this wouldn't, he rationalized abruptly, be drinking alone in his room, solely to ward off nightmares. This was being social, which was just what the doctor had, literally and gruffly, ordered.

"Aye, that's been my experience as well," he said, almost smiling. "I'd be honored to join you, if you'll tell me who you are—and have a second round on me."

"You can call me Guinan," she said with a barely discernible nod and smile as she turned and led him to an out-of-the-way table. She seemed to glide rather than walk, as if the floor-length gown concealed not legs but an anti-grav unit. Self-consciously, he set the sack of nightmare repellent out of sight on the chair next to him, but the woman didn't seem to notice as she settled herself on the opposite side of the table and signaled to the bartender.

A few curiously wordless moments later, they both held small goblets of Saurian brandy in their hands. The woman lifted hers in a motion that seemed to be half toast, half inspection of the amber liquid.

For just a moment, as her lips began to part, he was afraid she was going to come up with one of the oldest—and least welcome—of toasts: "To absent friends."

Instead, after a long moment of silence, she raised her goblet another millimeter and said, "To the future. As one of your world's more engaging charlatans often said a few centuries ago, that is where we will all spend the rest of our lives."

At once relieved and a little puzzled, he downed the drink, sipping it slowly, as it deserved.

"My world, you said? You're not from around here, then?" he asked as he signaled for the second round, his treat.

"No, but I've been here before—on your world. It's one of the more interesting ones. I like to check in every so often, see what's changed since my last visit."

Scotty found himself grinning. "Then you've come to the wrong country, lass. We Scots aren't noted for keeping up with the latest fashions. The local university is more than nine centuries old and hasn't changed its façade for three. Nor much of its curriculum." Which in fact had been one of the talking points of the oddly old-sounding young woman who'd invited him to "guest lecture" there instead of—or in addition to—Starfleet Academy.

The woman smiled wryly. "There's something to be said for tradition, properly employed. Personally, I like to think we can use it to guide ourselves into the future rather than chain us to the past." She glanced around the room, her eyes falling on a young man in a Starfleet uniform sitting with civilian friends a few tables away.

"Take Starfleet, for example," the woman went on. "I'd be surprised if it didn't have traditions that have their roots in the days of sailing ships, but if there's any organization that looks more toward the future, I couldn't name it."

It hadn't been a question, but her face invited a reply. "Aye, they have their moments," he said noncommittally.

"And what about your future?" she asked abruptly. "Do you have any plans?"

To survive, he thought, *whether I deserve it or not,* but he said nothing, only shook his head, hoping she wouldn't press the issue.

Then the second round was there. "To the future," she repeated, her cryptic smile making her look even more maddeningly familiar, and then added: "Keep a close eye on it. You never know what it has in store for you."

Moments later, to his surprise, she murmured something, set down her emptied goblet, and glided away, not back to the bar but out into the night.

Puzzled at the odd encounter and the woman's abrupt departure, Scotty sat for another minute, not quite able to resist the temptation of a third Saurian brandy, a double "for the road." Finally he picked up his nightmare repellent and headed for the door himself.

Halfway there, a slurred voice rose above the muted hum of a dozen soft-spoken conversations.

"C'mon, Matt, admit it. Only reason you went to Starflop Academy was because you knew you'd never hack it at a *real* school."

His inhibitions loosened by the drinks that still warmed his stomach, Scotty turned with a frown that quickly turned to a scowl as he saw the same young Starfleet ensign he'd noticed a few minutes before. The boy—he couldn't be more than a year out of the Academy—was lurching to his feet, knocking his chair backward onto the floor. Two casually but expensively dressed men about the same age were across the table from him, both leaning back and grinning broadly.

The ensign leaned forward belligerently, his hands flat on the table. "And you two think *you* could hack it at Starfleet? You'd be out on your cans before you got through the first semester. If they ever let you in in the first place." He laughed derisively, almost losing his balance as he shook his head. "I'd like to see one of *you* tear an impulse engine apart and then fix it!"

"We wouldn't have to," one of the others said. Scotty recognized the voice that had made the first taunt. "We'd just order our engineer to do it for us." Both of them broke into drunken guffaws as the ensign's hands clenched into fists.

Scotty's stomach knotted in sudden, remembered anger. For an instant, the ensign's face was his own from half a century ago, and the other two were masked by the condescending features of a pair of one-time "friends" of his own—Gregor Campbell and Sean Toricelli, two people he had never quite been able to forget. He'd come home from the Academy to show off his brand new ensign's uniform, but the congratulations hadn't been *quite* unanimous. Gregor and Sean, a pair just like these two had—

"Let it go, lad," he said, stepping up to the table next to the ensign and clapping a hand on his shoulder. "I know their wee-minded type, and you don't want to descend to their bloody level. It only encourages them."

All three faces swiveled unsteadily toward him, but only the ensign's showed any sign of recognition, his angry belligerence morphing unsteadily into wide-eyed surprise.

"Captain Scott?"

"Who's this, then, Mattie?" one of the others demanded. "One of your Starflop 'professors'?"

"*This*—" the ensign began emphatically, but Scotty, giving the boy's arm and shoulder a practiced twist that had come in handy in many a previous bar, surprised him into momentary silence and had him moving in the general direction of the door before he could recover.

"Just say I did not appreciate your ignorant remarks about Starfleet," Scotty said over his shoulder as he maneuvered the boy out the door.

At the same moment, he realized he'd left his nightmare repellent on an unoccupied table just inside the door. Too late now. There was no way he was going back in there, not for that.

"I—I have to apologize for my friends, Captain Scott," the young man stammered. "They didn't mean—"

Scotty cut him off with a snort. "Didn't mean what they said? Aye, lad, they meant it all right, and don't you ever think different. I've had dealings with their kind before. It's the mealymouthed things they say when they're sober that I would not put my trust in."

The young man blinked owlishly but didn't argue any further. Instead, he squinted, trying to focus on Scotty's face.

"You *are* Captain Scott! Aren't you? *The* Captain Scott?"

"I *was*," Scotty said pointedly, beginning to regret the impulse that had prompted him to interfere in something that had obviously been none of his business. "I've been retired for more than a year now."

The boy shook his head in alcoholic vigor. "I read all about how you saved those El-Aurians. And the new *Enterprise* itself! I've seen the interviews with Captain Harriman. He said it was a pure miracle, what you did! *Simulating* a photon torpedo—"

"Hardly a miracle, lad. Any engineer worth his salt would've done the same."

Another vehement head shake. "I've read everything there is to read about deflector shields in the Academy library, and I've never seen anything like that even mentioned."

"Aye, lad, and why should it be? That's not the way they're *supposed* to work. You have to rip out some of their guts and put them back wrong way 'round before they will. If you were telling someone how to use a sonic shower, would you bother to explain that you can modify *its* circuits to make it work as a low-power disruptor?"

"You can? How?"

Scotty sighed. "Did they not teach you *anything* at the Academy?" Not that they'd taught *him* many such things, Scotty thought, not in official classes, anyway. But for anyone who wanted to be an engineer—a *Starfleet* engineer!—the official curriculum was just a skeleton. It was up to the individuals to put flesh on the bare bones they were given. For every thousand words of assigned text, there were ten thousand more begging to be read and absorbed. For every instructor's formal lecture, there would be dozens of informal sources, inside the Academy and out. And it never stopped. For every bit of knowledge you had gained by the time you graduated, you'd learn a hundred more later, not only from your own experiences but from the experiences of your shipmates.

"What's your name, lad?" Scotty asked, softening his tone as he saw the stricken look on the ensign's face.

"Franklin, sir, Matt Franklin. And I would be deeply honored if you would allow me to buy you a drink, Captain Scott."

"I don't think that's what either one of us needs right now, laddie."

"I'm sorry. I just thought—"

"On the other hand," Scotty added with a sudden grin, "it might be just what we *deserve*."

Twenty minutes later, they were sipping their second highly social Saurian brandy at the bar in the boy's nearby hotel. As Scotty had guessed, Matt Franklin was barely a year out of the Academy. He was also at least as enthusiastic as Scotty himself had been at a similar stage in his career, even though the young man's only assignment so far had been on a transport ship, the *Jenolen,* delivering supplies and occasional passengers to a half dozen worlds throughout the Federation.

As they talked and sipped, one thing became glaringly obvious, at least to Scotty. Finally, as Ensign Franklin ordered a third round, Scotty sighed. "You have no idea, lad, how I envy you," he said softly, barely louder than the sigh that had preceded it.

Franklin's eyes widened, seeming ready to pop. "Sir?

You envy *me?* You've served on the *Enterprise!* You've done *everything!*"

"Not quite everything, lad. And even if I had, that's all in the past. For me, it's over." A wave of alcohol-enhanced self-pity swept over him. "For lads like you, it's just beginning. I'd trade places with you in a second. All that's left for me is one of those bloody retirement colonies. Or worse," he added, remembering the pathetic bottles of nightmare repellent that lately had become so much a part of his life.

Franklin seemed stunned, although that, too, was probably partly due to the Saurian brandy. "But surely, someone like you—" he began, then broke off, blinking. "And the retirement colonies, they're . . ." He blinked again. "They're *nice,*" he said earnestly. "I saw the one on Norpin V when we delivered supplies—and a half dozen new residents—last year. And—and the people couldn't be happier. Why, one of the new ones said that was the reason he came—friends of his were already there and they'd told him how great it was."

"Aye, it's a bloody paradise, I'm sure," Scotty said.

But even as he spoke, he found himself—and the Saurian brandy—wondering: How bad could it be? It might not be a paradise, but at least it wasn't the purgatory that Earth had become after the *Enterprise*-B.

Signaling to the bartender for yet another refill, he hunched forward over the table toward the still-distressed-looking ensign. "Norpin V, you said? Tell me more, lad."

As Guinan watched the two men, strangers only minutes before, move off into the night, deep in conversation, she still had no idea what, if anything, she had accomplished just then or in the six months since she had first glimpsed

Captain Montgomery Scott, beleaguered by a group of reporters who had finally run him to ground in an isolated corner of the *Enterprise*-B recreation deck. All she knew was that, whatever she had done, it had turned out right.

For those six months, she had, as she had intimated to Scott himself, done little but play the tourist. She hadn't dogged his footsteps or even kept track of where he had gone after he and the others transported down from the *Enterprise*-B. She had simply followed her "feelings," barely aware of their existence after that first, startlingly intense one that had gripped her like a vice in the aftermath of her "rescue." The only hint that they still existed was the chill mixture of apprehension and gloom that rippled up and down her spine whenever she found herself thinking about leaving Earth.

So she had given up trying to resist. She had even given up trying to outguess the feelings or to understand them.

And by not resisting those feelings, she had ended up here, at this Glasgow bar, when Scott had walked in. No one had been more surprised than she, or more irritated at whatever was the source of the feelings. Things would be so much easier if they would just come out in the open and tell her whatever the devil they had in mind for her, instead of playing this long-drawn-out cat-and-mouse game.

Not that she begrudged the last six months, of course. This peculiar—and peculiarly interesting—world of endless paradoxes had always fascinated her, even though she couldn't even remember who had first made her aware of its existence. It was as if she had always known about it.

Or perhaps it had been one of her "feelings," long before she had become conscious of their existence, that had steered her here. At the time of her first visit, the humanoid inhabitants hadn't even developed electricity or an internal combustion engine, let alone a star drive. If they had followed the path of other worlds she had known, they would have been millennia away from even the most rudimentary space travel. Nor would they have been within millennia of having the emotional maturity to accept the fact that they were neither alone in the universe nor even particularly remarkable, just one planet-bound civilization among tens of thousands.

Yet here they were only a few centuries later, the center of a full-fledged federation of worlds, most of which had preceded them into space by centuries.

And here, crossing her path again, was this Captain Scott, who had been associated with not just one but three starships with the all-too-familiar name of *Enterprise*.

So perhaps she shouldn't be surprised that Scott should be the object of one of the strongest and yet most ambiguous "feelings" she had experienced in the four centuries since she had first heard of a starship bearing that name, a starship that was apparently still several decades in her future.

She just wondered, as she so often did, what it all meant and what the source of her "feelings" was.

And if that source, assuming it existed at all, would ever reveal itself . . .

THREE

On Board the *Jenolen*
2369 Old Earth Date

AS THE TRANSPORTER room re-formed around Scotty, his disorientation was virtually complete. For an instant, he couldn't remember his own name, much less where he was or why. All that was real was the pain in his left arm, held to his chest with a makeshift sling.

For another instant, he wondered frantically why the *Enterprise* transporter room looked so different, then realized that this *wasn't* the *Enterprise*.

Finally, as the world came completely into focus, he saw two men standing before him. One was tall with a neatly trimmed beard while the other was inches shorter and had a metallic band fastened across his eyes like a blindfold. Both wore peculiar, form-fitting outfits he assumed were uniforms but which looked like nothing he'd ever seen in Starfleet.

For yet another instant, his thoughts whirled chaotically

as he heard himself automatically thanking the two men, whoever they were. Had the transporter malfunctioned and scrambled his brain? Was that why he didn't recognize the men? Why he couldn't even remember what places he had been transporting between?

Had his pattern degraded?

His stomach knotted in fear at the thought that his body and mind might *literally* be scrambled, that the few scraps he was remembering now were all he would *ever* remember. Anything was possible if, somehow, the transporter's pattern buffer had itself been damaged.

The pattern buffer!

Without warning, a splinter of memory glittered in the darkness of his mind.

The pattern buffer had been cross-wired to—

Franklin!

"We got to get Franklin out of there!" he blurted and lunged for the transporter controls.

Suddenly, the tiny shard of memory became an island, solid in the midst of the darkness that still clouded much of his mind: This was the *Jenolen!* They had crashed on a Dyson Sphere, of all things. He and Matt Franklin had been the only survivors, and Scotty had concocted this desperate scheme to keep them both alive until they could be rescued—

"Someone else's pattern is in the buffer?" the man with the metallic blindfold asked incredulously.

"Aye, Matt Franklin! We went in together!" The fingers of his still-functioning right hand darted across the controls.

But it wasn't working!

"Something's wrong! One o' the inducers failed!" Without looking up, he snapped an order to the others: "Boost the gain on the matter stream!"

The one with the metallic blindfold complied, but it did no good.

Finally, the ache in his heart sharper than the pain in his broken arm, Scotty forced himself to focus on the key readout on the transporter control panel, the readout he'd been purposely avoiding during his desperate efforts to retrieve the boy.

It confirmed his worst fears. The very fears he had had for himself moments before.

"His pattern's degraded fifty-three percent," he said, hanging his head. "He's gone."

Then the two men were introducing themselves and saying how sorry they were, but nothing penetrated until they came to the name of their ship: the *Enterprise*!

Of course! What other ship would it be? But the captain had retired. And the ship—

With a touch of returning panic, he realized he couldn't remember what had happened to the *Enterprise*. Crashed and exploded? Been retired to the Starfleet Museum? Images of different versions of the ship whirled through his mind, and he heard himself muttering something inane about getting it out of mothballs without really knowing what he was saying.

How long had he been *in* the pattern buffer, endlessly cycling? How much of the degrading of Franklin's pattern had been because of the failed inducer? And how much simply because of the jury-rigging, the constant cycling? How much *had* his own pattern degraded? Obviously enough to scramble his memory.

Unless he was still in there. A "pattern," not a person?

But still capable of dreaming? Hallucinating? No one's pattern had ever before been stored in a buffer for more than a few minutes, so no one knew *what* happened to a person's mind—to the person himself—over an extended period of time.

Then he realized he *must* be hallucinating. A huge Klingon was standing before him, and the bearded man was introducing it as a lieutenant.

A Klingon? *In Starfleet?*

"Captain," the one who called himself Riker said solicitously, "perhaps there are a few things we should talk about."

Aye, lad, Scotty thought silently as the man with the metallic blindfold signaled for them to be transported somewhere. *For instance, is any of this real? Or is it the figment of my addled brain?*

Resolutely, more than a little fearfully, he waited once again to be swallowed up by a transporter.

Her name was still Guinan, and she had finally caught up with the *Enterprise* she had been anticipating for more than four-and-a-half centuries. For over five years now she had dispensed drinks and occasional advice in the ship's bar while she observed the endlessly fascinating creatures, human and otherwise, that made up her clientele. She hadn't consciously thought of Captain Montgomery Scott since coming aboard, but neither had she forgotten him.

She couldn't.

The day she had first heard of the *Jenolen*'s disappearance and presumed destruction, she came closer than ever before to losing faith in her "feelings," even to rejecting them outright. How could it possibly be "right" that, through her own unwitting but deliberate interference, Scott should meet Ensign Franklin only to take an unofficial berth on the doomed *Jenolen?* If she had *kept* them from meeting, kept Scott safe on Earth—*that* would have made sense. And yet her "feelings" insisted that whatever she had done *was* right, no matter how it looked.

For a decade, she had fully expected the *Jenolen* to be found, all hands alive if a bit older and wiser. For another decade the expectation faded to a hope, then a wish, and finally to a regret.

Thus, she was more surprised—and more relieved—than anyone else on the *Enterprise* when the news filtered up to Ten-Forward: Captain Scott was still alive. Not only that, he apparently was still the same age he had been when she had last seen him and Franklin on the streets of Glasgow. The *Jenolen* had indeed crashed, just as everyone assumed. But Scott had survived the crash itself and had, through some kind of engineering legerdemain, managed to use the *Jenolen*'s transporter to save himself—to literally *store* himself in the pattern buffer for seventy-five years, until the latest *Enterprise* found him.

And now Riker and La Forge had retrieved him, completing the operation, essentially transporting him not across space but across three-quarters of a century of time.

And now that he had been rescued, at least one small part of the puzzle came clear to Guinan: Scott was *meant* to be here, in this time. Whatever far-reaching destiny she had originally sensed hovering about him required it.

Her first impulse was to pull a bottle of Saurian brandy out of her private stock and invite him down for a "welcome to the future" toast.

But she didn't.

Before her fingers even touched the scimitar-like bottle, she was gripped by a feeling almost as powerful as the one that had marked the beginning of her link to this apparently remarkable man. A feeling that told her to keep her distance—for now.

He would already be disoriented, she rationalized. Waking up to a world seventy-five years removed from his own, he couldn't help but be. And seeing her, as unchanged as himself, could only add to the disorientation. And lead to questions she couldn't have answered seventy-five years ago and still couldn't answer today.

No, he was here because he was meant to be here, in this time.

He was *needed* here.

But at the same time . . .

For just an instant, an uneasy chill rippled through her, coupled with a sourceless deluge of sadness that brought a lump to her throat and very nearly a tear to her eye.

It was not over, she realized with a start. Yes, Captain Scott was now here. He was *supposed* to be here. Something of great import *depended* on his being here.

But something could yet go wrong—terribly wrong.

What? she screamed silently in her mind, the word a curse hurled blindly at the infuriatingly elusive source of the feelings. *Tell me what you want of me!*

There was of course no response.

There was only a newfound certainty that—somewhere, somewhen—she still had a role to play in Captain Scott's fate. She had no idea what that role was, nor what she would be forced to sacrifice for it. She only knew that, when the time finally came, she would have no choice in the matter.

Whatever had forced these feelings onto her, driving them deep into her very soul, would see to that.

She could only wait with endless uneasiness, wondering, as each new feeling made itself known to her, if it was the one she now awaited, the one she now dreaded above all others.

FOUR

On Board the Shuttlecraft *Goddard*
2370 Old Earth Date

AFTER NEARLY six months of aimless wandering, Scotty was no more at peace with himself than when he had been resurrected from the *Jenolen*'s transporter system. For a few days after he had helped Lieutenant Commander La Forge rescue the *Enterprise*-D from inside the Dyson Sphere, his spirits had been as high as at any time since the black day he'd let Jim Kirk die. He'd felt that he was pulling his own weight, actually making a difference, but the feeling had quickly faded. Despite the repeated and seemingly heartfelt expressions of gratitude from La Forge and Picard and the rest, the truth quickly became obvious, at least to him. No matter what they *said*, they wanted him out from underfoot.

It was true that he had pulled off a minor miracle in resurrecting the *Jenolen*, but the "miracle" had been accomplished largely with the century-old technology of the

Jenolen itself. He was still a fish out of water with the *current* technology, with the new *Enterprise* itself.

But worse than that, it had been his fault that the *Enterprise* had been put in danger in the first place. If he had done what any self-respecting Starfleet officer *should* have done, this grand new *Enterprise* would never have gotten tractored inside the sphere in the first place. If he had given Picard and the rest a *thorough* account of everything the *Jenolen* had done, someone would have recognized the dangers and avoided them. Instead, he had wasted his time—and everyone else's—poking his ignorant nose in every nook and cranny of the candy-store of advanced technology that, to his twenty-third-century eyes, the new *Enterprise* was. He had gotten underfoot at every opportunity. He had interfered with the running of the ship, trying La Forge's not-quite-endless patience by making suggestion after suggestion, most of which were either blindingly obvious or scientifically ludicrous. For a time he'd been obsessed with holodeck technology. He had even gone so far as to pompously suggest that it shared a few principles with the cloaking technology he'd become thoroughly familiar with when he and Kirk and the rest had virtually rebuilt the *Bounty,* the Klingon bird-of-prey that had taken them from Vulcan to Earth after Spock's resurrection.

Finally, even La Forge's patience had given out.

And Captain Montgomery Scott, the one-time chief engineer of this very ship's ancestor, had been exiled from engineering.

But even then he hadn't done what he should have done. Instead of giving them the information that might have kept them from being pulled into the Dyson Sphere, he had retreated into drink—and into a holographic illusion of the original *Enterprise* bridge, where he sat alone, once again getting drunk and feeling sorry for himself.

In the end, Picard had "loaned" him the *Goddard,* its computer programmed with a special briefing covering the history of the skipped-over seventy-five years, and sent him on his way. A warp-two shuttlecraft was obviously a small price to pay for saving the *Enterprise* from what he had become: not only a technological dinosaur but a drunken Jonah.

In just a few short weeks in the twenty-fourth-century, he had disgraced Starfleet and betrayed the *Enterprise*.

Long before that, he had failed his friend Matt Franklin. And worst of all, he had failed Jim Kirk.

Both were long dead, but if there was any justice in the universe, Montgomery Scott was the one who *should* have been dead.

Had he been given enough time on board this new *Enterprise*, he would almost certainly have found a way to do something even worse than get them trapped inside a Dyson Sphere, something he couldn't "make right" later by some ego-driven piece of engineering sleight-of-hand. At least this way, off cruising the back roads of Federation space by himself in a low-warp shuttlecraft like the *Goddard,* the damage his bumbling could cause was limited.

Or so he felt each time he drank himself to sleep on the foul-tasting synthehol concoctions that were the best the *Goddard*'s replicator could manage.

And so he felt whenever his nightmares—now filled with two accusatory corpses rather than one—invaded his cocoon of sleep and eventually ejected him into painful reality.

Until one night . . .

The increasingly grisly corpses of Jim Kirk and Matt

Franklin were taking turns railing at Scotty for his failure to save them when a disembodied third voice invaded the grimly familiar nightmare and drowned them both out.

And woke him up.

After the usual moment of stomach-churning disorientation, reality clamped down on him. He was aboard neither the *Enterprise* nor the *Jenolen* but the *Goddard*. And the voice, a monotone that still held an edge of desperation, was not a part of his nightmare.

It was a distress call, originating out here, in the real world!

Abruptly, instincts born of half a century in Starfleet kicked in, and Scotty scrambled from his bunk as fast as his aching head allowed. Even before the bulkhead had completely closed over the smoothly retracting bunk, he was at the shuttlecraft's controls, simultaneously opening a channel to the other vessel and initiating a sensor scan. As his fingers flew over the controls, he was glad that one of the first things he'd done on the *Goddard* was improvise a way to impose some order on the multi-function control panels and display screens. In effect, he'd frozen them into a default configuration that bore at least a superficial resemblance to the seventy-five-years-out-of-date equipment he was accustomed to. The other functions and configurations, while still available if needed, obediently stayed out of his way unless he actually requested them.

"This is the Federation shuttlecraft *Goddard*," he said. "Please identify yourself."

The voice fell abruptly silent. At the same moment, a barrage of information flashed onto the main sensor display screen. Automatically, Scotty extracted the key bits of data from the jumble of letters and numbers as they scrolled up the screen and soon filled it.

Frowning, he leaned closer, wondering if his eyes were playing tricks on him. Or, worse, his mind! What he was seeing was obviously impossible.

But then the shuttle "windshield" switched over to viewscreen mode, and the source of the distress call appeared abruptly, wavered a moment, then solidified and filled a good quarter of the screen. It was, just as the sensors had indicated, a Federation shuttlecraft.

But not a shuttlecraft from *this* era! Instead, it was from *his* era, now seventy-five years dead.

Except for the number—NCC-1951—and the countless scratches and scrapes visible on all surfaces, it would've looked right at home in the shuttlebay of the original *Enterprise*. Even more remarkably, all systems seemed to be at least marginally functional.

Another time traveler, he wondered? Or a piece of junk that someone had managed to resurrect?

Then the anomalous image of the exterior of the shuttlecraft was replaced by the equally anomalous image of its equally scratched and scraped and downright barren interior. For several seconds there was no movement, no sign of life, but finally a young-looking humanoid with a widow's peak of short, mottled fur extending downward almost to the top of a broad, flat nose stepped nervously into range of the viewscreen. His startlingly green eyes were saucer-wide but with vertical, cat-like slits for pupils. His tattered clothes would have looked more at home on a nineteenth-century dirt farm than on a space-faring vehicle of *any* era. Although, Scotty realized belatedly, his own nightshirt-clad image wasn't the most dignified way for a Starfleet officer—even a retired one—to introduce himself.

"What's the problem, lad?" he asked when the young

humanoid remained silent despite the nervous trembling of his mouth.

"Are you one of the Wise Ones?" the other asked abruptly, almost cringing as the words emerged.

"I don't feel particularly wise," Scotty replied, stepping out of viewscreen range for a moment and grabbing a freshly replicated, seventy-five-years-out-of-date semi-dress uniform, the jacket of which at least partially disguised his middle-age spread, "but do you need assistance or not?"

"We most certainly do," a second voice broke in, *"no matter who you are!"* A moment later, as Scotty finished shrugging into his uniform and stepping back into range of the viewscreen, another humanoid, this one apparently female, stepped into the picture behind the male, who winced anew at the other's words and angry tone. She was wearing what looked like a military uniform. A small but nasty-looking wound just above her right temple and just below the razor-edged fur-line had been clumsily stitched shut but had no protective covering, not even an old-fashioned bandage. *"Our ship broke down and unless I miss my guess, the Proctors can't be more than an hour behind us, doing warp five. Our ship might've been able to outrun them, but this thing can barely do warp one."*

"Who—"

"Whoever you are, can you and this 'Federation' help us or not? If you can't, just say so. We can't waste what little time we have just chatting. If the Proctors catch us, they may not kill us but what they will *do is worse!"* She winced as she indicated the wound above her temple with an angry tap of her fingers.

The Prime Directive darted through Scotty's mind but only for an instant. His interpretation had never been all that strict to begin with, and the fact that these two were already riding around in a Federation shuttlecraft, even one so ancient, pretty much mooted the point so far as he was concerned.

But what could he do to help them? If their pursuers were indeed capable of warp five, then the brand spanking new *Goddard* had no more chance of outrunning them than did the ancient shuttlecraft they were currently using.

It was times like this that he *really* missed the *Enterprise*. In any of its incarnations.

"I'll do what I can, lass," he said, triggering a subspace call of his own at the same time he altered course to intercept the other craft, which continued limping along at an unsteady gait that averaged out at less than warp one-point-five. "For a start, I can probably beam you both aboard my own ship and—"

" 'Beam?' " The female frowned suspiciously.

Scotty blinked, wondering anew who these two were. For all he knew, they could be escaped assassins or terrorists, and the so-called "Proctors" could be the local police.

But he would have to sort that out later. For now, if the Proctors were as close and as dangerous as the pair said, there was no time to be wasted explaining transporter terminology or quizzing them in a fruitless effort to make sure they were the innocents they claimed to be.

On the other hand, there was no reason to take unnecessary risks. A quick check of the sensor readings told him there were indeed only two life-forms, both humanoid, aboard the ancient shuttlecraft, and neither one was armed, at least not with weapons of the type the sensors would automatically pick up. Old-fashioned projectile weapons and knives, however, were another matter, he thought as he activated a confinement field around the *Goddard*'s two-person transporter pad.

"Stand by," he said, which seemed only to make the male more apprehensive, the female more impatient. Still, they did nothing to sever the comm link as he brought the *Goddard* safely inside transporter range and synchronized its course and speed to precisely match those of the other ship.

"*What are—*" the female began but was cut off as Scotty locked onto the two and the transporter's stasis field froze them both. They vanished in the familiar light show and reappeared moments later on the *Goddard*'s transport pads.

"—you doing?" she finished with a startled blink when the stasis field released them.

"Welcome aboard the *Goddard*," Scotty said, "Captain Montgomery Scott at your service." Out of the corner of his eye he could see the responses coming in to his subspace call of a few moments before. The nearest Federation ship was more than twenty-four hours away at maximum warp, so whatever situation he'd stumbled into, he was on his own, for good or ill.

"I am Garamet," the female said, her entire tone changing from desperation to suspicion. "My brother is named Wahlkon. And you *must* be one of the Wise Ones," she added accusingly as she looked around at the interior of the *Goddard*. "Why have you returned *now?*"

"I'm sorry to disappoint you, lass, but I have no idea what you're talking about. And I thought you were in a raging hurry to get away from whoever was chasin' after you."

"Do not toy with us! You can deal with the Proctors as if they were clawless infants!"

Scotty suppressed a grimace of frustration. "Whoever or whatever you think me to be, I'm not. I overheard your distress call and—"

"But what you just did to us—it is precisely as it was described in Proctor Corlwyn's Journal of—"

"All I did was transport you from one vessel to another. I haven't the time to explain, but it's not unusual." *Although,* he thought with a belated shiver, *you have to be a wee bit daft to try it when both vessels are traveling at warp speed, even one this low. The slightest mismatch in either speed or direction could be disastrous.*

Garamet wrinkled her brow, causing a rippling motion in the mottled fur of her widow's peak, all of which Scotty took to be a frown. While she was apparently still trying to digest the information, her brother turned to look at her nervously.

"Garamet, if what you yourself have told me about the Wise Ones is true, this being could not be one of them. They have been gone for generations. And if they *did* return, do you think they would allow themselves to be seen? After going to such lengths as you described to remain *un*-seen for hundreds of years, why would they suddenly decide to reveal themselves?"

"*I* don't know, but surely—"

"Surely you are wasting precious time, Garamet. As you also told me only hours ago, if the Proctors capture us—"

"I know what I told you, Wahlkon!" she snapped, her not-quite-human features beginning once again to register the fear that had been so apparent on the viewscreen before the transport. "We won't be dead but we'll wish we were!"

Abruptly, she started to step off the transporter platform, away from her brother, but she stopped and jerked spasmodically backward as she made tingling contact with the confinement field.

"We are prisoners, then?" she demanded. "Are you after all in league with the Proctors?"

Hesitating only long enough for a tricorder to determine they were carrying neither projectile weapons nor knives, Scotty deactivated the confinement field.

"Sorry about that, lass," he said as the field shimmered out of existence. "Until I knew the lay o' the land, I had to take precautions."

Hesitantly, as if expecting more invisible barriers to spring up, the two stepped off the transporter pads.

Watching them out of the corner of his eye, Scotty adjusted the *Goddard*'s speed to compensate for the continuing slight variations in the other shuttlecraft's speed. The variations weren't quite as bad as he had first feared. A plan was beginning to form in his mind.

"If whoever's after you—Proctors, you said?—can do warp five, there's no bloody way I can outrun them. How far is it back to this ship you left behind?"

Garamet looked at him incredulously. "We can't go *back!*"

"We cannot go forward either if what you say is true. The *Goddard* is faster than what you had, but it cannot come close to warp five. You'll just have to trust me." He winced inwardly as the words reminded him of what had happened to the last two people who had trusted him. But he had no choice but to forge ahead.

Impatiently, Garamet answered his questions as best she could. When their ship's warp drive had failed, she said, they had abandoned it somewhere in what appeared from her description to be an Oort cloud of comet nuclei surrounding the system they were fleeing. The Proctors had by now almost certainly found the abandoned ship and were tracking the shuttlecraft's warp trail. She didn't seem to find it odd that the Proctors had sensors capable of such tracking while at the same time they didn't have even rudimentary transporters.

While he listened and questioned, he scanned for the ancient shuttlecraft's trail himself. As he had hoped for his evolving plan, the ship's poorly maintained, poorly shielded engines left a warp trail that he wouldn't be surprised to find was visible to the naked eye. Which meant that the Proctors would have an easy job of following it, even with what he assumed were relatively primitive sensors. With any luck, they might not even notice the *Goddard*'s far fainter trail, several thousand kilometers distant.

Extending the scan as far as possible back along the trail, he fed a stream of the trail's coordinates into the *Goddard*'s computer. Just as he was finishing, a ship came into sensor range. It was, as its would-be prey had indicated, doing just under warp five as it streaked along the shuttlecraft's spectacular warp trail.

A quick check of the *Goddard*'s sensor readings revealed both good news and bad. Good was the fact that the pursuer's own sensor field extended only a fraction of the distance of the *Goddard*'s. Bad was the fact that the ship was heavily armed with disruptor-like weapons, primed and ready to fire. The *Enterprise* could have brushed off that kind of firepower easily, even with her shields down to ten percent. The *Goddard,* however, was not the *Enterprise* and would likely be fried by the first blast.

And at warp five, the approaching ship would be within firing range in less than thirty minutes, sensor range in twenty.

But there still might be time, if he didn't waste any

more precious seconds dithering. And if the remote control he had jury-rigged while killing time between nightmares didn't fall apart on him. It had worked well the one time he'd used it, instructing the *Goddard* to beam him up from the surface of a planet he'd been doing a little sightseeing on, but that had been a considerably less demanding task. He had been motionless on a mountaintop while the *Goddard* had been in a low orbit, held stable by the impulse engines. This time both he and the *Goddard* would be careening through space thousands of kilometers apart.

His heart beating as rapidly as in his nightmares, Scotty locked the *Goddard*'s controls so that his guests couldn't, by intent or by accident, interfere with them while he was gone. Using the remote, he once again tweaked the *Goddard*'s course to bring the two shuttlecraft back into precisely matched parallel courses.

"I'll be back in a few minutes," he said, stepping onto the transporter pad and activating the transporters with a quick tap on the remote control, now nestled along with his tricorder in the utility belt whose pattern he had found months ago in the *Goddard*'s replicator.

The *Goddard* disappeared from around him, replaced a moment later by the shimmering, ghostly image of the interior of the other shuttlecraft. An unexpected mixture of sadness and nostalgia swept over him as the craft's barren and timeworn interior solidified and became fully real. Even the seats had been removed except for one bolted solidly to the corroded floor plates in front of the control panel. A small rectangle of blinking lights was mounted to one side of the control panel—a self-contained timekeeping device, the tricorder indicated, obviously designed for eyes different than his.

The controls themselves, he saw, were similarly worn

but appeared intact except for a couple of obvious jury rigs where switches from another type of craft altogether—Klingon from the look of them—had been substituted, presumably when the originals had been damaged. A quick diagnostic check revealed that the on-board computer still had enough functional circuits to do what needed to be done. In fact, he discovered as he ran a series of more detailed diagnostics, the malfunctions it *did* contain included a number of the very ones he would otherwise have had to introduce himself. For one thing, almost all the built-in safeguards, the circuits and sensors that would ordinarily keep the craft operating safely within its design parameters, were totally inactive.

Those same diagnostics also told him that the safeguards had not failed. They had been intentionally disabled. And his own experience told him why: to keep the craft itself in operation. If the safeguards *hadn't* been disabled, the shuttlecraft's warp drive would have long ago decided, sensibly, to shut down and wait for someone to repair it. The irony was, half of the required repairs weren't repairs at all, merely adjustments, things that could've been done in less time than it had taken to jigger the computer to shut down the safety circuits. But whoever was responsible apparently hadn't known how to make the adjustments, only how to disable the safeguards. It was like giving someone with a broken leg a massive dose of pain killers and telling him to keep walking rather than setting the broken bone and splinting the leg. Continuing to operate with disabled safeguards had of course only aggravated the problems, causing actual physical damage to systems which before had only been in need of adjustments.

But he would definitely have time to implement his plan, Scotty realized with relief. Before, he hadn't been all that certain, but half the work—disabling the safeguards—had already been done. He would need only to introduce a few key malfunctions before going on to program in a new course. That left him time to make some of the adjustments that should have been made originally, thereby at least partially eliminating some of the *un*wanted malfunctions. His engineer's soul longed to make some of the physical repairs, but those would have required not only time he didn't have but spare parts or a fully functional replicator, neither of which was immediately to hand either.

But it didn't really matter, he thought with a grimace as he finished the bare essentials, not for his purposes. The shuttlecraft's drive didn't need to keep working for long. After his tinkering, it would continue to operate—more efficiently and more reliably than before, in fact—for another hour or so before final overload. And that was all he needed.

He hoped.

"Sorry, old girl," he murmured as he began to program a series of delayed commands into the ancient ship's computer. "You did your duty and deserve better."

The programming complete, he gave the *Goddard*'s course and speed one final tweak to bring them back into precise synchronization with those of the doomed shuttlecraft, then triggered the *Goddard*'s transporters. The last thing he heard as the stasis field gripped him was the angry, piercing whine that erupted from the craft's engines as certain of his adjustments took hold and the ship began to wind itself up in preparation for the speed and course changes he had programmed into it.

As the *Goddard* took shape around him, his guests turned abruptly toward the transporter pad, away from the viewscreen they'd been watching intensely. Questions were plain on Garamet's face, uneasiness verging on open terror on her brother's. But Scotty didn't have time to hold their figurative hands, not yet. The moment the transporter's stasis field released him, he sprinted the few meters to the *Goddard*'s controls. As expected, the sensors showed the other shuttlecraft already veering from its previous course parallel to the *Goddard* and shooting away at a forty-five-degree angle, already millions of kilometers outside transporter range, moving faster than its original warp one-point-five, on its way, he hoped, to a well-out-of-spec warp two-point-five.

Most importantly, it hadn't exploded, which prompted a heartfelt sigh of relief. Scotty's unspoken fear had been that something both he and the eighty-year-old diagnostic routines had missed would turn the warp drive into a photon torpedo an hour sooner than he wanted. Such a premature explosion might not have killed his plan, but it would've crippled it. For this to work, he needed the pursuers to be distracted for as long as possible, giving him as much time as possible to see what could be done with the ship the two had abandoned.

Assuming he *could* do anything with it.

Assuming the Proctors hadn't destroyed it.

Bringing the *Goddard* about, he set in a course that would send it in a huge arc that would essentially leapfrog the *Goddard* over the area covered by the Proctors' limited-range sensors, then reacquire the warp trail at a point well behind the Proctors' ship. Then he could easily follow the trail the rest of the way back to the abandoned ship while the Proctors continued sniffing along the trail in the other direction like warp-drive bloodhounds. Until they caught up with the expanding cloud of elementary particles the ancient shuttlecraft would have by then become.

If the abandoned ship was what he hoped it was—the

Starfleet vessel whose shuttlebay the NCC-1951 shuttle-craft had once graced—he would try to jury-rig enough repairs to get it moving for at least a few hours. If he was *really* lucky, the Proctors would not detect the *Goddard*'s warp trail at all and would assume the two fugitives themselves had been turned into elementary particles along with the shuttlecraft.

With a little less luck, the Proctors would only be delayed, not fooled, and would ferret out the *Goddard*'s relatively faint trail and follow it. But even then, assuming he had found the abandoned ship and been able to at least partially restore its warp drive, he should still be able to elude them long enough to rendezvous with one of the Starfleet ships he'd earlier contacted via subspace. The nearest, the *U.S.S. Yandro,* commanded by Captain Buck Stratton, was by now less than twenty-two hours away.

Surprising even himself, Scotty managed to cajole and trick the *Goddard*'s warp engines into producing—more or less safely—just under warp three rather than the warp two that the manuals insisted was the maximum for any sustained period.

When they were finally underway, with sensors showing the Proctors nearing the point at which the shuttlecraft had shot off on its new and accelerated course, Scotty settled down to get what information he could about his two fugitive guests, starting with a computer check of the star system they were fleeing.

He learned little. While the system was well within what was now considered Federation space, it and a dozen other nearby stars were unknown except for their stellar coordinates. There weren't even notations about possible planets, Class-M or otherwise.

Not that it surprised him. With a strictly limited number

of Federation ships hopscotching through billions of cubic light-years, selecting their targets from among hundreds of millions of stars, it was no wonder that even here, little more than a hundred parsecs from Earth, there were more stars that were still only numbers on a star chart than there were that had actually been visited and scanned for life forms. Even a five-year mission like that of the original *Enterprise* could only scratch the surface of one small part of the almost incomprehensible population of stars in just the Alpha Quadrant alone. Warp drive is fast but it isn't that fast. If a world didn't call attention to itself through subspace communications, either intentionally or accidentally, it would likely not be noticed. And if it was accidentally noticed, it would even more likely be left alone because of the Prime Directive.

According to Garamet and her brother, however, their world of Narisia had been noticed about three hundred years ago by the so-called "Wise Ones," an otherwise anonymous race or group that either hadn't heard of—or had no use for—the Prime Directive. Whoever they were, they obviously preferred aggressive meddling to the inconvenience of having to stage an actual invasion and occupation. That could qualify, Scotty supposed, as a perverse sort of wisdom.

"And you have no idea who they really were?" Scotty wondered. Such apparently "covert" operations hardly seemed in character for either the Romulans or the Klingons, both of whom would've leaned much more toward open invasion. There were, however, any number of other less "honorable" enemies to cope with these days. The Cardassians, covered extensively in the *Goddard*'s briefing program, came instantly to mind. And the blue-skinned Andorians: Even though they had been a founding member of the Federation, there apparently were rogue factions that still went in for the same kind of underhanded tactics they had been known for in pre-Federation days. And there were of course the hive-minded Borg, seemingly roaming the Delta Quadrant at will in near-indestructible ships that looked suspiciously like massive compacted cubes of scrap metal.

From what Wahlkon and Garamet told Scotty, however, he doubted that the Borg or any of the others were the ones masquerading as the "Wise Ones." Narisia, a pre-technological M-class planet, had been co-opted several generations ago, or at least its leaders had been. Or perhaps "tempted" was a better term. No invasion force had descended on the planet. No armada had appeared in the sky, threatening fiery destruction from above, although it was understood from the start that such things were far from impossible—if they were ever needed.

Instead, a few leaders from various parts of Narisia had been secretly snatched up by what Garamet was now convinced was something very like the *Goddard*'s transporters, something she personally had never before experienced. On board what apparently were starships in high orbit, too high for them to be seen from the surface as anything but moving dots of light, these leaders were "given" a series of technological advances that not only helped them to remain leaders but helped them and their heirs to expand their domains until eventually all of Narisia was under their control.

That had been less than three centuries ago. With the help of these off-worlders, these so-called "Wise Ones," generation after generation of the now-hereditary leaders, calling themselves Proctors, had lived in comparative luxury while Narisia itself went from farming and wood fires to mass production and warp drive in record time. And even now the general population was unaware of the existence of the off-worlders. The only ones who knew were the Proctors and the select few who were involved in developing an understanding of the technological gifts. This included those like Garamet who had been, in effect, a test pilot for Narisia's gift-wrapped space program.

"And there's no danger any of them will let the secret out," Garamet said, grimacing as her fingers went reflexively to the wound at her temple, now almost invisible as a result of Scotty's clumsy but effective ministrations with a medical tricorder and a few items from the *Goddard*'s first aid kit. "Everyone who gets let in on the secret is also 'given' an implant. You can't see it or feel it but you know it's there. And don't ask me what it does or how it does it. All I know is, until mine was accidentally disabled, the very idea of telling any 'outsiders,' even my own family, about the Wise Ones made me physically sick. Literally! Even *thinking* about them, never mind talking about them, gave me the shakes. And I was luckier than most. When I was recruited, I learned that my grandmother Balitor had once been a recruit as well, so I at least had *someone* to talk to now and then."

"I don't suppose you still have the wee thing you extracted?"

Garamet shook her head with a shudder. "Once Wahlkon managed to pry it loose from my skull, we smashed the bloody thing and ejected it into space. But you'll see one soon enough if the Proctors catch us. They'll have new ones implanted in all three of us before we even get taken back to Narisia."

Scotty repressed a disappointed sigh. Garamet's action was understandable, but it would've been a help to have the device to analyze. He might even have been able to recognize the technology. At least then he'd have a better idea of who and what he was up against, who these so-called "Wise Ones" really were. And he could inform Captain Stratton, now twenty hours away, of the situation.

"And you've never seen these 'Wise Ones' yourself?"

They both shook their heads. "No one has, so far as I know," Garamet said and went on to explain that even the Proctors, the people actually taken into the ships, had never actually *seen* anyone. Each had just found himself in a plain, metal-walled room, being talked to by a disembodied voice. After the voice had explained—without *really* explaining—why they had chosen to help Narisia in general and these leaders in particular, objects began appearing on the floor in front of them, along with explanations of how to use the objects. When the voice was finished, the leaders found themselves back on Narisia, right where they'd been when they'd been picked up. Only now they had little treasure troves of weapons and other goodies, along with the information needed to eventually manufacture them themselves, assuming they were bright enough to either understand the information or seek out and control people who *were* bright enough.

The mottled fur on the sides of Garamet's head rippled momentarily, something Scotty had come to recognize as the Narisian equivalent of a shrug. "That went on until about a hundred years ago," she said. "Each new generation of Proctors would get more and more advanced gifts, but then the gifts stopped. So far as I know, no one has heard from the Wise Ones since then. There's been no contact at all. Whoever they are, they must have gotten bored with whatever game they were playing."

"Or they completed their plan for us when they gave us

a rudimentary warp drive," Wahlkon said. "Once they did that, we were apparently on our own. Unless," he went on, eying Scotty suspiciously, "they secretly send someone in every so often to take a look and see how we're doing."

Scotty almost laughed at the idea that he could be an agent for such interstellar meddlers, but after a moment he realized, uneasily, that he couldn't guarantee that the off-worlders had not, in fact, been from a Federation world— or at least a world that would someday become a part of the Federation. When the meddling had started, the Federation was in its infancy and the Prime Directive was neither fully defined nor fully accepted. Even so, no one involved in such a massive and long-term violation would want to be found out. They would, as the off-worlders had done, keep their identities and world of origin a secret. And once they had given Narisia the key to star travel, eventual contact with Federation worlds became virtually inevitable. Hence, the meddlers would have to pull back or have their secret exposed.

Scotty very much hoped his speculations were wrong, but he feared they were not. Back in his own dim past in the Academy and occasionally since then, he'd heard rumors of various do-gooder groups—often academics with a bent for social science—who wished they were allowed to "guide" fledgling civilizations through critical phases rather than being forced to sit back and watch the newcomers bumble through on their own, making the same sometimes disastrous mistakes that others had already suffered through. Some, it was rumored, had even gone so far as to advocate using primitive worlds as laboratories, nudging various groups of natives this way and that to see which actions had the most desirable results.

And under the right—or wrong!—circumstances no one

was immune to the temptation. Even Jim Kirk and the *Enterprise* itself had been drawn into violating the Prime Directive by engaging in a primitive arms race with the Klingons on Neural.

Vehemently denying any connection with the off-worlders, Scotty checked the sensors again and was relieved to see that the *Goddard* was nearing the end of its arc and was approaching the far end of the previous shuttlecraft's warp trail. There was still no hint of the Proctors except for a faint and fading warp trail that was almost obscured by that of the shuttlecraft it had been following.

Racing back along the glaringly obvious warp trail at a hair under warp three, Scotty pushed the *Goddard*'s sensors as far as he could and then pushed them even further by abandoning the standard pattern and focusing them directly ahead like a phaser burst. If the Proctors had already caught up with the shuttlecraft, had immediately figured out the deception, and were even now bearing down on the *Goddard*'s unseeing aft, there was nothing he could do about it. He couldn't push the *Goddard* any faster than he was already pushing it, and there was certainly no way he could fight back with an essentially weaponless shuttlecraft, warning or no warning. They would either catch him or they wouldn't.

On the other hand, if the sensors could reveal the nature of the abandoned ship ten minutes—or even a single minute—earlier than they would when scanning a normal pattern, it could help. Once the sensors revealed what kind of ship it was and what condition it was in, he could start planning, perhaps even start replicating parts he would need, if the *Goddard*'s replicator had the necessary—and necessarily obsolete—patterns still in its library. An extra minute with that kind of knowledge in his possession could conceivably give him the edge he needed. It could mean the difference between being captured by the Proctors and making a safe rendezvous with the *Yandro*.

Abruptly, a single line of data appeared on the screen, then another.

At least, Scotty thought as he squinted at the screen, the ship was still there. Almost invisible in the shadow of a kilometer-wide cometary ball of ice and rock and organic compounds, it hadn't been towed away or blasted into scrap metal by the Proctors as they'd passed by.

And it *was* a fairly large ship, he saw with relief, though far from big enough to be the *Constitution*-class he'd been hoping for. One of those he could field strip and reassemble blindfolded. But he could do almost as well with any ship of the line of that era, and surely—

He blinked, frowning in disbelief as another line appeared on the data screen, then a whole string of them as the sensors locked onto the ship's systems one after another and transmitted the data back to the *Goddard*.

Then the viewscreen lit up with an image, fuzzy at this distance but unmistakable. Scotty gasped even though the sensor readings had already told him what the image almost certainly would be. He had simply been unable—or unwilling—to believe that the readings were right and that there was no alternative explanation for them.

But the readings had been right and the explanation was the obvious, if near impossible, one. If he'd been startled when he'd first seen the ancient NCC-1951 shuttlecraft, he was dumbfounded now.

The ship was nearly as old as the shuttlecraft it had carried, but it wasn't a Federation starship, *Constitution*-class or otherwise. It wasn't a Federation ship of any type or age. But it was, for him, the next best thing.

It was a vintage Klingon bird-of-prey.

For a long moment, Scotty just stared at the image. If nothing else, it at least explained why the damaged controls in the shuttle had been replaced by what had looked like Klingon substitutes. But how the two had ever gotten together in the first place . . .

He turned to Garamet, who was also watching the viewscreen. "Is that the ship you abandoned?" he asked, trying to keep the utter puzzlement out of his voice.

"Of course," she said. "Is there some reason it should not be?"

Scotty shook his head. There were a thousand questions he wanted to ask, but there wasn't time. Later, when they were safely away from the pursuers, would be time enough.

He squinted once again at the sensor readings, now beginning to come in at full speed, revealing more and more detail, filling screen after screen. The warp core, he saw with relief, was sealed and functional, its containment fields at better than ninety percent. And there was no shortage of anti-matter. Even the Klingon no-frills version of an environmental control system hadn't deteriorated greatly. It wouldn't keep them comfortable, but at least it would keep them alive while he made whatever repairs proved necessary.

If he could indeed determine quickly enough what repairs *were* necessary. Unfortunately there were literally thousands of malfunctions that could cause a ship to drop out of warp as precipitously as Garamet said this one had. And only a small percentage of them would show up on a remote sensor scan. Pinpointing the problem would probably require hands-on access to the drive.

But at least he was thoroughly familiar with the ship.

He had virtually rebuilt one just like it, the *Bounty*, which had then transported him, Kirk, McCoy, Uhura, Chekov, and the newly reconstituted Spock from Vulcan to Earth, after which it had taken them on a round trip through time to the twentieth century to pick up a pair of whales. And this one, the sensor readings showed, obviously had far more working systems than that other one. And whatever repairs he needed to make, he wouldn't have to cope with the sulfurous heat of Vulcan, its great red sun daily turning the ship's interior into an oven. Of most immediate import, however, was the fact that a ship like this could leave Garamet's warp-five bloodhounds in the interstellar dust.

If he could get its drive working soon enough.

Despite a faint shiver that ran up and down his spine as he wondered just how close the Proctors were getting, Scotty for the first time began to feel they might actually all survive this impromptu little adventure.

FIVE

SCOTTY WAS finishing his work on the Klingon ship when the idea that could give him back his life exploded in his mind.

It instantly overwhelmed his every other thought, like a nearby supernova blotting out a sky full of normal stars. It hit him just as he slapped the bulkhead panel back into place after bypassing the last of the burnt-out couplers that routed the helm's commands to the bird-of-prey's computer. He froze for just a moment as his mind, unbidden, began converting the idea into at least the skeleton of a plan. Racing back toward the bridge—no effete luxuries like turbolifts here in Klingon territory—he marveled at his own thickheadedness even as the plan gained further form and substance. How could it have taken so long for such an obvious idea to occur to him? He *should* have thought of it the moment the Klingon ship appeared on the *Goddard*'s screen like the godsend it was.

His only excuse was that his mind had been focused totally on what the *Goddard*'s sensors told him needed repair and how he could do the work in the shortest possible time. But now—now that the repairs were completed—

If they were indeed completed.

He would know soon enough, he told himself sharply as he careened onto the dimly lit, cavernous bridge, moving faster than he had in years.

Garamet and Wahlkon watched, wide-eyed, as Scotty ran the computer through its paces with the bypassed couplers and pronounced the ship—the *Bounty 2,* he had just silently christened it—fit for duty. Moments later, a long-range sensor scan showed a ship—presumably the Proctors' warp five bloodhound—following the *Goddard*'s arcing path and nearing the point at which it rejoined the destroyed shuttlecraft's warp trail. Apparently the Proctors' sensors weren't quite as primitive as he had hoped, nor the Proctors as unobservant. They *had* picked up the *Goddard*'s warp trail and guessed what it meant. Worse, he realized a moment later, they had somehow managed to boost their speed to almost warp six.

But they still would arrive too late to stop him.

If the coupler bypasses held, *if* there weren't other problems he hadn't found, *if* his on-the-fly tune-up, adjusting the matter-antimatter mix to what should be an optimal ratio, had been successful.

Gingerly, hoping he wasn't simply asking too much of the ancient vessel, he routed nearly ninety percent of the output of the anti-matter generators to the warp cores. He could feel the deck vibrate beneath his feet as he watched the readouts to see if everything was, if not optimal, at least within acceptable limits.

The Proctors were two minutes away, their sensors repeatedly scanning the *Bounty 2,* when the warp engines finally shuddered into life. Hastily, with one eye on the approaching ship, he made one last check to be sure that the *Goddard* was firmly secured in the cargo bay.

Pointing the *Bounty 2* in the general direction of the nearest starbase, a course that would take it nowhere near either the pursuing Proctors or the approaching *Yandro,* he engaged the warp drive and carefully eased it up to just enough above warp six to keep out of range of the Proctors' weapons. He *thought* the Klingon shields would hold, but he'd be much happier if he didn't have to put them to the test.

Moving from one station on the bridge to another, checking every readout and status light again and again, Scotty at last decided that the ship, ancient as it was, really was going to hold together. Klingons might be nasty pieces of work, but they *did* know how to build a sturdy ship. He wasn't at all sure that a comparable-sized Federation ship, burdened with several tons of whales and water, would have held together during the slingshot run past the sun that had brought the original *Bounty* back to the twenty-third-century. Even structural integrity fields had their limits.

Boosting the speed to nearly warp seven, Scotty put the *Bounty 2* on automatic pilot and returned to the cargo bay and the *Goddard* and initiated a one-way subspace link with the *Yandro.* The message he sent was intentionally vague, indicating that the emergency he thought he had fallen into had in reality been little more than a misunderstanding. Everything was under control, he assured Captain Stratton. The *Goddard* no longer needed assistance, and he would submit a full report when the exigencies of his long-delayed but finally-achieved retirement allowed.

Ignoring Stratton's attempts to open a two-way link, Scotty set the *Goddard*'s comm system back to standby and returned to the Klingon bridge, where Garamet and her brother were watching the viewscreen with fascination as the stars streamed past at a rate they had probably never before experienced.

Bracing himself for their reaction, he told them he planned to keep the *Bounty 2,* going on to explain that he would of course transport them to the nearest starbase or, if they preferred, return them to the Narisian system and, once he'd checked out the Klingon transporters, beam them down to wherever in that system they wanted to go.

To his relief, they didn't seem to be at all troubled by the prospect of losing the *Bounty 2* or of being taken to a star-base. Garamet in particular seemed positively thrilled at the thought of seeing firsthand what Scotty's "Federation" was really like, while Wahlkon was apparently happy to go wherever his sister went. Both, however, refused to even consider being returned to Narisia. Garamet had been put automatically on a list of traitors the moment it was discovered that her implant had been damaged and she hadn't reported it. She would already be dead—or at least re-implanted—and Wahlkon either dead or a prisoner if they hadn't had the incredible good luck of having their distress call picked up by Scotty and the *Goddard.*

Since the off-worlders had vanished generations ago, the various Proctors had gotten even more paranoid and aggressive than before, Garamet explained. Each suspected that one or more of the others had managed to either monopolize the off-worlders' attention or destroy them and steal as much of their technology as possible. As a result, each Proctor had been pushing his own people to not only expand upon the technology they already had but to search the Narisian system and surrounding space for anything the off-worlders might have left behind.

It was on one of these searches through a particularly dense segment of one of two asteroid belts in the Narisian system that Garamet had stumbled across the derelict Klingon ship, invisible to her ship's sensors until she was nearly on top of it. Unfortunately, a searcher from a different Narisian faction had shown up not long after, and Garamet's ship had ended up colliding with the other ship as both tried to take possession of the prize.

Both ships were disabled by the collision, the other pilot killed. Garamet suffered only a few cuts and bruises, but one of her injuries was a blow to the head, which apparently disabled her implant. In any event, as she tried to repair her ship, thoughts that would have seemed unthinkable only hours earlier began to bubble up in her mind. She even found herself thinking that the secrecy that had surrounded the Wise Ones from the first day they had appeared was totally wrong-headed. And now that they were no longer around to keep all the Narisian factions under at least minimal control, the secrecy and the internecine warfare among the various Proctors had gotten immeasurably worse. As witness what had just happened between her and the other pilot. What was needed, she realized with a start, was for the truth to come out. Before her injuries, such a thought would have triggered a physical illness, forcing her to abandon it.

But there was nothing she could do about it, not in a disabled ship that was capable of communicating only with the Proctors.

In the end, after days of futile attempts to repair her own ship, she boarded the Klingon ship, still functional according to her ship's surviving sensors, and was eventually able to decipher enough of its controls to get its impulse drive working and, eventually, its warp drive as well.

But it all took time, too much time for the impatient Proctors, and when her superior contacted her, she was unable to conceal the fact that her implant was no longer functional. She was instantly ordered back to Narisia, of course, and when some hesitation was detected in her answers, her brother was threatened. If she didn't return immediately, she was told harshly, he would be the one to suffer. With the Klingon ship, however, she was able to get to Wahlkon before the Proctor's people and pick him up. She hadn't yet figured out how to operate the Klingon weapons systems, so she could only flee. And then the ship had blown the couplers and dropped out of warp drive, leaving Garamet and Wahlkon with only the shuttlecraft.

They had been sending out distress signals blindly, hoping they might somehow attract the attention of the offworlders, the Wise Ones whose ships they still assumed the bird-of-prey and the shuttlecraft to be. And that was where Scotty and the *Goddard* had come in.

Neither Garamet nor Wahlkon had any idea what either a Federation shuttlecraft or a Klingon bird-of-prey was, let alone how one had ended up inside the other, abandoned in the Narisian system. Scotty was equally at a loss to explain the latter, though he did have hopes of eventually accessing the Klingon logs. His immediate concern, however, was not where the bird-of-prey *had* been or what it *had* done. His only interest, now that he had control of the ship, was what it *would* be doing.

Captain Jean-Luc Picard's eyebrows inched upward in mild surprise as Captain Montgomery Scott's smiling face appeared on the *Enterprise* main viewscreen.

"Captain Scott," he said, returning a modest version of

the smile, "this is an unexpected pleasure. To what do we owe the honor of your return?"

"You remember suggesting I might want to try playing engineering catch-up? Well, if the offer of the use of the Enterprise *data banks is still open, I wouldn't mind getting started. At least I'll know just how much catching up I'll need to do."*

"Of course, Captain Scott. You're always welcome. Should I assume retirement didn't entirely agree with you?" Scott, Picard suspected, was, like himself, not one to appreciate the virtues of prolonged inactivity.

"You could say that, although you may have heard I haven't been entirely idle."

Picard nodded. He'd wondered if Scott would mention any of the reports that had been circulating through Starfleet. "Captain Stratton did file a report on a . . . false alarm, shall we say? He also made mention of a detailed report you indicated was forthcoming, as did the commander of Starbase—"

"Aye, and you'll have them. But if you'd like the short version . . . ?"

"If you please, Mr. Scott."

Scotty hesitated, as if he'd been expecting—or at least hoping for—a different answer, but then he pulled in a breath and launched into a bare-bones account of how he'd encountered two aliens and what he had learned from them. *"Whoever these Wise Ones were,"* he finished, *"they obviously violated the Prime Directive. But it all ended generations ago."*

"And you think it was someone from the Federation?"

Scotty shrugged broadly. *"I cannot say 'tis impossible, especially with the Federation shuttlecraft they had. Do you have any record of the ship it came from? NCC-1951?"*

"Mr. Data?"

Picard's android second officer spoke without hesitation. "NCC-1951, Captain, the *Antares*-class science vessel *Senzig*. It vanished at approximately the same time the *Jenolen* was lost. It was on its way to investigate an anomaly that, according to recent speculations, may have been related to an uncharted Borg Transwarp Conduit. There is no record of its having ever been found, nor of any survivors."

Picard frowned. *"Someone* obviously found it. But we're unlikely to ever learn the truth at this late date. Any extensive investigation in the Narisian system could only compound the violation."

"Aye, Captain. If what they told me is true, very few Narisians know the so-called Wise Ones even exist, just the leaders and the people working directly with them. Everyone else thinks that all the scientific advances of the last two hundred years were made by the Narisians themselves. To discover instead that the inventions were virtually all given to them, as if they were helpless bairns . . ." Scotty's voice trailed off suggestively.

Picard nodded again, this time with a slight grimace. "It could be traumatic for the Narisian psyche, certainly. I don't envy whoever will have to decide how to handle the situation when and if the Narisians do establish contact with the Federation. But such matters are not the responsibility of Starfleet captains, particularly not of retired ones. Although," he added with the barest trace of a smile, "this particular retired captain might consider expediting his official report of the incident. A thorough account, made before one's memory begins to play its inevitable tricks, could be of considerable help to whoever does eventually inherit the problem."

Scotty's smile froze for a moment but then widened as he shrugged. *"Aye, Captain, you'll have it in your computer before I come aboard."*

"Excellent, Mr. Scott. I look forward to your arrival, as I know Commander La Forge does as well."

Scotty let out a sigh of relief as the link to the *Enterprise* was broken. He was simply not accustomed to lying, even by omission, and it made him uneasy despite all the good intentions in the galaxy. All in all, though, it had gone as well as could be expected and far better than he had feared. He of course hadn't mentioned the existence of the *Bounty 2,* and Picard hadn't, for whatever reason, questioned him about how he had covered the distance from Narisia to the *Enterprise*'s current coordinates in the *Goddard,* which he still had not been able to push much past warp three. He'd been prepared to trot out as a last resort a story about how he had hitched a ride part way on the unnamed ship of a somewhat shady interstellar trader, a twenty-fourth-century equivalent of tribble mogul Cyrano Jones, but he was mighty relieved it hadn't been necessary. He was even more relieved that Garamet and her brother had apparently followed his instructions and had deleted the *Bounty 2* from their accounts as well.

With any luck at all, he could get what he needed from the *Enterprise* and be gone before anyone decided to ask him any really tough questions.

By then it would be too late. He'd be back on the *Bounty 2,* and no one could stop him from doing what he had realized he had to do.

He hoped.

SIX

SCOTTY FROWNED as a soft, chiming sound announced someone was at the door of the guest quarters to which Picard and La Forge had escorted him less than twenty-four hours earlier.

"Come in," he called, hastily blanking the screen of the terminal he was working at.

For a long moment nothing happened, but finally the door slid open with a barely audible hiss. His eyes widened as he saw the woman standing in the corridor, a Mona Lisa smile on her chocolate-brown face, a bottle of Saurian brandy in one hand. Guinan, she had called herself more than three-quarters of a century ago on Earth. And she still seemed to glide rather than walk, he realized as she crossed the threshold in a floor-length gown not unlike the one she had worn then. As the other gown had, this one only contributed to the illusion that she could defy gravity.

If it *was* an illusion, Scotty thought sharply as he watched her come to a stop in the middle of the room and turn toward him, her oddly regal features showing not the slightest sign of the passage of three quarters of a century.

"I'm older than I look, Mr. Scott," she said, her eyes now smiling as well as her lips.

"Aye, I would say so. Unless you managed to skip over a few decades the way I did."

She shook her head minutely. "No, although there have been some I wouldn't have minded skipping. Not the last few, however, since I joined Captain Picard here on the *Enterprise.*"

"You were here when they found me on the *Jenolen,* then?"

"I was. I thought of offering you another sip of Saurian brandy, to make up for the synthehol you found so objectionable when you first visited Ten-Forward. However, the situation soon became a bit hectic, as you may recall. And then you were on your way." She held up the scimitar-shaped bottle. "But now you're back, and the Saurian brandy never left."

As it had seventy-odd years ago, his mouth almost watered at the sight, but this time he shook his head. "I appreciate the thought, lassie," he said regretfully, "but when you're tryin' to make sense out of the last seventy-five years of Starfleet engineering advances, you'd best keep a clear head if you don't want to sink like a stone."

The woman shrugged, the motion as subdued as her smile. "Then accept it as my gift. Have a celebratory sip when you've made enough sense for one day." She paused and glanced at the blank terminal screen as she set the brandy next to it. "Are you making good progress?"

"As good as can be expected, I imagine. Do you understand such matters?"

"Only at a layman's level."

Scotty gave her what he hoped was a suitably rueful smile. "The last seventy-five years have almost turned *me* into a layman. I've a lot of catching up to do."

For a long moment she said nothing, her eyes fixed on his as if searching for something. There had been, he realized uneasily, a similar look about her in that Glasgow bar just before she'd disappeared into the night, just before he'd met the unfortunate Matt Franklin.

"Then perhaps I should leave you to your work," she said quietly, and once again she was gone.

As the door to the corridor hissed shut behind her, he realized he'd been holding his breath.

Guinan made her way slowly back to Ten-Forward, walking the corridors rather than taking the near-instantaneous turbolift system. She needed time to think.

Something was wrong.

She felt it but she didn't understand it any more than she had understood what she had felt that day, on an earlier *Enterprise,* when she had first become aware of Captain Scott's existence. Or what she had felt, barely six months ago, when he had been resurrected from the *Jenolen.*

Was this signaling the beginning of what the "feelings" had warned her about then? The beginning of whatever role she still had to play in Captain Scott's life?

But no answer came.

There was only the maddening frustration of utter helplessness, of knowing that *something* was coming but having no idea of its nature or its direction. Animals staked out as bait in those barbaric hunts that had been popular on nineteenth-century Earth must have felt this way, she thought with a silent grimace, when the first scent of a distant predator reached their nostrils.

But *she* was no helpless animal.

And she was not alone, despite how it often felt.

Stopping at the nearest companel, she linked to the bridge. "Captain," she said, her calm tone belying the feeling of urgency that gripped her, "I must speak with you."

Captain Jean-Luc Picard settled back on the couch in his ready room while Guinan stood silently in the middle of the room, her eyes not meeting his. Others would have thought her the epitome of calmness, but Picard knew better. He knew that, for her, the barely noticeable rigidity in her posture, the slightly compressed lips, the avoidance of eye contact—all these were the equivalent of anyone else's pacing the room on the verge of a panic attack. He had never seen her like this, not ever. Time and again, on the *Enterprise* and elsewhere, when events around her had been spinning out of control, she herself had never even come close to losing control. Sometimes she had been the *only* one, an island of wait-and-see calm in the midst of chaos.

"What do you know of Captain Scott's plans?" she asked abruptly.

Picard shrugged. "Nothing specific. As I understand it, his intent is to review the technological advances made while he was in the *Jenolen* transporter, although I suspect he is at the same time indulging in some innocent nostalgia."

"How so?"

"In addition to summaries of a few thousand articles only an engineer would understand, he's been accessing the logs of previous incarnations of the *Enterprise*. But I don't believe there's anything to worry about this time. He hasn't been drinking and he hasn't been spending any time in the holodeck simulation of the first *Enterprise*, even though he would have a legitimate reason to do the latter.

He's already had at least one offer from the Academy, suggesting he lecture to the cadets about his era in return for an accelerated course in all the engineering developments he's missed out on."

"And he has no other plans?"

"None that I am aware of."

"What of the Narisians? Are you certain his reports tell the entire story of what happened there?"

"I suspect they do not," Picard said with a faint smile, "but given his record I cannot but believe that any omissions were made for good cause."

"One man's good cause, even a *good* man's good cause, can be another man's disaster." For just an instant, her eyes seemed to glaze over. "To 'rescue' someone who doesn't want or need to be rescued, for example," she murmured, then blinked, as if consciously pulling back from whatever precipice her mind had unwillingly approached.

"Do you have reason to believe this is the case with Captain Scott?" Picard asked.

Guinan closed her eyes for a moment, as if marshaling her strength—or perhaps testing her balance. "No *reasonable* reason, just a feeling, a worry."

"You don't need me to remind you that you've had such feelings before," he said, the beginnings of a frown narrowing the corners of his eyes. "Or that they have virtually always been proven valid in some way."

"I know, Captain, I know. But it's different this time. The feelings are somehow related to Captain Scott and his being here, out of his own time. There's more, much more, but I don't know what it is, what *any* of it is." She shivered, something he had never seen her do. "It's like when you catch a glimpse of something out of the corner of your eye, a glimpse of something that terrifies you even more than death itself, like the first time someone sees a Borg cube. It's bearing down on you, but when you look directly at it, it's gone. But you know it's still there, just outside your range of vision, still coming. *I* know it's still there. And I know it's *meant* to be there, that Captain Scott is *meant* to be *here,* but . . ."

Picard watched her startling performance, fully realizing for the first time the true depth and intensity of the turmoil that boiled beneath her rigidly controlled exterior. He rose from the sofa and stood facing her, surprising himself by gently laying his hands on her shoulders.

"You've seen me through any number of dark times," he said quietly when she didn't draw back from his touch. "Your intuitions have saved me more than once, on the *Enterprise* and before. If there is anything I can do to help you through . . . whatever it is that's troubling you, please, let me do it. Let *me* help *you* this time."

The glint of a tear in her eye as she momentarily looked away startled him even more than all that had gone before, but before he could respond, it was gone, leaving him to wonder if it had existed only in his mind.

"I shouldn't have brought this up, Captain," she said, raising her eyes to meet his. Her voice was once again the way it had always been, her face once again a neutral mask. "There's nothing you *can* do, nothing anyone can do, not yet."

"Perhaps not," he said earnestly, "but you can at least *talk* to me about it. I can't pretend to understand these feelings you say you have, these premonitions or whatever it is that you can see that no one else can. All I know is that, in my experience, there is no problem so frightening that sharing it doesn't at least make it easier to bear."

She shook her head almost imperceptibly, then lay a hand lightly on his forearm as if *she* were comforting *him*. "You're most likely right, Captain," she said with a resigned smile, "but there simply isn't anything more to share. I've already told you virtually everything there is to tell. And there's nothing I can do, nothing you can do, nothing anyone can do—but wait."

"Are you positive about that, Guinan? You say Captain Scott is the focus of these 'feelings,' so perhaps for once the obvious approach might be worth trying. Tell *him* what you feel. Find out what *he* says."

She shook her head. "I'm sorry, but telling Captain Scott about these feelings is the one thing I know I can't do." She grimaced. "I should not even have told you."

"Is there a reason you can't tell him?" Picard had long ago learned to trust Guinan's unexplained intuitions, but there still were times when he couldn't help but think that she could handle them more . . . pragmatically. "Or is that restriction part of the 'feeling'?"

"Something like that, yes." She shook her head again, sighing faintly.

"Is there anything in your feelings that prohibit *me* from talking to Captain Scott?"

She was silent a moment, as if listening to some inner voice, then shrugged. "As you wish, Captain."

He watched her for a moment, half expecting her to change her mind, but she continued to stand silently, enigmatically.

"Captain Scott," Picard said, tapping his combadge. Scott, though he had protested he was merely a civilian passenger, had been issued his own combadge for the duration of his stay on the *Enterprise*.

But there was no reply.

As he tried a second time, then a third, Guinan turned to watch him, a frown beginning to narrow her eyes.

"Computer," he snapped as a fourth attempt went unacknowledged, "locate Captain Scott."

"Captain Scott is no longer aboard the Enterprise," the matter-of-fact voice of the computer informed him tonelessly.

SEVEN

"COMPUTER, HOW and when did Captain Scott leave the *Enterprise?*" Picard asked, turning abruptly and moving toward the ready room door and the bridge beyond.

"He departed aboard the shuttlecraft Goddard *twenty-one-point-three minutes ago,"* the computer informed him as the door hissed open.

With Guinan gliding close behind, Picard strode onto the bridge. "Mr. Data, why was I not informed of Captain Scott's departure?"

Data hesitated—that alone told Picard that something was wrong. "Captain Scott's departure was on your authorization, sir."

Riker stood and relinquished the captain's chair. "I take it you didn't supply that authorization?"

"No, Number One."

"The *Goddard* is no longer within sensor range, Captain," Data said.

"Display route taken by the *Goddard.*"

The starfield on the viewscreen blinked out and was replaced by another, this one with the *Enterprise* at its center and a string-straight, blinking path leading away. A moment later a series of figures appeared along the length of the blinking path, all extracted from the record the starship's sensors constantly and automatically made of all objects in its vicinity. The *Goddard,* the figures indicated, had gone into warp drive within seconds of clearing the *Enterprise* shuttlebay. It had immediately exceeded the shuttlecraft's design parameters by hitting warp three-point-one.

At a distance of approximately six billion kilometers from its starting point, ten billion from the *Enterprise*'s current position, the path ended.

But nothing, according to the sensors, was at the end of the path.

The thought that the shuttlecraft might have been destroyed darted through Picard's mind, but there was no indication of any significant energy release anywhere along the path, certainly not at its end.

Picard turned to Guinan, who had lowered herself gingerly into Counselor Troi's unoccupied chair on his left. "Guinan? What do your feelings have to say about *this?*"

"They're saying the same as before, but even more intensely. *Something* is happening that—"

"Captain," Data broke in, "sensors are detecting a subspace variance consistent with a cloaked ship, either Klingon or Romulan, moving at warp speed."

"Tag its location on the screen," Picard ordered. A moment later a flickering vector arrow appeared several billion kilometers from the far end of the *Goddard*'s indicated path. According to the figures that flickered in time with the arrow, it was moving at warp eight.

"Intercept course, maximum warp," Picard snapped to Ensign Raeger at the conn, then added unnecessarily,

"Don't lose it." Unless whatever it was, Romulan or Klingon, was employing a brand-new form of cloaking technology, there was little danger it could elude the *Enterprise* sensors.

He turned again to Guinan. "Does this help clarify anything?" he asked. When she only shook her head, he darted a look around the bridge. "Theories, anyone? Suggestions? Will? Lieutenant Worf?"

"It makes no sense, Captain," Riker said, still watching the screen, "but it certainly looks as if the *Goddard* was intercepted by a cloaked Klingon or Romulan ship."

"This deep in Federation space?"

"I told you it didn't make sense," Riker said with a grimace, "but what else could it be?"

"It is Klingon, Captain, not Romulan," Data spoke up. The flickering vector arrow had been replaced on the screen by a solid dot, which expanded into a tiny but equally solid image of a ship. "It is, in fact, a bird-of-prey." Data paused, looking from the image on the screen to a host of sensor readouts. "However, it is nearly a century old," he added. "That model has not been produced since the early twenty-fourth-century."

"Crazier and crazier," Riker muttered.

"Open a channel, Mr. Worf," Picard said.

"No response, Captain," Worf said a few seconds later. "However, readings indicate their communications system is activated."

"They're listening but they aren't responding?"

"Apparently."

The tiny image of the bird-of-prey vanished from the viewscreen.

"They have altered the phase of the cloaking field," Data said. "I am attempting to compensate."

"Mr. Worf, where would their last known course take them?"

"Directly to the nearest star, Captain," Worf said. "The Arhennius system is less than three hours away at warp eight. It contains no habitable worlds."

"And beyond the Arhennius system?"

"The next star on a direct line beyond Arhennius is approximately fifteen days distant, but a bird-of-prey of that vintage could not possibly maintain such a speed for more than a few hours. Anything above warp six was used only for emergencies of short duration."

"That is not entirely true, Captain," Data said. "In his memoirs of the House of Gorm, B'ator claims to have maintained warp eight-point-one for three days in order to take part in the final battle of—"

"The House of Gorm," Worf interrupted scornfully, "is far better known for 'making claims' than for the battles it actually fought."

"Let's not lose sight of our primary goal here, gentlemen," Picard reminded them, but even as he spoke, the bird-of-prey reappeared on the viewscreen.

"Compensation successful, Captain," Data said.

"It is still following the same course," Worf said, "and ignoring our hails."

"Mr. Data, can we be certain that the *Goddard* is being transported in the bird-of-prey?"

"We cannot. The altered cloaking field still produces a great deal of distortion. There appears to be a smaller vessel of some kind present, but it is impossible to determine anything further—except that it is completely powered down. No systems are operating."

"How long until we overtake it?"

Suddenly, Guinan's hand fell on Picard's arm, gripping

it tightly. "You have to overtake it *before* it reaches Arhennius, Captain," she said with quiet emphasis.

Startled, Picard turned toward her. "What is going to happen at Arhennius, Guinan?"

"I don't know. All I know now is that that is where it all starts. The *Enterprise* must be there."

"To stop it? To help it along? *What?*"

She shook her head, her fingers tightening even more on his arm. "I truly don't know. But we *must* be there. That much I *do* know."

"And if we aren't?"

"You're wasting time, Captain!" she said, a completely uncharacteristic flare of anger in her voice.

Or perhaps fear, Picard thought, a shiver momentarily gripping his own spine. The only time he had heard anything even remotely like this in her voice or seen her demeanor change so radically was when she had encountered Q, the thought of which only intensified his uneasiness. If there was anyone—or any*thing*—he did not want to ever again be involved with, it was that often childish and always infuriating creature of incalculable power and infinite perversity.

"Will we overtake the Klingon ship in time, Ensign?"

"I can't be certain, Captain," Raeger said, not looking up from the controls. "But we won't be more than a minute behind when it reaches the Arhennius system."

"Mr. La Forge," Picard said abruptly, activating the link to engineering, "can you give us any more? Safely?"

"*I doubt it, Captain, but I can try to tweak the warp core alignment and possibly the matter-antimatter ratio. Just don't expect the sort of miracle Captain Scott was famous for on the original* Enterprise."

"Understood, Commander."

In the end, the chief engineer managed to cut the time to Arhennius by approximately sixty-five seconds, but at the same time the fleeing bird-of-prey inched its own speed up, cutting over forty seconds from its own arrival time.

They would still be twenty seconds behind when Scott reached the Arhennius system.

With Arhennius now a glowing ball on the *Enterprise* viewscreen, the Klingon ship abruptly deactivated its cloaking field.

"Details, Mr. Data," Picard snapped a fraction of a second after seeing the image on the viewscreen leap into full clarity.

"Its present course will take it through the solar corona. Its shields may not be enough to protect it. Arhennius is only a quarter more massive than Sol, but it has more than twice the energy output."

"The *Goddard*—" Picard began, but Data continued.

"The *Goddard* is indeed in the bird-of-prey's cargo hold. It is still powered down. There is a single, humanoid life form on the Klingon ship's bridge."

"Not within the *Goddard?*"

"That is correct, Captain."

"And no Klingons? Anywhere in either ship?"

"As I said, Captain, there is a single humanoid life form."

"Captain Scott?"

"His presence would be entirely consistent with the readings," Data said.

"Then why—Mr. Worf, try again to open a channel."

"A channel *is* open, sir, but there is no response."

"But he can hear us?"

"If he is listening."

"Very well." Picard paused, pulling in a breath. "Captain Scott, if you are indeed on board the fleeing bird-of-prey, please respond. This is Captain Picard of the *Enterprise*. You are welcome to any assistance we can provide."

There was still no response. Data glanced up from the ops station readouts. "The life form's pulse has accelerated to an unacceptable level."

"Captain Scott, will you at least explain what you are hoping to accomplish? Our sensors show your ship heading directly into the star's corona. It is doubtful that your shields can protect you."

Still no response.

"The ship is once again accelerating," Data announced. "It will be entering the star's corona in—"

"You must follow him, Captain!" Guinan said abruptly.

"We *are* following him, Guinan. As soon as we're within transporter range, we'll beam him out."

"You don't understand! You won't get the chance. Arhennius itself is his goal. He intends to use its gravity well to slingshot back in time."

Picard blinked. Suddenly he saw Scott's earlier actions in a whole new light, particularly his seemingly nostalgic accessing of the logs of previous incarnations of the *Enterprise*. Those logs, Picard realized belatedly, contained not just the logs of the *Enterprise* itself but those of all *Enterprise* personnel—*even when they served on other ships!*

Including the *Bounty,* the Klingon ship that had carried Scott and Kirk and the others back to the twentieth century.

The *Bounty,* a bird-of-prey very much like the one Scott was at this moment piloting.

Guinan was right.

Scott *was* intending to go back in time, just as he had done before, when the alien probe had almost destroyed Earth because of the extinction of the whales. Using Spock's on-the-fly calculations, Scott and the others had sent the *Bounty* whipping through Sol's gravity well and back in time to when whales had still existed. And the calculations Spock had used to make the jump would have been included in at least one of the logs Scott had accessed!

But why was he doing it *now?*

And where in time was he going? Had he decided he couldn't catch up with the seventy-five years of new technology he'd missed out on? Had he decided he would sooner try to go back to a time when his knowledge was state of the art, not hopelessly outdated?

Unlikely. Despite some bad moments immediately after his rescue from the *Jenolen,* Scott was no quitter. And he certainly wouldn't risk upsetting the entire timestream for such a purely personal goal.

"Mr. Scott!" Picard said, his tone filled with as much authority as he could muster. "I *order* you to stop!"

"His communications system has shut down, Captain," Data said. "All power is being diverted to the warp drive and the shields. He did not hear your order."

"He didn't *want* to hear it," Riker muttered.

The Klingon ship was bulleting toward the Arhennius corona, once again accelerating despite the fact that it was already far exceeding its design specs. Picard half expected it to fly to pieces at any instant.

"Follow him," Guinan said, coming as close to shouting as he had ever heard her do. "If you ever trusted me, Captain, trust me now!"

He shook his head sharply. "Two ships will only disrupt

the timestream even more than one. And we *can't* follow him precisely, not without knowing a hundred times more than what the sensors can tell us. By the time we reach Arhennius—"

"Sensors are detecting increasing amounts of chronometric radiation, Captain," Data announced, bringing a sudden hush to the bridge.

"Origin?"

"Impossible to say, sir. There is no discrete source. It is simply *there*—and growing at an exponential rate."

"The radiation is there because the timestream is already changing, Captain!" Guinan said with even more intensity. "You *must* follow him—now! *Before we all forget that it has even changed!*"

For a moment, Picard's mind seemed to spin out of control. Even the image of Arhennius on the viewscreen shimmered and shifted as the Klingon ship accelerated directly into the corona. The ever-increasing warping of space caused by the ship's drive was, he knew, clashing ever more violently with the spatial distortion caused by the immense gravity of the star. Soon, the clash between the two essentially irresistible forces would literally squeeze the ship out of the here and now, sending it careening through time itself like a rocket shot up out of a planet's atmosphere, not into orbit but into a suborbital trajectory that would bring it plunging back like a meteor.

But these ships—the Klingon bird-of-prey and, if he heeded Guinan's desperate plea, the *Enterprise*—would be propelled not out of a planet's atmosphere but out of the entire space-time continuum, into a jagged arc through the unknown, an arc that would bring it plunging back at some distant time that only the most precise measurements and calculations could determine.

Measurements and calculations they had no time to make.

They could find themselves years or centuries distant from their own time.

If they survived at all!

Suddenly, the chronometric radiation intensified a hundredfold, setting off a klaxon-like alarm on the bridge, and Picard felt the universe—his *memory* of the universe—begin to shift like windblown desert sand.

With his last rational thought, he barked out the order that sent the *Enterprise* plunging into the Arhennius corona only seconds behind Scott and the Klingon ship. But even as the *Enterprise* shuddered under the strain, new images began to appear on the viewscreen, images beyond the corona they were shooting through at impossible speeds.

Images of a solid phalanx of Borg cubes.

Then that universe winked out and there was only the terrible shuddering of the *Enterprise* as the conflicting forces of the straining warp drive and the intense gravity field of Arhennius battered at each other and at the ship caught in the titanic crossfire. Finally, after microseconds that seemed to stretch into minutes, as if the *Enterprise* and its crew were relativistic particles descending the last few millimeters before plunging through a black hole's event horizon, the fabric of space-time was ruptured for the second time in less than a minute, and the *Enterprise* was sent hurtling through time.

EIGHT

FOR PICARD, the shuddering and kaleidoscopic roller-coaster ride seemed to go on forever, threatening to tear the *Enterprise* apart and scatter its fragments across centuries of time.

But all he could see in his mind's eye were the Borg cubes that had appeared—had *seemed* to appear, he told himself again and again—in the universe he had just been catapulted out of. Even though Scott had launched himself into the past only seconds before the *Enterprise* had followed, something Scott had done at the far end of his arc into the past had already disrupted the timestream, bringing the Borg—

Suddenly, the bone-jarring, eye-searing ride was over.

Like a plane emerging from the fury of a hurricane into the silent stillness of the storm's eye, the *Enterprise* re-entered the space-time continuum. Behind them, Arhennius was a rapidly shrinking ball of nuclear fire. Ahead was only a familiar and unremarkable star field.

"All stop," Picard snapped. The image on the viewscreen shimmered briefly as the *Enterprise* dropped out of warp.

"Where—" Picard began but broke off. *"When* are we, Mr. Data?"

"The computer's preliminary survey of the coordinates of nearby stars indicates we are in the latter half of the twenty-third century."

"And Captain Scott's ship?"

"Sensors indicate no ships within the Arhennius system, Captain."

Picard winced inwardly at the words, even though they were far from unexpected. If anything, they confirmed what he—what they *all* had been thinking as the *Enterprise* dove into the Arhennius corona: Slingshotting through time on the fly is not an exact science. Under these conditions, there was simply no way of determining the precise trajectory either Captain Scott or the *Enterprise* took. There was therefore no way of knowing precisely when either vessel had re-entered normal space-time with respect to the other.

"Can you at least estimate how far apart our arrival times might be, Mr. Data?"

"Not with any certainty, Captain," Data said as he consulted his instruments again. "Ensign Raeger appears to have come as close to duplicating Captain Scott's trajectory as is humanly possible. There was no way, however, to compensate for the *Enterprise*'s greater mass. I can only say that it is unlikely that our arrival was more than a few months before or after Captain Scott's."

"So he may not have arrived yet?"

"That is correct, Captain."

A flicker of hope brushed at his mind. "Check for warp trails, Mr. Data. If he is already here, he certainly would have left a warp trail, no matter where he went."

"He would." Data scanned a new set of readouts. "However, the only warp trail within the Arhennius system is that of the *Enterprise* itself."

Picard felt relief wash over him. "So he *hasn't* arrived yet. Perhaps we can lie low and wait for him, then stop him from doing whatever he was planning to do. And hope that no one from this era notices us."

He was silent a moment, looking at the deceptively familiar star field on the viewscreen. "Mr. Worf, maintain complete radio silence, but scan the subspace spectrum for any time-coded traffic."

"I have been scanning since we first arrived," the Klingon said, "but I have found no subspace traffic."

"Subspace frequencies in use in the twenty-third century—"

"I have already compensated for all known differences, Captain," Worf said, a touch of reproach in his I-know-my-job tone. "There is no subspace traffic on any of the frequencies used by members of the Federation or by either Klingons or Romulans during the second half of the twenty-third century."

The relief Picard had experienced moments before turned to a chill, his eyes drawn again to the viewscreen. "Mr. Data, how reliable is the computer's estimate of the current time? Could it be off by centuries rather than decades? Could we have gone back to a time before subspace radio was used in this quadrant?"

"It is highly unlikely, Captain, but I will know for certain in a moment," Data said, consulting a new set of readings that had just appeared on his control panel. "The computer has just completed a luminosity scan of the fifty nearest variable stars, including Sol, and is comparing these values with the values that Starfleet and other organizations have recorded continuously since before the founding of the

Federation. That will narrow it down to a period of a few months, and then—"

Data broke off as another set of readings appeared. "In terms of Old Earth chronology," he continued after a moment's study, "the year is 2293. Now that we know the year, the computer can scan remote galaxies for known supernovas whose light would have reached the Arhennius system during that year. Because of their distance and faintness, this will require more time, but . . ."

Data continued to explain, but Picard was no longer listening. Hearing the year—2293—had been enough.

It was not the year Captain Scott had signed onto the *Jenolen*.

It was a year earlier, the year the *Enterprise*-B had been launched.

The year that James T. Kirk, Scott's captain and friend, had died saving that other *Enterprise*.

For a moment Picard resisted the inevitable conclusion, but as his mind darted back to the conversations he had had with Scott in the days after his rescue from the *Jenolen,* all doubt vanished. The man's nostalgia for the first *Enterprise* had been huge, but his loyalty to its captain had been monumental.

Monumental and, no matter how noble, ultimately and obviously misguided.

There was no question in Picard's mind as to where and when Scott had *intended* to go.

And what he had intended to do.

But that knowledge, Picard told himself grimly, did nothing to resolve the one question that really mattered: Where and when had Scott *actually* gone?

And what had he done that could have changed history so drastically that the Federation no longer existed—or at least was not using subspace radio—in 2293 and had been replaced by the Borg by 2370?

Scotty cursed silently as he listened once again to the time-coded subspace messages he had finally been able to tap into with the *Goddard*'s comm system. Instead of several weeks, he had only *days* before the destruction of the *Lakul* and the near destruction of the *Enterprise*-B!

In his rush to slip away from Picard's *Enterprise* and then to keep from being overtaken by it, he must have miscalculated his trajectory. Or the actual mass of Arhennius or of the *Bounty 2* itself was a minuscule fraction different from the values he had entered. Or any of a hundred other possibilities. Even the formulae themselves, as recorded in Spock's log months of subjective time after the event itself, might have contained minute errors. Spock was, after all, half human.

He would probably never know which number or calculation had tripped him up, and in fact it didn't matter. It was done. He was where he was, when he was, and there was still a chance he could pull it off.

If the *Bounty 2* held up.

Against all odds, it had already survived the warp eight race to Arhennius and the bone-jarring, hull-plate-rattling passage through time, so there was no reason—other than a wee dose of common sense—to think that it would not survive the next five days. He could—and almost certainly *would*—spend his every waking hour monitoring the drive, nursing it along, adjusting each and every variable before any had a chance to drift even a micron off their optimum values.

And at least Picard had not followed him—or hadn't been able to. Either way, Scotty was grateful for small favors. He would need all he could get, not to mention some large ones as well.

Entering the coordinates at which, in little more than five days, the *Lakul* and the *Robert Fox* would be—had been?—destroyed, he murmured a prayer to whatever gods of the Highlands watched over errant engineers and engaged the warp drive.

As Picard had expected, Data's supernova survey revealed they were within two weeks—before or after—of the moment Kirk had died saving the *Enterprise*-B.

Briefly, he told Guinan and the bridge crew what he was virtually certain Scott had been attempting to do. Only Riker looked doubtful.

"Could he be that irresponsible? The man was a Starfleet officer for nearly half a century."

Picard could only shrug. "He was also three-quarters of a century out of his own time. His friends and family were almost certainly all dead, and everything he knew about engineering was seventy-five years obsolete. And it's not as if he hadn't done it before. Don't forget he was along when Kirk brought those two whales from the twentieth century."

"And saved Earth," Riker said, frowning. "You're saying this time he was planning to *risk* Earth, risk upsetting the entire timestream just to save one person?"

"There's no point in arguing the wisdom of his action, Number One. Nor of ours when we followed him. We can't take either of them back. What we *can* do—*all* we can do for now—is try to find out where and when he actually went and what he did that resulted in the timestream we find ourselves in. And then work from there."

Picard paused, looking around the bridge, his eyes lingering momentarily on Guinan, who, in a most uncharacteristic act, lowered her eyes. "To that end," he went on, "I'm open to any and all ideas. For a start, can we take it as a given that Mr. Scott overshot his intended destination and went further into the past than he intended?"

Riker nodded. "Based on what Mr. Worf's *not* hearing in subspace, I'd say we have to. Either that or he purposely made a second jump. Nothing he could have done here and now—or even a few weeks ago—could silence every starfaring race in this sector."

Picard nodded. "Mr. Data, is it possible for Mr. Scott to have overshot by not just years but decades? Even centuries?"

"It would be highly unlikely, Captain, but not impossible if something catastrophic occurred during the jump itself."

"Just how catastrophic?" Picard asked impatiently when Data paused for a moment.

"For example," Data continued, "anything that could cause his ship to unexpectedly gain a great deal of velocity or lose a great deal of mass. A change in either of those parameters would drastically alter his trajectory and—"

"And essentially destroy the ship and kill Mr. Scott. Is there anything *survivable* that could have thrown him that far off target?"

"Nothing that I have been able to hypothesize, Captain. However, neither Mr. Scott nor the ship would have to survive in order for the timestream to be affected. If something happened during the jump, whatever was left of the ship would complete the jump. And whatever was happening to the ship would continue happening wherever and whenever it emerged."

Picard's stomach knotted. "You're saying that if, say, a warp core breach or an anti-matter containment field breakdown was somehow initiated during the maneuver, the explosions could happen after it was completed? When it emerged into normal space?"

"Given the right timing, Captain, that is entirely possible."

Picard was silent for a long moment, his eyes on the familiar starfield on the viewscreen. Finally he looked back at Data.

"At least it gives us a place to start," he said. "Mr. Data, access all records of the Arhennius system."

As he waited for the results, he pulled in a deep breath and reached for the control that could send his voice to every corner of the *Enterprise*. He had a responsibility—a duty—to fulfill, and he had already put it off too long. Beyond the bridge, there were nearly a thousand crew members who still thought they were in a universe and a time that made sense.

Steeling himself, he lightly touched the control. "This is the captain," he said quickly, not giving himself time to have second thoughts, and then went on to explain as succinctly as possible what had happened and where he had, without their knowledge or consent, taken them.

There were no interruptions, only a pall-like silence as his voice echoed throughout the ship. Gradually, his face regained the color it had lost when the truth of their situation had first fully penetrated his consciousness.

When he finished, the silence was total, but after a few seconds voices began to emerge from the intra-ship comm system. No protests, no recriminations, only words of acceptance if not support. They had faced death with him any number of times, often in corners of the universe so remote they might as well have been in another time, and few had ever complained. They had known what they were signing up for when they had entered the Academy and even more so when they had signed on to the latest starship to carry the notorious *Enterprise* name. They weren't about to desert either Starfleet or their captain now.

Even so, Picard couldn't help but wonder if he himself had overreached.

And if that other captain of the *Enterprise,* who was unknowingly the cause of the current disastrous state of affairs, would be appalled at what he had "inspired" Captain Scott to do.

Or gratified.

Scotty's plan had been simplicity itself.

He would find the *Enterprise*-B, uncloak just long enough to transport the captain into the *Bounty 2,* and then return with him to the "present" via a second slingshot trajectory, already calculated. In the chaos surrounding the energy ribbon as it destroyed both the *Lakul* and the *Robert Fox* and almost destroyed the *Enterprise*-B, he would never be noticed during the brief time he was uncloaked. And during the journey itself, the improvements he had made to the *Bounty 2*'s cloaking mechanism would insure that no twenty-third-century sensors would get so much as a whiff of him.

And nothing would change.

That was the beauty of it, and the only reason he had gone ahead with it. As far as the universe of 2293 was concerned, Kirk would still have died while saving the *Enterprise*. The fact that, instead, he would be taken to 2370, could not possibly have any effect on the intervening decades.

That had been the plan, simple and straightforward.

Until, despite his round-the-clock monitoring of every aspect of the *Bounty 2*'s drive systems, Scotty found himself with time to simply think—and worry—about what could go wrong.

Grudgingly, he began to realize that, under the spell of an enthusiasm that had bordered on obsession, he had ignored—or at least rationalized away—many of the dangers that a mission through time entailed. Particularly a mission to a time in which the Khitomer Accords were only a few months old, a time when many in both the Federation and the Klingon Empire were still desperate for the Accords to fail.

A time when Admiral Cartwright, whose traitorous actions had come within a whisker of sparking a new war, was still seen by some as a hero.

Reports of even a glimpse of a Klingon bird-of-prey uncloaking within a parsec of Earth—reports that would almost certainly be confirmed when the *Enterprise*-B's sensor records were later examined—would be just what the Accord's diehard enemies wanted.

Anything could happen, including the war that Cartwright and his co-conspirators on both sides of the Klingon border had failed to ignite. Millions of lives would be lost.

That kind of chance, he belatedly realized, he simply could not take.

But neither could he bring himself to abandon Jim Kirk less than two days from his death.

In the end, after hours of agonizing, when it became clear he would reach his destination with more than an hour to spare, he swallowed hard and decided on a compromise.

He left the cloaked *Bounty 2* in the redundant concealment of a convenient pocket nebula, confirmed one last time that the *Goddard*'s jiggered sensors could indeed locate the cloaked ship, and continued the last few hours in the shuttlecraft. The *Goddard,* incapable of being cloaked, was more likely to be spotted than the *Bounty 2,* but with everything else that would be going on, it was still unlikely. And even if it were noticed, little attention would be paid to it since, despite its advanced technology, it was obviously a Federation craft, not Klingon. Even if the *Enterprise* sensor records were later examined, its presence would be a puzzle, not a provocation.

It would be filed away with other puzzles, not used by zealots as a pretext to break the Accords and start a new war with the Klingons. Time would heal itself of any minor wounds incurred in 2293, and the universe of 2370 would remain the universe of 2370.

The only difference would be that Jim Kirk would be there.

Alive.

NINE

THE HISTORY of the original timeline's Arhennius system, as sketchily outlined in the *Enterprise* computer records, provided no clues. Federation ships had scanned it at a distance for life signs and for habitable worlds, but all they found were two gas giants about the size of Saturn and two airless balls of rock a little smaller than Venus. There was no record of any ship—Federation or Romulan or Klingon—ever having entered the system itself. Therefore, Scott's bird-of-prey could have emerged at virtually any moment in the past two hundred years and undergone the most violent destruction possible, and it would have produced nothing more than a short-lived flare that wouldn't have been visible even to the most powerful telescopes in neighboring systems. The only time it would have even been noticed was during the few hours the Arhennius system was being scanned by long range sensors from almost a parsec away.

In any event, the *Enterprise* sensors had as yet found no indication that any such explosion had ever taken place in the Arhennius system, not in the last hundred years, not in the last million, although there *was* evidence of a half dozen low-yield photon torpedoes approximately a century ago.

"So," Picard said as the negative results of the scans continued to stream across the bottom of the viewscreen, "if he didn't accidentally overshoot catastrophically, what *did* he do?"

"There is one possibility, Captain," Riker volunteered. "Perhaps instead of overshooting, he *undershot* and had to make a second jump, and *that's* when he overshot, not because of something catastrophic but because of a mistake. Maybe his bird-of-prey was spotted by a Federation ship and he had to get out of there fast. Maybe he didn't have time to make all the calculations, maybe he missed the trajectory he was aiming for. He could've ended up anywhere—anywhen—alive and well. And if that's what happened, Captain, if he undershot, then he hasn't arrived yet. Perhaps we *could* do what you suggested earlier—just wait here for him to show up and beam him out before he has a chance to make a second jump."

Picard shook his head. "I doubt it, Number One. Even if everything you say is true, it wouldn't work. The timeline we are now in is almost certainly the timeline created by Captain Scott's interference decades or centuries in the past, no matter how or why he arrived there. It is *not* the timeline that Captain Scott would have emerged into at the completion of a first jump that fell short. He would have emerged into the original 2293, the one we are all familiar with, not into this one."

"That is essentially correct, Commander," Data said when Riker looked at the android questioningly. "Whether the original timeline still exists somewhere is debatable, but even if it does exist, we almost certainly cannot access it."

" *'Almost'* certainly?" Picard asked. "Tell us more, Mr. Data."

Data turned his attention briefly to a different set of readouts before answering. "It is perhaps significant that, ever since we arrived, there has been a massive amount of chronometric radiation permeating all space within sensor range."

"More than can have been generated by the arrival of a ship from three quarters of a century in this universe's future?" Riker wondered.

"There are no records of similar situations with which we could compare readings," Data said. "However, basic chronometric theory suggests that any such radiation triggered by the arrival of a chronologically alien object would be quickly damped out in a stable timeline, as would radiation triggered by any changes caused by the object."

"Which means what, Mr. Data?" Picard asked. "That *we* are seriously altering the timeline just by being here? Or that if Mr. Scott survived—either an overshoot or a second jump—he is still out there, still making changes?"

"Either is possible, Captain. Basic theory, however, suggests that a level of radiation this high and this steady is more likely the result of an earlier disruption so great that the timestream was rendered incapable of stabilizing itself and therefore continues to generate high levels of chronometric radiation."

"Or perhaps," Worf broke in, a touch of annoyance in his rumbling bass, "your theory is simply wrong."

"That is of course possible," Data conceded, unperturbed. "The theory should be considered tentative at best since it contains a number of unproven assumptions and has never to my knowledge been tested in a real-world situation, certainly never one of this complexity."

Riker snorted, almost laughing. "So what you're really saying is, you don't have a clue."

"Quite the opposite, Commander. In a sense, clues are all we do have. In theory, the level of chronometric radiation could be considered analogous to the ripples generated when a rock is thrown into a river. If the rock is large enough, it could even send the river over its banks or block it altogether. The radiation is believed to be directly— some say exponentially—proportional to the size and force of the 'chronological rock' thrown into the timestream. It could also be seen as a measure of the timeline's instability."

Picard nodded. "According to that theory, then, this timeline is highly unstable. Are you suggesting it is so unstable it might self-destruct? And do what? Allow the original timeline to restore itself?"

"Theory does allow for that possibility. However—"

Data broke off, his attention returning abruptly to the scan results still streaming across the viewscreen.

"There *was* an explosion?" Riker asked sharply.

"No indication as yet, Commander. The sensors have, however, detected traces of dilithium ore in the system's innermost planet. There are also indications of mining operations approximately one hundred years ago, which is also approximately the time at which the low-yield photon torpedo detonations occurred."

Picard frowned. "But the Federation never found dilithium here."

"That is perhaps because the Arhennius system was never closely examined. The dilithium deposits are beneath several kilometers of rock, undetectable by Federation sensors of that time unless the scans were done from low orbit. And records indicate that when long-range scans found no possibility of life of any kind, the Federation never actually sent a ship into the system."

"But in this timeline they did—*someone* did," Picard said. "Ensign Raeger, set a course for the planet in question, full impulse."

As the ensign complied, Picard turned toward Guinan, still seated in Troi's place. Though she had seemed to listen intently to every word the others had said since they had arrived in this time, she had spoken not a word herself.

"Guinan?"

Again she displayed uncharacteristic behavior by averting her eyes as she replied. "Yes, Captain?"

"You still have no . . . feelings as to what we should do? Or not do?"

"My feelings are irrelevant. You must do as you see fit."

"Your feelings are one of the major reasons we are here, Guinan," Picard said, unable to entirely suppress a brief flash of annoyance. "I don't recall your being at all reluctant when you asked—when you *demanded* that I trust those feelings, that I trust *you,* and follow Captain Scott through time."

She turned from the viewscreen to face him. As she looked up at him, she seemed more fragile than he had ever seen her. Instead of looking regal in her floor-length gown and the distinctive circular headgear that normally gave the impression of a crown, she looked small and beaten down.

Most of all, and most uncharacteristically, she looked uncertain.

"I'm sorry, Captain, I truly am, but nothing I say at this point could be trusted."

"Damn it, Guinan—" Picard began but cut himself off as she turned and hurried past him to the turbolift, her shoulders hunched as if to ward off invisible blows.

Anger flared through him for a moment but vanished as quickly as it had come when he remembered the state she had been in when she had urged him to follow Captain Scott. She was at least as lost as he. And it had been *his* decision, not hers, that had brought them here. She had urged, virtually demanded, but *he* had made the decision. She could in no way be blamed for what either Captain Scott or he himself had done.

Staring after her, he wondered darkly what could have had such an astonishing effect on her. Other than Data, no one he knew seemed so completely unflappable as Guinan. Even when faced by a creature like Q, she had not allowed herself to be intimidated. But now she was—

"An energy field is forming around the *Enterprise,*" Data announced.

"Shields to maximum," Picard snapped, but even as he spoke, even as Worf brought the shields to one hundred percent, the viewscreen filled with a soft glow. At the same time, a sharp tingling like static electricity enveloped Picard's entire body, inside and out. Riker grimaced, lurching to his feet next to Picard. Even Worf winced.

And the air within the bridge began to sparkle. Obviously the shields were having no effect.

For an instant, Picard thought Q was about to make another of his spectacular entrances, but this was different. Q put on visual pyrotechnics, but his arrivals had never been accompanied by physical sensations like these.

The prickling quickly turned into outright pain, as if he were being struck by thousands of tiny lightning bolts. Every attempt to move only intensified it. The sparkling haze itself grew brighter, denser, a thickening fiery fog.

"Engage, maximum warp!" It was all he could do to

issue the command. The words felt as if they were liquid flame, searing his mouth and throat as he forced them out.

At the helm, where the haze seemed even more intense, Ensign Raeger struggled to comply, her face contorted, her hands twitching spasmodically as they reached for the controls. Data turned toward her as she collapsed face down on the control panel, but his own effort to reach the controls failed as he twitched and went limp, a mass of sparks clustering around him as if attracted by the circuits he had in place of flesh and blood.

Picard and Riker lurched toward the controls through air that was still growing thicker with the crackling sparks every instant. Riker's body stiffened, every muscle frozen as he passed through a particularly dense patch. Like an axed tree, he toppled and hit the deck with a thud.

Picard, not fully enveloped by the patch that had felled Riker, lurched one last step toward the helm, tripped over Riker's outstretched arm and fell onto the still-twitching backs of Data and Raeger. The control panel, only inches from his face, was almost completely obscured by the intervening cloud of sparks, but he still managed, before the twitching of his own muscles turned to total paralysis, to hit the control that sent the ship lurching ahead on impulse power.

The air on the bridge cleared, the energy field and its effects vanishing even more quickly than they had come.

Picard and Riker gasped and lurched to their feet while Raeger jerked upright in her seat. Behind them, Worf still stood stiffly erect, but only because his massive hands had an unbreakable grip on the edges of the tactical station control panel.

Data's twitching ceased, but he remained motionless, still face down on the control panel.

Picard levered the dead weight of the android aside and hit the controls that switched the viewscreen to an aft view.

The image switched just in time for him to see a jagged oval filled with what looked like lightning bolts crackling in all directions while the entire display seemed to whirl like a nucleonic pinwheel.

And it was moving with them, following them.

Overtaking them!

"Maximum warp, Ensign!" he grated, his throat still raw from his last attempt to speak.

Wordlessly, Raeger complied, and the *Enterprise* began to pull away, even as the violence of the display continued to increase to what would have been a blinding level to the naked eye.

Suddenly, the display went through a final spasm, not spinning but giving the illusion of literally turning itself inside out.

Then it was gone, but where its center had been was now a tiny ship as unfamiliar as the energy display had been. No bigger than an *Enterprise* shuttlecraft, it had stubby, hawkish wings that had a Klingon look about them, but instead of a slender, arched neck leading up to a head, there was no neck at all, just an angular protrusion on what Picard assumed was the front of the body. What appeared to be a single warp drive nacelle was visible at the rear. For just a moment the ship was motionless except for a slight rotation on its axis, as if re-orienting itself. Then, abruptly, it headed directly for the Enterprise, taking up right where the ball of pyrotechnic light had left off. Within seconds, despite its size, it was moving at a warp speed only slightly less than the *Enterprise* was capable of.

Without warning, the object exploded. The viewscreen

went instantly blank as the protective circuits kicked in. Looking at the readouts on Data's control panels, Picard saw the energy signature of the explosion.

It had been a low-yield photon torpedo, similar to the ones used by the early Federation. Similar to the ones that had, according to Data's scans, exploded near the inner planet a hundred years ago.

But where had it come from?

And what had all the preliminary fireworks been about?

Under cover of the chaos created by the energy ribbon and the destruction of the *Lakul* and the *Robert Fox*, it was comparatively easy for Scotty to bring the *Goddard* within transporter range of the *Enterprise*-B without being noticed—or at least without being challenged.

The hard part, as he had known from the start it would be, was the timing.

Beam Kirk out a few seconds too early, and he would not have had time to make the necessary alterations to the deflector generators. The simulated photon torpedo would then not be produced, and the *Enterprise*-B itself would be destroyed, gobbled up by the energy ribbon.

And Scotty himself—the earlier Scotty, on the *Enterprise*-B—would be killed. The Grandfather Paradox, in spades.

A few seconds too late, and the *Enterprise*-B would be saved but its one-time captain would himself be swallowed up by the energy ribbon. And Scotty would have failed a second time to save the captain.

Tapping into the intra-ship communications, Scotty waited, his face grim, his stomach churning as he tried to blot out the tortured mental image of the hundreds he had once again let die on the other two ships.

Each second ticked by like a minute as he waited, listening.

Finally, they came, the words etched forever in his memory. First, Demora Sulu's urgent warning from the bridge: *"Forty-five seconds to structural collapse!"*

Then silence as he began counting down the seconds until he would again hear Jim Kirk's voice shouting the words that, the first time he'd heard them, had been Kirk's last.

This time, he vowed, they would be the words that would save him.

Everywhere on the *Enterprise*-D it had been the same. The energy field, whatever it was, had invaded every cabin, every corridor, struck every crew member no matter where he or she was. Luckily there seemed to have been no lasting effects from the energy itself, and the spasms and falls it had caused had resulted in less than a dozen easily treated injuries, from bruises and sprained fingers to one broken arm. Data, the only one to have been rendered unconscious, was the last to fully recover, but his built-in diagnostic and repair routines brought him back to full functionality in a matter of minutes.

Having no idea whether the deadly devices were limited to the Arhennius system or were scattered everywhere in this timeline, Picard brought the *Enterprise* to a stop after a few billion kilometers. Within minutes La Forge, up from engineering and working at the science station, quickly rigged an alarm system that would automatically engage the warp drive at the first sign that another of the inexplicable energy fields was invading any part of the ship.

At the same time, Data completed a sensor scan of the entire system, which showed only their own warp trail and the aftermath of the photon torpedo's detonation. There was no indication, he announced, of any more of the devices.

"Why doesn't that make me feel secure?" Riker asked sarcastically. "As I recall, there weren't all that many indications of the one that almost blew us up."

"If feelings of security are your goal, Commander," Data remarked, "you have chosen a singularly inappropriate profession."

"Gentlemen," Picard began, but he was cut off by La Forge, who had just begun skimming through the sensor records of their encounter with the device.

"Captain, there's something here you should see," the engineering officer said, tapping one of the science station controls. "You, too, Data."

Abruptly, the starfield disappeared from the viewscreen, replaced by an enhanced image of the jagged oval of the energy field as it had looked only moments before its final convulsions prior to vanishing and being replaced by the photon torpedo. A stream of figures raced across the bottom of the screen.

"I *think* I know what that energy display was all about," La Forge said after he'd let the others study the image for a moment. "You remember last year when we gave that stranded Romulan ship a hand, and Ensign Ro and I thought we'd been turned into ghosts but actually—"

"Their interphase experiments," Picard said, suddenly remembering.

"Exactly, sir. The Klingons and the Romulans both experimented with cloaking devices incorporating interphase generators. They hoped to not just cloak their ships but to shift them to a different spatial plane. That way they could not only become invisible but could travel *through* other matter like a ghost." He shuddered briefly at the memory of when he and Ensign Ro, as a result of an accident involving one of the Romulan experiments, had themselves been partially shifted into another plane. They had wandered the corridors of the *Enterprise* like technological ghosts, desperately searching for a way to communicate with the "real" world.

"But they both abandoned it," La Forge went on, "apparently because it was too dangerous. Well, in *this* timeline someone—the Klingons, from the look of that thing that was carrying the torpedo—must *not* have abandoned it."

Picard looked doubtful. "You're saying that that massive energy display before the device appeared was all part of the decloaking process?"

The engineer nodded. "That's one reason the process is so dangerous. At least the process this bunch uses. Whatever plane they displace these torpedoes to, it must exist at a much higher energy level than ours—also much higher than the one the Romulans were using. Ro and I would've been fried if they'd been using *this* one. Anyway, when they open a portal to send something through in either direction, some of that energy is forced through to our plane. It's like trying to move between the pressurized interior of a ship and the vacuum of space without using an airlock. If you open a door, the pressure is going to drive some of the air through the open door while you're going through. Only here it's pure energy, not air. They could never cloak an actual ship, with people in it, without massive amounts of protection to keep them from being incinerated whenever the ship transferred from one plane to the other. But for photon torpedoes . . ."

He shrugged. "They're kind of hard to destroy, but even

so the sensor records show that there *was* a protective shield around the one that nearly got us, a shield even more powerful than the *Enterprise*'s."

"It's no wonder this technology was abandoned in our timeline," Picard said. "But now that you know what you're looking for, can you devise a way to detect them, the way we can detect ships using standard cloaking? Or at least to warn us before another one starts to 'decloak' inside the *Enterprise*—which I am assuming is what this one was trying to do?"

The chief engineer shook his head. "Not here, and not without at least one interphase generator to work with. We're going to have to make do with the alarm system and a fast getaway."

TEN

SAREK OF Vulcan, Supreme Arbiter of the Alliance, looked up from the viewscreen in his uncomfortably luxurious shipboard quarters as the harsh yet deferential tones of the *Wisdom*'s commander, a Romulan named Varkan, erupted from the intercom.

"My apologies for disturbing you, Arbiter, but Deputy Koval insists he must speak with you."

"Put him through, Commander," Sarek ordered, controlling his annoyance at the obsequious commander's misguided protectiveness.

Turning back to the viewscreen, he watched as the flashing, crackling maelstrom that was the Vortex vanished and was replaced by Koval's granite-like features set against the background of his spartan office on Alliance Prime. The image flickered briefly, then took on a slight reddish tint, a sign that the Deputy Arbiter had initiated the ultra-secure link that was made possible by the special equipment that was always installed on any ship the Arbiter traveled on. Attempts to tap into the signal would now yield only static, even on the bridge of the *Wisdom* itself, where the tightbeam subspace signals were received and relayed to Sarek's quarters.

"What is it, Deputy?"

"Your suspicions appear to have been justified, sir. We have just learned that three of the Cardassian members of the Council have held at least one clandestine meeting only hours after your departure. Unfortunately, we do not as yet have any indication as to what was discussed."

"And Zarcot?"

"There is still no evidence that he has returned to Alliance Prime."

"But no evidence to the contrary, either, I imagine?"

"None as yet, sir. Nor is there any clear evidence of unusual activity within the Cardassian contingent of the Alliance fleet."

Sarek was silent a moment, considering. In the year since Zarcot had stormed out of the Council, the Cardassian had gained far more influence than he had ever exercised as a member. Unfettered by Council rules and traditions, he had also been provoking more confrontations than ever before, all seemingly designed to undermine Sarek's authority. In his latest efforts, Zarcot had convinced the gullible and thoroughly illogical majority of Council members that "no one could possibly claim to be a true leader of the Alliance without personally observing the object that could well prove even more dangerous than the Borg."

Zarcot himself had "set an example" and traveled to the Vortex to make just such a "personal observation" several weeks ago and had sent back reports filled with dire but totally unfounded warnings that "worlds would likely be destroyed by the Vortex long before the Borg made their next move." He was supposedly on his way back to Alliance

Prime with more information and the beginnings of a plan he wanted to present to the Council, but no one knew for certain *where* he was. As he had on the journey out, he was maintaining radio silence, supposedly for security reasons but actually, Sarek was almost certain, in order to enhance the drama of his so-called mission.

And perhaps to allow him to make a sidetrip to meet secretly with other Cardassians.

In any event, the need for "personal observation" by Zarcot or by Sarek or any other official was of course utter nonsense, as all Vulcans knew. Unfortunately, the vast majority within the Alliance and on the Council were not Vulcans and were therefore all too often ruled not by logic but by that most destructive and most easily manipulated force in all of nature: emotion.

And Zarcot, obviously, was a master manipulator.

Logically, everyone knew that the scientists who had been tracking and observing the Vortex ever since it first entered Alliance space decades ago were far more qualified observers than any politician or soldier. Unfortunately, Zarcot could claim—with only slight exaggeration—that in those decades the scientists had learned essentially nothing beyond the blindingly obvious: The Vortex destroyed or absorbed anything and everything in its path without being slowed, diverted or weakened to any observable degree. Nor did weapons have any effect, neither the phasers and photon torpedoes of Alliance cruisers like the *Wisdom* nor the disruptors favored by Klingons and Cardassians.

Even so, Alliance scientists from a dozen worlds assured Sarek that the Vortex was a distraction and nothing more. Unlike the Borg, it was a natural phenomenon and posed no danger to any Alliance worlds—unless, of course, it departed radically from its projected trajectory, something it had shown no inclination whatsoever to do. The most effective way to "deal" with it, therefore, was simply to study it from a safe distance and stay out of its path, which was precisely what the scientists had been doing and continued to do. A half dozen automated probes constantly monitored the Vortex and transmitted all data to Alliance Outpost No. 3 for analysis and storage, and its projected path was recalculated continually. Other than minuscule refinements, there had been no changes to that predicted path since the observations had begun.

But those who opposed Sarek and lusted for his title— particularly Zarcot and the other Cardassians, whose worlds likely wouldn't be threatened by the real menace, the Borg, for millennia—would have none of it. Logic be damned, the leader of the Alliance had to *demonstrate* his concern over this spectacular but easily avoidable danger.

And so he was here, parsecs from Alliance Prime and Vulcan, wasting precious time while the *Wisdom* cautiously eased its way closer to the Vortex and he learned absolutely nothing other than the utter futility of urging non-Vulcans to act logically.

And wondering how much longer the Alliance could be held together, with or without Sarek himself as Supreme Arbiter.

In truth, he was amazed that it had held together as long as it had. The sole reason for its existence was the presence in its midst of the Borg. There had been no choice but to unite against a common enemy so powerful it could destroy any individual world with no more effort than it would take to swat a fly.

Even the threat of total annihilation at the hands of the Borg, however, had not been enough to eliminate opportunism and backstabbing and a hundred other thoroughly illogical behaviors, particularly among the Klingons and Cardassians and even now and then the Romulans.

Part of the problem was the extremely deliberate pace at which the Borg moved. They would take decades to complete their assimilation of a world before moving on to the next. This took away from the sense of urgency that was essential to keep Alliance members from each other's throats as they competed for short-term advantages that would prove utterly meaningless in the long run if the Borg were not stopped.

The Klingons, for example, had kept their success with interphase cloaking a closely guarded secret for decades, using the technology only to "protect"—i.e., to surround with interphase-cloaked space mines—Klingon-claimed worlds whose resources they also refused to share. As a result, a golden opportunity to destroy the embryonic Borg fleet in its cradle, the Terran system, had been lost. And by the time the rest of the Alliance developed the technology, the Borg fleet was no longer embryonic, nor was it even accessible. Dozens of cubes watched over each of the worlds that had since been assimilated, and an unknown number were hidden behind the sensor-opaque shield they had erected around the entire Terran system, enclosing even its Oort cloud of comet nuclei. Behind it, Terra and every other body in the system almost certainly continued to be strip-mined for the raw materials needed to construct more Borg cubes.

And every few decades, the shield would vanish, just long enough for a new fleet of those cubes to emerge and head for another nearby world. Vulcan, if the pattern of the last two centuries continued, would be next.

Vulcan's only hope—the Alliance's only hope—was that, before it was too late, they could build and deploy

a sufficient number of interphase-cloaked photon torpedoes to carry out a belated and much more difficult version of the plan that the Klingons had thwarted
originally by their illogical refusal to share their cloaking technology.

And the Alliance fleet would have only one chance.

If any Borg ships escaped the attack, they would soon
return.

And they would be immune to the cloaked torpedoes.

That was how the Borg operated. The Alliance had
learned this early on when they had made the mistake of
"testing" a new weapon on a lone Borg cube parsecs away
from the others. The test had been successful, the cube destroyed, but the next time the fleet attacked an even more
isolated cube, the weapon had no effect. That cube—and
presumably all the others—had somehow adapted and
were no longer vulnerable. The attacking ships were of
course destroyed.

So, now, all the Alliance could do was continue to build
as many photon torpedoes and as many cloaking devices as
possible.

And hope.

And all Sarek could do was try his best to retain control
and prevent ambitious and myopic fools like Zarcot from
fragmenting the Alliance and throwing away the one small
hope they all had for long term survival outside a Borg
Collective.

"Very well, Deputy Koval," he said at last, "keep me informed and keep trying to locate Zarcot. I will cut this so-
called mission as short as I can. In the meantime, if any
Cardassian ships approach Alliance Prime, keep them in
high orbit, out of transporter range. And if Zarcot reap-
pears, assign him a bodyguard detail. For his own protec-

tion, of course. Do the same for the Cardassian members of the Council."

Signing off, Sarek deactivated the ultra-secure link and allowed the chaos of the Vortex to re-form on the screen.

It took Picard and the others—with the notable exception of Guinan, who had not reappeared since she had retreated from the bridge—only a few minutes to reach a decision: Set a course for Earth.

First, that was where, in 2293, Starfleet Headquarters had been located for decades. If anything was left of Starfleet, with or without subspace radio, it would be there.

Second, records showed that Kirk's death had occurred less than a parsec from Earth. That was where he had encountered the energy ribbon that had killed him and very nearly destroyed the *Enterprise*-B.

If Scott was going to show up anywhere in this timeline, it would be there.

After what seemed like an eternity, the words Scotty had been waiting for came. *"That's it!"* Kirk shouted to Demora Sulu on the bridge of the *Enterprise*-B. *"Go!"*

Scotty instantly activated the *Goddard*'s transporter, which was already locked onto Kirk's coordinates. In the split seconds he had to operate, he would not have had time to achieve a lock as well as perform the actual transport.

Kirk's dematerialization was barely completed when a klaxon-like alarm, deafening in the confines of the shuttle-craft, assaulted Scotty's ears.

Heart suddenly pounding even more violently, he tore his eyes from the shimmering energies that were forming above the transporter pad and looked down at the control panel—and saw a red light flashing in time to the alarm.

Radiation! The intense, wildly fluctuating gravimetric radiation generated by the energy ribbon must have—

But it wasn't gravimetric!

The gravimetric radiation was high and fluctuating wildly, but that wasn't what had triggered the alarms.

It was a sudden surge of chronometric radiation.

Chronometric!

And it was dozens of times higher than even in the first moments after he and the *Bounty 2* had emerged from the slingshot trajectory that had deposited them in this era!

Belatedly, his eyes darted up to the forward viewscreen. Only moments before, it had been filled with the *Enterprise* as the ship began to pull away from the coruscating space-borne tornado that was the energy ribbon.

Now there was only the ribbon, itself receding.

The *Enterprise* was gone!

Impossible! The ribbon *couldn't* have swallowed it up! It *hadn't!*

And yet the *Enterprise* was gone!

But there *was* something else out there, the sensors indicated. Two somethings, and they were *huge,* hundreds of times the size of the *Enterprise!*

Hastily, Scotty redirected the scanners, and the other objects appeared on the viewscreen.

They weren't where the *Enterprise* had been, but a hundred eighty degrees around, apparently trailing the energy ribbon from a safe distance.

He recognized the behemoths instantly from the images in the *Goddard*'s briefing program, and they were virtually the last thing he had expected—or wanted—to see.

Borg cubes.

What had he done that could possibly have resulted in *this?*

A hand on his shoulder almost sent his heart into his mouth. Turning, he found himself facing a smudge-faced and very puzzled looking Jim Kirk.

Commander Varkan's image had just appeared on Sarek's viewscreen when the world seemed to go mad around him, setting his heart to pounding. The Romulan commander's image blurred almost into anonymity and the lushly carpeted floor undulated beneath Sarek's booted feet. For just an instant, the entire *Wisdom* seemed to vanish, leaving him floating helplessly in the darkness of empty space, surrounded only by thousands of pinpricks of starlight.

But almost before the images of the stars could register in his mind, they were gone, leaving him to wonder if it had all been illusion. Logically, it had to have been.

He was obviously still surrounded by the thankfully solid walls of—

Of what?

A jolt of pure terror shot through him, turning his muscles to rubber as he realized he didn't recognize anything around him, not the face peering at him from the meter-wide viewscreen, not the holo-portraits on the walls, not *anything!*

Where was he?

How had he gotten here?

Somehow controlling the panic that threatened to overwhelm him, he tried to think back to the last thing he remembered.

And realized he had no conscious memory at all.

No past.

Not even a name!

For what seemed like an eternity, he stood frozen, unable to move or even to generate a rational thought beyond the obvious:

Where am I?

Who am I?

But then, almost as quickly as his mind had emptied, a torrent of memories came flooding back, threatening to drown his still-struggling consciousness.

Limp with a relief that did not question the source of the memories, he thought: I am Sarek of Vulcan, ambassador to—

No! Not ambassador! Arbiter! Supreme Arbiter of the Federation and—

Alliance, not Federation!

He shook his head violently as he tried to make sense of the returning memories: The Borg. The Vortex. The Alliance Council.

But what was this "Federation" that had suddenly appeared in his mind, like a parasite that had attached itself to his returning memories? What—

But it was *not* something that had just appeared, he realized, and with the realization came the beginnings of calmness and control. The "Federation" was just one small part of a long string of illusory memories that had plagued him for decades.

Memories of dreams.

Dreams that were not even dreams, merely shadows of dreams that he *must* have had even though he could not remember ever actually having them.

How could he have forgotten, even for an instant? He had been victim to them throughout most of his adult life, he now remembered. At odd times, day or night, on the rare occasions when he allowed his mind to wander, he would find himself "remembering" events that had never happened, events that *couldn't* have happened, events totally at odds with his true memories and with the world around him but otherwise virtually indistinguishable from his real memories.

He had, he remembered now, tried at various times to dismiss them as visions, which Vulcans, having limited telepathic abilities, were sometimes subject to, but that illogical effort had always failed. The most he could logically say was that they might conceivably be *memories* of visions, but of visions he could not consciously remember having had in the first place.

In the end, his only salvation had been to tell himself, as he did now, that the false memories were simply products of his subconscious and that therefore they were nothing more than a rare and peculiar form of dreaming, a series of wish fulfillment fantasies produced by his subconscious. What else could they be *but* fantasies, he had asked himself a thousand times? They had simply seeped up from his subconscious through the imperfectly formed barriers all Vulcans erect early in life to keep their emotions from breaking free of the prison of their inner, secret selves and into the real world of their logical, conscious minds.

He could not allow them to be anything else, just as he could not allow the momentary lapse of memory he had just suffered to be anything more than that: a lapse, a brief misfire of a cluster of otherwise healthy neurons.

It was his only choice if he wished to retain his sanity, if he wished to retain his ability to make logical decisions and act upon them.

And now—now, with the possibility of a Cardassian attempt to unseat him growing daily—he needed that ability more than ever.

Without it, without all the logic and decisiveness he

could muster, the Alliance could well be doomed. Without it—

"Arbiter Sarek?" Commander Varkan's uneasy voice penetrated his whirling thoughts. *"What is it you wish?"*

Sarek came to himself with a start as he realized how long he had been standing silently before the viewscreen.

And remembered why he had contacted Varkan. He had decided to cut this ludicrous "mission" short.

"Prepare to return to Alliance Prime," he said. "I will join you on the bridge in a moment."

Signing off, Sarek broke the connection and thumbed open the door to the corridor. He had wasted more than enough time on this fool's errand, he thought grimly as he strode toward the bridge, the memory of his recent lapse slipping more deeply into his subconscious with every step.

ELEVEN

PICARD, HAVING decided a private conversation with Guinan was essential, had just exited the turbolift a few dozen meters from her quarters when Riker's voice came through his combadge.

"Captain, to the bridge."

Wondering briefly if he should summon Guinan to the bridge for whatever was happening, he spun about and stepped back through the still-open doors of the turbolift.

"On my way, Number One. What is it?"

"Andor has just come within sensor range, Captain."

"And—?" Picard prompted impatiently as the turbolift shot upward.

"And you'd better have a look, sir," Riker said, his grim tone changing Picard's annoyed impatience to stomach-twisting apprehension.

The door opened on the bridge, and he strode through.

And stopped abruptly as his eyes went from Riker, rising from the captain's chair, to the viewscreen.

The image filling the screen was fuzzy, indicating the object—the planet Andor, the first Federation planet that lay along their path from Arhennius to Earth—was barely within sensor range.

But the image was clear enough—and growing clearer by the second as the *Enterprise* drew closer at nearly warp eight.

Borg cubes, dozens of them, hovered around the planet like a malignant cloud.

His heart pounding, Picard could not keep from shuddering visibly. To him the Borg were not only the impersonal evil they were to most who encountered them, even to Guinan, who had been parsecs distant from her homeworld when the Borg, having apparently found it unassimilable, destroyed it overnight. To Picard, they were a very personal evil as well, a horror that had lived on in his nightmares since those terrible days when he had *been* a Borg. Again and again he had relived those times, cringing inwardly as his will was relentlessly beaten down by the networks of implants and by the neverending pressure of the legions of slave minds in the collective, which itself had been anathema to the tiny fragment of humanity that he had somehow managed to hold onto throughout the entire ordeal. There were still nights when he awoke to find himself screaming silently as he struggled to pull free, like a man submerged in carrion-infested quicksand that was not drowning him but was leaching its way into his body, literally absorbing him bit by bit while he remained fully conscious, aware of each and every sickening moment.

Pulling in a deep breath, he forced himself to at least *appear* calm.

"How many, Number One?"

"Sixty-seven so far. There may be more hidden in the shadow of the planet."

"And the status of the planet, Mr. Data?" he asked, his voice as flat as his body was tense.

"The conversion of the planetary ecosystem is not yet complete, Captain. There is still five percent free oxygen, but increasing levels of methane, fluorine, and carbon monoxide have already rendered the atmosphere unbreathable for anything but a Borg."

"How long . . ." Picard began but, uncharacteristically, let his voice trail off.

"We have never before observed the Borg's planetary transformation process in action," Data said, "so there is no reliable method of estimating the time remaining before the transformation is complete."

"Nor how long it's been going on already," Riker said, his face a stony mask as he watched the image. He swallowed. "How many Andorians are there?"

"None," Data said, studying the sensor displays. "There are, however, approximately two billion Borg. Sensors indicate most were, before their assimilation, Andorians."

Alone in her dimly lit quarters, Guinan listened to Picard's brief announcement concerning the fate of the Andorians. She knew it was time—*past* time for her to tell him the whole truth. Every moment she waited, the chances grew greater that he would learn it elsewhere. If that happened, the trust they had shared for even longer than he remembered would be, if not broken, severely damaged. It had already been damaged, but not, she hoped, beyond repair.

And yet even now, knowing she had no choice, she could not entirely free herself from the paralysis induced by the oil-and-water combination of emotions that had been eating at her like acid from the moment the *Enterprise* had emerged from its jolting passage through time.

For it was in that moment she had felt history rearranging itself around her, felt its countless elastic threads shift and intertwine and stretch almost to the breaking point as they were woven into new and radically different patterns.

Patterns that filled her simultaneously with elation and despair.

In the hours since that moment, her thoughts had been like a pendulum being swatted violently back and forth. One moment she hoped with all her heart that what she had seen in the patterns was right, and then, a moment later, she hoped with equal fervor that it was not only wrong but a delusion, that the "feelings" that had plagued her for centuries had finally reached an intensity that had simply driven her mad.

But now . . .

Now, with the fate of Andor confirmed, she could no longer summon up any tenable hopes that the patterns she had seen were either false or induced by her own madness. There was no longer any doubt that they truly reflected the reality in which the *Enterprise* now existed.

And if she did not act now, if she did not regain Picard's total trust, everything could be lost . . .

Closing her eyes, she gathered together all her strength, strength that had seen her through countless crises before but only one that had tested her as severely as this. With the feeling that she was stepping off a precipice, she opened her eyes, waved the door open and stepped from her quarters into the corridor.

Not daring to hesitate, she glided rapidly toward the nearest turbolift and, seconds later, emerged onto the bridge. As the doors hissed shut behind her, every eye darted toward her, even Data's. On the viewscreen, the malignant cloud of Borg ships still hovered around the dying Andorian world.

The newest addition to the Borg Collective.

"Captain," she said, approaching him and bringing her eyes up to meet his directly for the first time since the *Enterprise* had emerged into this universe, "there is something I must tell you."

Picard frowned and glanced questioningly toward the door to his ready room, but Guinan shook her head. "This is something you all need to know."

She paused, looking around at the entire bridge crew, then drew in a deep breath. "Earth as you knew it," she said softly, "does not exist in this timeline. Where it once was, there are only Borg."

The blood drained from Picard's face, as it did from Riker's, until both were nearly as pale as Data. Even La Forge's mahogany features took on a greyish, corpse-like pallor, while Troi winced under the painful pressure of the emotion radiating from the Terrans. Only Worf, already scowling, seemed unaffected.

"How do you know, Guinan?" Picard's voice was so brittle it threatened to snap. "I don't doubt that it's true, but how do you know?"

"I've known since the moment we emerged into this continuum, but—"

"How do you know, Guinan? How?"

"I can't explain it, Captain," she said despairingly, her voice laden with apology. "You of all people should know that. All I can tell you is that there have been other times when I have been shifted into another timeline, but this is different. Those other times, I sensed that something was different, that something was wrong, but that was all. This time there is more. This time I can sense *both* timelines and some of the differences between them. It's as if they were closer together, or as if I were somehow linked more intimately to both than in any of those other incidents."

"Captain," Data broke in before Picard could continue his uncharacteristically harsh questioning, "I do not have a rational, scientific explanation for Guinan's special knowledge, but I believe there is something you might want to consider."

"Yes, Mr. Data?" Picard, still frowning, turned toward the android.

Data paused, as if reluctant to continue, but after a moment he said, "It is not really an explanation at all, Captain, but it is part of a category of utterances that nevertheless seem to have meaning to humans. Guinan may be aware of more than the rest of us because . . . Guinan is just Guinan."

Riker let out a brief snort of harsh laughter. "No one's ever argued with *that*."

Picard's features relaxed slightly. "I've always known it to be true," he said, his eyes meeting Guinan's again, his momentary anger turning into a sigh. "In any event, shooting the messenger is virtually always counterproductive. Tell us, Guinan, what else do you know about this place?"

"Just one other thing for certain, Captain. It's the reason I told you before that any advice I might give you in this timeline could not be trusted." She paused, lowering her eyes for a moment, then raising them to once again meet Picard's.

"In this universe," she went on, forcing the words out, "your world is gone, but mine is not. Here, the Borg did *not* destroy El-Auria."

"Not that I don't appreciate what you were trying to do, Scotty," Jim Kirk said, "but there are no two ways about it. You screwed up royally."

The engineer flinched under the words, not because he resented them but because he knew they were absolutely true. His halting attempt to explain his actions to Kirk had only made his rashness more glaringly apparent. Worse, listening to his own words as he spoke them had made him begin to wonder if, in the final analysis, he hadn't done it all for a purely selfish motive. Had his primary concern *really* been to save the captain's life?

Or had it been to save *himself* from the guilt and the nightmares that that death had inflicted on him?

"I cannot say how sorry I am," he began bleakly, but Kirk held up a hand to block the words.

"Like I said, you screwed up," Kirk repeated, this time with a rueful grin. "That's the bad news. The good news is, you survived and so did I, so we've got a chance to do something about it. For a start, how about finding out what it was that brought these—Borg, was it? What kind of name is that, anyway?—that brought these Borg into the picture? Obviously they're not here simply because you saved me."

Scotty blinked in confusion. "But you just said—"

"I said you screwed up and you did. You never should have taken off on this wild goose chase. You never should've taken a chance on corrupting the timestream just to save one person—even if that person *was* me. I *didn't* say that saving me was what brought these Borg monstrosities down on us."

"Then what—"

"What *did* cause it?" Kirk shrugged. "I have no idea, Scotty, not yet. But whatever it was, it wasn't your rescuing me. You said it yourself. As far as the *Enterprise*-B and that timeline are concerned, you were right: You didn't change anything. With or without your 'interference,' I disappeared. The energy ribbon got me in one case, you got me in the other, so I was taken out of the picture either way. And if that isn't enough, just use a little of your engineering-style common sense. The effects of what you did here and now, in 2293, whether it was saving me or something else you did accidentally, would begin here and now. Worst-case scenario, the effects would grow larger and larger until the here and now you came from—2370, you said?—would be drastically altered. But not *this* here and now. Whatever caused *this* change happened a long time ago. As our mutual friend always says," Kirk added with a more genuine grin, "it's only logical."

A wave of irrational relief swept over Scotty. It was indeed only logical, and he would surely have realized it himself if he hadn't been so rattled. "But if it was *not* something I did, then what—"

"Tell me about this future captain of the *Enterprise*. Is he impulsive?"

"I did not spend that much time with the man, but I seriously doubt it. Although he did let the *Enterprise* get trapped inside the Dyson Sphere the *Jenolen* had crashed on."

Kirk nodded. "And you said he 'gave' you this shuttle-craft, just like that, no promise to return it on a given date, nothing. That sounds pretty impulsive to me, Scotty."

"Aye, I suppose you could look at it that way."

"And you said he was right behind you back there in 2370, trying to get you to stop. Did he have any idea what you were planning? Did he know about our own little adventure on the first *Bounty?*"

"We'd not discussed it, but I can't imagine that he did not."

"Me neither. So when he saw you were heading almost

directly into a star, he must have realized you were going to try to slingshot *some*when." Kirk paused, grinning again. "Ten to one, he followed you. Care to bet?"

Scotty blinked. Was it possible? From what he had seen of the *Enterprise*-D captain, Picard was far more by-the-book than Jim Kirk had ever been. He didn't even lead his own landing parties the way Jim almost always had.

On the other hand, the woman calling herself Guinan had been on the bridge with Picard. Scotty had heard her voice once or twice before he'd closed the incoming channel.

And strange things happened when that seemingly age-less woman was around.

She had somehow popped up in Glasgow, and because of her delaying him a few minutes in that bar—which was still nearly a year in the future in this timeline, he realized with a shiver—he had met Matt Franklin and decided to join him on the *Jenolen*, which was the only reason he'd been on board when it had crashed on the Dyson Sphere and the only reason he'd ended up seventy-five years in his own future.

And now—now she had been on the bridge of the *Enterprise* when it had been pursuing him, and here he was, almost back where he'd started, but in a world not of the Federation but, apparently, of the Borg.

Scotty shook his head. "I don't know, but, aye, it's pos-sible. He could've tried to follow me."

"I'm certain of it!" Kirk said triumphantly. "And he couldn't have had time to do any serious calculations, not nearly as many as Spock did on the first *Bounty*. All he could do was stick as close to your tail as possible, and that wouldn't be nearly close enough. Which means he showed up back here at a slightly different time, maybe before you arrived, maybe after. But no matter when he arrived, he must've made a *second* jump even further back, and—"

"But why would he do *that?*"

Kirk shrugged. "Who knows? Probably looking for you. It just stands to reason that he *did*. And that he made that second jump at the same moment that you were beaming me out of the *Enterprise*-B. That's why everything changed right then. Something he did at the far end of that second jump—another fifty or a hundred or a thousand years back—changed *this* here and now. Maybe all he did was catch the attention of the Borg a few hundred years back and they followed him home. And decided to stay. From what you said, they'd have been powerful enough to wipe out the whole Federation without breaking a sweat."

Scotty blinked, his stomach knotting as he realized Kirk was right. It was the only thing that even marginally made sense.

"If that's true, then we cannot do anything about it."

Kirk brushed Scotty's words aside with a curt and dismissive shake of his head. "Come on, Scotty, you don't really believe that. You turned the galaxy on its ear just to try to save *me*. Don't tell me you're turning cautious *now*, when the whole Federation is at stake!"

"But what—"

"What can we do?" Kirk asked with a rhetorical flourish. "Simple. We do whatever it takes to keep those things from wiping out the whole Federation. For a start, we find out what Picard and *his Enterprise* did that caused all this. And we keep him from doing it."

The knot in Scotty's stomach tightened painfully at Kirk's words, but he managed a weak smile. "Aye, is *that* all?"

"That's the spirit, Scotty."

The engineer shrugged, the faint smile gone. "You do realize, Captain, that coming back here to try to save you was a bairn's errand compared to what you propose? I knew exactly when and where I had to jump to, but we haven't any idea how far back Picard jumped or what he did when he got there."

"Don't sweat the details," Kirk said as he glanced around at the interior of the shuttlecraft. "What*ever* we do, we'll need something with a little more speed and range— and shielding—than this, so the first step is a transportation upgrade. We retrieve the *Bounty 2*. You *do* remember where you put it?"

Scotty nodded without enthusiasm. "If it didn't disappear along with the *Enterprise*."

"We won't find out if we don't go look, now will we?"

Scotty grimaced. "Aye, I don't suppose we will," he said, reaching for the control that would send the *Goddard* on its way to where the cloaked and silent *Bounty 2* might or might not be waiting for them.

"And now that we've got some time on our hands," Kirk said, glancing at the control panel readouts, then back at Scotty, "maybe you'd like to tell me a little more about the Borg. Who and what are they and where the blazes were they when we were cruising around in *our Enterprise?*"

TWELVE

IN ORDER for his report to the Council to be at least technically true, Sarek grudgingly spent several minutes "personally observing" the Vortex's nearly blinding energy
display on the bridge viewscreen before ordering Varkan to
bring the *Wisdom* about and return to Alliance Prime, even
though his original schedule had called for them to spend
another two days circling it on impulse power and observing it from all sides.

"As you wish, Arbiter," the Romulan said, not entirely
able to hide his disappointment at the abrupt truncation of
the *Wisdom*'s role as the Arbiter's personal transport.

Before he could issue the orders, however, a muted
klaxon sound erupted from the communications station at
the rear of the bridge. The image of the Vortex dissolved
into a chaos of dancing lights. The commander turned an-
grily toward the Narisian communications officer.

"Emergency override signal, sir," the Narisian said
apologetically, her cat-like eyes widening as she scanned
the readouts that darted across the tiny screen embedded in
the communications console.

"The *Wisdom* is on special duty," the commander snapped. "If some fools have managed to attract the attention of the Borg, there is nothing *we* can do to help."

"It's not from a ship, sir, it's from Outpost No. 3."

Even as the Narisian spoke, the visual static on the viewscreen vanished, replaced by the image of a Vulcan civilian. Sarek recognized him instantly as Kasok, one of the scientists he had personally appointed to the Vortex observation team.

"We need your help," the scientist said without preamble. *"Yours is the only ship in the vicinity of the Vortex, and we—"*

"Whatever your problem is, there is nothing we can do," Commander Varkan said, plainly irritated. "Arbiter Sarek is on board, and—"

"That is all the better, Commander. Please allow me to speak with him."

"I am here, Kasok," Sarek said, stepping into range of the screen before the Romulan could object. "Have you discovered something about the Vortex?"

It would be ironic, Sarek thought, almost smiling, if scientists parsecs from the Vortex were to make an important discovery while Sarek himself was within a few million kilometers of it and could see absolutely nothing worthwhile.

Ironic and, of course, quite logical.

"No, Arbiter. But a ship unlike any known to the Alliance appeared out of nowhere only a few thousand kilometers from the Vortex."

"Appeared? Came out of warp, you mean? Or decloaked?"

"No, Arbiter, neither. There were no—" The scientist broke off, turning momentarily to tap a series of com-

mands into something out of range of the screen. *"Here, Arbiter,"* he said, turning back to the screen, *"you can see for yourself. This is the visual image sequence from observation platform number two. Watch the right edge of the screen, just beyond the edge of the Vortex itself."*

"Kasok—" the commander began, obviously annoyed at the scientist's presumption, but Sarek silenced him with a wave of his hand.

"Please continue," Sarek said.

An instant later, Kasok's image was replaced on the screen by a section of the Vortex, the image uncomfortably bright and far more detailed than the "direct view" Sarek had gotten earlier on the same viewscreen. Smoothly but rapidly, the image dimmed, transforming the Vortex from a raging inferno to a swirling but still detail-laden fog.

As the Vortex faded, the background of stars that had been obscured by its brilliance emerged and an arrow-shaped pointer appeared and scurried across the screen to a point about halfway between the edge of the Vortex and the edge of the screen.

"There," Kasok's voice informed Sarek as the arrow became a circle enclosing half a dozen faint stars, *"that is where the object will appear."*

And within seconds, it did. For a moment, it flickered, as if it were an image being transmitted to the viewscreen through a faulty connection, coming into existence and then fading out and returning again and yet again. Kasok had been right, Sarek thought. This "appearance" did indeed bear no resemblance to an object emerging from warp or de-cloaking.

Then the object was solid and unwavering, a tiny rectangle, essentially motionless with respect to the Vortex.

"What is it?" Sarek asked.

Kasok hesitated, but only a moment. *"We have no idea, Arbiter. That is why I contacted the* Wisdom. *It is the only Alliance vessel within range and therefore the only one capable of investigating."*

"Out of the question," the Romulan commander snapped, but once again Sarek gestured him to silence.

Two possibilities had occurred instantly to the Vulcan. First, because the ship had appeared not only close by the Vortex but in an unknown manner, it could very well be associated with the Vortex in some way and might therefore be a source of information *about* the Vortex. Second, the ship might be a trick, something created by Zarcot and the Cardassians and staged for Sarek to see and report to the Council. In either case, logic dictated that he learn as much as possible as soon as possible about the intruder.

"Do you have its present coordinates?" Sarek asked.

"Unfortunately we do not, Arbiter, but we do have its course. When the automated analysis systems alerted us to the object's presence, we were able to reorient observation platform number four in time to determine the course it took when it departed a few minutes later. The platform, of course, could not follow."

"Of course. Transmit the course coordinates, Kasok, and we will investigate. In the meantime, what more can you tell me of this object?"

The image on the viewscreen fluttered and changed. *"This is from platform four,"* the scientist's voice informed them. In the new image there was no sign of the Vortex, only the background of stars. In the foreground was the object, now obviously a ship but equally obviously not an Alliance ship. Boxy with a pair of large tubes running along the bottom like runners on a sand sleigh, it looked more like a planetary hovercraft than any kind of starship. Then the ends of the tubes were enveloped in a harsh, pulsing glow. An instant later, the object began to move rapidly and then, in a spectacular flash for so small a craft, it vanished into warp drive.

"That was the last image we were able to obtain," Kasok said as his own image reappeared on the screen. *"Its warp trail indicated it was moving at slightly less than warp three on the course whose coordinates we have just transmitted."*

"Commander," Sarek said, turning to the Romulan, "intercept course."

"With all due respect, Supreme Arbiter, do you think it wise to—"

"Without knowledge, there can be no wisdom, Commander. Now lay in an intercept course before the chance to gain some possibly invaluable knowledge is lost."

"As you wish, Arbiter," the Romulan said, lowering his eyes momentarily in formal but grudging obeisance.

While the commander issued the necessary orders, Sarek returned his attention to Kasok. "Assuming it maintains its last known course, what could its destination be?"

"Unknown, Arbiter. The nearest inhabited stellar system situated directly along its course is more than a hundred light-years distant."

"What of Borg vessels? Could it be planning to rendezvous with one of them?"

"Unlikely, Arbiter. It is moving almost directly away from the two Borg that follow the Vortex. And it will miss the Andorian system by more than a quarter parsec, so unless some of that system's sentinels come out to meet it—"

Kasok shrugged. *"Anything is possible, but they've stayed put for a hundred years."*

"Is it possible other such vessels have appeared near the Vortex in the past but were not observed by the platforms?"

"That is definitely possible, Arbiter. As you know, the platforms are located so as to provide complete and uninterrupted views of all aspects of the Vortex itself, but there are any number of blind spots in the surrounding space."

"Theories, Kasok?"

"Nothing worthy of the name, Arbiter, merely unfounded guesses."

"And those guesses?" Sarek persisted.

"Little more than you yourself suggested, Arbiter: a new type of cloaking device or warp drive. The latter seems unlikely, however, in light of the fact that the ship departed using what appeared to be a conventional warp drive. But whatever the object is, the most logical possibility is that it has some connection with the Borg. It not only appeared in Borg space but within a million kilometers of the only two Borg vessels not hovering around one of the worlds they've assimilated."

"Agreed," Sarek said, nodding almost imperceptibly, "although I would not be quick to discount the possibility that the Vortex itself is somehow involved. Inform me immediately if anything else unusual occurs in the vicinity."

"Of course, Arbiter. And my colleagues and I would appreciate it if you would keep us informed of your progress in the investigation."

"Of course, Kasok."

A moment later the scientist's image vanished, this time replaced only by a moving starfield. Sarek stood silently watching it for several seconds. Perhaps this misbegotten "mission" would actually produce something of value after all.

Picard's eyes narrowed as he took in the full import of what Guinan had said: In this timeline, El-Auria survived. "Despite what you said before, you're now saying that your advice *can* be trusted?" he said finally. "Your 'feelings' can be trusted?"

"I don't know, Captain, I truly do not. I believe they can. I *fear* they can."

"Fear? What is there to fear if, as you say, you have been given back your world?"

"Because the one other thing those feelings have told me from the moment of our arrival, the one thing they have told me with absolute clarity, is that something is terribly wrong about this timeline. They tell me that we are right to try to undo whatever caused it to come into existence."

"And you would assist in that undoing? Even though it meant your world would again be destroyed by the Borg?"

She was silent for a long moment, the acid of her conflicting emotions once more eating at her mind. "At this moment I don't know. But I can tell you this. Whatever happens, I won't lie to you. And I won't hide the truth from you, as, I'm ashamed to say, I've been doing since our arrival here."

For several seconds there was complete silence on the bridge as Picard's eyes bored into hers. This time, she didn't avert her gaze but kept her eyes focused directly on his, neither defiantly nor obsequiously but as if to provide him with a pathway into her mind, even into her soul.

Finally, Picard lowered his own eyes, closing them for a moment in a soundless sigh as he acknowledged the inevitable. Despite her uncharacteristic behavior of the last few hours, despite her overwhelming motive to protect rather than destroy this timeline, he still trusted her above all others. He couldn't imagine *not* trusting her.

"Very well, Guinan," he said. "I believe you, of course. But do you have any idea of what actually happened in this timeline to bring it to this point?"

She hesitated before shaking her head regretfully. "I know virtually no more than what I have already told you and what you have yourself observed. Earth and some nearby worlds have been assimilated by the Borg. El-Auria has not yet been destroyed. And there is something terribly wrong with this timeline, something of far greater importance than the existence or non-existence of a single world, either yours or mine."

"And you know nothing of what caused this change?" he persisted, turning again to the grim image on the viewscreen.

"No more than you. But if Captain Scott's actions are responsible for El-Auria not being destroyed, he has to have gone back at least thirty years further than we did."

Picard nodded. "Obviously. But no matter how far back he went, how could a single man's actions bring the Borg all the way from the Delta Quadrant at least a hundred years ahead of their schedule? The Borg aren't known for their spontaneity or flexibility. It would take something of major proportions to have altered their behavior to this extent."

He looked around at the others. "But the immediate question is, how do we go about finding out what Captain Scott did? And when?"

"It would be logical to continue on our present course, Captain," Data volunteered. "Even if Earth no longer exists, the energy ribbon that took Captain Kirk's life almost certainly still does. And, as you said when we first chose this course, if there is any one place and time Captain Scott will be drawn to, it is there."

"He's right, Captain," Riker said, the color only now returning to his bearded face. "And even if Scott doesn't show up there, we won't have lost more than a few days. Then we can get out of this—this Borg zone and start looking for worlds they *haven't* destroyed, worlds that may know when and why the Borg arrived ahead of schedule. El-Auria, for example," he added. "At least we know it's safe in this timeline."

"I think, Number One," Picard said deliberately, "that other worlds might be a better choice. Considering the fact that what we would be trying to learn from them is, in effect, how to impose a death sentence on their entire world."

Riker stiffened as he realized what he'd said. "I'm sorry, Guinan," he said, turning toward her, but she waved his apology away.

"Actually," she said softly, "that is quite possibly what we *will* have to do. El-Aurians have traveled and listened, not just in what was to become Federation space, but everywhere they could reach. If anyone in this timeline knows what Captain Scott did, it would be an El-Aurian."

"We can discuss—"

"Captain," Data interrupted, "the chronometric radiation is increasing precipitously."

"Source?" Picard snapped, relieved at some level for the distraction.

"There is no identifiable source, Captain. It is everywhere."

"Could it be caused by Captain Scott's arrival?"

"I do not know, Captain."

"What does your theory say will happen if the level continues to increase, Mr. Data?"

"As I noted before, basic theory cannot be considered reliable regarding such matters."

"Guinan? Suggestions?"

A frown narrowed her eyes as she glanced toward the viewscreen. "I do not belong here," she said abruptly. Just as abruptly, she turned and glided toward the turbolift.

A new sense of uneasiness, as if his last link to reality were being severed, clutched at Picard's stomach as he watched Guinan retreat from the bridge for the second time in twenty-four hours.

"Captain," Worf said almost the moment the turbolift doors closed behind her, "we are being hailed."

Picard spun back toward the viewscreen. "So subspace communications do exist in this timeline. Mr. Data, is there a ship within sensor range?"

"No, Captain."

"The source may be outside sensor range," Worf said. "The signal itself is tightbeam, being directed toward the *Enterprise* and nowhere else."

"Do what you can, Mr. Data," Picard ordered, frowning. Starfleet had experimented with tightbeam technology, which sent signals through subspace like a laser beam rather than broadcasting them in all directions, but they had never deployed it. Instead, the Federation had chosen to boost the power of their omnidirectional subspace transmitters and to place subspace relay stations throughout known space. Tightbeam transmissions could have extended the range even further, but they had been considered impractical. For one starship to hail another via a tightbeam transmission, it would have to know the other ship's precise subspace coordinates, an obvious impossibility unless they were already in contact.

But in this timeline . . .

"Captain," Data said, "I have been able to key the long range sensors to the tightbeam transmissions and obtain some limited information. The ship is of no known type but has a number of characteristics that indicate a Romulan origin."

"Weapons?"

"Photon torpedoes and disruptors."

"Powered up?"

"Under these conditions it is impossible to tell, Captain."

Picard was silent a moment, wondering again why Guinan had absented herself from the bridge so suddenly. Wondering what her "feelings" had been telling her this time.

Or if it had simply been a delayed reaction to the suggestion that her home world might be asked to help engineer its own destruction.

"Mr. Worf," he said abruptly, "open a channel, on screen."

The viewscreen wavered a moment, as if having to adjust itself to properly utilize the incoming signal.

Then, suddenly, the image was crystal clear.

There were two people on the screen, standing on a starship bridge similar to the Romulan bridges Picard was familiar with but smaller, with an even more utilitarian look. In the foreground was a Romulan, sharp-faced with a skullcap of tightly curling gray hair, wearing a uniform that was and yet was not that of a Romulan commander.

In the background, standing just to one side and a meter behind the Romulan, stood a chocolate-skinned woman in a dark floor-length gown and a large, attached, elliptical head covering.

Unless his eyes—or his mind—was playing a vicious trick on him, it was Guinan.

THIRTEEN

KIRK OF COURSE was full of questions after seeing what little there was to see in the *Goddard*'s briefing program about the Borg, but Scotty could only shake his head in reply.

"I asked the same questions and more," he explained, "but I got blessed few answers."

No one even knew for certain how the Borg had begun, Scotty went on. A race somewhere in the Delta Quadrant must have, for reasons no one could even guess at, decided to turn themselves into a "collective" of mentally linked cyborgs. What one Borg learned, they all soon knew. And once the collective had been created, apparently its only interest was in expanding. However, instead of simply contacting and trying to work with other races, or even invading or destroying them, they chose to "assimilate" them, taking total control of everything—bodies, minds, technologies, resources, entire biospheres, everything. No one—perhaps not even the Borg themselves anymore—had any idea what drove them to continue or what determined their "strategy" or much of anything else. Except that the Borg idea of a perfect universe was a universe that was one hundred percent Borg.

To make matters worse, the Borg apparently had the technology—transwarp conduits—to "jump" the tens of thousands of parsecs from their domain in the Delta Quadrant in a matter of hours or days, but it was rarely used. Slow and steady expansion seemed to be their long-term plan, moving outward inexorably like the event horizon of a black hole that grew by eating every star in its path, except that this black hole ate not stars but civilizations, swallowing them whole and, in effect, digesting them, transforming their billions of individual members into billions of interchangeable cells in the body of the Borg Collective.

Kirk grimaced. "They make the Klingons look downright benevolent by comparison, don't they? All the Klingons do is conquer and plunder. They don't steal your mind. But if the Borg are so hell-bent on taking over everyone they run into, why didn't one of them assimilate *us?* They had every chance in the world, but they acted as if they didn't even know we were there."

" 'Tis likely they did not. Oh, they can see us well enough, but as long as we don't match what the bloody things are programmed to look for, they just don't notice us."

Kirk nodded thoughtfully. "So they run on autopilot, like a bunch of big, high-tech ants. As long as we don't crash into one of their ships or do something stupid that forces them to notice us, they won't bother us. Right?"

"Aye, I'm no expert, but that's the way I understood it."

"Then we likely have all the freedom we need."

"Freedom to do *what?* If the Borg have wiped out the entire bloody Federation, what can—"

"From loose cannon to fatalistic stick-in-the-mud in one

easy leap?" Kirk said, shaking his head in mock despair. "Scotty, old friend, if you'd had this attitude back on the old *Enterprise*, we'd have all been dead a hundred times over. And from what you told me about that little adventure of yours with the Dyson Sphere, that brand spanking new *Enterprise* of Picard's would be nothing more than a plasma cloud if you hadn't pulled a rabbit out of the *Jenolen*'s hat. Now snap out of it before I'm forced to have the Engineers' Guild revoke your Miracle Worker permit!"

"You have a plan, then, Captain?"

"Of course, Scotty. A starship captain, even one without a starship, *always* has a plan. It's included in the job description. In any case, who says the Federation has been wiped out? The *Enterprise* disappears and those two space-going ant hills show up in its place, and you jump to the worst possible conclusion. But no matter how many worlds have been 'assimilated,' there has to be *someone* out there still on their own. You're certainly not going to tell me that *no* one ever eludes them or falls through the cracks."

When Scotty didn't argue, Kirk continued. "Once we find a world they haven't gotten around to yet, we talk to people and find out when the cubes showed up. And, if we're lucky, *why* they showed up. At the very least, we find out about anything unusual that might've happened just before they started showing up, something that Picard and his *Enterprise* might have been responsible for. And then—" He paused and shrugged.

"Then I guess we play it by ear and hope for the best," he finished with a grin obviously intended, like much of what he'd been saying in the last few minutes, to buck up the troops. "Will that new *Bounty* of yours hold up to another slingshot maneuver or two?"

"Do you really think—" Scotty began, the worried frown that had never quite gone away still creasing his brow.

"Nothing's a sure thing, Scotty," Kirk said, cutting him off with a wave of his hand, "but I frankly don't see what other choice we have. You certainly can't want us to just throw our hands up and do nothing. I wouldn't think that would have much appeal for you either. Or maybe you have a plan of your own that you haven't told me about?"

When Scotty only shook his head, Kirk went on. "All right, then. We're agreed. Any plan is better than nothing. Now let's see if we can come up with something even better. For a start, fill me in on everything else. For instance, how the devil did you end up in that Klingon bird-of-prey? It's not the same one we used to snatch those whales, is it?"

Scotty shook his head. "Not unless someone removed the tanks and put everything back the way it was."

"Then where *did* you find it? It's not the sort of thing you normally find floating around waiting to be picked up."

"Aye, it's not, and that's not the half of it," Scotty said, going on to explain about the fleeing Narisians and the equally ancient shuttlecraft.

Kirk was frowning thoughtfully by the time Scotty finished. "If I didn't know it was impossible, I'd say it was a setup. It's almost as if someone *wanted* you to have it."

Scotty suppressed a shiver as Guinan's cryptic smile flashed through his mind. "You could be right," he said, remembering. "I don't see how she could have managed it, but there's a woman on Picard's *Enterprise* called Guinan, and strange things happen when she's around."

Scotty went on to tell a bemused Kirk about his seventy-five-years-apart meetings with Guinan. He was almost finished when a light started blinking on the control panel and the shuttle dropped out of warp. A moment later the computer's voice announced that the coordinates of the *Bounty 2* had been reached.

Kirk briefly eyed the starfield, noticeably dimmed by the dusty presence of the pocket nebula. "It's a little late to ask, Scotty, but you *do* have something on board that's able to spot a cloaked ship. Right?"

"Aye, I tweaked the *Goddard*'s sensors a wee bit when Picard first gave me the keys, but we shouldn't need to use them," the engineer said, tapping a command into the control panel. "I set the *Bounty 2*'s controls so I can de-cloak it from here."

But the viewscreen remained empty except for the stars.

Scowling, Scotty tried again.

And again.

"Maybe we should try Plan B," Kirk suggested after the fourth try produced no more evidence of a de-cloaking bird-of-prey than had the first three.

Scotty swallowed uneasily as he turned to the sensor controls and tapped in the code that would switch in the "tweakings" he had programmed back in the future. The "normal" sensor readings would lose a little of their precision, the way an image seen in infrared isn't as sharp as an image seen in visible light, but anything that was cloaked would become visible, the way that any heat source would become visible, even in total darkness, to an infrared sensor.

The already fuzzy image of the nebula grew even fuzzier, turning the stars beyond it from pinpoints to pin heads. Otherwise, the viewscreen remained blank.

"I don't suppose you have a Plan C, old friend?"

His stomach twitching painfully, Scotty began making

further adjustments to the sensors, going well beyond anything that could be called "tweaking." The swirls of the tiny nebula alternately thinned and thickened, completely blocking the stars at one point.

But no matter how many nudges and tweaks he inflicted on the controls, there was no indication that anything was out there other than the nebula and the stars.

The *Bounty 2,* the increasingly leaden feeling in his stomach told him, had probably accompanied the *Enterprise*-B into whatever space-time limbo it and the rest of the Federation now existed in.

If any of it existed at all anymore.

His shoulders slumped, feeling older than he had ever felt, Scotty was starting to turn toward an expectant Kirk when the starfield on the *Goddard*'s viewscreen was suddenly blotted out by the distinctive burst of energy that indicates a ship has dropped out of warp drive.

Another instant, and his eyes recovered enough to see a ship about the size of a bird-of-prey but with a decidedly Vulcan look appear in the center of the viewscreen.

So the Borg do *have other ships beside their city-sized cubes,* Scotty thought but did not have the time to say before the *Goddard*'s comm system, totally silent until that moment, crackled into life.

"This is the Alliance vessel Wisdom," a muted sounding voice proclaimed. *"Identify yourself."*

Scotty, provisionally relieved that the words and voice sounded totally unlike what he imagined the Borg would sound like, moved quickly to one side, gesturing for Kirk to take his place and respond. They'd agreed shortly after setting out that any contact would be better handled by a captain with moderate diplomatic and first contact experience than by a retired engineer with limited interpersonal skills and a sometimes counterproductive penchant for telling the unvarnished truth.

"This is the shuttlecraft *Goddard*," Kirk said but froze a moment later as the ship on the viewscreen vanished and was replaced by an image that was as startling to him as the first glimpse of a Borg cube had been to Scotty. This image, however, was infinitely more welcome. Over his shoulder, he could hear Scotty gasp at the sight.

"Sarek!" the engineer blurted out before his mind caught up with his tongue or Kirk had a chance to signal him to stay quiet.

On the screen, the Vulcan looked as startled as a Vulcan could look in the brief moments before his familiar but disturbingly haggard features resumed their normal impassive facade.

An instant later, the screen went blank.

"Now what?" Kirk wondered aloud, frowning puzzledly as he turned toward Scotty.

But before the engineer could more than shrug his shoulders, they both felt the anticipatory tingle of a transporter field locking onto them.

Picard tried with limited success to keep his racing thoughts from descending into chaos. First and most obvious was the simple realization that if this timeline had its own Guinan, she could be an immeasurably valuable source of information. And if she was anything like *his* Guinan—not that he or anyone else could actually lay claim to her—it was no accident that she was here. It wouldn't surprise him to learn that she had prevailed upon this Romulan to bring her to this particular place, just as her other self had prevailed upon Picard to follow Captain Scott through time.

Then his mind darted back to San Francisco on nineteenth-century Earth and their "first" meeting, and he wondered for an instant why she didn't appear to recognize him. Even if Captain Scott had made a second jump, surely he had not gone back *that* far, another four hundred years, and changed history so much that Guinan had been kept from visiting nineteenth-century Earth.

But then the obvious answer slammed into him. It was *he* who had been kept from visiting Earth of that era!

In this timeline, Starfleet did not exist in the twenty-fourth century. Therefore the *Enterprise* did not exist. Most likely Picard himself did not exist, except perhaps as a Borg drone. And if he and the *Enterprise* didn't exist in the twenty-fourth century, he could hardly have gone back to the nineteenth to meet Guinan for the first time.

Then the Romulan on the screen was speaking, and Picard wrenched his thoughts out of the labyrinth that this Guinan was rapidly becoming. *"I am Commander Tal of the Alliance vessel* D'Zidran," the Romulan said. *"Who and what are you?"*

"Captain Jean-Luc Picard of the starship *Enterprise*," Picard said, recovering, wondering what the "Alliance" might be. This timeline's version of the Federation?

"And where are you from?" the Romulan asked, his eyes darting momentarily toward that other Guinan, whose own eyes revealed a moment of surprise.

When Picard did not respond instantly, the Romulan continued. *"From the warp trail you left as you fled the Arhennius system, I can tell that your ship is not one I am familiar with. Nor is the bridge I see around you now. And the fact that your warp trail seems to begin somewhere within the Arhennius corona also strikes me as . . . unusual."*

"Captain," Data broke in, "I have been able to penetrate the planet's shadow with our sensors. In addition to another twenty-two Borg cubes, there are eleven ships similar to Commander Tal's. Their weapons appear to be powered up and ready."

"Thank you, Mr. Data," Picard said evenly, never taking his eye off the Romulan on the screen. "Commander?"

The Romulan's startled eyes still looked directly, if a little uncomfortably now, at Picard. After a moment, he lowered them, then cast another brief glance at the Guinan standing behind him.

"I told you," she said, mild sarcasm in her tone, *"that these people are not agents of the Borg."*

The Romulan flushed slightly but did not rebuke her.

"Is that why we were attacked in the Arhennius system?" Picard asked. "Someone thought we were associated with the Borg?"

Tal shook his head. *"You were not attacked. You simply triggered one of the space mines the Klingons deployed during their dilithium mining operations in the system."*

"Our sensors showed only traces of dilithium," Picard pointed out. "And no mining operations, no activity of any kind, for nearly a century. Why haven't the things been removed? Or at least deactivated?"

Tal's eyes shifted toward Lieutenant Worf briefly. *"As I'm sure you know, Captain Picard, Klingons do not gladly hand over their food bowls, even after licking them clean."*

True enough, Picard thought, ignoring the faint bass rumble—the Klingon equivalent of mumbling under one's breath—that came from behind him.

Tal, after another moment of silence, turned to speak to someone out of range of the viewscreen. *"Tell Subcommander Volak to have all ships stand down. And to come out of their obviously ineffective hiding place and resume monitoring the Borg.*" He turned once more to face Picard. *"Is that satisfactory, Captain Picard?"*

Picard nodded. "Thank you, Commander," he said, then shifted his gaze to the Guinan on the screen. "Are you the commander's advisor?"

"In some matters," she said softly, *"when he desires it."* For an instant their eyes met, and a shimmer of puzzlement—perhaps recognition?—rippled across her face. *"I am called Guinan."*

The Romulan waved her aside as he leaned closer to the viewscreen, half blocking her image. *"You have told us your name and the name of your ship, Captain,"* he said brusquely, *"but you have not yet named your native world. One of your officers is obviously a Klingon, but you and your second in command are not as easily identified. You obviously cannot be what you appear to be."*

"Why is that? What do we appear to be?"

"Terrans. Are you familiar with that unfortunate species?"

Picard nodded expressionlessly. "We are."

"Then you certainly understand why we would find it difficult to believe you are what you appear to be."

Picard hesitated as he realized what the Romulan meant. He thought briefly of professing ignorance but, after a brief glance at that other Guinan, decided against it. "Terra has been assimilated by the Borg," he said. "Therefore we cannot be Terrans unless we are agents of the Borg."

"Precisely," the Romulan said, nodding in approval.

"Does this mean, then," Picard went on, "that *no* Terrans survived the Borg invasion? None were offworld when the Borg came?"

"We were not witness to the first Borg incursions, but we have always assumed Terrans had not yet developed a star drive when the Borg assimilated their world. They had certainly not made official contact with any who are now in the Alliance. Nor has anyone in the Alliance ever encountered a Terran who was not also a Borg drone. So, if you cannot be a Terran, what is your homeworld?"

Picard hesitated again, his eyes once again drawn to that other Guinan's enigmatic face. He could hardly tell the truth, at least not the whole truth—that he had come from the future with the sole purpose of wiping this entire timeline out of existence. While Guinan, in any guise, might be able to accept it, he doubted there were many others that were similarly capable, particularly among the Romulans. He needed a story that was not entirely true but was true *enough* to pass muster.

"Surely, Captain," Tal prompted, *"identifying your homeworld is not that difficult a task."*

"Actually, Commander," Picard admitted, bracing himself inwardly, "it *may* be somewhat difficult, not because we do not have the information but because you may find it hard to believe."

The Romulan arched his eyebrows in what was obviously mock curiosity. *"Indeed? And why is that?"*

"Because we are from another . . . reality," Picard began, carefully watching that other Guinan out of the corner of his eye. "We—"

A bark of laughter erupted from the Romulan's throat. *"Another reality? You are spirits, then? You are very solid spirits, if we are to believe our sensors."*

Picard shook his head, still watching Guinan as much as the Romulan. "We of course are not 'spirits.' By 'another reality,' I mean an alternate universe, one just as real and solid as this one, but different in many ways. Surely your scientists have suggested the possibility that such things exist."

"Perhaps," the Romulan said with a shrug, *"but the Alliance has little time for such theoretical esoterica. We must focus our energies on more practical matters, for example finding a way of stopping the Borg."*

Picard managed a small smile. "Oddly enough, that is precisely what we ourselves are doing."

The Romulan frowned skeptically. *"Explain."*

And Picard did, cautiously spinning out the story his subconscious had apparently been working on ever since Riker's jolting remark about El-Auria,

In their own universe, Picard explained quite truthfully, the Borg, while not yet invading the Alpha Quadrant, were as much a long-term threat as they were here. If a way wasn't found to stop them, they would almost certainly, given time, turn the entire galaxy into one massive collective.

Recently the Federation had stumbled onto a method of traveling to alternate universes, Picard continued, beginning to bend the truth in earnest.

"That is why your warp trail began in the Arhennius corona?" Tal asked with a frown. *"Your method of travel involves a star's gravity well?"*

Picard nodded, relieved that the Romulan had jumped in to supply a part of the explanation. "An interaction between an intense gravity well and the warp drive, yes."

"And you are out exploring? Looking for what? A universe where the Borg don't exist?"

Picard shook his head. "A universe where they have been defeated," Picard said slowly. "In our universe, the Borg have not arrived in this sector of the galaxy, but they soon will, and we are powerless to stop them. The *Enterprise* and several other ships are searching for a universe in which a way to defeat the Borg has been found."

"This is obviously not the universe you seek," the Romulan said. *"I assume you will soon be on your way."*

"Not necessarily," Picard said, still watching that other Guinan out of the corner of his eye. She had been listening intently, looking as if she were about to interrupt any number of times, but always restraining herself. "There is a major difference in Borg behavior in this universe. In our own universe—indeed, in every universe we have visited— the Borg have for millennia steadily and systematically expanded in their home quadrant. Here, however, they appear to have broken that pattern and leaped hundreds if not thousands of parsecs to take over Terra and expand outward from there."

"And how do you know this?"

"I don't know for certain, not as yet. Based on what we have seen so far, however, it seems to be the only logical conclusion. I am of course assuming that the Borg in this universe originated in the Delta Quadrant, as they did in ours."

"They did," said the Guinan on the screen.

The Romulan turned to scowl at her. *"I realize you know many things, Guinan,"* he said stiffly, *"but I did not know you were more of an expert on the origins of the Borg than are those who have made it their life's work to study them."*

"There are many things you do not know about me, Tal," she said in a tone so familiar it sent chills up and down Picard's spine. Then she turned to look out of the screen at him. *"Captain Picard, would it be possible for me to visit the* Enterprise? *I would like to learn more about*

this universe you say you are from. It could be most useful for the Alliance," she added, glancing at Tal.

Picard hesitated, remembering how his own Guinan had fled from the bridge moments before the hail from the Romulan ship and the appearance of this Guinan's image on the screen.

"I don't see why not," he temporized, "but we are far outside transporter range."

"Of course," she said, looking again toward the Romulan, whose scowl faded into a look of resignation.

"Very well, Guinan," Tal said, *"but someday you will go too far, even for you."* Turning back to the screen, he said, *"You are welcome to her, Captain, at least for the time being. In the meantime, I will be making a complete report of this incident to Alliance Prime, which may well have further questions. I trust you will have no objection to answering them."*

"None," Picard said, and the images wavered and disappeared from the screen. The moment the connection was broken, he stood up from the command chair and strode to the turbolift. "Number One," he said over his shoulder, "let me know if our friend Tal—or anyone else—makes contact. And Mr. Data, keep me informed of any changes in the level of chronometric radiation. I'll be wherever Guinan is."

FOURTEEN

NOT EVEN the discipline that came from a hundred-plus years of iron self-control could keep all traces of shock and surprise from Sarek's face when the two creatures appeared on the *Wisdom*'s viewscreen.

They were doubly impossible.

First, they *appeared* to be Terrans, but Terrans no longer existed except as mindless Borg drones. The only existing records and images of that lost race were contained in the thoroughly studied logs and diaries of the few travelers that had sporadically and unofficially visited the world in earlier, less troubled centuries.

Second, Sarek recognized them not only as Terrans but as specific Terrans that he had until this moment believed existed only in his own hallucinatory memories of a life he could not possibly have lived.

One was named Kirk, those memories told him. He had been a captain and then an admiral in the fleet of starships maintained by the "Federation," which Sarek had long ago decided was nothing more than his rogue subconscious's idealized version of the constantly-coming-apart-at-the-seams Alliance.

The other Terran, he "remembered," was named Scott. For many years he had been an engineer on the ship the one called Kirk commanded.

Logically, neither one could exist here, in the real world.

But, equally logically, it was pointless to deny their existence, just as it was pointless to doubt his own sanity. He had to assume he was sane despite evidence to the contrary.

And he had to find out who and what these beings really were.

It was the only logical course.

But before he could even begin to formulate a plan, one of the beings, his eyes widening in seeming surprise, blurted out Sarek's name.

For a fraction of a second, the Vulcan froze. How could this creature from his own hallucinations know his name?

Abruptly, keeping his hands out of range of the viewscreen, he signaled for Varkan to break the connection.

As the impossible image was replaced by the sensor-provided image of the aliens' tiny craft, the commander turned toward Sarek in puzzlement. "What—" he began, but Sarek cut him off.

"Transport them both to Interrogation."

Varkan hesitated but only for a moment. Stepping forward, he spoke the security code that only a ship's commander possessed, then activated the transporters and watched the lines of data that streamed across the bottom of the screen.

"Transport complete, Arbiter."

"Now program it to respond to my voice rather than yours, Commander."

The hesitation was longer this time, but finally Varkan complied, speaking the code again and adding a transfer sequence. Sarek repeated the code, watching the screen as the computer indicated its acceptance.

"Arbiter—" Varkan began but again was cut off.

"I will speak with the prisoners myself, Commander. Signal me immediately if there is any further communication from Outpost No. 3. Or any communication whatsoever regarding the prisoners or the Vortex."

"As you wish, Arbiter. But I urge you not to interrogate them alone."

"Are you suggesting the chamber's security is insufficient? Or malfunctioning in some way?"

"Of course not, Arbiter," Varkan said hastily. "All mechanisms are checked regularly. It is just that—"

"I appreciate your concerns, Commander, but you will serve the Alliance best by remaining on the bridge."

The Romulan looked for a moment as if he were going to continue his protest, but he finally nodded an uneasy assent. "As you wish, Arbiter," he repeated.

Sarek turned and strode from the bridge, making his way down a dimly lit secondary corridor to the auxiliary transporter cubicle that provided the only means of access to Interrogation, itself buried deep in the *Wisdom,* as were similar rooms in all Alliance ships.

"Enable entry," he said distinctly, waiting a moment for the newly reprogrammed computer to recognize his voice and accept his command.

The door slid open and he stepped through, onto the single transporter pad that made up most of the cubicle's floor. "Interrogation," he said, unable to entirely suppress a shiver as the transporter field gripped him.

A moment later, he found himself in another small room, this one with no entrances or exits. The only way in or out was by transporter. A control panel and a meter-wide viewscreen took up half of one wall. He was, he realized, probably the first person to occupy this space since the *Wisdom* had been commissioned, just as the two beings from his false memories were the first to occupy the chamber on the far side of the still-opaque wall opposite the viewscreen.

The so-called "drone chamber."

One was built into every Alliance vessel, all in the so-far-vain hope that a Borg drone could be captured and totally isolated from the collective.

And interrogated.

As yet it had never happened.

Unless these two were themselves Borg creations, Sarek thought. Could the Borg have learned how to extend their mental links beyond the collective? Could they have eavesdropped on his thoughts and then modified two of their Terran drones to match his false memories?

Or could they have somehow *created* those false memories in the first place?

Anything, he feared, was possible. After more than a century of observation, no one in the Alliance could do more than make wild speculations about the Borg's true capabilities.

"Enable automatic extraction mechanism," he said.

"Enabled," a soft voice replied from the walls. Until the mechanism was disabled, any significant change in his life signs would be detected and would trigger the transporter.

"Security protocol *alshaya*."

"*Security protocol* alshaya," the computer confirmed. Until Sarek removed or altered the protocol, the only connections to the outside world were a hard-wired incoming link from the bridge, allowing the commander to signal him in an emergency, and a hard-wired two-way link allowing him to access the *Wisdom*'s records.

"Enable iso-vision," he said. The wall he faced faded to one-way transparency.

The two beings—Terrans? Modified drones?—were both looking in his direction, frowning. Could they have heard his voice despite the force fields that separated them? Or had the faint hum of the transporter alerted them?

Sarek could not entirely suppress the chill he felt as he saw that these two did not just *resemble* the beings from his false memories, as he had hoped this up-close, detailed inspection would reveal. Other than the stubble on the face of the one called Scott, he could detect no differences between these two and the two from his "most recent" false memories.

Finally, he turned and inspected the bio readouts on the control panel beneath the viewscreen. There were dozens, but collectively they showed two things:

The beings were one hundred percent organic, which meant they were not Borg—at least not in any way that Alliance technology could detect.

And they *could* be Terrans. None of the readouts conflicted with any of the biological parameters that had been assembled from the records of pre-Borg visitors to the world.

"Full vision and sound," he said.

A moment later, the beings' eyes widened. With the

sound baffles down, he could hear their accelerated breathing.

Kirk and Scotty lurched and almost fell as the transporter field released them and they found themselves in a featureless, gray-walled room—box?—with no doors, no windows, nothing. The only light source was a square glowing patch above their heads.

"Sarek!" Kirk half-shouted, but there was no response.

At the same time, Scotty snatched the remote control unit from the utility belt at his waist, studied its readout a moment, then entered his security code.

Nothing happened. The *Goddard*'s computer did not respond.

This was not good, Kirk thought. Even if Sarek reappeared and took the time to talk with them, Scotty's ill-timed exclamation had committed them to something at least vaguely resembling the truth, which unfortunately was, in its simplest form: *"We're here to radically alter the past and present of dozens of worlds, including your own."*

Not that they would ever have a chance to do any such thing, not if their present situation was any indication.

"Ideas, Scotty?"

The engineer shook his head, frowning as he replaced the remote control in his belt and extracted what Kirk assumed was a tricorder, even though it was closer in size to a communicator. Scotty's frown deepened as he scanned slowly in all directions.

"There's another room not much bigger than this one on the other side of this wall," he said, pointing, "but there's no way out of either one, except by transporter. And there's a force field to block *that*."

Kirk grimaced. "A maximum security dungeon? But where? In Sarek's ship?"

"Aye," the engineer said after a moment's study of the tiny tricorder screen, "we're in *a* ship, at least. There are more than a hundred life forms, including Vulcan and Romulan and half a dozen others. I wouldn't—"

Scotty broke off, directing the tricorder toward the wall that concealed the adjacent room. "The force field is going down," he said. An instant later the silence was replaced by a faint, directionless hum.

Hastily he grabbed his remote control, but before he could re-enter his code, the humming stopped and the tricorder indicated the force field was back.

And that the adjoining "room" now contained a life form.

A Vulcan life form.

Hastily, Scotty stowed the tricorder while Kirk nodded his approval. The last thing he wanted to do was call attention to that or the communicator and possibly have the devices confiscated.

As they watched the wall, its entire length wavered like a viewscreen going out of focus.

Suddenly, then, it was transparent, and they found themselves facing not a viewscreen image but a seemingly real and still-haggard-looking Sarek less than two meters away. In the otherwise featureless wall behind him were a small viewscreen and control panel.

"Are we prisoners?" Kirk asked sharply.

"That depends on who and what you are and how you come to know my name," the Vulcan said, his voice indistinguishable from that of "their" Sarek.

Suddenly, Kirk had an idea. The truth!

But not quite the *whole* truth . . .

"What the devil are you talking about, Sarek?" he asked, putting on his best puzzled frown while surreptitiously laying what he hoped was a restraining hand on Scotty's arm. "Scotty and I've known you for thirty years. Your son is one of our best friends."

Watching Sarek's eyes closely, Kirk was virtually certain he saw a flicker of reaction but couldn't tell if it was surprise, anger or disbelief. Sarek—*his* Sarek—had always been even harder to read than his half-human son, and this version was obviously no easier.

"Explain," the Vulcan said. "I have no son, and, to the best of my knowledge, I have never seen either of you until a few moments ago."

"What is this, some kind of Vulcan mind game?" Kirk asked, escalating his frown to a scowl. "Damn it, Sarek, there's more than enough craziness going on without you pretending not to know us!"

"To what 'craziness' are you referring?"

Kirk snorted, chancing a sideways glance at Scotty to see if the engineer was on board yet. "You mean besides you beaming us into some kind of high-tech dungeon for no reason? Where do I start? For one thing, there aren't supposed to be any Borg within thousands of parsecs, but there they are. Worse, they just *appeared*, quicker than a bird-of-prey can de-cloak. Where'd they come from? For another, what kind of ship is this *Wisdom*? That is where we're being held, isn't it? You said it was an 'Alliance' ship, whatever that is. Did Vulcan pull out of the Federation when Earth wasn't looking and start its own—"

"I assure you I am not playing games of any kind," Sarek interrupted. His voice was still under tight control but his face was beginning to take on a pallor Kirk had never seen on a Vulcan. "Tell me what you were doing when you say the Borg vessels 'appeared.' "

Kirk let out an exasperated sigh but inwardly he exulted. "We were investigating that *thing* back there, that ribbon of energy," he said, giving his voice the angry impatience of someone being forced to waste his time answering foolish questions. "Whatever it is, it's already destroyed at least two ships and killed hundreds of people. We were trying to get a closer look at it, trying to find out what it is, but mostly we were looking for a way to get rid of it before it had a chance to incinerate anything else!"

"The Vortex," Sarek said, half turning to the viewscreen behind him and entering a series of commands into the control panel beneath it. A moment later, the screen was filled with the now familiar maelstrom of crackling energy.

Visual aids, no less, Kirk thought as he nodded with feigned impatience. "If that's what you Vulcans call it, yes, that's what we were trying to get a good look at. We were observing it from what we thought was a safe distance when . . . something happened. That thing—the Vortex—must've reached out and done something to us. For a second, it flickered, and the next thing we knew, there were those two Borg ships. Obviously, we weren't inclined to stick around to see what they were up to."

"Do you have sensor records of the events you describe?"

"We'd just *gotten* there, Sarek. We were just getting set up when things went crazy. Now are you going to tell us what the devil is going on? And why you're treating us like strangers? Or enemies, even?"

Sarek turned abruptly back to the screen. "Here," he said as his fingers tapped in more commands, "is an enhancement of what one of our observation platforms recorded in the vicinity of the Vortex at the time you say the Borg ships appeared."

The image of the Vortex vanished, replaced by a motionless starfield. Within seconds, something flickered into existence and vanished, but it was enough to draw their eyes to that spot on the screen. A moment later, the object appeared again and again faded, but this time Kirk recognized it, and he didn't have to fake his look of astonishment.

It was the *Goddard*.

Another appearance, another fade, and finally it remained, solid.

"It would seem," Sarek said as the image of the *Goddard* froze on the screen, "that you are the ones who appeared out of nowhere, not the Borg."

Which should not have been a surprise, Kirk realized abruptly. From his and Scotty's point of view on the *Goddard,* this entire universe had suddenly appeared around them, brought into existence by something Picard had done far in the past. It was only logical that, from this universe's point of view—from Sarek's point of view—Scotty and he were the ones who had come into existence, suddenly and inexplicably.

Which would, Kirk realized with relief, fit perfectly with the idea that he had been trying to hint at—the idea that the *Goddard* had accidentally been transported here from an alternate reality, perhaps by some side effect of the energy ribbon, which looked to be the only thing that existed, unchanged, in both universes. If he could sell that idea to Sarek—or better yet, if Sarek came up with it himself—it would then be only logical for Scotty and himself to try to find out where and when the two realities had parted company. Scientific curiosity would demand it. They could simply lay out the history of their reality and compare it to the history of *this* reality, with particular emphasis on when and where the Borg first appeared.

Kirk put a look of suspicion on his face as Sarek turned away from the screen to face them again. "I thought you said you weren't playing games with us, Sarek," he said accusingly, gesturing at the viewscreen. "Then what the devil do you call *that?*"

"It was precisely what it appeared to be: a record of your arrival. What we have yet to determine is where you arrived from and by what means you traveled."

Kirk snorted. *"We* didn't arrive from anywhere. Unless it's from a whole different universe, a *sane* universe where—"

He stopped abruptly, scowling at Sarek. "Is *that* what you're trying to tell us? That we *are* from a—from an alternate universe? That's ridiculous."

"Under normal circumstances I would agree, even though our scientists have long suggested that realities alternate to our own could theoretically exist. However, the circumstances I find myself confronting now are hardly normal. That you came from an alternate universe appears, in fact, to be the only logical explanation—if, that is, you are telling at least an approximation of the truth when you say you have known a Vulcan named Sarek for three decades."

"And if those images you showed us are real." Kirk shook his head stubbornly. "Look, Sarek—"

"The images are quite real, I assure you. As are these." Once again Sarek's fingers darted across the controls and the image on the viewscreen changed. The miniature *Goddard* vanished and was replaced by—

Earth.

But not an Earth Kirk had ever seen before.

The shapes of the continents and oceans were instantly recognizable, but all traces of green and blue were gone, as was the pristine white of the clouds Kirk had seen from orbit a thousand times. Continents and oceans from pole to pole were smothered in a mottled brownish-yellow haze streaked with cancerous gray clouds.

"This is the last image we have of Terra before the Borg erected a sensor shield around the Terran system," Sarek explained. "The transformation to a Borg world had been underway for several years at that time. It has almost certainly been completed in the century since."

Kirk's stomach knotted. He had long since accepted the likelihood that, in this universe, Earth was a Borg slave world, a part of their so-called collective, but until that image appeared on the screen, his acceptance had been at a sanitized intellectual level, the way one can intellectually accept the reality of the bodies buried beneath the neatly mown grass and flower-bedecked headstones of a cemetery without actually visualizing the decaying bodies in the darkness below or considering the grisly multitude of ways they had died. But now the image of the actual dying Earth—a *murdered* Earth—shattered the fragile barrier between intellect and emotion and brought with it a vivid image of the grotesque Borg cubicles he had seen in the *Goddard*'s briefing program. For a moment all Kirk could see in his mind's eye were the zombie-like faces of the friends and family he had left behind on Earth, now nothing more than cyborg slaves that had once been human but now retained only enough of their humanity to be aware of the nightmare in which they were trapped.

If any of them had even been born in this universe.

This universe that had come into existence at the very

moment when *he* should have been going *out* of existence, consumed by the nucleonic fury of the Vortex.

His stomach knotted even more painfully in a sudden spasm of guilt. Was the logic he had outlined to Scotty both facile *and* faulty? There was no way, it said, that his own rescue could have caused this universe-shattering change. It had to be something that Picard and that other *Enterprise* had done, centuries further back in time.

But no one truly knew what kind of logic governed the rules of time travel. No one even knew if such rules existed.

Above all, there was the disconcerting "coincidence" that the changes had occurred—the *Enterprise*-B had vanished, the Borg cubes had appeared—in virtually the same instant Scotty had snatched him out of the path of the Vortex.

The everyday logic of cause and effect had plenty to say about *that*. However, if you got deep enough into the mathematics of quantum physics and all the other arcane disciplines that theoreticians dabbled with in hopes of learning how the universe really worked, you would find evidence that even normal time—whatever "normal time" was— didn't necessarily have to flow in one direction only. That which was cause when time flowed in one direction became effect if time flowed in the opposite direction. Overlay that with the mathematical descriptions of warp drive and slingshotting through high intensity gravity fields, and theoreticians in even the most ivory of towers could only speculate on how it all would apply to the so-called "real world."

All of which was several light-years over his head and even over Scotty's, not to mention the heads of virtually everyone else he had ever known. As far as Jim Kirk was concerned, it all came down to a resounding: "Who knows?"

And what it all led Kirk to was the inevitable question he had been avoiding since the moment he had learned what this timeline contained: *If I were to go back and pitch myself into the Vortex, would that put things back the way they're supposed to be? Would it rescue those billions on what had once been Earth from the Borg hell it had become?*

If he was certain that that was the case—and if he could get out of this seemingly escape-proof prison—he would do it in an instant. Not gladly, not even without regret, but without hesitation. He literally couldn't live with himself if he didn't.

But what if, he couldn't help but think, his being saved from the Vortex wasn't the key? What if he'd been right all along? What if it was Picard's doing, not his and Scotty's? Or something different altogether, unrelated to either of them? What if he allowed himself to be plunged into the Vortex and the timeline continued unchanged, ignoring his sacrifice altogether?

Or what if the timeline did change—but into something even worse?

No, the time might come when they would know enough to say with certainty that his own death was required to set things right, but that time hadn't come yet, not by a long shot, not until they found out what Picard and that other *Enterprise* had done.

But in order to find that out—in order to do *anything*—he had to get Sarek to let them out of this cage.

"It looks like you're right, Sarek," Kirk said somberly, for once not having to disguise or exaggerate his true feelings when he spoke. "This *is* an alternate universe, one in which our whole world has been destroyed. I hope you won't mind if we try to find out why."

With an eagerness she hadn't felt in centuries, yet with an almost equally intense uneasiness, the woman calling herself Guinan waited on the *D'Zidran*'s bridge for the *Enterprise* to come within transporter range.

She had lived with the ghost of the one who called himself Picard for more than four hundred years. Until a few minutes ago she had assumed it had been a dream, despite the fact that her people seldom dreamed. It was likely a result of her many years on Picard's world, she had often told herself. Humans were—had been—a dreaming race if nothing else, and it wouldn't be the first time she had temporarily acquired traits of the races she observed and listened to. Some inner part of herself, she had always suspected, was listening as intently as her outer shell, temporarily adapting itself to different worlds in ways that made her observations, her "listening" more . . . complete.

After all, what better way to understand a race than by not only participating in the conscious lives of its members but by also emulating their generally more honest inner lives? This would have been particularly useful on a world like Earth, where inner and outer lives were often so different as to be almost irreconcilable.

But this particular dream had been so vivid that for decades she had had only to close her eyes for it to return and play itself out on the russet glow of her lowered eyelids.

And in her heart.

In the dream, the one who called himself Picard and a strange, artificial companion had come from hundreds of years in the future, on an errand that she could never quite remember. What she did remember was that he declared with absolute certainty that the two of them would meet in that same distant future he had come from, that they would develop a relationship deeper than any she had experienced even in her long life. She also remembered that, in the dream, she had been injured, and Picard had not only risked his life to save her but had risked being trapped for the rest of that life hundreds of years in his own past.

In the centuries that followed she had often been driven, inexplicably, to return to Earth, not only to observe or listen but to search for anything that would indicate the dream had been more than a dream.

But there had been nothing.

And then Earth itself was no more. In its place was only the utter desolation of a Borg world, its billions of newly created drones toiling mindlessly on the poisonous remnants of the planet they were systematically destroying.

All hope that the dream had been more than a dream ended with Earth.

And she had moved on, finding herself drawn to the Alliance as it slowly and contentiously brought itself into existence, hoping someday to do battle with the Borg.

And now . . .

Now not only had her dream, dead for centuries, been resurrected, but it had brought with it the possibility that she had been wrong all those years. If this Picard was telling even an approximation of the truth, perhaps the "visit" she remembered *had* been more than a dream. Perhaps Picard and the pale almost-human had come to her not from her universe's future but from another's, from the future of a universe in which the Borg had not yet come and Earth still had a future.

The universe that *this* Picard claimed to have come from.

A universe that might no longer exist.

The bridge wavered around her as the *D'Zidran* dropped out of warp and an alien craft with startlingly graceful lines filled the viewscreen.

A craft which, to her relief and dismay, looked eerily familiar.

Tensing, she waited for the touch of the alien transporter.

FIFTEEN

BALITOR, THE *Wisdom*'s Narisian communications officer, was barely able to keep the fur on the back of her neck and shoulders from rippling like grass in the wind, so great was her feeling of eager anticipation. From the moment the Proctors had accepted her into the Inner Circle, she had known that a moment like this *might* come, but she had never truly thought that it *would* come, not for her. Her mother had spent half her life on Alliance ships and Alliance worlds, working alongside explorers and scientists and warriors of all kinds, and not once in all those decades had she encountered anything that prompted her to consider, even for a split second, attempting to establish a Link with the Wise Ones. Nothing had come even remotely close to meeting the criteria drummed into her during her months of training and conditioning.

But now, after less than two years, Balitor herself had been presented with the most clearcut case she could imagine: a never-before-seen craft, appearing out of nowhere and containing never-before-seen beings who nonetheless appeared to know the Arbiter and were now being held prisoner. This was precisely the sort of "unexpected" or "unpredictable" thing she had been instructed to watch for. There was no doubt in her mind that her Link would be accepted and that she would soon experience that which even the Proctors are denied.

Until now she had assiduously avoided even wondering what the Link itself would be like, knowing as she did the overwhelming odds against her ever having the chance to actually experience it. Her mother had thought about it—dreamed about it, *longed* for it—for all those empty decades, growing ever more dispirited as it became ever more evident that her opportunity was never to come. Balitor had seen it happen, had seen the hope gradually fade from her mother's eyes, replaced by steadily growing disappointment. Her mother should have lived another thirty years after leaving the service of the Proctors, but she was gone in five, her fur as dull and lifeless at the end as a woman decades older.

It wasn't fair, Balitor thought, a twinge of bitterness over her mother's fate dulling her own elation, but it lasted only seconds. Nothing—short of having this opportunity snatched from her at the last minute—could dampen her barely-controlled euphoria for long. In a few hours, as soon as her shift on the bridge was over, she could retreat to her quarters where, safe from prying Alliance eyes and constant interruptions, she could, at last, initiate the process that would give her life meaning.

Just a few short hours . . .

Guinan—*his* Guinan—was waiting for Picard behind the bar in a darker than usual Ten-Forward. Even the luminescence of the bartop itself was dimmer than he had ever seen it, but the scimitar-shaped bottle and two half-filled

triangular Denebian glasses that waited with her were plain
enough. Saurian brandy, he remembered, had been one of
Captain Scott's favorites. Not surprisingly, the two of them
were alone in the bar.

"Have a seat, Captain," she said, nudging one of the
glasses toward his side of the bar. "I can't say I haven't
been expecting you."

"I rather imagined you would be," he said, picking up
the glass, savoring the aroma for a moment and then setting it back down without drinking. "Do you have any answers?"

"None that you want, I imagine. Certainly none that will
make the situation any less difficult for either of us. For
one thing, since I left the bridge, I've realized that I wasn't
as open with you as I promised I would be."

"Something to do with that other version of you?" he
asked with a slight smile.

Guinan shook her head almost imperceptibly. "I didn't
know she existed, although I suppose I should have. No,
it's something I should have told you the moment Captain
Scott was rescued from the *Jenolen*." She paused, lowering
her eyes for a moment, then bringing them back up to meet
his. "You see, Captain, I was very likely responsible for his
being on the *Jenolen* in the first place."

"*You?*" Suddenly his mind was spinning again. "How?
And for God's sake, *why?*"

"The 'how' is easy," she said and quickly told him about
her meeting with Scott in the late-twenty-third-century
Glasgow bar and his subsequent meeting with Matt
Franklin, the young ensign from the *Jenolen*.

"As for the 'why,' " she went on, "I'm sure you're as
tired of hearing it as I am of saying it, but I simply do not
know. All I know is, if it hadn't been for me—and those

damnable feelings that brought me there—Captain Scott would in all likelihood have lived out his retirement peacefully, if unhappily, on Earth. But he didn't. And now he's somewhere in the past turning history inside out, causing your homeworld to be destroyed and mine to be saved."

Picard was silent a moment, trying to take in this latest revelation. "And you think that was the ultimate reason for what you did? To bring your world back from the dead?"

"I have no idea, Captain. That's what is so frustrating about the feelings. They never include a reason. What's worse, I have no idea where they come from or why. For all I know, they could be bubbling up out of my own subconscious. But wherever they come from, I don't see how saving my world and destroying yours could be the reason for my meddling in Captain Scott's life."

"Because those same feelings now tell you that the current timeline is 'wrong' in some way? That we should try to set it right?"

She nodded silently.

Suddenly, Picard couldn't help but smile at the utter absurdity of the situation. Her "feelings"—or more likely whoever or whatever was responsible for them—had caused a cosmic train wreck and now they were hoping things could be put back the way they were.

Or perhaps Q or one of his ilk was being more subtle and less self-aggrandizing than usual and was perpetrating his biggest prank yet. He wouldn't put it past Q, a creature with an infinitely large ego and the nearly infinite power to indulge it. Virtually everything Picard had seen Q do had been, at one level or another, a prank.

But without knowing for certain, knowing only that Guinan and her feelings had been right more times than he liked to remember . . .

"Well, then," he said, "I suppose we'll just have to try to do what they want."

As Sarek listened to Kirk describing the universe he and his companion claimed to have come from, two things became increasingly clear and increasingly disturbing.

First, everything they said about it matched his own supposedly false memories, sometimes in details he hadn't even been consciously aware of until they were mentioned. And the creatures themselves matched their counterparts in those same memories. Each time one of them spoke, particularly the one called Kirk, the uncanny similarity notched upward in Sarek's mind. Movements, gestures, tiny details of their features, even their patterns of speech as their words emerged from their version of a universal translator, everything matched his spurious memories.

Second, their universe had diverged from Sarek's more than a century before his birth. That was when, according to the one called Kirk, Terra—Earth, as they insisted on calling it—had developed a warp drive and established contact with Vulcans and other starfaring civilizations. The warp signature of Earth's very first test flight had been detected by a Vulcan ship that happened to be cruising the stellar neighborhood. Within hours, that Vulcan ship was on Earth, its passengers earnestly welcoming the newcomers into the interstellar community. Within a century, the upstart Earth had progressed to playing a major role in their version of the Alliance, a group of allied worlds called the Federation.

In the real world—in Sarek's universe—none of that had happened. Either the test flight hadn't been conducted, perhaps because Earth had already been assimilated by the Borg by then, or there hadn't been a Vulcan ship near enough to detect the resultant warp signature. In any case, the first "official" notice Vulcans or anyone else took of Earth was decades later when a fleet of Borg ships swept out from Terra and surrounded the Alpha Centauri system, setting up a death-dealing blockade that destroyed any ship that tried to enter or leave.

A few years later, the sensor shield was erected around the Terran system, although Vulcan ships had in the meantime managed to survey Terra and record the images Sarek had shown them earlier. Alpha Centauri, however, was never isolated in that way, nor were the subsequently assimilated worlds. They were left—as examples?—open to long-range sensors, which were able to monitor the entire process as their atmospheres were gradually changed from a breathable oxygen-nitrogen mix to a corrosive blend of methane, carbon monoxide, and fluorine.

It was assumed that the conversion—and planet-wide strip-mining—of Earth had continued to completion after the shield was raised.

No one knew where the Borg had come from or precisely when they had arrived. Because the approach of their asteroid-sized ships had totally escaped detection, some had suggested that the Borg, like Kirk and Scott now claimed to have done, had emerged from an alternate universe. In those pre-Alliance days, however, there were no regular patrols, and sensors were more limited, which meant that if an alien ship—or even a fleet—didn't intrude directly on territory claimed by another world or accidentally encounter an exploratory or trade ship in deep space, it was unlikely that it *would* be detected.

None of that, however, was of any help to Sarek in deciding what to do with these two interlopers. If they were telling the truth and were *not* Borg creations, they and the technology represented by their tiny craft might well be of help against the Borg.

On the other hand, if they *were* Borg creations, their every thought being instantly shared with the collective—

An amber light at the bottom of the control panel flashed brightly, cutting off his speculations. It took him only a fraction of a second to realize that it was a signal from Commander Varkan, sent through the same hard-wired connection that allowed the *Wisdom*'s computer to bypass the shields and respond to the control panel and provide the images Sarek had ordered up to show his "guests."

"We will continue this discussion later," he said, opaquing the wall and, a moment later, initiating transport.

"Enable exit," he said as soon as transport was complete. The door of the auxiliary transporter cubicle slid open and he strode rapidly up the narrow secondary corridor toward the bridge.

A new shiver of uneasiness rippled through Guinan's body as the transporter on Picard's ship gripped her. She couldn't be sure, but she *thought* it felt different from the Alliance transporters she was accustomed to. More likely, she told herself, the difference was a result of her own nervousness, a compounding of the faint prickling sensation that had been quietly assaulting her since Commander Tal had agreed to allow her to be transported to the *Enterprise*.

Then the *D'Zidran* bridge vanished in a faint cascade of colored lights, replaced an imperceptible moment later by a room three times that size. Picard himself stood at what she assumed were the transporter controls. He looked up, smiling, albeit with a slight stiffness.

After no more than a couple of seconds, he stepped up

onto the massive transporter platform—there were at least six separate pads—and reached out to take her hand.

"Welcome aboard the *Enterprise*, Madam Guinan," he said, his tone warm but wary.

"Just Guinan." No one since Mr. Clemens had used that form of address.

"As you wish," Picard said, releasing her hand as a door slid open, hissing softly. "This way to the bridge."

Following him through the door, she found herself in a broad corridor that curved gently out of sight in either direction. How big *was* this ship? The *D'Zidran*'s sensors had undoubtedly provided that information, but she hadn't thought to ask Tal. Such statistics were normally of no interest to her, and the graceful image on the viewscreen had not hinted at great size.

Another door hissed into being in the opposite wall of the corridor, and Picard motioned her through it, into a small room. "Bridge," Picard said, apparently to the walls. But whatever or whomever he'd spoken to must have been listening. Moments later the door reopened, and the corridor outside had been replaced by the bridge. It was even more spacious than it had appeared on the *D'Zidran*'s viewscreen, large enough to swallow up a dozen bridges the size of the *D'Zidran*'s. The first thing she saw was the huge viewscreen and the detailed image of the *D'Zidran* centered in it. The second was the pale humanoid seated at a control panel in front of the screen.

The same being that had accompanied Picard to nineteenth-century Earth in her dream!

A name sprang unbidden to her lips: "Mr. Data—"

The humanoid turned smoothly from the control panel before him and looked at her questioningly. "Do you know me?"

For once in her long life, she was at a loss for words. A moment later, the tall, bearded man who had been watching the viewscreen intently turned toward her.

Riker!

The name flashed through her mind but went no further. Her eyes, however, must have betrayed her, she realized as she felt Picard's hand on her arm and heard his murmured, "Perhaps you would like a moment to rest?"

Silently, she nodded. Despite her intentions to speak openly about the "dream"—at least with Picard—she realized she hadn't been prepared for *this*. Not only Picard himself but virtually everyone else from that "dream" was here. The artificial humanoid named Data. Riker. Troi. And there a few meters behind Riker, she saw now, was the dark-skinned man with the metallic blindfold-like device covering his eyes, apparently enabling him to see. The only person missing was the red-haired woman, the oddly named Dr. Crusher.

"This way," Picard was saying, gently guiding her away from the others toward a door that was already hissing open in the smoothly curving back wall of the bridge. Expecting another conveyance like the small room she had just emerged from—an elevator, she assumed, a luxury she had never, in the Alliance, associated with a starship—she stepped through and was startled to find herself in a large, luxuriously furnished room with desk and couch and wall decorations and, of all things, an aquarium bathed in soothingly soft light.

"Make yourself comfortable," Picard said, still standing in the open door, making no move to follow her inside. "If you'd like a few minutes alone to—"

"No, please, stay," she said abruptly, her determination returning now that the situation was more nearly the way she had pictured it, just the two of them. "We must speak."

For just an instant he was motionless, then visibly relaxed as he stepped across the threshold and let the door hiss shut behind him.

"As you wish," he said. "And you're quite right. We really do need to speak, perhaps more urgently than either of us knows."

SIXTEEN

DURING THE series of wary exchanges between Kirk and Sarek, Scotty had realized that the situation was even more hopeless than he had imagined. First and foremost, this Sarek obviously wasn't going to release them, no matter what.

But even if he did . . .

Even if he did, there was nothing he and Kirk could do to repair the damage to the timeline. Finding approximately when the timelines *seemed* to diverge had been remarkably easy but it wasn't nearly enough. They still had no idea when the real divergence had taken place.

Obviously Picard had done something that brought the Borg from the distant Delta Quadrant to Earth in the twenty-first century, but the actual deed, the triggering event, could have taken place in the twentieth.

Or the nineteenth.

Or any time whatsoever. According to everything he'd learned about them, the Borg tended to act slowly and deliberately. It could have taken them centuries to decide to travel the thousands of parsecs to Earth.

Without knowing *what* Picard had done, there was no way of knowing *when* he had done it.

If he had done anything at all.

Perhaps the mere presence of a twenty-fourth-century Federation starship in the twenty-first century or earlier had somehow attracted the attention of the Borg. Perhaps, centuries in the past, before the collective had grown so large and so inflexible, their attention was easier to gain. Perhaps they had captured the *Enterprise,* learned of Earth's location and come to investigate.

And decided to stay.

Picard's second jump could have taken him back a hundred years or a thousand. The *Bounty 2*—even if it did magically reappear—might be capable of another slingshot maneuver before it literally flew to pieces. With a great deal of luck and even more jury-rigged repairs, it might hold together for two or three—but no more. Hardly enough to search even the twenty-first century for the *Enterprise,* let alone the previous millennium.

But then, as Scotty listened, his mood growing darker by the minute, Sarek abruptly ended the conversation.

"We will finish this discussion later," the Vulcan said without warning.

An instant later, the wall again went opaque and the faint hum they had heard before returned.

Recovering, Scotty grabbed the tricorder from his utility belt.

"A transporter," he said as he pointed the tricorder at the wall and scanned the instrument's tiny screen. "He's gone."

"How far?" Kirk wanted to know.

"A dozen meters, no more, but now—" He paused, shaking his head. "The shielding around this 'cell' was down for a wee bit, again," he said, "but it went back up as soon as the transport was completed."

"Makes sense," Kirk said. "Not helpful, but it does make sense. What can you tell about the shielding? Is there any way through it?"

Scotty studied the tricorder, frowning at first, then raising his eyebrows in surprise. "Aye, there just might be."

"What is it, Commander?" Sarek asked as he emerged onto the bridge.

"We have received a distress call," Varkan said, gesturing at the viewscreen, where a less-than-clear image of ex-councilman Zarcot breathed heavily, the massive cords in what passed for a neck among Cardassians standing out even more than normal.

"Sarek! At last! Tell this fool who I am!"

"He knows who you are, Zarcot. What is it you wish?"

"Transport me aboard the Wisdom! *My own ship was destroyed, and this lifepod must have been damaged as well. The life support system is failing."*

"Explain."

"There isn't time! Just lower your shields and—"

"There will have to be time, Zarcot." Sarek looked toward Varkan. "Commander, what do your sensors show?"

"The signal is indeed coming from a lifepod," the Romulan said, studying the sensor screens over the operator's shoulder, "and the life support system is clearly malfunctioning, as is the impulse engine. There does not, however, appear to be any immediate threat to the occupant's life."

"Thank you, Commander," Sarek acknowledged, turning back to the viewscreen. "Now explain your presence here, Zarcot. In your alarmist dispatches regarding the dangers posed by the Vortex, you indicated you were about to return to Alliance Prime. You even hinted you had devised a plan to deal with the Vortex."

"Sarek, please. This is no time for petty retribution. My opposition to some of your policies—"

"It is caution, Zarcot, not retribution. Do you deny that your Cardassian colleagues still on the Council have recently held secret meetings?"

"Obviously they were not secret if you know of them. In any event, strategy meetings are standard procedure. You will know the results at the next Council meeting. Now please, get me—"

"That is good to know, Zarcot. In the meantime, I repeat: Explain your presence here. Why have you not returned to Alliance Prime? What happened to your ship?"

"The Vortex did something to it, I don't know what. We were taking a last set of readings before leaving, and we must have gotten too close. A tendril of energy of some kind snaked out farther than any had before, and the next thing we knew, it had hit us, penetrating our shields as if they didn't exist. We lost all control, and the anti-matter containment field became unstable. Or so our engineer told me. We had to abandon ship."

"Where are the others?"

Zarcot's wavering image lowered its head. *"I don't know. I haven't been able to raise the other lifepods. I fear they may have been destroyed."*

"You alone survived, then?"

"I hope not, but I have no way of knowing."

"How did you get this far from the Vortex in just a lifepod?"

"I don't know, Sarek. I'm not an engineer. Perhaps the Vortex energy threw my lifepod here. All I know is, if I don't

get out of it before life support fails, my death will be on your *conscience.*"

Unperturbed, Sarek turned to the Commander. "Is there any sign of other lifepods? Or of the parent ship?"

"None, Arbiter," the Romulan said, again studying the sensor displays over the intimidated crewman's shoulder. "There is only the craft belonging to the two beings you transported into Interrogation."

"Open a channel to Outpost Number Three. I will speak with Kasok."

Zarcot opened his mouth to protest but his image vanished before any sound emerged. Seconds later, Kasok appeared on the screen.

"Kasok," Sarek began abruptly, "Zarcot's ship was recently in the vicinity of the Vortex. What records do you have of its activities?"

Kasok's eyes widened but he said nothing as he consulted several rapidly scrolling screens of data. *"A ship, possibly Zarcot's,"* he said, looking up, *"circumnavigated the Vortex several times in several different orbits."*

"And when it left?"

Kasok shook his head, frowning. *"Unknown, Arbiter. Its departure occurred in one of the blind spots."*

"Thank you," Sarek said, turning away from Kasok's vanishing image. "Commander, status of Zarcot's life support?"

"Still deteriorating but—" Varkan broke off, frowning, as the stranded Cardassian's image returned to the screen. "The deterioration is accelerating. If it continues at this rate, only minutes remain, not hours."

"And there are still no other ships or lifepods within sensor range?"

"None, Arbiter."

Sarek stood silently, his eyes fastened on Zarcot, who had by now adopted a look of stoic resignation.

Finally the Vulcan spoke. "Proceed with the transport, Commander.

"Very well. Commander, proceed with the transport."

"As you wish, Arbiter," the Romulan acknowledged, then began issuing the orders.

Moments later the shields went down, and the Tellarite at the transporter controls began the lock-on procedure. After several seconds, he looked up from the controls. "There is interference of some kind, Commander," he said. "I'm having trouble locking on."

At the same time, a hissing sound erupted from the communications station.

"Commander," the Narisian communications officer began, but before she could say more, Zarcot's face vanished from the viewscreen in a burst of static.

And was replaced a chaotic moment later with another face.

Sarek was barely able to conceal his surprise as he recognized the anxious features of one of his prisoners, the one who claimed to be a Terran called Kirk.

Scotty's heart was pounding as the information streamed across the tricorder's tiny screen.

In the minute following Sarek's abrupt departure, the engineer had scanned the entire spectrum of the shield around the cell *and* the shield around the ship itself. They were each almost as powerful as the old *Enterprise*'s deflectors, but they were also comparatively primitive, the data on the tricorder screen now indicated.

Primitive, that is, compared to the twenty-fourth-century deflector technology he had developed a nodding acquaintance with during his first few weeks on the *Goddard*. For one thing, the spectrum of the main shields, while not quite Swiss cheese, did have holes, as, luckily, had the *Jenolen*'s, which discovery on his part was the only reason the *Enterprise* had been able to transport him and La Forge off the doomed ship while its shields were holding open the Dyson Sphere's door. The shield that surrounded their cell, however, was not nearly so porous.

But both were limited by the twenty-third-century-or-earlier technology that had produced them. And the frequency spectrum that could be covered by twenty-third-century technology was considerably more limited than what could be covered by twenty-fourth-century technology.

Holding the tricorder in one hand, Scotty snatched up the remote with the other. When he had originally cobbled the remote together, he'd given it at least ten comm channels, "just to be safe." Under most circumstances, one would have been enough, but he knew there were far too many ways individual frequencies could be blocked for him to take it for granted. Storms in a planet's atmosphere or in space could generate interference. Radiation could distort certain frequencies, and unknown chemical compounds could absorb or block them. Emission nebulas could swamp others. The list went on and on, and there were any number of other things that he couldn't possibly foresee.

Like the shields that now held them trapped.

Switching on the remote, he held it in front of the tricorder and quickly scanned across the available frequencies.

Suddenly, his heart was pounding even faster. The highest frequency channel just barely skirted the upper edge of the shield spectrum.

But that should be enough.

"Are you ready to get out of here, Captain?"

Kirk broke into a broad grin. "Let's go! I guess it's a good thing I didn't have your Miracle Worker's permit revoked after all."

"Aye," Scotty replied, stowing the tricorder and selecting the uppermost comm channel on the remote, "and a wee bit of dumb luck doesn't hurt, either."

After only a couple of seconds, the remote display indicated it was linked to the *Goddard* computer. Hastily, Scotty entered the commands that would reprogram the transporter to operate at the high end of its own frequency range.

Another few seconds and he felt—or imagined he felt—the whisper-light touch of the transporter as it scanned the space whose coordinates the *Goddard*'s computer had extracted from the remote's memory.

A moment later the familiar tingle of the stasis field gripped him, just as he noticed the beginning of the captain's thumbs-up gesture.

The featureless cell vanished, replaced in the blink of an eye by the interior of the *Goddard*. Both men stepped off the transporter pads and hurried to the controls.

"I don't suppose you can mask our warp trail," Kirk said hopefully as Scotty raised the *Goddard*'s shields.

"A wee bit, but likely not enough to—"

Scotty broke off as he glanced at the viewscreen.

A ghostly image flickered in and out of existence. Remembering that he had left the sensors set to detect the cloaked *Bounty 2,* he thought for an instant that it had reappeared. But this was a totally different ship, squat like the *Wisdom* but with sharper edges.

"Scotty, what the devil is *that?*" Kirk asked. "And that," he added a moment later, pointing at a tiny, lifepod-size vessel, uncloaked.

Scotty didn't answer, just began tweaking the sensor pa-

rameters the same way he had done when he'd been looking for the *Bounty 2*.

Within seconds, the ghostly image steadied, though it
didn't become any less ghostly.

"Whatever it is," Scotty said, scowling, "it's using a
primitive Klingon cloaking device. And its weapons are
charging, almost ready to fire."

"What kind—" Kirk began but broke off as he saw the
indications on the screen himself.

Disruptors—trained directly on the *Wisdom*.

"Sarek's ship is lowering its shields," Scotty exclaimed.
"They're tryin' to beam someone off that lifepod!"

His eyes darting back to the sensor readings, Kirk saw
that the cloaked ship's disruptors were now almost fully
charged.

Suddenly, memories of Spock and Sarek—*his* Sarek—
flashed through his mind, and he realized the truth: If there
was anyone he should instinctively trust in any situation, in
any universe, it was them.

"Hail them!" Kirk almost shouted, but Scotty was already initiating a signal that would blanket all frequencies
in both normal space and subspace.

The ghost image of the cloaked ship and the lifepod
vanished into chaos that quickly resolved itself into the
same image of the *Wisdom*'s bridge they had seen just before they had been beamed into the dungeon. Sarek, standing behind a Tellarite at what looked to be transporter
controls, turned abruptly toward the viewscreen.

"Sarek!" Kirk shouted. "Raise your shields! There's a
cloaked ship out here about to fire on you!"

Sarek froze but only for a moment. Even as he opened his
mouth to demand to know how this so-called Terran had

escaped, a flood of memories—*false* memories—darted through his mind, as if crying out for his attention. False memories that, he suddenly realized, he had been purposely shunting aside, not only because of the pain they brought him but because of the shamefully illogical actions he himself had taken in them.

But now . . .

Now they held a message.

An urgent message telling him that, regardless of the logic of the situation, he should place his trust in these beings, no matter who or what they claimed to be.

"Raise the shields, Commander," he ordered, then looked toward the Narisian. "Tell Zarcot to stand by."

Virtually simultaneously, the shields flickered into life and a Cardassian cruiser wavered into existence less than a dozen kilometers away, its disruptor banks spewing out destruction.

The *Wisdom*, more than twice the size of its attacker, lurched slightly, then steadied as its shields reached full strength.

"Target their weapons," the Romulan commander snapped, but before the *Wisdom*'s phasers could be powered up to fire, the Cardassian ship sped away on full impulse. Before tractor beams could be brought to bear, it was out of range. An instant later, it vanished with a blinding flash as its warp drive engaged.

Sarek thought briefly of pursuing the fleeing ship but decided against it, signaling Varkan to stand down. He was virtually certain what Zarcot's plan had been and that, thanks to the Terrans' interference, it had failed and would not soon be resurrected. If the *Wisdom* had been destroyed—by the Vortex, as far as anyone on distant Alliance Prime would ever know—Zarcot would have returned, claiming that his warnings about the Vortex had been confirmed. He would doubtless have been hailed as a prophet and allowed, perhaps even "forced" to take Sarek's place on the Council.

Sarek turned back to the viewscreen where the one called Kirk still waited tensely. "Are there more such vessels nearby?"

"None that we can detect," Kirk said, and Sarek caught a glimpse of the other ex-prisoner in the background.

"I will require an explanation of these events," Sarek said.

"Of course. If you promise not to put us in the lockup again."

Sarek didn't hesitate in his reply. "You have my word. In any event, I have other use for the 'lockup,' as you call it."

He turned to the Romulan commander. "Transport ex-Councilman Zarcot aboard," he said, "directly to Interrogation. I will deal with him when I have concluded discussions with our other visitors. And contact Deputy Arbiter Koval on Alliance Prime. There is much I must tell him."

SEVENTEEN

WITH A mixture of relief and renewed apprehension, Picard heard the door close behind him, cutting off the doubtlessly curious gazes of virtually everyone on the bridge.

Guinan—*this* timeline's Guinan—stood in the middle of the room, almost precisely where her counterpart had stood a few subjective days earlier, a few very real decades in the future. This Guinan was even more uneasy than the other had been, or perhaps she just didn't conceal it as well.

"In your world, did we meet again?" she asked abruptly. "As you promised we would?"

The question took him by surprise, but it also, he realized with another gust of relief a moment later, resolved his own dilemma. When she had first appeared on the transporter pad, he had had to restrain himself from asking similarly obvious questions. If she had never before laid eyes on him in this timeline, such questions would brand him as a madman in her eyes, and that was the last thing he wanted. If anyone in this timeline knew what had brought about the change, it almost certainly would be her, and he would need her trust in order to get such information. She, however, like his Guinan, apparently had no concerns about what people thought of her. Or, in this particular instance, she was simply too curious to care.

"We did," he said. "And did our first meeting take place in your universe the same as it did in mine? In San Francisco? In the 1890s?"

He could see the tension drain from her face and body as she nodded. "In a manner of speaking," she said. "I don't actually remember it happening, but I remember remembering it, if that makes any sense. I'd always assumed it was a dream, but now I don't know what it was. I don't suppose *you* have an explanation?"

He smiled. "Just that you're a very remarkable . . . being, perhaps even more remarkable than you know. Tell me, do you occasionally feel impelled to do or say things for which you can find no logical reason?"

Her eyes narrowed and some of the tension returned to her stance. "How did you know?" she asked, a new suspicion in her tone. "I haven't told even Tal about *that.*"

"It's all right," he said, still smiling. "I suspect it's because I've probably known you—your counterpart in my universe—longer than you've known Tal. And Romulans, particularly Romulans in the military, are often more rigid in their thinking than humans, more likely to dismiss such things out of hand. But it *is* true, then?"

She nodded, looking around uneasily. "It was one of those . . . impulses that brought us here, in fact, although Tal doesn't realize it, of course. Should I assume that this . . . other Guinan has acted on similar impulses?"

He nodded. "She has. They've saved my life more than once."

"You believe in them, then?"

"I don't have a choice. She's been proven right time and again."

"So have I. It's the only reason Tal tolerates me, I think. But you were right about his rigidity. Luckily he has encountered enough beings with 'legitimate' mental powers such as telepathy and precognition to accept the idea that my occasional 'advice' comes from a similar source. But tell me, did your Guinan come with you on your quest to find a way to defeat the Borg? Is she here? On this ship?"

Before Picard could devise an answer, he was interrupted by Data's voice coming from his combadge. *"Captain, the level of chronometric radiation is increasing."*

"Thank you, Mr. Data. I'm on my way." Picard had turned toward the door while he spoke but now he turned back to Guinan for a moment. "Wait here if you like," he said. "I'll be back as soon as I can."

Striding toward the door, he wondered if the rise in radiation level was good news or bad. If it meant the appearance or approach of another "chronologically alien" object, it *might* mean Captain Scott was finally about to put in an appearance despite all the logical reasons why it was impossible, but—

He lurched to a stop as the door hissed open and he almost bumped into someone about to step into the ready room.

Guinan.

The Guinan from *his* universe, about to come face to face with her counterpart.

That could certainly account for the chronometric radiation, he thought, wondering what the readings would have been if anyone had been monitoring them when he'd met his own future self in the *El-Baz* five years ago.

He stepped to one side and turned in time to see this

timeline's Guinan's eyes widen in something that wasn't quite surprise. The Guinan in the doorway was smiling faintly, looking more relaxed than she had at any time since the *Enterprise* had emerged in this timeline.

"I presume," he said, easing past the Guinan in the doorway and onto the bridge, "no introductions are necessary."

On the bridge everyone's eyes but Data's were once more on the door to the captain's ready room as it hissed shut, leaving the two Guinans inside, alone.

"Mr. Data?"

"The new chronometric radiation has leveled off, Captain. It is also extremely localized, unlike the other radiation, which extends at least as far as our sensors can reach. The new radiation appears to be centered—"

"—on the *Enterprise* itself," Picard interrupted, "perhaps specifically on my ready room." So much for any hopes that Captain Scott was about to appear.

"Exactly, sir, and it decreases rapidly with distance." Data studied the readouts another moment. "Now it is decreasing overall."

Picard glanced back at the ready room door. "They're just getting used to each other, I imagine, Mr. Data."

Or merging into the single being they had once been, he thought uneasily, wondering what Data's "basic theory" had to say about such things but not really wanting to know.

Kirk's eyes widened in startled amusement as the door to Sarek's luxurious quarters on the *Wisdom* opened before the three of them.

"The furnishings are not of my choice," Sarek said, stating the obvious.

"Somehow," Kirk said with a faint smile, "I didn't think they were."

"Tell me, Kirk," Sarek said virtually the moment the door slid shut behind them, "is Spock the name of the son you claim your Sarek has?"

The question jolted Scotty, reminding him of the "alternate universe" idea that Kirk had tricked Sarek into believing. But surely, he thought, after what had just happened, the captain was going to tell Sarek the truth. The *whole* truth.

"As a matter of fact," Kirk said, "he is. But how did you know? Is that *your* son's name?"

Obviously, Scotty realized with a sinking feeling, Kirk wasn't quite ready for the whole truth yet.

"As I told you when you first suggested that your Sarek had a son, I have none, though once I did. He and his entire crew were killed by the Borg more than fifty years ago."

"But his name was Spock?"

"It was not."

"Then what—" Kirk began but broke off, his eyes widening in that look of sudden understanding that Scotty had seen so often before.

"Sybok," Kirk said softly. "Of course." When Sarek did not respond with a denial, Kirk went on: "If that's true, how did you come up with the name Spock?"

"Answer my questions and I will answer yours," Sarek said, his voice seeming even more toneless than before.

Scotty suppressed a grimace. If the captain kept this up . . .

Kirk shrugged. "Fair enough. Just remember, you told us a few minutes ago you weren't playing Vulcan mind games with us."

Sarek ignored the implied warning and asked: "Did the Sarek you know once request that you retrieve his son Spock's body from a distant star system and return it to Vulcan?"

Scotty's heart was suddenly pounding as violently as

when he'd discovered a way out of their recent prison, but Kirk only nodded a wary affirmation.

Sarek went on. "Did you, at great risk to your own life and those of your crew, including Captain Scott here, do as that Sarek requested?"

Kirk nodded again. "Of course. Spock was—*is* one of my closest friends."

"He was returned to life, then?"

"As you seem to know. Once we reached Vulcan with his body, you—that other Sarek—requested *fal tor pan*, a re-fusion of his regenerated body with his soul, his *katra*. Spock had given it over to another human friend shortly before his death." Kirk paused, eying Sarek more closely. "Do you know—remember?—what that other Sarek said when the logic of his request for *fal tor pan* was questioned by his fellow Vulcans?"

Sarek was silent for several seconds, his eyes narrowing almost imperceptibly.

" 'My logic falters where my son is concerned,' " he quoted, then watched as Kirk nodded. "It would appear," he continued softly, "that logic falters as well when applied to the present situation." Another extended moment of silence and then: "Is the one known as McCoy still well? Spock's *katra* caused him no permanent ill effects?"

"He fully recovered."

"That is good." Yet another extended pause, as if the Vulcan knew where he logically had to go and yet still did not wish to go there.

"The *fal tor pan* was performed on Vulcan, as it had to be," Sarek continued. "Then you returned to Terra—to Earth. Spock chose to return with you."

Kirk nodded again. "You said you would tell us how you knew—"

"And I will. But there is one more question to answer."

"What more do you want to have confirmed? You seem to know as much about those events as we do."

"Instead of returning directly to Earth," Sarek continued remorselessly, "you used your ship—a Klingon ship—to travel back in time approximately three hundred years. Is that also true?"

"We didn't have a choice," Kirk said. "Earth was being destroyed by an unstoppable alien vessel, more powerful even than the Borg. Apparently it was destroying the planet because we humans had caused whales to go extinct centuries before. Going back in time to retrieve a pair of whales was the only chance we had. If we hadn't—"

"The reason is irrelevant," Sarek interrupted. "The fact is, you *did* travel back in time."

Kirk nodded. "We did."

"Is that what you have also done now? Have you traveled through time again? Have you come from the future rather than the contemporary alternate reality you claim to be from?"

For a long moment there was total silence, Kirk's eyes locked with Sarek's as his mind undoubtedly raced to find a believable yet not quite true explanation that did not include the fact that they were here to erase this entire timeline.

Scotty, on the other hand, was suddenly almost limp with relief. The engineer had an instinctive distrust of politicians and diplomats and had always been uneasy whenever Kirk himself took on that role, even though this time, Scotty himself had initially encouraged him to do it.

"You always were too clever by half when you put on your diplomat's hat," he muttered to Kirk under his breath, then added aloud, "I believe 'tis time for a wee bit of the truth, Captain, now that Sarek's figured it out for himself anyway."

Without waiting for a reply, Scotty raised his eyes to meet Sarek's.

"Captain Kirk's not the bloody time traveler this time," he said. "I am."

The chronometric radiation was back to what Picard had come to think of as the normal background level for this apparently unstable timeline by the time the two Guinans emerged from his ready room, unsmiling, even somber.

"I will return to the *D'Zidran*," one of them said. Picard assumed it was the one from this timeline, but even he couldn't be sure. As far as physical appearance went, they could have switched clothes, differing primarily in color, and no one would have been the wiser. "I will ask Tal to get word to Alliance Prime asking to have every ship in the fleet be on the lookout for Captain Scott."

"And it would be helpful, Captain," the other Guinan said, "if you or Commander La Forge could give Tal the technical information the Alliance will need in order to adapt their sensors to detect Captain Scott's ship, should he be using the cloaking device. Somehow, neither the Romulans nor the Klingons developed that form of cloaking here, only the interphase variety you already encountered."

Picard nodded, not really surprised at the turn things had taken once Guinan—his Guinan—had stopped hiding and decided to talk to her counterpart. "Have Tal contact us as soon as one of you has had a chance to . . . explain the situation to him." He turned toward the engineering station. "Commander La Forge, I assume you can have the necessary information ready to transmit."

"From what I've seen of their sensor capabilities, the conversion shouldn't be a problem, sir," he said, no indication of approval or disapproval in his purposely neutral tone. "I can have the data assembled in a few minutes."

Picard silently accompanied the two Guinans to the transporter room, where he watched the one who remained behind as *she* watched her almost-twin shimmer out of existence. In the turbolift on the way back to the bridge, he finally spoke.

"Did you learn what we need to know?"

"I learned what she knew. And she learned what I knew."

"I rather suspected that's how it would be, from what she said about the search for Captain Scott. But does she know the whole truth? That we're from the future, not an alternate universe?"

She shrugged, a slight movement of her hands, as the turbolift doors opened on the bridge. "If you can't trust yourself, who *can* you trust?"

"And how does *she* feel about 'correcting' the timeline?"

"It disturbs her as greatly as it does me, but she knows it has to be done. If it *can* be done. She's had the same feelings of 'wrongness' that I have, but she's had them for so long that she hardly notices them anymore."

"And the destruction of her—of *your* world?"

"It's not as if we have a choice, Captain. You of all people should know that she will do what we both know must be done."

Picard was silent a moment. They were before the viewscreen now, everyone's eyes on them both.

"Of course, Guinan. I'm sorry."

"It's all right, Captain," she said after a moment. "Despite all appearances, to you she *is* still a stranger."

He shook his head. "Not entirely. A number of us do seem to have met both of you four hundred years ago, when you were still one."

"Before the timelines diverged," Guinan said, smiling faintly. "As best we could determine, the split was sometime in Earth's twenty-first century."

"Was that when she first detected the 'wrongness'?"

"That was one indicator, yes, but she can't remember precisely when it started. She—we were involved in other things, nowhere near Earth, for several decades. The last time we visited Earth was early in the twenty-first century. It was another fifty years before she attempted to return, and by then it had been assimilated. We assumed it happened before your ancestors developed warp drive, because no one outside your solar system officially knew you existed and certainly not that the Borg had arrived."

Picard nodded. "And they *would* have known if the Borg had come *after* we developed warp drive. The Vulcans made contact with Earth within hours of Cochrane's first test flight. But why would the Borg bypass every other world between Earth and the Delta Quadrant in order to take over Earth? And then begin spreading out—very slowly—from there?"

"I have no idea, Captain, but that appears to be precisely what happened. El-Auria was one of the worlds they bypassed, together with hundreds, perhaps thousands of others."

Each of which, Picard thought but refrained from saying, *will either be destroyed or turned back into Borg Collectives if we manage to "correct" this timeline out of existence.*

EIGHTEEN

MUCH OF Scotty's explanation to a stone-faced Sarek was taken up with an attempt to convince Sarek—and perhaps himself—that Picard and the crew of that future version of the *Enterprise* were the ones responsible for the premature arrival of the Borg, not Kirk and himself. When he finished and fell silent, the Vulcan continued to watch him expressionlessly, saying nothing, until the engineer began to squirm uncomfortably, wondering if he'd made a massive mistake admitting the truth this way. Maybe Kirk *could* have found a way around it. Maybe the captain was right in keeping the truth to himself—the truth that they were here to find a way to, essentially, eliminate this Sarek's entire universe. Could even someone as logical and as principled as Sarek accept that kind of truth and not see them as enemies? Enemies who, despite having saved his life and his ship, had to be kept from carrying out their purpose, even if it meant jailing or killing them?

Scotty shook his head dismally. He was used to working with engines, not people. With engines you knew where you stood. If you did something wrong, they let you know in no uncertain terms: They stopped working. Or blew up.

People, on the other hand, even the logic-driven Vulcans—

"If you'd like to confirm what I told you," he said abruptly, screwing his courage up another notch, "I'd not object if you wanted to look inside my head."

One of Sarek's eyebrows arched in a subdued version of an expression he'd seen on Spock's face a hundred times. "A meld would not be advisable," the Vulcan said. "When other species are involved, the procedure is difficult at best, debilitating at worst. And if you are lying, I would be playing directly into your hands."

"I beg your pardon?" Kirk looked at Sarek quizzically.

"If you are agents of the Borg, there would be no better way for you to learn every Alliance secret than by taking it directly from my mind."

"I see. Would you feel any safer melding with *me?*"

"Because you once melded with your Sarek?"

"You know about that, too? That was my thought, yes."

"Since I am not 'your Sarek,' it is irrelevant."

Kirk sighed, seemingly unworried. "That reminds me. You did promise to tell us how you know these things. We've kept our part of the bargain and answered everything you've asked."

Sarek nodded a brief acknowledgment, looking more toward Scotty than Kirk. "Of course."

Quickly, the Vulcan told them of his false memories and his brief suspicion that they were a result of some kind of cross-time link between himself and the Sarek in their universe. "However," he concluded, "since it now appears that this universe replaced that universe rather than co-existed with it, it would seem that my twin and I did not co-exist either and therefore could never have been linked in any way."

"That's an easy one," Kirk said with a slight grin. "You just have to think of it in a slightly different but equally logical way. I obviously don't know all the rules about time travel paradoxes, but our universe probably wasn't *replaced* by yours when the *Enterprise* did whatever it did. More likely it was *transformed into* yours. Which means that you *are* 'our Sarek.' It's just that you—and all your memories—were transformed, right along with however much of the rest of the universe was affected. But, for whatever reason, not all of the memories of that other life were completely eliminated. Some of the strongest of them must still be there, hidden behind the new ones. You're getting glimpses of your original memories, that's all. Ghost memories, so to speak."

"Very facile, Kirk," Sarek acknowledged, then paused as his eyes narrowed infinitesimally. "However, I must admit there is an appealing logic to your theory. And a certain comfort in the implication that if you were to be successful in your quest to repair the damage you say the *Enterprise* caused, our universe would be restored to its original form rather than destroyed."

"I hoped you'd see it that way."

"However," Sarek continued, "I find your argument for blaming the *Enterprise* for the change less than convincing. The fact that, seen from your perspective, your rescue from the Vortex immediately preceded the change is *prima facie* evidence that the one was the cause of the other."

Kirk grimaced. "Don't think I haven't thought of that. And if I were certain it was true, I'd let the Vortex take me in a second. But how could saving my life *now* have brought the Borg here over two hundred years ago?"

Sarek eyed Kirk expressionlessly. "I would think it would be obvious. You have already admitted to traveling back in time once, and my so-called 'ghost memories' contain a number of other similar occasions."

Kirk grimaced. "Therefore I may do so again, now that I've been saved? Is that what you're suggesting?"

"It is only logical. Perhaps *you* will be the one to bring the Borg to this quadrant two hundred years prematurely."

"Impossible!" Kirk snapped, although the knot that suddenly tightened around his stomach belied his show of certainty. "I would never do anything so insane."

"But your successor, this Picard would?" Sarek asked.

"I would not dismiss either possibility too lightly, Captain," Scotty said uneasily. "You never know what you might be capable of under the right circumstances. Remember Edith Keeler."

The knot grew achingly tight. As if he could ever forget! Even after all these years, the memory of that terrible moment on the bleak and grimy streets of Depression-era New York had the power to take his breath away. He had watched her die—*caused* her to die only meters in front of him because he had seen the horrors that would come if he allowed McCoy to save her. The Guardian had shown him: For decades, perhaps centuries, Earth would be ruled by Hitler and his bloodthirsty Nazi disciples. There would be no *Enterprise,* no Starfleet, no Federation.

"All that you knew is gone," the Guardian had said moments after McCoy, sick and delusional, plunged into the past.

And then . . .

Then the Guardian had allowed—even encouraged— Kirk to follow McCoy and set things right, to cause time to "resume its shape."

And the ancient entity had, from its first words, seemed almost eager. For billions of years, it told Kirk and Spock when they first arrived, it had "awaited a question."

And when they returned from the past: *"Many such journeys are possible,"* it said. *"Let me be your gateway."*

That seeming eagerness, more than anything else, almost kept Kirk from reporting the Guardian's existence to Starfleet.

Almost.

The danger it posed was incalculable, as McCoy's adventure had proven, and he was just one man, a man with the best of intentions. If someone—or thousands of some-ones—with evil intentions found the world and were given similarly unrestricted access to the past, nothing and no one would be safe. They could snuff out civilizations in the blink of an eye and, by sealing off the Guardian's world from the rest of the galaxy, make certain that whatever they changed in the past was not undone.

In the end, he had reported its existence and its threat to Starfleet. If it was going to be found and controlled, inevitably, by someone, better it was Starfleet than the Klingons.

The Guardian's existence was clsssified immediately, at the highest levels.

But that was in a different universe. "Sarek, has your Alliance discovered the Guardian's world?" he asked, focussing on Sarek's face, his eyes, for even the slightest hint of recognition.

Not surprisingly, there was none. "I know of no world so designated, but perhaps we know it under another name. What are its coordinates?"

Kirk shook his head. "I don't *have* the coordinates. I doubt if anyone outside the very top level of Starfleet would. If Starfleet existed in this timeline." He turned to Scotty. "I'm assuming its existence wasn't declassified in the time you came from?"

Scotty shook his head. "I cannot imagine it was," the engineer said, taking the remote from his utility belt. "But it's easy enough to find out. Computer, give me the coordinates of the Guardian's world."

The expected reply from the *Goddard*'s computer came instantly. *"No data available."*

Kirk took the remote. "Computer, summarize all existing data on the artifact known in the seventh decade of the twenty-third century as the Guardian of Forever."

"No data available," the computer repeated.

Sarek, who had been observing, silent and motionless except for his eyes, asked: "What is this 'Guardian' of which you speak?"

Kirk swallowed away the returning knot in his throat and gathered his thoughts for a moment. Then, in terms as accurate and impersonal as he could manage, he explained what little he knew about the Guardian and its world.

"I see," the Vulcan said when Kirk finished. "You believe that if you can find this artifact, it will show you what caused this timeline to come into existence? And then send you back in time to prevent it from happening?"

"I believe there's at least a chance. *If* we can find the Guardian. *If* it's in the mood to answer questions and give us a hand. *If* a hundred other things. But for any of this to happen, you'd have to be willing to help us find it. Are you?"

Sarek studied the two a moment, then nodded almost imperceptibly. "If you are telling the truth and if my own 'false memories' of a Borg-free Alliance—your 'Federation'—are indeed fragmentary memories of that other universe, then it is only logical that I help you. All Alliance worlds will benefit if we are successful. On the other hand, if you are lying . . ."

The Vulcan fell silent for a moment, his face revealing nothing. Again he offered a minuscule nod. "If we find that the so-called Guardian does exist in this timeline and can be located, I will go there myself and attempt to communicate with it. If all is as you say, you will be allowed to pose your own questions. Is that agreeable?"

Kirk breathed a sigh of relief. "Perfectly. Now, how complete and how extensive are your computer's charts of space in and around Alliance territory?"

"All stellar systems within a hundred light-years of Alliance Prime—"

Sarek broke off abruptly as the viewscreen in the far wall flared into life. The Narisian communication officer's cat-like face appeared briefly before being replaced by that of Commander Varkan.

"What is it, Commander?"

"A fleet-wide alert has just been issued by Alliance Prime. All Alliance vessels are requested to report any sightings of the being I believe to be one of the two you insisted we bring on board the Wisdom."

Sarek glanced at the two humans. "Who initiated this request, Commander? Who knows of their existence?"

"The initial request to Alliance Prime was from Commander Tal of the D'Zidran. *Tal had a peculiar story about tracking down an unknown vessel that had triggered one of the Klingon mines in the Arhennius system. He said—"*

"A vessel called *Enterprise*?" Sarek asked sharply.

The Romulan's eyes widened in surprise. *"How did you know that?"*

"Patch me through to Commander Tal," the Vulcan ordered, ignoring the commander's question. "Immediately."

"As you wish, Arbiter," Varkan said, obviously as displeased at this turn of events.

For a moment, the Narisian's face reappeared as the Romulan relayed Sarek's order. Sarek's screen momentarily lapsed into visual static as his personal comm unit was linked directly into the Alliance subspace network. As Sarek waited for Tal to appear, he said over his shoulder:

"Apparently your *Enterprise* did not make a second jump after all, gentlemen."

After several minutes of discussion, Picard and the bridge crew—including Guinan this time—were no closer than before to having a workable plan. *Something* that Captain Scott had done at some indeterminate time in the past had brought the Borg to Earth centuries ahead of schedule. Only the Borg knew what and when that something was. And no one, not even Guinan, had yet come up with a possible, let alone practical, way of obtaining that knowledge. Picard, despite the revulsion the idea inspired, had suggested somehow exploiting the nightmarish link that still existed between himself and the Borg, but he had no idea how to proceed. It was not as if he could tap into the collective at will. And even if he could make a connection, he would more likely be taken over long before he had a chance to systematically search through the Borg memories—even if he knew how to make such a search.

But then they were hailed by the *D'Zidran.*

"On screen, Mr. Worf," Picard snapped.

Commander Tal, the other Guinan in her customary position a meter behind his left shoulder, appeared on the viewscreen a moment later. The rest of the *D'Zidran*'s bridge crew, however, were conspicuous by their absence, giving the bridge the deserted look of a derelict. Tal's lips parted to speak but he froze in silence for a moment as his narrowing eyes fell on the *Enterprise*'s Guinan, who this time had not scuttled out of range of the viewscreen.

Tal glanced over his shoulder at his Guinan, then looked back to the screen. *"I see that she was not exaggerating."* He was silent another moment before continuing, once again leaning forward, as if the motion could provide even more confidentiality than the empty bridge. *"Tell me, Captain Picard, just as a matter of idle curiosity, do I have a duplicate in your universe?"*

"There is a Tal," Picard said cautiously, "who has had quite an interesting career. Whether he is your duplicate, however—"

"Never mind," Tal said abruptly, waving a hand in dismissal. *"It is not important."*

"As you wish, Commander," Picard said. "I assume you would like us to transmit the information required to adapt your sensors to detect a cloaked ship."

Tal smiled. *"I would, I imagine, if you would also be willing to give me the design for the cloaking device itself. From what Guinan tells me, it is considerably safer and certainly less spectacular than our own methods. But no, that is not why I contacted you. It is to let you know that the Alliance has already located your Captain Scott. And that the . . . individual who found him would like to speak with you."*

NINETEEN

SHE WAITED.

Somewhere in what remained of the solar system that had once been home to Species 5618, the Borg Queen, the One Who Was All, waited.

And listened.

All around her, their rudimentary thoughts an incessant, mind-numbing murmur she never dared entirely block out, billions of drones on the remnants of nine worlds, scores of moons, and thousands of asteroids carried out their unending synchronized tasks, slowly but inexorably bringing into being the greatest single Borg armada of all time.

Like all the others of her kind left behind in the Delta Quadrant, she had no name that she could remember or wanted to remember. She had once had a name, of course. Or, more accurately, the organic shell that had once housed the intricately interconnected collection of nerve cells that had been her pathetically isolated pre-assimilation brain had once had a name. For centuries, however, there had been no reason to recall that name, or even to acknowledge that it had ever existed.

Unlike other Queens, however, this one had discovered during the early centuries of her existence that, with or without a name, she had ambitions. Those ambitions of course did not conflict with the overriding ambition of all Queens to bring the Borg Collective ever closer to perfection. That would be unthinkable. Her ambitions were supplementary to that overriding, collective-wide ambition. She in fact saw them as being solely in the interests of achieving that perfection more quickly, with less risk to the collective. That she withheld knowledge of certain of her plans from those parts of the collective outside her own matrix did not strike her as traitorous, nor did the mere fact that she was *able* to confine that knowledge to her own matrix strike her as strange. The time to share her plans would be when they had reached fruition, when the unprecedented size and success of her matrix would alone prove the rightness and efficiency of her methods.

Such secrecy had, after all, been virtually forced upon her. It had been the only way she could put her ideas to the test, the only way she would ever be able to use those ideas in order to better serve the collective's drive toward perfection. When those ideas had first begun to come to her, centuries before she had discovered the trick of keeping occasional thoughts within the confines of her matrix, the stultifying disapproval that spread glacially throughout the collective made it obvious that no idea of hers would ever be considered, let alone implemented. With thousands of races already successfully assimilated, with more being assimilated all the time, it was utterly obvious to the collective that no fundamental changes were needed.

But she knew better. She had known better for more than three hundred years, ever since the failure with Species 874, which had, despite all her matrix's efforts, chosen death over assimilation. From that supremely disappointing moment on, she had known: The old ways were *not* the best ways if they resulted in the loss of even one species. Changes *were* needed.

One particular way, she soon came to believe, was very far from being the best way. In the name of short-term efficiency, all drones were programmed to do specific tasks, sometimes many specific tasks. Included in that programming were parameters defining all objects and beings the drones needed to interact with in order to successfully carry out those tasks. In order to carry out those tasks in the most efficient manner possible, they needed to be shielded from distractions. Therefore, they were programmed not only to do their assigned tasks but to ignore all distractions, "distractions" being defined as anything falling outside the parameters of the objects and beings they were programmed to interact with.

In short, if a drone didn't need a particular object for the immediate task at hand, it literally would not notice that object's presence. The images of the excluded objects would form in the inputs to a drone's optical system but would go no further, never reaching the brain of the drone, let alone that of the Queen and the hive mind that was the collective.

As a result, alien ships that fell outside those parameters could move freely within the very shadow of a Borg ship, unnoticed unless they attacked and forcibly drew attention to themselves. Alien beings could move about *inside* Borg ships, literally brushing shoulders with millions of drones, and not be truly seen.

To remove that programming and allow drones to notice and interact with whomever and whatever they came in contact with would of course be disastrous. It had been attempted once in the early days of the collective, and the entire matrix that had been used as a test site had slowly and literally ground to a halt as more and more of the drones, long ago robbed of their ability to think independently, first fell behind in their assigned tasks and then became essentially catatonic as they found themselves unable to cope with the insoluble puzzles created by having to deal with so many objects and beings unrelated to their tasks.

At the same time, the collective dared not fully restore the drones' ability to think independently, even if it were still possible. That would give each and every drone the capability of refusing to follow their programming, if only briefly. It would be like giving each individual cell in a muscle the option of whether or not to obey the signal from the brain telling that muscle to contract. It could only result in utter chaos, each and every cell in the muscle going its own way, sending the muscle into paralyzing spasms.

The idea she had shared with the collective centuries ago addressed that problem, perhaps not entirely solving it but at least alleviating it. The Collective, however, had ignored her and her idea almost as completely as drones ignored objects they were not programmed to notice.

But then she had stumbled upon the mental trick that allowed her to limit her thoughts to within her own matrix, keeping them secret from the rest of the collective, from the other queens and their matrices. At that point she realized she could test her idea—but not in the Delta Quadrant, where her matrix operated cheek by jowl with countless other matrices. In such close quarters there was far too much danger of discovery, and discovery would mean, at the very least, the end of the test, perhaps the loss of her matrix. Conceivably she could suffer the ultimate punishment: being purged from the collective's near-infinite memory banks, guaranteeing that even her thoughts and memories would be erased. It would be as if she had never existed.

But elsewhere, beyond the Delta Quadrant . . .

In a small ship with only a few dozen drones from her matrix, she had used abandoned transwarp conduits to make repeated trips over the next two centuries to both the Alpha and Beta Quadrants, selecting several pre-space worlds and transforming them gradually into worlds that would, all unknowing, act as eyes for the Borg—or at least for her own matrix when and if it arrived in their part of the galaxy.

But then, as if delivered up by some trickster god, had come Species 1429 and a technology that seemed to render all those carefully prepared worlds superfluous. Suddenly all the work she had invested in those worlds was transformed into a total waste of her resources.

Or so she had thought at the time, and so she had thought when she prematurely abandoned them and left them to their own primitive devices.

A hundred years later, she had learned how wrong she was. The first time she had attempted to use the technology of Species 1429 for anything other than test runs, something had gone wrong. She had no idea *what* had gone wrong, or why. All she knew was that the technological legacy of Species 1429 was not the panacea she had envisioned and that, except in the direst of emergencies, she dared not make use of it again.

The mishap had, however, presented her with a new and perhaps even greater opportunity than the one she had lost. And to make sure *this* one wasn't lost, she had cautiously reestablished contact with the worlds she had abandoned. They became once again her first line of defense against the unpredictability of this peculiar corner of the galaxy.

One had already proven its worth, bringing information that would, when the time came, save billions of drones, perhaps the entire Borg armada, perhaps even herself.

And so she continued to wait.

And to listen . . .

Picard was barely able to maintain his neutral expression as the grainy, *D'Zidran*-relayed image on the *Enterprise* viewscreen steadied and he recognized the face staring solemnly out at him. Out of the corner of his eye, he noticed that Guinan was volunteering no help, only watching with a deceptively disinterested look. He assumed that the other Guinan was presenting a similarly inscrutable exterior to Tal as the two of them watched and listened on the otherwise deserted bridge of the *D'Zidran*.

"Do you know me as well, Picard?" Sarek asked without preamble. The Vulcan's features looked considerably younger than when Picard had last seen them not long before Sarek's death seventy-odd years in this world's future, but there was also a haggard look he had never seen on that other Sarek's face, not even when he knew he was dying.

"I do, Ambassador Sarek," Picard said, inclining his head minimally in a gesture of respect.

" 'Ambassador . . .' *Yes, that is what I understand Sarek is in your universe. Here I am Supreme Arbiter of the Alliance."*

"I was told you had found Captain Scott."

"Indeed. He is with me now. Is he the only Terran you are searching for?"

Picard hesitated before answering cautiously. "He is the only one whose presence in this universe I am aware of."

"There is no need to continue the pretense that you are from an alternate universe, Picard. Captain Scott has admitted what I will assume for the moment to be the truth: that you and he are both from the future, though not one which I would recognize."

"I see," Picard said, though he obviously didn't. "May I speak with Captain Scott?"

"In a moment, Picard. First, tell me how you came to be here."

"But you said you knew that we—"

"That you come from the future, yes. That tells me little. Please explain how and why."

"So you can compare my story to Captain Scott's?"

"Would you not do the same?"

Picard nodded. He would indeed, though perhaps not as openly. As quickly as he could, he explained. When he finished, Sarek gave a barely discernible nod.

"Let me be certain I understand, Picard. You followed Captain Scott into his so-called slingshot maneuver and arrived here, in this timeline, approximately three days ago."

"Precisely," Picard said. "We knew something was drastically wrong the moment we saw Borg ships in the area."

"From your vantage point, then," Sarek continued, *"there has been no major change in this timeline since you arrived. Is that correct?"*

"It is. What—"

"And you yourself made no more such maneuvers? You traveled to no other times since your arrival?"

"We did not," Picard said. "We assumed Captain Scott himself had made a second maneuver, further into the past. Or that he had overshot, perhaps hundreds of years. We could see no other explanation for the presence of the Borg."

"Captain Scott assumed the same about you."

Picard frowned. "If both of us came directly here and *stayed* here, then how did this timeline come to be?"

Sarek stepped back, motioning to someone out of range of the screen. *"I have my own opinion,"* he said, *"but I will allow you to discuss the matter with Captain Scott."*

A moment later Scott stepped into range of the screen, followed by a second man, this one wearing a smudged and slightly torn Starfleet dress uniform from the late twenty-third century. Picard didn't immediately recognize the man's grim features despite a look of nagging familiarity. The man's eyes widened as he looked past Picard to take in the rest of the bridge.

"And here I thought the Enterprise-A *was too spacious for its own good,"* the man said, a faint smile briefly softening his features as he returned his eyes to Picard. *"I'm James T. Kirk, captain—*one *of the captains—of the original* Enterprise."

Suddenly, Picard's mind was spinning.

He had been right: Scott *had* slingshotted into the past with the intention of saving his commander and friend.

But he had also been wrong: Scott had *not* failed, had *not* overshot hundreds of years and brought the Borg to Earth. He had apparently done precisely what he had intended to do.

And yet the Borg were here.

And the Federation was not.

"This *was* your purpose, then, Captain Scott," Picard said, "to save your one-time captain from the energy ribbon."

"Aye, it was," Scotty acknowledged, momentarily lowering his eyes. *"I know now how daft it was, but once I had the* Bounty 2 *in my hands, once I knew there was even a*

wee chance of saving him, it would have been defying fate not *to try. Or so I told myself."*

And *tempting* fate *to* try, Picard thought but did not say. Recriminations would be pointless at best, even though he could not keep himself from wondering once again if Kirk himself, one of Starfleet's legendary mavericks—or loose cannons, depending on whom you talked to—was appalled or gratified at what he had inspired Scott to do.

"I know the feeling, Scotty, believe me," Kirk put in, apparently sensing Picard's disapproval. *"As the old saying goes, 'It seemed like a good idea at the time.' "*

He turned his eyes to Picard again, all remnants of the smile gone. *"Don't worry, Picard. You won't have to throw me back into the Vortex, or whatever they call it in your era. I'll dive back in myself—if it can be determined for certain that Scotty's saving me is what caused all this."*

"And who is to be the judge of that certainty?" Picard asked, trying to keep the skepticism out of his voice. He couldn't imagine Kirk willingly surrendering his life as long as even the most minuscule chance of a non-fatal solution existed. The man had virtually made a career out of beating the odds.

"I'll accept whatever you and Scotty decide," Kirk said, his tone now subdued. *"And Sarek, of course,"* he added with a glance offscreen toward the Vulcan. *"But before anyone decides anything, it would be nice to have a few facts, not just hunches and speculations, no matter how logical."*

"Agreed," Picard said, "but whatever brought this timeline into existence could have happened anytime since the Borg came into existence and anywhere in the galaxy. How do we determine where or when to even start looking for facts?"

"We visit the Guardian," Kirk said. *"If we can find it."*

"Guardian?"

"The Guardian of Forever," Kirk said. *"Scotty and I were hoping you might be one of the people entrusted with its world's coordinates."*

Picard frowned. "What is it?"

Resignedly, Kirk gave him the same sketchy explanation he had given Sarek minutes before, but Picard could only shake his head.

"When I was at the Academy there were rumors of dozens of miraculous lost worlds and races, but I remember nothing of the sort you describe. If it does exist, though, I can certainly see why it would be kept a secret."

"It existed in my day, believe me," Kirk said grimly. *"I only hope it exists in this timeline as well."* He turned to Sarek. *"Are you ready to start looking?"*

Within minutes, using Kirk's and Scotty's memories of that long-ago mission, Sarek zeroed in on a remarkably anonymous star in the *Wisdom*'s data banks. It was less than a parsec from the route the original *Enterprise* had been following when it had been diverted to investigate the "ripples in time," distortions that would most likely register on the new Enterprise's more advanced sensors as chronometric radiation. In this timeline, it was the only star in that sector that had never been surveyed at close range. It wasn't even known if any planets orbited the star.

They arranged to rendezvous, the *Enterprise* and the *Wisdom*. Picard and Guinan would beam over to the *Wisdom*, in the hope that they could convince a reluctant Sarek to transfer both himself and his two "guests" to the faster *Enterprise* for the journey to the coordinates he had found.

As the *Enterprise* to *D'Zidran* to *Wisdom* connection

was finally broken, the images of Tal and that other Guinan flickered across the screen, vanishing almost before they were fully formed, but not before the eyes of the two Guinans met for one brief, intense moment.

A chill swept over Guinan in the split second that her eyes met those of her counterpart on the distant *Enterprise*. Suddenly, she realized what she must do.

As she had admitted to Picard, similar wordless "intuitions" had gripped her countless times before, but never had one come over her as suddenly or gripped her as powerfully as this one, not even in those long-ago centuries when the two had been one.

And never—*never* had the reason for the action she must take been so immediately obvious. Sometimes it took years or decades before the reasons came clear. Sometimes they remained obscure forever.

But this time, the reason was *so* obvious that, even before the exchanged glance, as she had listened to Picard and Sarek talk, listened as they determined the coordinates of the so-called Guardian's world, she had been on the verge of breaking in and suggesting the very thing that the feeling now demanded.

Putting her hand lightly on Tal's shoulder, something she had done perhaps only twice in their years together, she said: "If you have ever trusted me, my friend, trust me now."

Balitor could not believe her good fortune as her shift finally ended and she made her way toward her quarters, barely able to keep from breaking into a run. For hours that had seemed like years, she had waited, resenting every second she was forced to delay her attempt to Link with the Wise Ones.

But then had come the message from Alliance Prime and the contact with the second alien vessel, and she realized the delay had been a gift, not a hardship. This new information was even more important, more vital than what she already had. She *knew* it was. There was no longer even the tiniest sliver of doubt in her mind. Her Link *would* be accepted!

Her only regret was that her mother would never know. The knowledge could not have made up for the disappointment her mother's life had become, but it could at least have reassured her that, through her daughter, her life would be given meaning. It had not been lived entirely in vain.

Balitor was trembling, every square centimeter of her body tingling with anticipation by the time she palmed open the personal security lock on her door and let it click shut behind her. Leaving the lights off so as to have nothing to distract her, nothing to dilute the coming experience, she removed her uniform and lay down on her sleeping pad, her fur-covered body free now of all restrictions, all distractions.

Instead of curling up, knees to chin, as she normally did to sleep, she lay on her back, bringing her left hand up to gently stroke her left temple as she concentrated on the series of thoughts and words that would, she had been taught so long ago, initiate the Link.

At first she could feel nothing happening, and she began to fear that her very eagerness was interfering with the process. The Wise Ones, the Proctors had told her again and again during her training, did not possess emotions nor did they value them in others. Even so, it had been the Narisians in whom the Wise Ones had chosen to place their trust, not the seemingly emotionless Vulcans. The Narisians, not the Vulcans, were the Chosen—despite their frailties, not because of them, the Proctors said.

Finally, faint lights began to come into being, swirling in the darkness around her, and she could feel a growing warmth in her temple.

Suddenly, the lights blossomed into a glow that enveloped her like a cocoon and then faded into darkness. An instant later, despite the warmth that still bathed her temple, an icy chill enveloped the rest of her, as if the very air around her had congealed, freezing her in place. As the darkness returned, she sensed the presence of the Wise Ones all around her, as if their minds hovered in the very air of the darkened room in which her now-chilled body lay. She could feel them brushing against her mind, bringing the outer, physical chill inside, as if to freeze her very thoughts.

And a voice, not in her ears but in her mind, said: *"Welcome, Balitor. Share with us the knowledge that you bring for our enlightenment."*

Shivering both with cold and with pleasure, Balitor opened her thoughts to the Wise Ones.

Captain Jean-Luc Picard tossed restlessly on his ready room couch, drifting in and out of that unsettling twilight between sleep and wakefulness where dream cannot be distinguished from reality. He had hoped to get a little much-needed rest while the *Enterprise* raced to rendezvous with the *Wisdom*, but his mind had refused to halt the constant stream of wildly varying images of what he imagined the Guardian's world to be like.

But those increasingly hallucinatory images were not now the primary source of his uneasiness.

It was the voices that had begun whispering in his mind,

bringing with them wordless feelings of disorientation and dread. In fleeting moments of clarity, he wished he could fully awaken and find the whispers gone, a forgotten dream, but he could not.

The whispers, he knew in those moments of clarity, were not a dream, not an hallucination.

The Borg were once again whispering in his mind.

It had been thus ever since Locutus's brief existence.

Every physical trace of the Borg additions and modifications had been painstakingly removed from his body and brain, but whatever allowed him—*forced* him—to now and then Link with the Borg, to eavesdrop on some segment of the collective, was apparently not a physical object that could be located and excised. Like so many other modifications, it had most likely been created by a small cadre of the countless nanotech devices the Borg had introduced into his body, but once the work of this particular group had been completed, it was apparently self-sustaining and undetectable, at least by Federation medical science. He suspected it was nothing more than a series of neural patterns, no different from the other patterns that made up his subconscious mind.

No different, that is, except for its origin—and its purpose.

But this time, he realized as the whispers built to a crescendo, something was different. Very different.

The whispers were not emotionless, wordless directions being issued to a swarm of drones to repair or modify or defend some part of the ship of which they themselves were a part.

This time the whispers were laden with emotion. They also conveyed a straightforward series of messages, messages that jolted him fully awake the moment their meaning penetrated his drifting consciousness.

His eyes snapping open, Picard lurched upright as if jerked by a giant puppeteer, almost tumbling to the floor before he could regain full control of his body and get to his feet. Heart pounding, he crossed the ready room to the door, already hissing open at his approach. With difficulty, he held his pace to a smooth but rapid stride as he made his way down the ramp and onto the bridge.

"Ensign Raeger," he said, coming to a stop directly behind the conn officer, "how long until rendezvous with the *Wisdom?*"

"Approximately seventy-seven minutes, sir."

"Shorten that if you can. Mr. Worf, are there any Borg ships nearby?"

"Other than the two accompanying the Vortex, none within standard sensor range, sir."

"Initiate a maximum range scan, Mr. Worf. Start with the immediate vicinity of the *Wisdom.*"

Tensely, Picard waited, watching the viewscreen as the warp factor inched higher and Worf initiated the scan. To his relief and puzzlement, the scan revealed nothing remotely Borg-like in the vicinity of the *Wisdom.* There might still be time to warn Sarek.

But to deliver that warning without also alerting the Borg would not be easy.

TWENTY

ORDINARILY the Borg Queen would have paid scant attention to the Link that had just been initiated. She preferred to review the information such a Link would provide only after it had been filtered and stored and the Link itself terminated. Entering directly into a Link was often both unpleasant and counterproductive. It would expose her directly to the emotions that totally organic creatures were subject to, and the very presence of those emotions could easily obscure vital aspects of the message the creatures were trying to transmit through the Link.

But this, she saw immediately, was a member of Species 642. Another member of that Species had once provided her with what promised to be truly invaluable information, so she decided to enter directly into the Link.

At first, the information itself was, if looked at logically, unremarkable. A small ship with two sentient beings aboard had supposedly "appeared out of nowhere." Not a startling occurrence, given the variety of star drives that were in use throughout the galaxy, and the ship itself obviously presented no threat. Later, this pair claimed to have come from an "alternate universe," though the creature Linking the information did not seem to have a clear concept of what the term even meant.

Sometime later, a second, much larger alien ship of unknown design and origin had made itself known, its commander professing an interest in one of the beings aboard the earlier ship.

Until that point, she had been less involved with the information itself than with her efforts to isolate herself from the emotions in which the creature constantly shrouded itself. But then an image virtually erupted from the creature's mind, an image far more vivid than anything that had come before: an image of the larger ship's commander as the creature had seen it briefly on a viewscreen.

She recognized the alien commander instantly, even though she had not seen him for nearly three subjective centuries.

His name, when she had captured him, had been Picard.

She had hoped he would willingly act as bridge between the Borg and his troublesome species, 5618, but he had stubbornly and irrationally resisted despite all the rewards she had offered, not the least of which had been power and authority almost equal to her own.

And so, in order to gain access to his knowledge and memories, she had been left with no choice but to transform him into the drone Locutus.

But then, during her failed first attempt to assimilate Earth, the Federation had somehow stolen him from her and then used what he had learned of the Borg to defeat her, at least temporarily.

She was never able to determine precisely what had happened to Locutus after that. She had studied the fragmentary records snatched from Starfleet computers during her second—and successful—attempt to assimilate Earth, but she had been unable to find anything beyond the fact that he and his ship had gone missing and was presumed destroyed in the interim.

Then, in her abortive attempt to minimize the massive losses suffered in the assimilation of Earth, she had unexpectedly been given an opportunity to assimilate not just twenty-fourth-century Earth but more than three hundred years of its history.

She had of course taken immediate advantage of that opportunity despite the obvious potential pitfalls. In one simple operation, she was able to eliminate an increasingly troublesome thorn in the side of all Borg before it had even begun to sprout. And now, in this universe which had come about because of her actions, the planet on which Picard had been born—would someday have been born—no longer existed. It had not existed for centuries except as part of her matrix. He could not have been born on that Earth, could not have grown up to enter a Starfleet that had never existed, could not have found a way to travel back to a point decades before his now-nonexistent birth.

He simply could not exist.

Unless, somehow, that other universe in which Picard *had* been born still existed.

Somewhere.

But wherever or whenever he was from, he was almost certainly here to destroy her and the universe she had created. It had been his goal at their first meeting and throughout that long-ago series of encounters that had not yet come to pass in that other universe, and there was no reason to think that it was any different now.

She had no choice but to stop him, to destroy him before he destroyed her.

But in order to be certain that that destruction would be final and complete, she had to learn where and when he had come from.

And how he had gotten here.

Without knowing at least *that* much, she could not be certain that, when she destroyed him, he would not simply reappear yet again.

With great deliberation, she turned her attention once more to the Link.

The *Enterprise* had barely dropped out of warp when Scotty, waiting with Kirk and Sarek for Picard and Guinan to beam over from the *Enterprise,* felt the telltale tingle of a transporter beam locking onto him. He had no time to react, only time enough to wonder what the blazes Picard was up to, before the *Wisdom*'s spartan transporter room disappeared in the fleeting sparkle of the transporter energies.

A moment later the spacious transporter room of the new *Enterprise* materialized around him. Kirk and Sarek were on the pads on either side of him, Kirk looking as startled as Scotty felt. Traces of anger and surprise managed to crack through Sarek's normally impassive mask, his eyes narrowing as they fell on a grim-faced Picard standing next to the ensign operating the transporter controls.

"Shields up," Picard snapped to someone on the distant bridge.

"Picard," Sarek began, his tone stiff even for a Vulcan, "I demand an explanation for—"

"Arbiter Sarek," Picard interrupted, "please accept my apology for changing plans without warning you. I know I promised to transport onto the *Wisdom* for our first meeting, but I have obtained new information since that promise was made, information that makes it essential that I speak with you privately, away from the *Wisdom*'s crew."

"What could possibly justify—"

"I have reason to believe there is a Borg spy aboard the *Wisdom*," Picard interrupted again, overriding Sarek's protests.

"Captain," Riker's voice came over the intercom, *"the* Wisdom*'s commander—"*

"—wants to know what is going on, I'm sure," Picard finished for his first officer. "Tell him Arbiter Sarek will speak with him in a few minutes."

"What leads you to conclude that such a thing as a Borg 'spy' even exists, Picard, let alone exists on the *Wisdom?"* Sarek demanded, though he didn't resist as Picard shepherded them all into the nearest turbolift. "Is it part of the special knowledge you bring with you from the next century?"

Picard shook his head. "Not in the sense you mean, I'm sure, Arbiter. Suffice it to say that the *Enterprise* has the means to occasionally intercept certain Borg communications. One was intercepted little more than an hour ago, and—"

"Precisely how were you able to intercept these alleged messages, Picard?" Sarek interrupted. "Every transmission from the *Wisdom,* both in and out of subspace, is automatically monitored, and we have detected nothing."

"These weren't 'normal' subspace transmissions, Arbiter."

"And yet you are able to detect and intercept them. In what sense were they 'not normal'?"

"It is difficult to explain," Picard said with a mixture of uneasiness and impatience. He could hardly admit, at least not yet, that he had once *been* a Borg and still occasionally experienced ephemeral links with nearby segments of the collective.

"You wish me to assume, then, Picard, that in the future you claim to have come from, you have developed a technology that makes such detection possible?"

"You could assume that," Picard said uncomfortably, "although it is not a technology, per se."

Sarek studied the *Enterprise* captain for a moment, then seemed to come to a conclusion. "You have found a way to tap into the thoughts of the collective," he said, his voice as uninflected as if he were discussing a missing uniform button.

Picard cast a startled look at Sarek. "Only in a very limited way," he admitted. "I will gladly explain as much as I can, but later. At this point—"

"What was contained in this intercepted message?" Sarek interrupted. "And what leads you to believe that it originated on the *Wisdom?*"

"I can't be *certain* it originated on the *Wisdom,* but it did inform the Borg of the presence of two beings who had 'appeared out of nowhere' and who claimed to be from an alternate universe. It also told of the imminent arrival of another, larger ship from that same universe."

"What possible interest could that information have for the Borg?"

"I have no idea, Arbiter, but that doesn't matter. What *does* matter is that you and I were openly discussing the Guardian. It is therefore likely that this spy will learn—may already have learned—not only of the Guardian's existence but of its potential value."

"If the communication you intercepted said nothing of the Guardian, is it not logical to assume that the so-called spy was not aware of it?"

"Perhaps, but it is also possible that I did not intercept the entire message. Or that the spy was not yet aware of the Guardian's nature or its importance."

Before Sarek could reply, the turbolift doors hissed open on the bridge and Picard gestured them out.

Sarek and Kirk and Scotty came to a halt outside the turbolift doors, their eyes taking in the bridge and its crew. Kirk said nothing, just pursed his lips in a silent whistle. Sarek, not surprisingly, showed no reaction whatsoever, while Scotty, suddenly excruciatingly conscious of what his rash actions had caused, flushed and lowered his eyes, wishing he had his own personal cloaking device.

As the turbolift doors hissed shut, Riker stood up to relinquish the captain's chair, but Picard gestured for him to remain where he was.

"The commander of the *Wisdom* is getting impatient," Riker said, indicating the viewscreen and the angular, Romulan-like ship belligerently facing the *Enterprise*.

"I will speak with him," Sarek said, stepping forward.

"On screen," Riker acknowledged as Sarek made his way to stand before the screen, by which time Commander Varkan's image had appeared, replacing that of the *Wisdom*. Picard remained behind, near the turbolift with Kirk and Scott, silently guiding them toward his ready room.

"*Arbiter, are you—*" the Romulan commander began with a scowl, but Sarek cut him off.

"As you can see, Commander, I am unharmed. Open channels to Alliance Prime and to Outpost No. 2, then stand by for orders. I will contact you when I have completed my dealings with Captain Picard." He turned abruptly away from the screen. A moment later, at a gesture from Riker, the commander's image vanished, replaced once again by the *Wisdom*.

Rejoining Picard and following him into the ready room, Sarek asked without preamble, "What can you tell me of this so-called Borg spy?"

"Very little," Picard admitted as the door hissed shut behind the four of them. "The message itself was surprisingly clear but there was little to identify the one sending the message. He was, however, highly emotional and obviously not a Borg, at least not a Borg like any I have ever encountered. In fact, I suspect he didn't even realize he was communicating with the Borg."

"How is that possible? If this being was in direct mental contact with the Borg, how could he not know?"

"I don't know," Picard admitted. "All I know for certain is that he thought of the beings he was contacting as virtual gods and was almost overwhelmed with gratitude for being allowed to serve them. He addressed them only as 'Wise Ones.' "

Scotty suppressed a gasp as he heard the words. Suddenly, a collection of what had until then been unrelated facts stored haphazardly in odd corners of his mind seemed to magically rearrange themselves into a simple and blindingly obvious pattern, not unlike the way the inner workings of some complex new piece of engineering equipment would suddenly reveal themselves to him when he finally unearthed a key piece of data.

"The Narisian!" he blurted. "She's the bloody spy!"

Sarek turned toward him abruptly while Picard and Kirk only looked puzzled. "Explain," Sarek demanded.

"The communications officer, sir," Scotty said. "She *is* Narisian, isn't she?"

"She is, but what would lead you to think—"

"Did the Narisians develop space travel a wee bit faster than everyone else?"

"They did," Sarek admitted after a moment's reflection, "but why would that point to their being spies for the Borg or for anyone else?"

"They had help, that's why! The Narisians had help— from the Borg!" Scotty raced on to tell them of Garamet and Wahlkon, the Narisians he had encountered in the future of the original timeline, and how he had feared it might have been someone in the Federation that had violated the Prime Directive and given them their boost from gunpowder to warp drive.

"But it was the Borg," he finished. "In both timelines! It *has* to be! But in our timeline, the Borg abandoned the Narisians generations ago, don't ask me why. Here, they didn't. Or haven't yet."

"It's possible," Picard admitted with a frown. "Perhaps in our timeline, their invasion was delayed for some reason, so they abandoned their 'spies.' But here they established a major beachhead much earlier and kept their spies active."

"Or the other way around," Kirk said. "Their invasion was more successful here *because* they kept their spies active. Or they just made more and better use of them. As I understand it, the Borg *need* someone else's eyes and ears to let them know what's going on. That bunch isn't particularly observant when it comes to spotting anything new or unexpected."

Sarek nodded. "Once they do become aware of something that poses a threat, however, they quickly modify themselves and their ships to become virtually invulnerable to it."

Picard nodded his uneasy agreement. "It is the same in my experience. Members of my crew and I have been inside Borg ships more than once, unnoticed. If any so-called spies had alerted the Borg to our presence, we would almost certainly have been killed or assimilated long ago. The Borg certainly had the power to do whatever they wanted with us."

Sarek turned abruptly to Scotty. "Assuming Picard is correct and this spy does exist, can you identify it for certain? The communications officer is not the only Narisian on board. I am aware of at least one other, in engineering."

"A sensor scan *might* do it," Scotty said. "Garamet had a neural implant of some kind. Among other things, it kept her from revealing the truth to anyone outside the 'inner circle.' Proctors, she called them. Before the implant was damaged and her brother removed it, it literally made her sick to even *think* about giving away any secrets."

Or a scan might not *do it,* Picard thought, remembering back to his own experiences after escaping from the Borg. Scans had been able to pinpoint all the discrete nano-devices the Borg had implanted in his brain and body, allowing them to be removed. But whatever it was that still enabled him to "overhear" occasional Borg thoughts and messages had never been detected by any device other than his own mind.

"It is certainly worth a try," he said, standing up and leading the way to the bridge.

As he had feared, however, a remote scan revealed nothing. Both Narisians on board the *Wisdom* registered as being completely normal, with no implants of any kind, as did everyone else.

"So you play it safe and lock them both up," Scotty said as the last readout vanished from the *Enterprise* screens. "And stun them so they can't let the Borg know they've been found out."

"It may come to that, Mr. Scott," Picard said. "However,

the Borg will almost certainly link with them again, and there is no guarantee that they cannot extract information from unconscious minds as easily as they can from conscious. It might even be easier for them," he added, remembering the dream-like state he himself had been in during much of the link. "Nor is there any guarantee that the Narisians—if they are indeed Borg spies—are the only ones."

"What are you suggesting, then, Picard?" Sarek asked. "Surely you do not propose that we allow them to continue passing information to the Borg."

Picard shook his head. "Of course not. What I am suggesting is that we determine for certain who the spies are before we proceed to tip our hand."

"Have you not already tried and failed? Your sensors were unable to detect anything useful, or am I mistaken?"

"You are correct, Arbiter, but there is another method we could use," Picard said and went on to explain. When he had finished, Sarek was silent for several seconds.

"Very well, Picard. If you will transport me back to the *Wisdom,* I will make arrangements with Commander Varkan. When you can assure me the spies, if they indeed exist, have been nullified, we can then attempt to find this so-called Guardian."

With a brusque nod, Sarek strode to the turbolift. Behind him, Picard began issuing the necessary orders.

Commander Tal had not been happy with Guinan's request, but he had not been able to bring himself to deny it. She rarely requested anything, particularly something as specific as this, but whenever she did, interesting—and often beneficial—things happened. Most recently, it had been her suggestion that had caused him to alter his patrol pattern in such a way that the *D'Zidran* had been the ship closest to the Arhennius system when the detonation of one of the Klingon interphase mines had been detected. And it had been at her insistence that instead of simply following the unknown ship's warp trail, he try to contact them.

Above all, however, if it had not been for his first chance encounter with her a decade ago on Alliance Prime, Tal and the entire crew of the *Cormier* would be dead, their bodies vaporized along with the ship and the spacedock in which the botched repairs had been carried out.

He had never been able to explain her "talent" and she had never more than hinted at an explanation. Some odd form of telepathy or precognition, he had often told himself, not so much to explain it as to simply give it a needed label, a label that made it easier for his logical conscious mind to accept.

She had never been officially a part of his crew, was not even from an Alliance world, but she had been with him on three ships since the *Cormier,* part passenger, part confidant, and part unofficial adviser.

And, though he would never publicly admit giving credence to such superstition, something of a good luck charm.

At least until now, when he found himself racing to beat the Supreme Arbiter to the so-called Guardian's world, an uncharted planet whose coordinates Sarek himself had determined using information given him by the two self-professed Terrans. Despite his best efforts he had not yet been able to imagine how this action could bring him either good fortune or career advancement.

And yet, despite his misgivings and despite Guinan's own unwillingness—or inability?—to tell him why this trip was necessary, why it couldn't be left to Sarek to make the journey, he was doing it. He was, to put it mildly, uneasy, but he was following her lead, largely because he knew he would be even more uneasy if he refused.

Balitor had risen and dressed, the ecstasy of the Link finally beginning to fade, when she felt the pulsing warmth in her temple return. Startled, she turned toward her bed, but before she could even lie down, the immaterial lights that had so gently enveloped her before returned, no longer soft and comforting but blazing with eye-searing brightness. A moment later, the chill returned as well, but with bone-chilling intensity. Simultaneously she felt the Wise Ones return, but their ethereal bodies this time did not brush gently against her mind, responding to her efforts to initiate the Link. Instead, they smashed against it like battering rams—as if attempting to destroy her!

Her mind reeled as she realized what must be happening: She was being punished! Desperately, she tried to think what she could have done to offend.

Her terror escalated as she realized she could not even *ask!* Her body, her lips, her vocal cords were paralyzed. She could not move, could not even speak.

Stifling the scream that echoed silently in her mind, she mentally prostrated herself, begging to be told what she had done, pleading for a chance to redeem herself.

But this time there was no response, no softly welcoming voice, nothing.

Until . . .

She felt the same presence she had felt before, but this time it didn't envelop her like a life-sustaining womb. Instead it gripped her like a steel fist.

And her body began to move, not in response to her own frantic commands but of its own volition.

Or the volition of the Wise Ones!

Terrified but resigned to whatever punishment the Wise Ones saw fit to impose, Balitor could literally do nothing but watch and listen as her body turned and took a tentative step, then another, its movements stiff and uneven.

Suddenly, the attempts to walk stopped and her body swayed unsteadily. Her hand darted out, its palm slamming hard against the wall as if to keep from falling. For several seconds her body stood motionless, and the mindvoice that had previously welcomed her to the Link with soft and soothing tones returned, but this time it was sharp and demanding.

"Balitor," it grated, *"if you wish to continue to serve the Wise Ones well, do not resist."*

For a moment her terror only increased, but then, as the meaning of the words came clear to her, relief and joy flooded over her.

She was not being punished! She was being honored!

She was being given yet another opportunity to serve the Wise Ones. Her very own *body* had been chosen to serve as vessel for Them! She had not known such a thing was *possible*. The Proctors had never even hinted at anything beyond the Link, which they had maintained was the ultimate honor, the ultimate opportunity!

A helpless but suddenly ecstatic prisoner in her own body, Balitor watched with rising anticipation as it began to move again, unsteadily pacing back and forth in her cramped quarters, the movements becoming smoother and less stiff with each step it took.

TWENTY-ONE

WITH MORE difficulty than she had imagined possible, the Borg Queen endured the creature's rampant emotions and yet continued to function, continued to silently walk the creature's body back and forth as she consolidated her control and adjusted to its limitations, to its maddeningly slow reaction times and fragile structure. It threatened to collapse at any moment, and undoubtedly would do precisely that if she relaxed her painfully tight control for even a moment.

The augmented Link required for complete control was far worse, far more intense than any normal Link she had ever undergone, immersing her so deeply in the creature's mind that its thoughts and memories became almost indistinguishable from her own. Even worse, her own distant memories of that bleak time before she herself had been assimilated were resurrected, floating back into her conscious mind like sediment being stirred up from the lightless depths of some forgotten seabottom. Having not reviewed those memories for centuries, she had logically assumed they had long ago been purged, but she had obviously been mistaken. Particularly disturbing was the realization that the mind and body to which she herself had long ago been limited had been no better and no worse than those of this pathetic creature.

How, she wondered, could any sentient being prefer that state of self-destructive chaos and painful loneliness to the organized efficiency, the completeness of the Borg Collective? It was literally incomprehensible to her despite the fact that those same resurrected memories told her that she herself had resisted assimilation, had even been terrified of it.

Until the process had been completed and she understood.

But such concerns were irrelevant, she told herself. The creature's emotions were irrelevant as well, except insofar as they hindered her attempts to control its body.

Only one thing was immediately relevant: the origins of the being who called himself Picard.

The memories of the Balitor creature told her little beyond what she had already gleaned through the original Link. Worse, she wasn't even certain how she could gain access to the information she needed. Using her host to question Picard from a distance would almost certainly be futile and could, in addition, raise suspicions in his mind. Her best hope at this point was to gain access to his ship's data stores, but in order to accomplish that, she would have to be transported to his ship. Once there, she could utilize Picard's memories, extracted en masse and safely stored while Locutus had been part of her matrix. Those memories would give her quick and easy access to virtually anything on board.

The problem would be getting her host transported from this ship to the *Enterprise* without arousing suspicion. She was not accustomed to using deception. Like all Queens, she was accustomed to simply taking what she needed and destroying or assimilating anything or anyone that presented an obstacle.

But this situation was different.

She could easily call up a Borg ship and destroy the Picard creature and his ship, but that would not be enough. Such action could even, conceivably, precipitate the very disaster she feared, though she had no idea how or why. Picard, by all the laws of logic, could not be here, could not exist, yet he did. Therefore, the laws of logic—at least as she understood them—did not apply, and until she knew considerably more than she knew now, she could not take what would, according to normal logic, be the obvious course.

But then, as she continued to perfect her control of the creature's body, a voice emerged from the *Wisdom*'s comm system and changed everything.

"This is Sarek, Supreme Arbiter of the Alliance," it said. *"I have just returned from the alien vessel, the* Enterprise, *where I was given disturbing information. They have had more experience with Vortex-like phenomena than we, and their medical personnel are of the opinion that the length of time the* Wisdom *spent in proximity to the Vortex has very likely caused undetected but potentially serious damage to the health of everyone on board. They assured me, however, that their medical science is such that they can not only detect any such damage but treat and reverse it. I myself, in fact, have already undergone the tests and treatment."*

Sarek fell silent. After a moment Commander Varkan's voice replaced the Vulcan's. *"All off-duty personnel will report to the transporter room for transport to the Enter-*

prise. *As soon as the tests and any indicated treatments are completed, you will be returned to the* Wisdom *to relieve the crew currently on duty."*

It was, she realized in amazement, an order to do precisely what she wanted—needed—to do.

Hastily searching Picard's stored memories, she found nothing to indicate that the subtle alterations to the Narisian's brain could be detected by any technology that the *Enterpise* possessed. The crude implants that she had used in her earlier efforts would have been obvious to the most cursory of scans, of course, but those had been supplanted generations ago. Certainly a routine physical examination of the Balitor creature would reveal nothing. It was of course possible that this vessel had upgraded its technology. She had no way of knowing.

But to gain immediate access to the *Enterprise* was obviously worth whatever risk was entailed.

The decision made, she palmed open the door and stepped out into the corridor, her control of her host's body now so nearly complete that it required virtually no conscious effort.

As she made her way down the corridor toward the transporter room, other compartment doors opened and other off-duty personnel emerged and headed in the same direction, some looking puzzled, others worried, others as stone-faced as the body she herself inhabited.

She noted that both Sarek and the *Wisdom*'s commander were waiting in the transporter room, watching as three of the crew stepped apprehensively onto the pads, their eyes carefully averted from the commander, as were those of every other crew member except herself. From the Balitor creature's memories, she saw that this was not surprising. Commander Varkan was feared as much as he was respected, and the thought of meeting his stern gaze directly, thereby calling attention to themselves, was more unsettling than the prospect of being transported to an alien ship. The presence of the enigmatic Supreme Arbiter only reinforced the tendency to simply follow orders as efficiently and inconspicuously as possible.

The Balitor creature's turn came quickly as the commander motioned for her and a pair of Romulans to step onto the pads. Acknowledging her presence with a nod—she was the only member of the trio that was part of the bridge crew—he gestured to the transporter operator the moment her feet settled on the pad. Almost instantly she felt the tingling paralysis that preceded transport by these comparatively primitive devices.

As the *Wisdom*'s transporter room vanished behind a glittering curtain, a feeling of vertigo startled her until she saw in her host's memory that, for her, it was both normal and familiar. Then the curtain faded and she gave a mental sigh of relief as she saw that this *Enterprise*'s transporter room was identical to the one in Picard's memory. The crew was also the same. The ship's counselor, who was a mixed-breed of Species 5618 and the telepathic Species 1599, and Riker, Picard's second in command, both stood not far from the controls, watching the new arrivals. Three medical ensigns whose faces were familiar to Picard, even if their names were not, stood to one side, also watching.

If the rest of the ship was as familiar as this transporter room, she quickly concluded, she would have no trouble accessing its data banks from virtually anywhere, including the sickbay to which she assumed they would all be escorted. With Picard's knowledge instantly available, it would take only seconds to access a complete history of the ship and the logs of its captain. Her dull-witted host would serve as little more than a conduit, seeing little and comprehending less of the data that would simply be relayed at lightning speed through its sensory system into the matrix's data banks, where she could later study it at her leisure and decide on a course of action.

Looking around, wondering why the ensigns had not yet stepped forward to escort herself and the two Romulans to the sickbay, she noticed the counselor, a slight grimace on her face, tapping her combadge and murmuring something into it.

Was something wrong?

Could they have somehow detected her presence? The counselor's empathic talents *might* be capable of such a feat, the Locutus memories told her, but only if she knew precisely what she was looking for. But that would mean they already suspected a Borg presence on the *Wisdom*, which was of course impossible. For hundreds of years, no one had suspected the Borg of having anything to do with the Narisians or any of the other "observer" races. Even the creatures themselves did not know that their races' benefactors were the Borg.

No, it was just her host's rampant emotions, so powerful she could not entirely block them out.

Unless the Picard creature—

As if cued by her thoughts, the door to the corridor hissed open and someone stepped through.

Picard himself!

Suddenly the Borg Queen found herself as close to panic as her physical body, the product of the technologies of a thousand assimilated worlds, would allow.

Memories flooded her mind, just as they had at the initial sight of Picard's face on the *Wisdom*'s viewscreen. But those relatively bland memories had been triggered by a mere image, a two-dimensional representation that had been heavily diluted and distorted by Balitor's limited mind and imperfect memory.

This was Picard himself—*Locutus!*—and the memories this time were incomparably more intense.

But these memories, unlike those involving his transformation into Locutus, were of things that had not happened, things that could not possibly have happened.

In these, she remembered dying!

She vividly remembered screaming in pain and frustration, something she hadn't thought herself capable of, as the flesh-and-blood portions of her chosen body were literally eaten away. She remembered seeing her attendant drones disintegrating around her, remembered feeling her entire matrix going the way of her own body, dying with her.

She remembered lying helpless yet still alive, still fully conscious and acutely aware that, even though she was reduced to nothing but a brain and spinal column encased in protective metal sheaths, she was still capable of being resurrected in a new body.

She remembered this same Picard, drenched in sweat, looming over her. She remembered him picking up the thing she had become, remembered the mixture of revulsion and pity that filled his eyes and his mind as he held it briefly in his hands.

She remembered the grisly metallic snap as he broke her spine in two, taking from her her last chance for true resurrection.

She remembered her consciousness fading as he dropped the quivering segments to the deck. She even remembered accepting, in the final moments of that consciousness, the previously incomprehensible notion that she herself, not just her individual, replaceable bodies, could come to an end. The only form of resurrection now possible was to be duplicated from her stored memories, but it would not be *her*. It would be a being exactly like her, a being who *remembered* being her but in truth had never been.

She herself would be no more.

She remembered all that and more in disturbingly vivid detail.

And yet she knew—knew without the slightest doubt—that none of what she remembered had happened.

Yet!

Suddenly, the truth exploded in her mind. These memories were not of what *had* happened but of what was *yet to come!*

She neither knew nor cared which ability from which assimilated race had provided her with these premonitory "memories." She knew only what she herself had to do.

She had to cease her obsessive search for irrelevant details of Picard's past, for meaningless clues as to how he could still exist and why he was here.

All that mattered was that he be destroyed.

Now!

Before those "memories" became reality. If yet another Picard appeared out of nowhere, so be it. She would deal with it when and if the time came.

Ignoring the physical limitations of her host's frail body, she launched it toward Picard and the security detail that had followed him into the transporter room.

Moments earlier, just outside the transporter room, Picard suppressed a grimace as Troi's muted words came through his combadge: *"It is worse than Mr. Scott suspected, Cap-*

tain. I sense that the Narisian is not alone in her mind.
Something *is controlling her."*

"Borg?"

"Perhaps. It feels Borg, but there is far more emo-
tion—"

"Thank you, Counselor," he said, cutting her off as his
eyes met those of Worf, who led a security detail that included Ensigns Porfirio and Houarner. "You heard?"

The lieutenant nodded. "If one of them is already possessed by the Borg, then anything we do will be known to
the entire collective."

"Indeed." Tapping his combadge again, Picard spoke to
Data, still on the bridge. "Mr. Data, inform Sarek that the
Narisian is apparently being actively monitored if not controlled, almost certainly by the Borg. Tell him we will do
our best not to betray our suspicions and to learn as much
as we can from our medical scans before returning her to
the *Wisdom* along with the rest of the crew. With luck, the
Borg won't realize we suspect anything."

With Data's acknowledgment, Picard returned his attention to Worf. "Put away your weapons but stay alert when
you escort her to sickbay."

He waited a moment until the three officers holstered
their phasers, then stepped forward as the doors to the
transporter room opened. Two Romulans and the Narisian
were still standing on the transporter platform, looking
around uneasily, as Picard entered.

The Romulans paid him no attention, but the Narisian
froze the moment she saw him. Her face betrayed no emotion, but her vertically slitted eyes locked unwaveringly on
him. Picard couldn't be certain if it was an illusion, but the
fur on her head seemed to bristle.

Pretending not to notice, he turned toward Riker and

Troi. The counselor, her eyes still riveted on the Narisian, gasped.

At the same moment, perhaps a split second earlier, the Narisian, in expressionless silence, leapt with startling speed, not at Picard but at the security detail two or three meters behind him. Her movements were so sudden and so blindingly fast that she had her hands on Porfirio's loosely fastened phaser before he or any of the others could react.

As if thoroughly familiar with the weapon, she had it set to full power in an instant, without having to even look at it. Even before the weapon was completely raised, she pressed the firing stud. The beam lashed out, charring the deck bare meters from Picard and starting to sweep toward him.

At the same time, Worf fired his phaser at the Narisian.

For a moment, the Narisian wobbled, her own deadly phaser beam twitching backward onto the already scarred area of the deck, but almost instantly it steadied.

The split-second hesitation and retreat, however, had given Hovarner time to act, and a second phaser beam, set to heavy stun, staggered the Narisian.

But it did not fell her.

Worf and Houarner fired again until finally, with startling abruptness, the Narisian collapsed, thudding to the deck as if every muscle had gone flaccid simultaneously. For a moment that seemed to go on forever, the fingers that somehow still held Porfirio's phaser twitched as if they had a mindless life of their own but could not manage the strength or coordination to press the firing stud. Finally the fingers were as still as the rest of her body, and Porfirio retrieved his weapon as Picard himself knelt next to the body.

Troi grimaced as if in pain. "It is gone, Captain," she said, her voice trembling.

Picard scooped the Narisian up in his arms and said to

the transporter chief, "Two to beam directly to sickbay."
He glanced briefly at the haggard-looking Troi. "Join us
there, Counselor, immediately," he said in the moment before the transporter beam enveloped him and Balitor.

Without warning, agony engulfed Balitor, as if her entire
body, inside and out, had burst into flames. In the same
moment, that body literally collapsed, every muscle going
limp as she thudded to the deck. Not one would respond.
She couldn't move, she couldn't scream.

She couldn't even lose consciousness.

She could only endure—and realize that the Wise One
was gone.

What madness, she wondered through the pain, had
overcome the Wise One to produce such a burst of violence, to virtually destroy her own body in a vain attempt
to kill one single person?

Then the one called Picard was looming over her and
she understood. A ghostly image of another Picard, an
image that only the Wise One could possibly have sent,
blotted out everything else, even softened the pain, as it
came closer and reached down as if to strangle her and—

Instead of strangling her, the real Picard picked her up
even as he barked orders into the air. The transporter room
vanished, replaced by another, unfamiliar room, and her
pain-deadened nerves barely felt her body being laid on a
soft, flat surface.

Someone else, a female with long red hair, was standing
over her then, running a small, hand-held device over her
body, then holding it almost touching her head and—

Her heart faltered, and she realized in dull horror that
these beings were trying to kill her, probably in retaliation
for the attack they had seen her body carry out.

But the Wise Ones would protect her, she told herself. She had served them well. She knew they would not abandon her.

Then the woman was doing something else, pressing another object against her chest and someone else was fastening a small metallic object to her forehead. Behind them, she could still see the one called Picard, watching intently as he directed the efforts to kill her.

Her heart faltered again, skipping a beat and another, and the edges of her vision began to draw in, and she couldn't tell if her heart was still beating or not, if she was breathing or not. Suddenly she realized the Wise Ones could not—or *would* not—protect her after all, not from these creatures from another universe. But at the same time a voice spoke in her mind, a voice she recognized though she hadn't heard it in years.

You have done me honor, my daughter, it said. *I would give anything to serve as you have served.*

The pain was gone, banished by her mother's presence, by the words she had feared she would never hear.

Her last thought as both vision and consciousness faded was one of gratefulness for the fact that her mother had been allowed to know of the service she had been privileged to give.

She had failed!

The Picard creature still lived, its terrifying features looming over her almost the way they had in the nightmarish pseudo-memories of her own death. For a moment it seemed to be looking *through* the Balitor creature's eyes, through the Link directly to the Queen herself, warning her of what was still to come.

Spasmodically, before the Picard creature's mind could

reach through and take her own in its mental grip, she terminated the Link.

And triggered the command she had long ago provided for, the mental command she had believed, until that moment, would never need to be given.

She waited as it was wordlessly transmitted, as it touched countless minds all over the quadrant, bringing briefly to life the message that had lain buried there for much of their lives.

One by one, she felt those minds lapse into unconsciousness and then death. Like Balitor, they had all done the jobs they had been conditioned to do, but now, suddenly, each one had become a potential danger, the magnitude of which she was no longer able to rationally estimate. Pure rationality, which she had until now adhered to in her every decision, was no longer possible, not as long as the Picard creature continued to exist.

When the process was complete, when all the creatures that had served her were dead, she did what she now knew she should have done when she first became aware of the Picard creature's presence in this era.

She took direct control of the Borg vessel nearest to the Picard creature's ship. With far less effort than had been required to take over Balitor, she insinuated herself into every aspect of the vessel until it literally became a part of her, much the way the cybernetic bodies that she routinely donned became a part of her.

Dr. Beverly Crusher stepped back from the biobed, her shoulders slumping in defeat. "She's gone, Captain. I don't understand why, but she's gone."

"The phasers—"

The doctor shook her head. "They don't cause lasting

physical damage even at heavy stun. In any event, all readings indicate virtually no physical damage at any level. I'm not familiar with Narisian physiology, of course, but everything in her body appears fully functional. It just isn't functioning. It's as if something in her mind simply overrode the body's autonomic system and shut down her entire nervous system. Even neural stimulators had no effect."

"Could there be a symbiosis of some kind?" Picard asked. "Narisian and Borg?"

Crusher shook her head. "I doubt it. She was obviously not a drone."

"Not the kind of drone we're used to, but perhaps in this universe . . ." He turned to Troi and Riker, who had just entered sickbay. "You heard?"

"A poison pill, Borg variety," Riker said as Troi nodded her silent agreement. "Something in her mind. She was found out, so she had to die. The bastards couldn't allow her to survive and spill their secrets."

Picard was silent a moment, looking down at the body, knowing that his first officer was right. One more victim of the Borg, one among the billions.

Straightening, he nodded tersely to Riker and Troi as he tapped his combadge and headed for the nearest turbolift. "Mr. Data, we're on our way to the bridge. Locate Guinan and—"

"I'm here, Captain," Guinan's voice assured him. *"At least I think I am."*

"I'd appreciate it if you could decide for certain, Guinan. Data," he continued as the turbolift doors slid open, "reestablish contact with the *Wisdom* and Arbiter Sarek."

The Vulcan's unreadable face greeted them on the main

viewscreen as they emerged onto the bridge. Picard ignored the questioning looks directed at him by Scott and Kirk, who had reluctantly remained on the bridge throughout the incident.

"What is it, Picard?" Sarek asked. *"Your android did not—"*

"The Narisian Balitor is dead," Picard said as he strode to the captain's chair, flanked by his first officer and counselor. Briskly and concisely, he summarized the events that had led up to the death. As he did so, Worf entered the bridge, having left the security of the transporter to Porfirio and Houarner.

"The other Narisian is dead as well," Sarek said when Picard finished. *"I have also just now received word that the same is happening to the Narisians attached to Alliance Prime."*

A sick feeling clutched at Picard's stomach at the thought that his actions were what had somehow triggered not only Balitor's death but that of these others—and who knew how many more throughout the Alliance—as well. Spies or not, the Narisians were victims of the Borg as much as any of the members of the thousands of fully assimilated races across the galaxy.

"Only Narisians?" Picard asked.

"Those are the only ones reported so far." Sarek spoke emotionlessly.

"Can someone familiar with Narisian physiology determine precisely what caused the deaths? We have so far been unable to find any cause for Balitor's death."

"I have already ordered a thorough examination of the other Narisian. Transport Balitor's body to the Wisdom *and we will examine it as well."*

"I don't want to stick my nose in your business, Picard,"

Kirk said, "but isn't it more important to find out why she tried to kill you than how she died?"

"Obviously the Borg were controlling her," Picard said.

"As you say, that's obvious. The real question is, what set them off? Why did they suddenly decide to kill you, particularly in such an inefficient way? And what can you do if they try again, maybe with a little more efficiency?"

"He's right, Captain," Riker said quietly. "And unless—"

"Captain," Data broke in, "the chronometric radiation is decreasing rapidly. It has dropped fifty percent in the past thirty seconds."

Automatically, Picard darted a look at Guinan as the level of chronometric radiation continued to drop. "It isn't me this time, Captain," she said, all traces of her usual cryptic smile gone.

"Sarek?"

"To the best of my knowledge, Picard, we have done nothing that could logically result in such a decrease."

"Hail the *D'Zidran*, Mr. Worf," Picard snapped. "Perhaps Guinan's local counterpart has some ideas."

"No response, sir," Worf announced moments later.

"Chronometric radiation has leveled off at twenty-two-point-seven percent of the previous level, Captain," Data said.

A sinking feeling gripped Picard. "The timeline is stabilizing?"

"That is what theory suggests, Captain," Data responded, his fingers continuing to dart across the control panel as he spoke. "However, I would point out that, even after this decrease, the radiation level is still more than five times what one would expect to find in a stable timeline."

"Keep trying to reach the *D'Zidran*, Mr. Worf. Meanwhile, I'm open to any and all ideas." He glanced briefly at Kirk before going on. "Captain Kirk was right when he said our immediate concern should be why the Borg have decided to come after me, and what measures we can take if they do try again. Sarek, you're more familiar than any of us with these particular Borg. Do you—"

"Captain," Data broke in, "one of the Borg cubes following the Vortex has broken away. It is now on an intercept course with the *Enterprise*. And we are being scanned."

A chill washed over Picard. Vivid images of the warren-like interiors of other Borg ships, swarming with thousands upon thousands of grotesque cybernetic zombies, threatened to push everything else out of his mind.

"It appears," he said after a moment, "that at least one of our questions has been answered. They *are* going to try again."

TWENTY-TWO

"PICARD," Sarek said abruptly, "attempting to flee will be futile. Additionally, there is as yet no firm indication that the Borg ship means you harm. Except during assimilation of a world, no Borg ship has ever attacked an Alliance ship unless that Alliance ship attacked the Borg ship first."

Without waiting for an acknowledgment, Sarek cut the connection to the *Enterprise* and stood up from Varkan's command chair.

"Do not move from our current position without my direct authorization, Commander Varkan," he said. "Do not follow the *Enterprise* if it unwisely attempts to flee the Borg ship. Do not respond to their hails. There is much I must consider. I will be in my quarters."

Turning from an uneasy and puzzled Varkan, Sarek strode from the bridge. Less than a minute later he was seated before the viewscreen and control panel in his quarters. The screen still showed the unmoving image of the *Enterprise*.

At least they appeared to be heeding his warning and were not making a vain attempt to flee. Any such attempt would only make the situation even more perilous than it already was. And there *was* a chance, no matter how small, that the Borg ship would not attack despite the fact that the *Enterprise*—and the *Wisdom,* he now noted—were being scanned. The Borg had finally "noticed" them both.

The question was: Why?

Obviously, something fundamental had changed in the last few hours. The most disturbing possibility was that Picard's claimed link with the Borg had been a two-way affair. When Picard had learned of the existence of the spies, perhaps the Borg had learned of something in return, perhaps even Picard's intent to "restore" the timeline to what he considered Borg-free normalcy. Was that why one of their spies had tried to assassinate him?

And were the Borg themselves now coming to do what their Narisian surrogate had failed to do? Logic told him it was a virtual certainty, despite what he had told Picard. The only sliver of doubt came from the fact that the Borg *could* have sent a ship to make the first attempt. Instead, they had sent one of their spies, a most illogical action if the Borg's only purpose was to kill Picard and/or destroy the *Enterprise*.

He watched as the Borg cube drew nearer. It would be within weapons range in less than ten minutes. He wished he could have told Picard the complete truth, but he had not dared, not as long as there was the slightest possibility that Picard's link with the Borg was a two-way street.

He considered the logic of the decision he needed to make before those ten minutes were up. Should he destroy the Borg ship if it became certain that it would otherwise destroy the *Enterprise?* And the *Wisdom?*

Normally he wouldn't hesitate to accept the loss of a single ship, even one which he himself was aboard, if the only alternative was to prematurely reveal the weapon that was their only hope to eventually destroy *all* the Borg vessels. But the *Enterprise,* if Kirk and Scott's story of the so-called Guardian could be believed, provided a chance to do something far better than simply destroy the Borg fleet. They could, if successful, restore the "original" timeline and, in effect, destroy the Borg before they ever came to Alpha Quadrant, not at some nebulous future date that might never come. And if they were able to do *that,* they would not only eliminate the Borg from the Alpha Quadrant but restore to meaningful life all those billions the Borg had assimilated and turned into drones in the last two or more centuries. And give those same billions two centuries of time to prepare for when the Borg *did* cross into the Alpha Quadrant.

If . . .

For just an instant, Sarek's "dreams" of that other universe flashed through his mind more vividly than ever before. It was obviously a universe infinitely preferable to the one that existed around him now.

And it was a universe that he would almost certainly be consigning to oblivion if, in the next few minutes, he allowed the *Enterprise* to be destroyed.

With implacable logic, he made his decision.

Kirk could no longer hold it in. For what seemed like an eternity, he had stood by silently while the Borg cube bore down on them, growing ever larger in the viewscreen.

"Picard," he said, leaning close, his voice less than a whisper but knife-sharp, "I need to talk to you. Privately."

Picard scowled briefly but nodded. "You have the bridge, Number One."

Seconds later the captains of two different *Enterprises* entered the ready room.

"I don't mean to step on another commander's toes," Kirk said the moment the door hissed shut behind them, "but don't you think it's about time to *do* something?"

"You heard Sarek as well as I."

"I did. And I trust him—*have* trusted him—with my life. But what *I* heard him say was that, unless you count what the Borg do when they're taking over a planet, they've never made an unprovoked attack on any Alliance ship. *Yet!* And that if we're lucky as hell, they won't start now, despite the fact that they're already scanning us, which—correct me if I'm wrong—is *also* something they've never done before."

Picard nodded grimly. "I am well aware of that."

"And I assume that sending a spy to try to assassinate you isn't something they do every day, either. A couple things strike me as being pretty obvious. First, the Borg have departed from their usual routine. And second, they're out to get you."

"What would you have me do, Captain?"

"For a start, how about doing whatever it was you did when you 'intercepted' whatever it was that told you the Borg had infiltrated the *Wisdom.* Intercept something that tells you why the devil they're suddenly on a collision course with us."

"Believe me, I've tried. I'm *still* trying, but the chance of success is remote."

Kirk grimaced. "All right, then, Plan B: Get us the hell out of here as fast as possible."

Picard shook his head. "Sarek was right. Trying to run would be futile. The Borg ship is already moving faster than the *Enterprise* could, even for an instant, even if Commander La Forge tuned every system in our warp drive to perfection and diverted every joule of energy from shields and life support. They would overtake us in minutes."

"Even so, it's better than sitting here doing *nothing!*"

"I am well aware of your reputation, Captain," Picard said sharply, "and it is my considered judgment that Sarek was right. Unlike you, I am quite familiar with the Borg in my own time, and my experience tells me that, slim as it is, our only chance for survival is to follow Sarek's advice."

Kirk pulled in a deep breath that did nothing to calm him. "All right," he said. "Maybe you *can't* outrun them, but what about just evading them? They may be fast, but something that size has to have a pretty lousy turning circle. Can't the *Enterprise* at least *outmaneuver* them?"

"Perhaps, but only for a short while."

"How long? Long enough to get within transporter range of the so-called Vortex?"

Picard frowned. "Possible but not likely."

"Then let's do it, before it goes from unlikely to totally impossible."

"To what purpose?"

"Isn't it obvious, Picard? Beam me back in there, into the Vortex."

"You're willing to sacrifice yourself without being certain it will accomplish anything? You said you wanted to establish the facts before you—"

"That *would* be preferable, I'll admit, but how do we establish them? I'm wide open for ideas."

"The Guardian—"

"Forget the Guardian. We can't get there unless we can outrun the Borg, which you say is impossible. And even if we could, there's no guarantee it would help us. The very best we can hope for is to be able to outmaneuver that cube out there for a few minutes, which *may* be long enough to beam me into the Vortex. In any event, given the circumstances, I don't see how letting you beam me into the Vortex is that much of a sacrifice on my part. Either we all get fried by that *thing* out there and accomplish nothing or *I* get fried by the Vortex and *maybe* save the *Enterprise,* not to mention Earth and a few other worlds. Don't tell me you wouldn't do the same thing."

"If that were truly the choice, of course, but—"

"Come on, Picard, we're wasting time," Kirk said, brushing past him toward the ready room door. "That cube will be all over us in a few minutes, and *then* we won't have any choice at all."

His DNA and neural scans completed and his identity verified by the computer-controlled neurobiosensor he had attached loosely to his forehead, Sarek carefully entered the code that only he and four of his most trusted advisors—Vulcans all—knew. The *Enterprise* and the starfield behind it vanished from the viewscreen before him but not from the one on the *Wisdom*'s bridge. There, the viewscreen would continue to operate normally under the control of the bridge crew, totally unaware of Sarek's activities.

He watched patiently as a new image built up: nearly three thousand tiny specks of light, each representing a hyper-powerful, interphase-cloaked photon torpedo attached to a warp drive that could outrace even the Borg. Most were in clusters of a few hundred. One cluster, he knew, surrounded Andor, another Alpha Centuari. The largest cluster by far surrounded the Borg sensor shield that in turn surrounded the entire Terran system.

After the recent example of Cardassian treachery, even Sarek's Vulcan mental discipline was hard pressed to keep him from shivering inwardly at the sight of so much destructive power. No one, not Cardassian, not Klingon, not any Alliance race, had found a way around the security system he had designed and now controlled, but they had tried, just as Zarcot had tried to destroy the *Wisdom* and kill Sarek for his own short-term gains. If Zarcot or someone else of his ilk *did* gain control of them—

"Vortex," he said, wrenching his thoughts back to the task at hand. As he spoke, the major clusters vanished as the screen zoomed in on two tiny clusters of only five specks each. One cluster, he saw, was moving rapidly away from the other.

"Targets." At his word, a pair of ghostly Borg cubes appeared. One was in the midst of the more distant, comparatively motionless cluster of lights. The other was a short distance ahead of the moving cluster, as if being pursued by it. Which was, in truth, precisely what was happening.

Like every other known Borg ship, this one was constantly accompanied by a small cluster of the cloaked torpedoes, each one equipped with sensors that could track the Borg even while cloaked. The next time the Borg lowered the sensor shield around the Terran system, every interphase-cloaked photon torpedo would, at the command of Sarek or one of the four trusted advisors, maneuver inside the nearest Borg cube, de-cloak, and detonate. Those surrounding the Terran system would attempt to do the same with the unknown number of Borg vessels that would suddenly be revealed to their sensors. The energy leakage that was an unavoidable part of the decloaking process would inflict major damage itself. The photon torpedoes, it was hoped, would finish the job, reducing the cubes to metal scraps and vapor.

If every aspect of the plan were executed perfectly, a few minutes after the Terran shield went down, the quadrant would be free of Borg ships for the first time in more than two centuries.

But even then there would still be the billions of planet-bound drones, the drones that once had been humans and Andorians and Alpha Centaurians.

But if Kirk and Picard and Scott were telling the truth, as he was gambling they were, if they survived long enough to reach the Guardian's World, if the Guardian agreed to help them—

Without warning, the *Enterprise* darted away, first under full impulse, then going to warp.

Kirk, pacing the bridge nervously, winced as the pursuing Borg ship once again changed course far more sharply than anything that massive had any right to do. Not as sharply as the *Enterprise,* but there wasn't nearly the difference in maneuverability he had hoped for. No matter how many times the *Enterprise* zigged and zagged, no matter what kind of evasive maneuvers Picard ordered the computer to execute, the cube followed, never once losing ground for more than a few seconds. They weren't being overtaken as fast as they would've been in a straight flight, but the cube *was* steadily closing the gap.

And they were little closer to the Vortex than when they had started.

"Four minutes to weapons range, Captain," Worf announced. Over the last twenty minutes the distance to the Borg ship had been cut in half. Unless they found an evasive pattern that worked better than the ones they had been using, it would be cut to zero in another twenty or less.

As the computer angled the *Enterprise* into another sharp turn, something caught Kirk's eye as the star field swept across the viewscreen.

"There," he said, pointing to a smudge that had appeared near the left edge of the screen, "is that a nebula?"

"It appears to be," Data agreed as the *Enterprise* once again hit maximum warp on its new course. "It is not, however, large enough to allow us to elude the Borg. Even if it were entirely sensor-opaque, which it is not, it would be useless to attempt to hide there. The range of Borg weapons is such that if the Borg were to station themselves just outside the nebula, they would need only to sweep the entire nebula, and—"

"Picard," Kirk said sharply, his voice suddenly filled with hope, "I know my last suggestion hasn't worked out all that well so far, but that nebula gives me another idea."

"Explain, Captain."

"No time. Just take us in there, quickly. I'll explain as we go. Please."

Picard scowled at him for a moment, then glanced at the figures streaming across the viewscreen, quantifying the overall rate at which the Borg ship was overtaking them.

"Very well," he said abruptly. "Give Ensign Raeger the details of what you need."

At least, Sarek thought as he watched the ultra-secure viewscreen in his quarters on the *Wisdom*, Picard's unwise attempt to flee had proven one thing: It was the *Enterprise* the Borg were after, not the *Wisdom*. Unless it meant only that the *Enterprise* had attracted attention by moving, and the *Wisdom* had not. But whatever the reason, the *Wisdom* had not been touched by the Borg sensors since the *Enterprise* had launched itself into flight.

Sarek was uncertain what he would do if the *Enterprise*, in its increasingly desperate maneuvers, took itself and its pursuer out of sensor range. While the cloaked torpedoes could—and would—easily keep pace with the Borg ship, the *Wisdom* could not. He was also uncertain—puzzled—as to what Picard was thinking. He was buying a little time, but to what end? He couldn't keep the *Enterprise* out of range of the Borg weapons forever, not even for another hour.

If it weren't for the real possibility that Picard was permanently linked to the Borg, he would have answered the *Enterprise*'s hail long ago, letting Picard know that the Borg ship could be destroyed at any time, but—

His puzzled frown deepened. What was Picard doing *now?* The *Enterprise* had entered one of the tiny nebula that dotted the region of space the Vortex was passing through.

And it wasn't coming out, not if the *Wisdom*'s sensors could be trusted. They could distinguish only vague shadows within the nebula, but the surrounding space was crystal clear. And empty.

Was it time? he wondered. With the *Enterprise* motionless, the Borg ship would be within weapons range in less than a minute. Its weapons were fully charged and ready. Certainly Picard could not be foolish enough to think that the nebula would provide a safe hiding place. Not only was it far too small, but there were numerous voids, some running through it like meandering river canyons. All the Borg ship needed to do—

Suddenly, a set of symbols flashed on the viewscreen and vanished. Calling them back onto the screen, Sarek saw that a ship, presumably the *Enterprise,* had just passed through one of the narrow, canyon-like voids, exposing itself to the outside world for a fraction of a second. But that fraction of a second was enough for the *Wisdom*'s sensors— and, almost certainly, for the Borg's. The *Enterprise* was moving, Sarek saw, at full impulse on a course that was only a few hundredths of a degree from being a collision course with the oncoming Borg ship.

For an instant he thought that Picard must have realized he couldn't escape and was planning to do as much damage to the cube as he could—by attempting to ram it.

A foolish maneuver at best, but then Sarek saw the *true* endpoint of the *Enterprise*'s present course: the Vortex. And he realized what Picard *was* attempting. If the *Enterprise* went from full impulse to maximum warp the moment it emerged from the nebula, it would pass well within weapons range. But at that speed, with the cube moving at an even greater speed in the opposite direction, the *Enterprise* would be through that range in too short a time for the cube to react effectively.

By the time the cube was able to make a complete one-hundred-eighty-degree turn, the *Enterprise* would have gained enough time to reach the Vortex before the cube could catch up.

They would then have time—at least a few seconds—to do what Sarek should have realized they were planning from the start of the evasive maneuvers: transport Kirk into the Vortex.

Which might restore the timeline without the help or advice of the Guardian.

Perhaps it would not be necessary to give away the Alliance's secret weapon after all.

Despite the urgency that was driving the Borg Queen's actions, a kind of exhilaration she had forgotten the very existence of gripped her as she raced after the Picard creature's ship. Like the capacity for fear, it was something that must have, all unknown, lain dormant in some vestigial corner of her still-largely-organic brain, only to be resurrected by her more-than-intimate contact with the Balitor creature and its out-of-control emotions.

One small part of her was disappointed that the chase would soon be over. The Picard creature's ship, while agile, was steadily losing ground. Soon it would be within weapons range, and that would be the end of it. The concentrated firepower of her ship would reduce the entire structure and all its occupants to a spreading cloud of plasma in a matter of seconds.

Ahead, the fleeing ship made an abrupt turn, nearly ninety degrees, but it would do the Picard creature no good. No matter how maneuverable the tiny craft was, it would be—

Abruptly, the *Enterprise* slowed. A moment later, it began to fade from the sensors. But even as it did, something else was revealed to her through the visual interface: a nebula, a small cloud of interstellar dust.

She watched in disbelief as the *Enterprise,* now on impulse power, faded entirely from the sensors as it crept into the heart of the nebula. Surely Picard couldn't think he could hide in such an obvious way?

At her current speed, she would be in weapons range in less than thirty seconds, at the nebula itself in little more. Once there, she could simply sweep the entire nebula. It might be largely opaque to her sensors, but it would present little obstacle to her weapons.

But then, for just an instant, the *Enterprise* reappeared as it moved—still on impulse power—through one of the voids in the nebula. In that instant, she saw the projected course of the *Enterprise,* showing precisely where it would re-enter open space. It had essentially made a U-turn and was on a near-collision course with her ship.

If she had not been in direct control of the ship, that piece of information would have been noted and used only to pinpoint the spot where the *Enterprise* would most likely emerge from the nebula. Without her guidance, the ship would have continued racing toward the nebula, altering its course just enough to bring it even closer to that exit point than its present course would. And its sensors would continue to monitor all space surrounding the nebula in case the fleeing ship reappeared at some other point.

But she was not bound by the limitations of the drones who normally controlled the ship. Their orders were narrow and rigid, while hers were, basically, whatever she said they were.

In less than a second, she saw two things. First, if the *Enterprise* went to maximum warp the moment it emerged, the combined speeds of the two ships would be such that they would pass each other so rapidly she might not have time to fire.

Second, the course the *Enterprise* appeared to be following led directly to the Vortex.

And she realized something that would have meant nothing to any drone but which meant everything to her.

The two—the ones called Scott and Kirk—had "appeared" near the Vortex, and now Picard was apparently attempting to return them to that same spot. Would they then vanish the same way they had appeared, going back to wherever or whenever they had come from, taking Picard with them?

And how, she wondered as a new possibility suddenly arose out of her Locutus memories, could she even be certain that they were still on board? The three of them and any number of others could very easily have left the *Enterprise* and remained behind in the nebula in one or more of the smaller craft the *Enterprise* carried.

Craft that a normal Borg ship would ignore once the main craft had been destroyed.

But with her in control, this was *not* a normal Borg ship. Whatever their plan, they would not escape.

With a renewed sense of urgency, she slowed the vessel, dropping out of warp just as the *Enterprise*'s projected emergence point came within weapons range. At this lower relative speed, she would have more than enough time to disable the *Enterprise* when it emerged, no matter how rapidly it was moving, no matter what evasive maneuvers it undertook. She could then determine whether the Picard creature and the other two were still aboard or had remained behind in the nebula in one of the smaller craft.

There was no way any of them could escape now.

TWENTY-THREE

SAREK'S HOPE of keeping the Alliance's secret weapon a secret was short-lived. Seconds after the *Wisdom*'s sensors had picked up the *Enterprise*'s motion within the nebula, the Borg ship altered course slightly and dropped to sublight.

But Picard, Sarek realized instantly, would have no way of knowing the Borg ship had slowed prematurely. The *Enterprise* sensors would be as blinded by the nebula as the Borg's. If, as Sarek expected it to do, the *Enterprise* emerged from the nebula at maximum warp, heading almost directly at the Borg ship, it wouldn't shoot through the danger zone nearly fast enough to avoid Borg fire. Not only that, even if the Borg ship, now almost at a standstill, somehow failed to destroy the *Enterprise* and let it slip past, it would now be able to overtake it long before it reached the Vortex.

It was time to act. He had no choice.

Deliberately but rapidly, Sarek entered another code into the control panel. The neurobiosensor quickly verified his identity once again.

And cleared the signal to be sent.

On the screen, the five specks of light swarmed toward the Borg ship like angry insects, burrowing into it in the seconds before the *Enterprise* emerged from the nebula.

Now continuously monitored by the neurobiosensor, Sarek sent the de-cloak and detonate signals.

Focusing her entire attention on the *Enterprise*'s projected exit point from the nebula, the Borg Queen impatiently suppressed the countless unrelated signals that were clamoring for her attention. There would be time enough for them when her objective was accomplished. For the next few seconds, she wanted no distractions, nothing that would take even a tiny fraction of her attention from that objective: the complete and final destruction of the Picard creature and his ship.

But then, an infinitesimal instant after the *Enterprise* finally emerged from the nebula and went immediately to maximum warp, just as the intensity of a particularly insistent signal spiked violently, the ship's sensors went dead.

A fraction of a second later, she was enveloped in something the remaining organic portions of her brain interpreted as searing pain.

The Borg ship reappeared on the *Enterprise* viewscreen, indistinctly at first as the sensors struggled to pierce the last fringes of the nebula. The cube wasn't, Picard noticed with alarm, at the predicted coordinates or moving at the predicted speed. But there was no time to do anything but what they had hastily planned and programmed into the computer.

With virtually all power temporarily diverted to the

warp drive and the shields, the *Enterprise* surged ahead, the Borg ship now crystal clear on the viewscreen, its course and position pinpointed by the sensors. While they had been inside the nebula, it had altered its course so that the *Enterprise* would pass within hundreds of kilometers, not the tens of thousands they had calculated. Worse, the Borg ship had dropped out of warp, which meant the relative velocity at which it and the *Enterprise* would pass each other would be far too low to—

Picard gasped as he suddenly felt invisible flames searing his flesh. For an agonizing instant he thought it might be some weapon the Borg of this universe used, but then, through eyes that barely functioned because of the pain, he saw what was happening to the Borg cube on the screen: It was expanding, beginning to disintegrate, shards of blinding light pouring out through dozens of widening fissures. Somehow, the cube was being destroyed!

And he knew the source of his pain: the Link to the Borg. Through that Link he was experiencing a feeble specter of what the tens of thousands of drones—and the ship itself?—were experiencing as they were vaporized.

As suddenly as it had descended on him, the agony was gone, shattered into a thousand bearable fragments that faded rapidly from his consciousness.

And the Borg cube was no longer a cube, not even a disintegrating one. It was little more than an expanding shell of fragments being vaporized by the massive fireball that was propelling them outward even as it destroyed them, like the shockwave of a miniature supernova.

"All stop!" Picard ordered sharply.

The *Enterprise* dropped out of warp, the image on the viewscreen wavering momentarily as the sensors adjusted to the sublight environment.

Then the viewscreen dimmed as automatic filters kicked in to protect the screen and its watchers from the eye-searing glare as the fireball consumed the last remnants of the shell before beginning finally to fade.

A moment later, Sarek's voice erupted onto the bridge. *"Picard, is it your intention to return Kirk to the Vortex?"*

After a moment of shocked silence, Picard recovered his voice. *"Wisdom* on screen," he snapped, and Sarek's face appeared instantly. "What happened, Sarek?"

"If you wish to restore your timeline, Picard, answer my question."

Darting a look at Kirk, who seemed as puzzled as himself, Picard scowled. "That *was* the plan," he said, "but if you can—"

"There is no time for discussion, Picard," Sarek said, more tension in his voice than Picard had ever heard in any Vulcan's. *"Proceed to the Vortex if such is your wish."*

"I won't *know* if it is or not—unless you answer my question: *Did* you destroy that Borg ship? If you did, I would say we have more options than you led us to believe."

Before Sarek could reply, his image vanished from the viewscreen.

For a seemingly interminable moment the Borg Queen was paralyzed with shock and pain as the distant ship that had for a few minutes served as her body was torn apart and vaporized. Like the equally impossible sensation of exhilaration, it had been resurrected from a past that, until these last few hours, she had thought dead and forgotten.

But then it was over, and she was once again whole, once again fully rational.

And she knew instantly what had happened.

The ship she had been controlling had been destroyed—
because of her!

Anger—yet another unwelcome ghost from that distant past—swept over her. But not anger at the Picard
creature or whoever had triggered the destruction of her
ship but at herself, at her rashness, at the sheer *irra-
tionality* of her actions.

The alarms she herself had put in place decades ago
in every Borg vessel had been warning her. She had
sensed those warnings, but she had brushed them aside.
She had been so absorbed in her obsessive pursuit of Picard that she had failed to instantly comprehend their
meaning or their importance. Worse, her control of the
ship had been so complete, the ship so much an integral
part of herself, that she had, unknowingly, kept the *ship*
from reacting.

She had kept the ship and its thousands upon thousands
of drones from saving themselves.

It would not happen again.

Her actions from this point on would be dictated by
strict logic.

And that logic now overwhelmingly dictated that, in
order to be absolutely certain that she would achieve her
primary goal, she would have to scale back the magnitude
of her intermediate goal by hundreds of worlds. Instead of
waiting another hundred years for thousands more ships to
be built, she would have to be satisfied with the thousands
already built. Without the assistance of the Narisians, she
would no longer have any way of learning what new
weapons some Alliance world might secretly devise in
those hundred years, and that kind of uncertainty was unacceptable. To accept it would be to accept the very system

that she had spent the last several subjective centuries proving wrong.

No, she had no choice. She had to initiate the final phase of her plan not a hundred years from now, but *now!*

The shrunken image of the *Enterprise* bridge vanished abruptly from the corner of Sarek's viewscreen, leaving only the full screen display that indicated the locations of the interphase-cloaked photon torpedoes. At the same moment an ear-piercing alarm erupted from his control panel, sending even his heart racing.

Because he knew instantly what it meant.

He had never before heard it except in simulations, but its meaning was unmistakable: Someone, somewhere had broken through the layers of security that surrounded the interphase-cloaked fleet.

With the neurobiosensor still continuously confirming his identity, he sent the signal that would freeze the entire system, locking out all incoming signals until everything could be analyzed and the source and nature of the intrusion determined.

Automatically, the system began spewing out teraquads of data, detailing the status and history of every interphase-cloaked device, including source, destination and content of every signal they had ever sent or received.

But before Sarek could even begin to search through the avalanche of data, another alarm went off.

And one of the specks of light on the screen winked out.

Followed by another.

And yet another.

As close to panic as a Vulcan could come, Sarek zeroed in on the final readings transmitted from the now-missing ships, scanning them rapidly. Everything appeared completely normal until—

Impossible! With the system frozen, not even *he* could force a detonation command through.

But *someone* had.

Milliseconds before the datastreams ended abruptly, all three devices had received—and accepted—an unauthorized detonation signal.

And on his screen, still more lights were winking out.

His heart only now beginning to slow, he re-transmitted the signal that would—*should!*—freeze every single device, making it impossible for them to detonate or decloak or even *move*.

But it had no more effect than the first such signal. The remaining thousands of lights continued to vanish in ever greater numbers until, after less than sixty seconds, every single one was gone, leaving only the muted specks that were the Borg vessels.

Though he knew it wouldn't help, Sarek called up another set of readings and yet another.

The same detonation signal appeared in every one, just milliseconds before the readings ended.

But no decloaking signals.

The photon torpedoes had been detonated, every one, but not in *this* dimension, where the explosions would have at least *damaged* the Borg cubes they were clustered around. Instead, their deadly power had been released in that other dimension, where it had no effect whatsoever on the Borg or on anything at all in this dimension—except for extinguishing the specks of light on his viewscreen.

They knew, Sarek thought bleakly. *All this time, they knew.*

They must have known for years, perhaps from the very beginning of the program. Even the Borg couldn't have found a way to defeat the fleet's entire security system in the few minutes that had passed since he had revealed its existence by destroying the one Borg ship.

It had been the spies, of course. There were Narisians on every Alliance world and on virtually every Alliance ship. They must have long ago informed the Borg of the interphase-cloaked torpedoes. And the Borg had devised a way to destroy them despite the security measures. They had been watching and waiting ever since, letting the Alliance waste its resources on a weapon they knew they could destroy in seconds.

If only he had destroyed *both* nearby Borg vessels, the *Enterprise* could at least have reached the Vortex, and there would have been a chance to restore the timeline Picard and Kirk and Scott and the rest had come from.

But now, with that remaining Borg vessel more than capable of destroying any Alliance ship—any *fleet* of Alliance ships!—there was no way Kirk could be returned to the Vortex.

But the being they called Guardian . . .

Sarek was reaching for the control panel to enter the command that would re-open the channel to the *Enterprise* when yet another alarm went off.

Contact had still not been reestablished with the *Wisdom* when a rapidly flashing readout clamored for Data's attention. Kirk abruptly cut off his restless pacing and peered over the android's shoulder.

"Captain," Data said as he scanned the information, "chronometric radiation is once again decreasing. The timeline would appear to be achieving even more stability."

What now? Kirk wondered as Picard turned toward Guinan.

"Could the destruction of the Borg cube be causing this?" Picard asked.

"I do not know, Captain."

"Your feelings—"

She shook her head, momentarily lowering her eyes. "They are telling me nothing."

"Captain," Data broke in, "this may be the cause. The sensor shield around the Terran system has just fallen."

Kirk's stomach suddenly knotted and he involuntarily averted his eyes as the image on the viewscreen shifted, centering on distant Earth. For a moment all he could see in his mind's eye were the zombie-like faces of his friends and family, even of himself, now nothing more than creatures that had once been human but now retained only enough of their humanity to be sickened by what had happened to them.

And all apparently because of him.

With an effort that he hoped was invisible to Picard and the others, particularly Scotty, Kirk regained control of himself and raised his eyes to the viewscreen, where Data was rapidly increasing the magnification, zooming in on a single point of light at the center of the screen.

"That is Terra's sun," he said, pointing out the obvious.

But then, as the magnification continued to increase, countless tiny dots began to appear all around the brightening star, all moving relentlessly outward.

For a timeless moment, Picard felt as if he were paralyzed, suffocating in a poisonously unbreathable atmosphere, unable to either resist or die.

As if he had once again been absorbed by the Borg, whose ships now swarmed across the *Enterprise* viewscreen by the hundreds, perhaps thousands.

For that was what each dot represented: a Borg ship.

He knew without having to ask. In the aftermath of the pain inflicted on him by the one Borg ship's destruction, he had once again heard the Borg whispering in his mind. The link forged by that destruction had persisted, outlasting the destruction itself for a brief moment. There had been no specific words like those that had filtered into his half-waking mind earlier, nor even the wordless intuitions he had reluctantly become accustomed to. Instead, it had been a myriad of distant voices, like the murmur of a vast and invisible crowd, rising and falling, imparting nothing but an overwhelming feeling of restlessness, of apprehension.

Orders, his Locutus memories told him, an ocean of orders sweeping out in massive waves, setting in zombie-like motion millions of drones and the ships they controlled and maintained.

"How many?" he asked when he was once again able to speak.

"Two-thousand-three-hundred-eleven, Captain," Data said.

"Borg?" Kirk asked, somehow keeping his voice steady.

"Almost certainly," Data agreed, glancing briefly at Picard, "but we are too distant for a reliable visual identification. The sensor readings, however, are consistent with Borg cubes."

"And what of Earth?" Picard asked, his voice barely above a whisper.

"Its atmosphere matches that of other Borg worlds," Data said matter-of-factly as the now-unblocked sensors began to take the measure of the distant star and its attendant worlds. "Its overall mass is approximately five percent less than in our universe. The other terrestrial planets have also lost—"

"We get the picture, Data," Riker snapped. "They've been strip-mining the solar system to build their damn cubes. And using what's left of Earth as a breeding colony to fill them."

"From what you people told me about this bunch," Kirk said, "I can't believe you were expecting anything less." He pulled in a ragged breath. "But what's important now is, where the hell are they going?"

"They are moving in several directions," Data said as his eyes darted across the readouts. "However, ninety-three of them are heading directly for the *Enterprise*."

"*Picard!*"

Sarek's image reappeared abruptly on the viewscreen.

"Sarek, what—" Picard began, but the Vulcan cut him off unceremoniously.

"*Proceed to the Guardian's world immediately, Picard. It is your only chance.*"

"But if you can destroy the Borg ships—"

"*I cannot. I did destroy the one, and I believed I could destroy others, but I cannot. The weapons capable of doing so no longer exist. The Borg destroyed them all just moments ago.*"

"How—" Picard began, but again Sarek cut him off instantly.

"*You are wasting time, Picard.*"

"Arbiter Sarek is correct," Data said, not looking up from the data that streamed across his station's displays. "Even if we proceed at maximum warp, we may not be able to reach the Guardian's world, assuming it exists, before the Borg overtake us."

"Go!" Kirk broke in. "I'm no fan of the Guardian, but like the man says, if you can't throw me into the Vortex, it's your only chance!"

Picard suppressed a scowl, but he knew they were right, Sarek and Kirk both.

"Very well. Ensign Raeger, maximum warp on a course to—to where we *hope* the Guardian's world is."

As the ensign briefly acknowledged the order and the coordinates that followed, Picard returned his attention to Sarek. "I assume," he said after a moment's silence, "that you fully understand what will happen if we succeed."

"*Of course, Picard. If you succeed, this timeline will cease to exist.*"

Picard nodded in grim apology. "And you also understand that there is no guarantee that it will either be replaced by or transformed into one that is more palatable."

"*I am logical, Picard, not naive. And logic indicates that the chance is worth the taking. If you do not take it— or if you fail—you and I and the entire Alliance and dozens of other worlds will either be destroyed or assimilated, apparently within days at most, if the fleet now emerging from the Terran system is any indication. You and I have both seen enough of the Borg to know that that is not acceptable. Now go while you have the chance. I will do what I can to delay pursuit.*"

Sarek raised his right hand in the familiar Vulcan gesture. Like Vulcan logic and honor, it was, not surprisingly, common to both universes. "*Live long and prosper,*" he said in an oddly soft voice in the moment before his image vanished from the viewscreen.

TWENTY-FOUR

SAREK CUT the link to the *Enterprise* and contacted Alliance Prime immediately, no longer making use of the ultra-secure channels he had used with Deputy Arbiter Koval. At the same time, he patched the image on his own viewscreen through not only to Alliance Prime but to the bridge of the *Wisdom* and to all other Alliance ships. During the seemingly interminable moments it took for the links to snake their way through subspace, Sarek hurried to the bridge where an uneasy Commander Varkan awaited him.

When all reachable ships were linked, Sarek implacably overrode all questions and gave every commander the projected path and velocity of the cluster of ninety-three Borg ships that were setting off after the *Enterprise*.

For an instant, just an instant, despite what he had told Picard only minutes before, despite all logic, Sarek could not help but think of telling them to gather all ships around Alliance Prime or even Vulcan and fight to the finish.

But any such action was obviously pointless. No more than fifty ships could be mustered for each world, and fifty *thousand* ships would not be enough.

So he gave them their orders.

Their logical but suicidal orders.

To the commanders' credit, virtually all obeyed without question, the Vulcans, Trill, Tellarites, and Klingons immediately, the Romulans after a brief hesitation. The only defectors were a half dozen Cardassians, who began an immediate race to return to Cardassia.

In the silence that followed, Sarek once again checked the progress of the *Enterprise* and of the leading Borg cubes. It was as he had feared: Unless the Borg were delayed several minutes, they would overtake the *Enterprise* before it could get within transporter range of the hypothetical Guardian's world. The *Enterprise* had managed to nudge its warp factor up by a minuscule fraction, but it would not be enough.

Everything depended on the hundred or so Alliance vessels that could, at one point or another, fling themselves in the path of the Borg fleet.

With the ships underway, including the *Wisdom*, it was time to explain.

But first he spoke the words that would transport ex-councilman Zarcot from Interrogation directly to the bridge. Even an illogical, short-sighted fool such as he deserved to know why he was about to die—and a few moments to prepare for that death. Or to have the time to wonder, as Sarek himself wondered: Even if a new timeline was created to replace the disastrous one they believed they had inhabited all their lives, would they or anyone else ever know?

Even in dreams?

Kirk, like everyone else on the bridge, winced inwardly as the last of the distant Alliance ships—a scattered school of minnows throwing themselves in front of an oncoming swarm of sharks—flared and vanished from the *Enterprise* viewscreen. The Borg, except for a single temporarily disabled cube, were back to full speed by the time they swept through the last of the clouds of molecular debris that were all that remained of Sarek's fleet.

"Sarek's delaying action gained us approximately two minutes, Captain," Data said. "However, unless our speed can be even further increased, the Borg will still be within weapons range before we can reach the Guardian's world."

Picard grimaced but did not contact engineering. Any such action, Kirk knew, would only be a distraction to Commander La Forge, who was already doing everything humanly possible to squeeze the last ounce of speed out of the warp drive. The chief engineer had already disabled a half dozen automated safeguards, trusting to his instincts to know when to throttle back temporarily, when to give one particular weak link a brief rest before pushing it once again past its design limits. He suspected that Scotty himself couldn't have done better on the old *Enterprise*.

"At least Sarek and his people won't be turned into Borg zombies," Kirk muttered. His own so-called sacrifice—a single life that, by all rights, should already have ended—seemed pitifully small by comparison. Even if the *Enterprise was* able by some miracle to reach the Guardian, even if the Guardian did require something more of him than his death—

An almost inaudible moan cut into his dismal chain of thought. Looking to one side, he saw Scotty, his lips pressed tightly together, his eyes barely slits.

"We're not lost yet, Scotty," he said automatically but so softly no one else could possibly hear, though he couldn't help but notice that the one called Guinan glanced momentarily away from the viewscreen as he spoke. "We've gotten out of worse."

But as he reached a hand out toward the engineer's arm, Scotty turned abruptly and, with lowered eyes, hurried to the turbolift.

Stifling an impulse to follow and give the engineer a probably useless pep talk, Kirk turned back to the viewscreen.

And forced himself to face the truth.

They couldn't reach the Vortex.

They couldn't reach the Guardian, even if it *did* exist.

But one obvious possibility remained, a possibility that had been in the back of his mind from the start, as it doubtless had been in Picard's and everyone else's.

His own death, not in the Vortex but here and now.

It *might* do the trick.

Or it might not.

But it was better than no chance at all.

He leaned down and spoke softly in Picard's ear.

"No! Kirk must not die *here!*"

The words erupted from Guinan's lips like a cork from a bottle, driven by the sudden pressure of a "feeling" so intense it literally sent chills through her entire body.

And brought her own burden of guilt crashing down on her shoulders, making her physically sway under the weight. Picard, standing next to Kirk just inside his ready room, reached out worriedly to steady her.

"Guinan?"

She shook her head helplessly. Barring a miracle beyond even anything she could imagine, they were all doomed to spend the remaining few hours of their lives in this misbegotten universe that should never have come into existence in the first place.

And wouldn't have, except for her interference.

Suddenly, a sharp pain knifed through her temples, sending her lurching sideways, her knees almost buckling. Automatically grasping Picard's still-outstretched arm to keep from falling, she felt the pain spread out through her head like a clinging spray of acid. In the same moment Picard's ready room seemed to fade and ripple as if seen through a distorting lens, and a shadowy alien landscape wavered into existence in the near distance, completely surrounding her, extending to a distant, indistinct horizon.

"Jean-Luc," she heard herself say as she collapsed into darkness, not sure if she was whispering or shouting, pleading or apologizing for the disaster that was enveloping them.

"Guinan!"

Brushing Kirk aside, Picard dropped to his knees at her side on the ready room floor. She was still breathing, but her pulse was elusive. Her eyes, squinting in pain when she had fallen, were now wide open.

And utterly blank.

His heart pounding, Picard tapped his combadge. "Dr. Crusher, transport Guinan directly to sickbay. Whatever's happening—"

He broke off and hastily stood up as her body was enveloped in the glimmer of a transporter field.

"You have the bridge, Number One," he said as he emerged onto the bridge and headed directly for the turbolift with Kirk close behind.

By the time they arrived in sickbay, Guinan was stretched out on a biobed, Beverly Crusher standing over her with a medical scanner.

"What is it?" Picard asked without preamble as he hurried to stand on the opposite side of the biobed while Kirk remained near the door. "What's wrong with her?"

Dr. Crusher shook her head with an impatient "don't-rush-me" look as she continued to move the scanner over Guinan's head and torso.

After what seemed like hours to Picard, Crusher looked up. "Well?" he prompted when she didn't immediately speak.

"All readings for which I have El-Aurian referents are normal, but—"

"Like the dead Narisian," Picard snapped. "That's *not* what I want to hear."

"It *isn't* what you're hearing, Captain. Or at least it's not what I'm saying. The Narisian's organs were all completely functional but they weren't functioning, like an engine that had been turned off. And she was dead. Guinan's organs all appear to be not only functional but functioning perfectly. And she is entirely alive."

"But unconscious. Why—"

Crusher cut him off with a shake of her head. "Not unconscious, Captain, at least not according to a neural scan. All indications are that she is fully conscious. If anything, her level of neural activity indicates she's considerably *more* conscious than normal, even for an El-Aurian. Although that could just be *her* normal level of activity. I've never run a neural scan on her before."

"So what do we do? Can you wake her up?"

She sighed impatiently. "I told you, Captain, she *is* awake. She just isn't *here*."

Picard was silent a moment as he looked down at the face of his friend. "If you could get comparison readings," he said, "from her alter ego in this universe—would that help?"

"I honestly don't know, but it couldn't hurt. And talking

to that other Guinan might be a good idea, anyway. Assuming the same thing hasn't happened to her."

"I'll see what I can do." Tapping his combadge, he turned to the nearest turbolift. "Number One, I'm on my way to the bridge. Try again to contact the *D'Zidran*—if it still exists."

"The *D'Zidran* is on screen, Captain," Riker half shouted as Kirk and Picard erupted from the turbolift onto the bridge.

A chill gripped Kirk's spine like an icy hand, overwhelming all his other conflicting emotions, as he looked at the viewscreen and realized what he was seeing there: the *D'Zidran* was close to, perhaps even in orbit around the Guardian's world.

He had no idea how or why it had gotten there, but there was no question in his mind but that it *was* there. Nothing else could account for the way the image of the *D'Zidran*'s bridge undulated in and out of focus as if seen through the rippling surface of a wind-blown sea.

Which, in a sense, it was: a sea not of matter but of time, its very fabric warped and re-warped by the unfathomable power of the object on the surface of the planet; *the Guardian of Forever.*

Kirk had seen those undulations, had felt them as the old *Enterprise*—his *Enterprise*—sped through them. There could be nothing else in the universe—in any universe—quite like them.

The fact that the face of the *D'Zidran*'s commander was one that he recognized, not fondly, from his own past barely registered as Picard, a couple paces ahead of him, said:

"Commander Tal, let me speak with Guinan."

Tal's undulating image stared out of the screen silently, expressionlessly, while Picard's words ricocheted through the subspace network to the distant ship. Finally, abruptly, Tal shook his head. *"She is not here. She has transported down to the surface of a planet she called the 'Guardian's world'."*

Kirk's stomach lurched at the words as he remembered what Scotty had said about this odd and ageless woman, about how she had been present at—had been instrumental in—each and every key incident that had led inexorably to the present situation.

And now she was on the Guardian's world, where all time was, if the Guardian felt cooperative, instantly accessible.

What, he wondered with a new chill, was she up to now?

The view from space of the Guardian's world had not prepared Guinan for the somber reality that enveloped her when the shimmer of the transporter energy faded. From the relative safety of high orbit, she had looked down on the sensor-produced images of the endless ruins, observing them objectively, noting with interest the countless different styles of buildings, the lack of any city-like pattern to their distribution. Even the so-called time ripples of which she had been warned had seemed less a danger than a distraction as they swept across the face of the planet, warping her vision as they now and then reached out and sent waves of distortion through the orbiting *D'Zidran.*

But here on the surface, low-hanging slabs of rainless, lightning-streaked clouds, threatening a storm that never came, seemed to isolate her not only from the *D'Zidran* but from the stars themselves. She was not just surrounded by the planet-spanning ruins but felt in danger of becoming a prisoner of this strange world, of being somehow absorbed by it.

And yet, despite the fear, despite the utterly alien surroundings, despite the bleak wail of an unseen, unfelt wind—a wind that blew through time itself?—she felt as if she was somehow familiar with this world, as if she was *already* connected to it in some way that was as inexplicable as the feelings that had brought her here.

At the same time, again without knowing how or why, she realized that more of her "ghost memories" had emerged from whatever shadowy corners of her mind they had been lurking in.

Particularly real and vivid were those associated with the one called Picard and with his world. It was as if she had lived two lives simultaneously, both leading inevitably to this time and place. She was barely able to tell where one life began and the other ended, which was real and which was imagined.

And there was more, she knew, far more than the memories of those two lives. She could sense the existence of other memories, other lives in other times, but they were still beyond her reach, like shadowy creatures that moved, not quite silently, through a dense fog that swirled all around her.

You are not a stranger to this place, a voice said in her mind, and she looked around, startled.

And saw the Portal.

There was nothing else the misshapen torus *could* be.

In the midst of a chaos of ruins from a thousand different eras, a thousand different civilizations, it alone was . . . functional?

Alive?

It pulsed with energy, seen and unseen.

"How is it that you know me?" she asked, clothing the thought in words only out of recent habit. "I have never visited your world before."

Not in your current form, perhaps, but the shell you wear is irrelevant. It is you I recognize.

"Are you the source of the . . . 'guidance' I occasionally find myself subjected to?"

You receive guidance from no one but yourself.

"A future self?" she asked.

For you, as for me, there is no future and no past. There is only the eternal now.

She grimaced. This so-called Guardian of Forever was even less helpful than her feelings, what*ever* their source. The feelings at least told her *what* to do, even if they didn't tell her why.

"Can you help us to restore this universe to what it was before the stranger from the future interfered?" she asked.

The play of energy around the irregular torus that was the Portal intensified, as did the lightning displays in the rainless clouds, now roiling and darkening even more, as if the coming storm could no longer be held at bay. Even the keening of the unfelt wind grew louder.

Finally, the voice returned to her mind. *Through me it is possible to make all as it was. It is not possible to make all as it must be.*

"I do not understand."

You do not, and yet you do. You must look into yourself. The answer you seek is there, and there alone.

"You speak in riddles," she said, uncomfortably conscious of the irony of the accusation. "I still do not understand."

You must look more deeply. You must open the self you are now to all the selves you have been and will be.

And the Portal shimmered, seeming to become a mirror with a dozen facets, each reflecting a different image, but even as she tried to focus on them, they shattered into a hundred, then a thousand facets, until each facet was only an intense spot of sparkling light, and the entire Portal became a chaos of pulsing, crackling energy that part of her longed to plunge into while another part recoiled in terror.

The Vortex, one part of her mind screamed at her.

It is the Nexus, another part of her mind—another Guinan—whispered. *You/I/we have never left.*

Suddenly, she/they knew it was true.

And knew what the Guardian meant.

Tal's Guinan, Picard's Guinan and a thousand others on a thousand worlds in a thousand eras.

All were linked through that one brief instant when they had been trapped in that seductive domain beyond space, beyond time, in the heart of pure joy and contentment.

All were linked in that one brief instant before her/their physical body was torn free and plunged back into a reality she/they had by then come to despise.

All were linked in that one brief instant that was also forever.

You must look into yourself for the answer, the Guardian of Forever had said.

At last, she knew what it had meant.

She must look into that part of herself that still existed there, in that eternal instant that stretched from the beginning of time to the end and perhaps beyond—that part of herself that was, she realized, the source of her feelings.

In this life and all others.

Allowing herself to remember that which she had struggled for decades to forget, she let fall the barriers she herself had erected in those agonizing moments of her "rescue."

And was overwhelmed once again by the memory of what she had lost when the *Enterprise*-B's transporters had torn her physical shell free of the Nexus: an eternity of unimaginable bliss.

But with the memory of that lost bliss came also the answer she sought.

An answer that spanned more than three centuries.

Kirk must return to the Vortex.

The Nexus.

Not to be killed but to be called forth to help Picard seventy-five years later.

For Picard was himself essential to restoring what was. He and he alone, with his rudimentary link to the Borg, could pursue the Borg back in time and prevent them from assimilating Earth and creating this abortive yet essential timeline.

Do that, and her world would die. El-Auria would die and Earth would live, and all would be as it was.

But not yet as it must be.

The words came not from the Guardian but from the deepest core of her selves, that self that always had and always would exist within the Nexus. The words flared through her entire being, tearing aside the final veil and exposing the horror of what yet could be, a horror beside which the destruction of the world she had for a few brief centuries thought of as her home was of no more consequence than the death of a single drone would be to the entire Borg Collective.

She/they knew what must be done.

And, for the first time, received a fragmentary and soul-chilling glimpse of *why*.

TWENTY-FIVE

GUINAN'S EYES snapped open to find Picard and Crusher standing over her worriedly. Kirk stood to one side, his face unreadable.

As she realized she was once more alone in her mind, a bleak feeling of loss and isolation swept over her, just as it had when she had been torn from the Nexus. But this was far less intense. She had been separated now only from another part of herself, not from a universe of endless bliss. And her sense of urgency was so strong that, this time, she was able to force the feeling aside in an instant.

Sitting up, she swung her legs off the biobed. "We have to return to the Vortex," she said, standing up before either of them could press her back onto the bed.

"What the devil—" Picard began while Crusher brought the medical scanner back into play.

"I'll explain later," Guinan said, "if I can still remember it later."

"But what happened?" Picard persisted.

"Her readings are unchanged," Crusher said, shaking her head.

"I—*we* spoke with the Guardian. The only way to restore the original timeline is to—" She paused, turning her head to look directly at Kirk. "The only way to restore the original timeline is for you to be sent into the Vortex you were rescued from."

Kirk nodded, his expression unchanged. "I can't say I'm surprised. Can I assume that just killing me still isn't acceptable?"

She shook her head, repressing the urge to tell Kirk that it wasn't death that awaited him in the Nexus but something far more wondrous, something she envied him more than she had ever envied any living being. Feelings aside, however, she knew that for the true nature of the Nexus— the Vortex—to be known could be nearly as dangerous as for the existence of the Guardian to be public knowledge. And Kirk, knowing that the only alternative was to be destroyed or captured by the Borg, had already indicated his unequivocal willingness to surrender himself to the Vortex.

"No matter how willing he is, Guinan," Picard said, "it can't be done. The Borg are everywhere. It would take a miracle to get within a parsec of the Vortex now."

"I know that's what you think, Captain, but it is essential that we do."

"But you have no suggestions as to how?"

"I'm sorry. All I know is that the Guardian claims there is no other choice. And that there is even more at stake than you know, more than you can imagine."

Picard continued to look at her, directly into her eyes, for a second, then another and yet another. Finally he nodded, not so much in agreement as in capitulation, but before he could more than tap his combadge to speak with the bridge and order the necessary course change, she lowered her eyes and swept past them all to the turbolift.

*   *   *

So, Kirk thought as Picard headed for the turbolift himself, issuing orders as he walked, *the Guardian really* doesn't *want me dead. It wants me sent into the Vortex.*

Which at this late date just happens to be impossible.

Without a miracle.

And isn't it a remarkable coincidence that I happen to know just where to find the number one card-carrying miracle worker in all of Starfleet?

"Captain Scott, I owe you an apology."

Scotty looked up from the drink that had been sitting before him for several minutes, his hands clasped around the glass as if it needed to be held down in order to keep it from leaping, unbidden, to his lips. Guinan stood across the Ten-Forward bar from him. Somehow it didn't surprise him that she had gotten there without his noticing.

"Aye, perhaps you do, lassie. If you had not been at that Glasgow bar . . ." He shrugged, lowering his eyes and renewing his grip on the drink.

"If I hadn't delayed you those few minutes," she continued for him, speaking softly, "you wouldn't have met that young ensign and you wouldn't have—"

"His name was Matt Franklin," he said, his eyes still on the drink, a touch of anger in his voice. "And if I hadn't met him, I would not have been on the *Jenolen* and I would have lived out my life in my own time. I would not have been on *this Enterprise,* I would not have found that Klingon ship, and I could not have come back here and caused all this with my bloody meddling!"

He broke off, his stomach knotting even more tightly as the urge to down the drink in a single swallow, then grab the bottle and drain it in stinging gulps grew more powerful.

"Tell me something I do *not* know!" he grated, the anger boiling up.

"Very well," she said, her already soft voice becoming even quieter, almost a whisper, as she leaned closer over the bar. "In this timeline that you created by saving your friend Kirk, my world survived. The Borg bypassed it. You could say that, by delaying you those few minutes, I traded my world for yours—and for the entire Federation."

"But you couldn't have known—" he began, then stopped as he remembered what he had told Kirk about this seemingly ageless woman. *Strange things happen when she's around.*

"You *did* know?"

Guinan hesitated, steeling herself. The "feelings" had, over the centuries, demanded many things of her. They had driven her to warn friends and enemies alike of known and unknown dangers. They had forced her to keep secrets from friends while blurting them out to strangers. At their behest, she had ordered and cajoled and pleaded and tricked. She had even withheld information and used words to obscure the truth rather than reveal it.

But she had never been required to lie.

Until now.

"I did know," she said. "I don't know how I knew, but I did. I knew my world would be saved. What I didn't know was the price for its survival."

And she waited, knowing that what Captain Scott would do in the next few hours was crucial, not just for a few dozen worlds in and around the Alliance but for billions. In those hours, he had to decide whether he would continue his slide into the depths of guilt and self flagellation that had started on the bridge of the *Enterprise*-B or pull himself together and become again what he had once been.

For it was only then that he could fulfill the destiny she had glimpsed on the Guardian's world, the destiny that was the reason they were both here, the reason she had, all unknowingly, shepherded him to this time and this place, all to insure that he would, somewhere and someday, do or say or inspire something that would tip the balance of the universe for all time. The effect of that action, whatever it turned out to be—or perhaps the effect just of his presence— might not be seen for a dozen years or a dozen generations, but it *would* come, directly or indirectly.

He *would* make his indelible mark.

If he somehow pulled himself together in the next few hours.

And she, by uttering that meager handful of words, by shouldering part of the burden of guilt he had until then borne alone, had done her small part in nudging him toward recovery, even rebirth.

Or so her "feelings" told her.

What they did *not* tell her was how he—or any of them, no matter what decision he made—could survive the next few hours, let alone elude the Borg and deliver Kirk to the Nexus.

A mixture of relief and anger swept over Scotty as the meaning of the woman's words sank in: relief that he had not been solely responsible for this Borg hell, anger that she had tricked him.

"And now that you *do* know the price?"

"The original timeline must be restored."

"Aye," he said, his voice filled with sarcasm, "is *that*

all? I don't suppose you'd have any idea how that wee task might be accomplished?"

"It's simple, Scotty," a familiar voice said from just behind him. "You have to put me back where you should have left me—in the Vortex."

Scotty spun around on the bar stool. "Don't be daft, Captain, I couldn't—"

"You have to," Kirk said flatly. "Or *somebody* has to. The decision is in. Your friend here just talked to the Guardian, don't ask me how, and *it* says getting me back into the Vortex is the only way." He looked questioningly at Guinan. "Right?"

She nodded but remained silent.

"And you trust her word?"

Kirk's eyebrows shot up quizzically. "Is there some reason I shouldn't?"

For a moment Scotty was ready to blurt out what Guinan had just told him, but he held his tongue. Even if her delaying him in that bar *had* been a deliberate act, *he* was the one who had made the final and indefensible decision to slingshot back and disrupt time. She had merely given him the opportunity.

Scotty shook his head, his stomach churning at the thought of actually doing what Kirk had just told him was necessary to remedy his "mistake."

Kirk looked from one to the other. "All right, then. It's agreed?"

"Aye, Captain, but—"

"But me no buts, Scotty. If we don't do *something* in the next few hours, we're all going to be either dead or, if we're *really* unlucky, a bunch of Borg zombies. And tossing me into the Vortex is the only idea on the table. Unless you have something else in mind."

Scotty shook his head desolately.

"Besides," Kirk went on, giving Guinan a momentary glance, not quite a wink, "now that I've had a little time to think about it, I'm not all that sure that a dive into the Vortex is necessarily fatal. If all the timeline needed to snap back was for me to be dead, there are a lot easier ways of accomplishing that than by running a Borg gauntlet. As an old friend of ours likes to say, Scotty, 'It's only logical.' And Guinan tells me the Guardian specifically vetoed the idea of simply having me killed. Just like her own 'feelings' did."

A twinge of hope tugged at the knot in Scotty's stomach. It *was* logical.

But it was also hopeless. "Even if you're right, it can't be done. The Borg—"

"The Borg are an obstacle, I admit. But you've overcome obstacles before and saved my hide more times than I like to remember. One time too many, in fact, so now you have to *un*save me."

"But how—"

"*I* don't know," Kirk said with a laugh. "You're the miracle worker. And this superdeluxe version of the *Enterprise* you have to work with is practically a miracle in itself."

"Aye, and that's the bloody problem! I don't even know how this *Enterprise* works. I told you what a mess I made of things when they first brought me on board. If you don't believe me, just ask Commander La Forge."

"So when did not knowing how something works stop you before? You think I've forgotten how you jury-rigged the *Bounty?* You hadn't had so much as a basic Klingon Technology 101 course, and still you practically rebuilt that bucket of bolts and made it do things the Klingons never even dreamed of—like hauling a pair of whales back from the twentieth century!"

"But—"

"I told you, Scotty, but me no buts. Look, maybe you'll fail, but so what? You've failed before, not often, but you have. The one thing you've *never* done, old friend, is give up without even trying! *And you're not going to start now!* There's a lot more than just Earth at stake, so get yourself down to engineering and plant yourself in front of a terminal or rip some control panels apart or do whatever it is you engineers do when you want to find out how things work or you're looking for inspiration. You've got all of six hours to find a way for Picard to get us past the Borg, or through them, or whatever!"

Impossible, Scotty thought, but he knew—had known all along, somewhere deep inside—that the captain *was* right about one thing. He never *had* given up without at least trying, and now of all times was *not* the time to start, especially since he was the one who had, albeit with a little help, created the problem in the first place. He might—probably would—die in the next few hours, but he would at least die *trying*.

Standing up abruptly, before he lost his nerve yet again, he pushed the still-filled glass and the bottle across the bar toward Guinan.

"If you have any influence on this *Enterprise,* lassie," he said, "you may have to use it with Commander La Forge to get him to let me back in engineering at all."

Scotty stared in frustration at the words and formulas and diagrams as they flashed by on the screen. After Guinan's promised intercession, a harried La Forge had reluctantly directed him to an out-of-the-way terminal in engineering, where he had been rooted ever since, almost three hours now, but it was looking more hopeless by the minute. It was true he now had a better idea how the *Enterprise*-D's version of the warp drive worked, but compared to La Forge, he was still in kindergarten. If La Forge hadn't been able to nurse a few more decimals of warp speed out of it by now, there was certainly nothing Scotty could do to help.

In theory, Kirk had been right, but not in reality. In theory, no one should give up without even trying, but in reality there was damned little chance that it was going to do any good. Even if there *was* a miracle waiting to happen somewhere in the new *Enterprise,* Montgomery Scott wasn't the one to find it. Every "miracle" he'd pulled off on his *Enterprise* had been grounded in solid scientific and technological knowledge and reasoning, even if his so-called intuition had allowed him to now and then skip a few steps. He had had a deep, hard-won understanding of the equipment, an understanding of what the rules were and *why* they were, and that had given him the freedom to bend or break those rules in order to get results the designers never intended. Even on the original *Bounty,* the rules had been the same and even most of the Klingon technology had not been all that different from that of Federation starships.

But even if the Borg's speed could be matched or exceeded—as La Forge was still struggling unsuccessfully to do—there was no way the lone *Enterprise* could flash past dozens or hundreds of Borg ships without being vaporized. And even if it *could* get past them by sheer speed alone, it would have to drop out of warp, lower its shields and become a sitting duck long enough to transport the captain into the Vortex. Even if he could find a way to bypass the shields with the transporter, as he had in the *Jenolen* and again in the *Wisdom,* transporting from a ship moving at warp speed to someplace *not* moving at warp speed hadn't worked in the days of the original *Enterprise* and it still didn't work. There was simply no way a transport could be completed in the milliseconds they would be within transporter range. That was one rule that was neither bendable nor breakable.

It was not even possible—according to Guinan and the Guardian, at least—to send the entire *Enterprise,* with Kirk on board, into the Vortex at maximum warp. It had to be Kirk and *only* Kirk.

No, the only way to get at the Vortex was to get the Borg to go back to ignoring the *Enterprise.* Or to become invisible, which would have been easy enough if he hadn't mislaid the *Bounty 2.* Since no one in this timeline except one small group of Cardassians had stumbled across "standard" cloaking technology, the Borg had probably never developed a defense for it, only for interphase cloaking, which wasn't, technically speaking, cloaking at all but a form of dimensional shifting.

But the *Bounty 2* was gone, probably wiped out along with everything else in that now-defunct timeline, and there was no way of building a cloaking device for the *Enterprise,* not even if he had six months instead of six hours.

Unless . . .

Suddenly, as if pulled by a mental rubber band, his mind shot back to the days immediately after the *Jenolen,* when the entire *Enterprise* had seemed like a giant technological candy store. Before his ham-handed ways had gotten him exiled from Engineering, one of his seemingly misguided enthusiasms had been holodeck technology. And one of the questions he'd asked, one of the questions that La Forge had politely laughed off as being too ridiculous to even consider—

Excited for the first time since this misbegotten universe had sprung into being around him, Scotty wiped the warp drive data from the terminal screen and began racing through specs and schematics of the holo generators.

After five minutes, his heart was pounding as if he'd run a mile, not sat transfixed as he scanned dozens of schematics and engineering specifications.

Standing up abruptly, he started to search the walls for the nearest intercom but then remembered the tiny device—combadge, they had called it—that Picard had given him.

"Bridge," he said, giving it something closer to a slap than a tap, "I cannot be sure, but I may have found a wee something."

TWENTY-SIX

"WELL, Mr. La Forge, will it work?" Picard asked as Scotty lurched to a verbal halt. They were gathered not on the bridge but in central engineering where a still-harried La Forge was constantly monitoring and occasionally adjusting several critical parameters in the warp drive.

"I honestly don't know, Captain, but one thing *is* obvious. If we adjust the deflector fields to block sensor scans rather than incoming particle and energy weapons, we'd be defenseless. A single phaser hit in the right place, unhindered by the shields, could destroy the warp core or turn the *Enterprise* into the biggest photon torpedo on record."

Kirk, standing next to Scotty, shook his head, almost laughing. "And just how long would the deflectors, at full strength, hold up against what one cube, let alone dozens of them, can throw at us? I seem to recall that Sarek's entire fleet didn't last very long."

"We've never had to find out," La Forge began, "but—"

"Less than a minute," Picard interrupted, drawing automatically on Locutus's remaining memories, "if we were to be extremely lucky and only one Borg ship attacked. A matter of seconds if several fired on us simultaneously."

"So what do you have to lose?" Scotty looked from one to the other while Kirk nodded his agreement.

Picard pulled in a breath, his eyes meeting Guinan's for an instant, looking for an assent that may or may not have been there.

"As you say, Mr. Scott. Make it so. Quickly. At best, we have two hours before the nearest Borg ships are within weapons range."

Unlike on the ill-fated *Enterprise*-B, the majority of the modifications and reroutings on the *Enterprise*-D could be done via the computer once the necessary safeguards were disabled.

The first and easiest step was to take some images—including that of a Borg cube—from the main computer memory and transfer them to the holodeck computers. Somewhat trickier—but right down La Forge's alley—was overriding several additional, hard-wired safeguards in order to be able, at the last possible moment, to modify the phase and frequency of the deflectors, making the field opaque to subspace sensor scans rather than to the usual array of particles and energies.

Scotty himself, of necessity, took on the task of modifying the outputs of the holographic imagery subsystem, which normally drove the billions of holo diodes that lined the walls of the holodeck. What he needed the subsystem to do now was what La Forge had, a seeming lifetime ago, politely derided as impossible: provide a modulating input to the conformal transmission grids that lined the exterior hull and produced the spacial distortion that made the deflectors possible. Normally the distortion and hence the deflector field itself conformed to the shape of the hull, essentially producing an impenetrable "skin" covering every square centimeter of the ship's exterior. With the inputs of the transmission grids modulated by the imagery subsystem, however, the grid system would be fooled into producing a deflector field not in the shape of the underlying *Enterprise* but in the shape of whatever image was being provided by the imagery subsystem computers.

In this case, a Borg cube.

Or so Scotty believed, based on what he feared might be a comparatively superficial understanding of the technology involved. He just hoped that it wasn't, as some had suggested, a case of not knowing enough to understand why it wouldn't work.

But it felt right, just as the countless shortcuts and "tricks" he had pulled off on the old *Enterprise* had felt right and had, when the crunch came, been proven right.

Unfortunately, no matter how well it worked, this particular trick would not produce a visual image of a cube. That would require lining the outside of the ship with specially augmented holo diodes, something that *might* be accomplished in a well-equipped spacedock but never in deep space under warp nine conditions. The transmission grids would, at best, produce a deflector field that would look to Borg sensors like a Borg cube. To someone near enough to get a visual sighting, however, it would look like what it really was: the *Enterprise*.

According to Picard's Locutus memories, that *might* be enough.

If the nebula they had located in the *Enterprise* data banks existed in this universe.

If they could reach that nebula before the Borg reached them.

And if they were very, very lucky.

In any event, nobody had come up with a better idea.

For the first time since her arrival more than two hundred subjective years ago, the Borg Queen emerged, physically, from the solar system that had once been the home of Species 5618. She had faith in her armada for most things, but it was no better equipped to deal with the unexpected than was any other collection of Borg ships.

And the Picard creature's very presence was the epitome of the unexpected. By all tenets of logic, he could not exist, and yet he was here. By those same tenets, "memories" of events that had not yet happened, "memories" of her own destruction, could not exist, and yet they existed.

Waiting to happen—unless she could prevent it.

In the time since the idea had first occurred to her, she had only become more convinced that she was right despite the fact that under ordinary circumstances she would have dismissed it as impossible.

But the current situation was far from ordinary, even farther from predictable. Making use of the time sphere harvested from Species 1429 was by itself enough to introduce a measure of unpredictability, but that was only the beginning. When she had used it, in the aftermath of her matrix's takeover of Earth, she had intended to go back only a few days to warn her earlier self about the unexpectedly effective defense of Earth the Federation had mounted. The damage it had inflicted was such that, when the inevitable second wave of Federation ships would attack, her entire matrix would almost certainly be destroyed, and that was simply unacceptable. But instead of taking her back a few days, the time sphere had somehow malfunctioned, sending her back more than three centuries.

And now she was living through those three centuries again while—she assumed—her earlier self simultaneously lived through them for the first time. Knowing what her earlier self had done, she had for the most part been able to keep from interfering with that earlier self, particularly her work with the Narisians and others. Once the earlier self had obtained the time sphere and abandoned the Narisians and all the others, she had taken them over, continuing the control, knowing that her earlier self would never contact them again.

But the mere fact that she *was* living two lives simultaneously, the fact that she had crossed three centuries of time, meant that time was not inviolable. If she herself could physically travel back in time, then her mind, perhaps altered by that travel, could do the same—but without the assistance of the time sphere.

Therefore it was only logical that these "memories" of her own death at the hands of Picard were nothing less than a warning of that death sent back by her own future self, its final conscious act.

It was essential, therefore, that she tend to this matter herself, that she make absolutely certain that Picard *was* destroyed, once and for all.

The latest information indicated that Picard's ship, instead of continuing to flee, had turned about and was once again on a direct course for the Vortex. Which strengthened another of her theories, that Picard was attempting to reach the Vortex so that he and his ship could "disappear" the same way the other ship had "appeared" there. The ship, the *Enterprise,* would almost certainly be intercepted and destroyed, reduced to a spreading cloud of dissociated atoms by other Borg ships long before it could reach the Vortex.

She was, however, taking no chances. If the impossible came to pass and Picard's primitive ship eluded the dozens of Borg ships closing in on it, she and more dozens of ships would be waiting at his destination, the Vortex.

She would be waiting, and this time she would make no mistakes . . .

TWENTY-SEVEN

PICARD could almost feel the impatience radiating from Kirk as Ensign Raeger guided the *Enterprise* into the nebula. The Borg were still almost five minutes distant, but Kirk, seated where Counselor Troi normally sat, was leaning forward tensely, gripping the arms of the chair as if he thought he could speed up the ship by sheer force of will.

"All stop," Picard ordered as the last vestige of the external universe disappeared from the now completely blank viewscreen.

"The nebula is essentially identical to its counterpart in our own timeline, Captain," Data said. "Its extremely high levels of ionization severely restrict the range of our sensors as well as the Borg's. In most areas, the range appears to be less than one hundred thousand kilometers. However, because of the size and energy differentials between the *Enterprise* and the Borg ships, we will be able to detect approaching cubes at least twenty thousand kilometers before they can detect us."

Picard nodded tensely as Data switched to a broad-sweep, directional sensor scan, giving them, they hoped, a few additional thousands of kilometers of warning. Once that was done, there was nothing to do but wait and hope that the fragmentary memories left behind by Locutus were reliable and that his own extrapolations from those memories were valid. If not, the nebula they had searched out would be the grave not only of the *Enterprise* but of the Federation and the Alliance and probably much more.

Ten minutes later, the first cube appeared on the screen, moving toward them through the nebula at the Borg equivalent of minimum impulse. At a word from Picard, Raeger maneuvered the *Enterprise* laterally, keeping out of the hypothetical range of the Borg sensors. Soon a second cube appeared, its nebula-limited sensor scan overlapping that of the first.

Then a third appeared, and a fourth. The Borg were doing just as the Locutus memories had suggested: using the bulk of the fleet to methodically sweep the entire nebula while a smaller number remained outside, waiting to vaporize the *Enterprise* the moment it was flushed out, like a rabbit out of a briar patch.

Picard pulled in a breath as Raeger positioned the *Enterprise* halfway between the projected paths of two of the approaching Borg. "Now, Mr. La Forge," he said.

Picard waited, hardly breathing, as Scott's and La Forge's jury-rigged modifications were switched in, routing the outputs of the holodeck computers through a maze of buffers to the circuits that controlled the deflectors.

Abruptly, the viewscreen shimmered and went blank.

An instant later a half dozen warning lights flared. The *Enterprise* was, according to the sensors, surrounded by an impenetrable cube-shaped shell.

Which was precisely what they had been hoping for.

"Go to visual subsystems," Picard ordered.

The viewscreen remained blank, but the warning lights went out.

"Computer," La Forge said, "show projected positions of approaching vessels."

The four cubes reappeared, their images blinking to indicate they were not real, merely an indication of where the computer thought the actual objects were.

They waited.

Finally, Data spoke. "We are almost certainly within the area in which their sensors overlap."

Picard held his breath for another few seconds, as did almost everyone else on the bridge, until the images of the two nearest Borg cubes drew even with the *Enterprise*.

"Match their speed and course," Picard said even though Ensign Raeger was already doing precisely that.

Finally, the nebula began to thin and the blinking images vanished, replaced by real images provided by the visual observation subsystem. A dozen more cubes came into view in rapid succession as the nebula continued to thin. Finally, the stars reappeared.

By now the Borg sensors had almost certainly regained full function.

And directly ahead, well outside the nebula, another Borg cube came into visual range. One of the sentries, waiting to blast the *Enterprise* when it emerged.

Still holding his breath, Picard waited.

Nothing happened except that the cubes that had just emerged from the nebula turned and reentered at a different angle so they would sweep a different corridor.

Picard resumed normal breathing. Captain Scott's jury-rigging had worked.

And the fragmentary Locutus memories had been right. None of the cubes, not even the ones posted outside the nebula where their sensors were fully effective, had "noticed" the one additional cube that all their sensors must have detected. Like drones that were not programmed to detect humans inside a Borg ship unless they tripped over them, these ships were programmed only to detect the *Enterprise* or other similar ships. They were *not* programmed to detect a Borg ship that appeared out of nowhere—unless that ship was on a collision course with one of the others or posed some obvious, programmed-for threat.

"Set a course for the Vortex," Picard said into the relieved silence, "impulse power until we're past the sentries." Standing up abruptly, he looked down at Kirk, still seated in Troi's chair. "Could I speak with you a moment, Captain? In my ready room?"

Kirk glanced at Data and the viewscreen in front of him. "Sure, if there's time. This is one deadline I don't dare miss, much as I might like to."

Annoyed at himself for feeling uncomfortable, Picard watched as Kirk leaned close to the ready room's softly lit aquarium and the fish gliding gracefully back and forth. He had brought Kirk here to—

To what? Not apologize, but . . . make sure that they . . . understood each other? Kirk, he suspected, would be far better at this, whatever "this" was. Kirk might be too impulsive for Picard's taste, but the man's obvious skills in dealing with people—

"Its own containment field?" Kirk asked, looking up from the aquarium.

Picard nodded, relieved that the other had spoken first. "We would've lost it a hundred times over if it didn't have one."

Kirk grinned. "So things still get shaken up when something gets through the shields." He looked back at the shimmery-finned swimmers. "They are sort of soothing. I could've used something like that now and then in the old *Enterprise*. But I can't imagine that you got me in here to show me your fish."

Picard pulled in a deep breath, a sigh in reverse. "I just didn't want you to think that, when I first saw you and Captain Scott—" He paused, sucking in another breath. "You no doubt sensed occasional . . ."

"Disapproval?" Kirk asked, smiling.

"That's as good a word as any," Picard admitted.

Kirk made a sound just short of a chuckle. "Understandable. Scotty and I had just screwed up an entire quadrant of the galaxy, maybe more."

"Understandable, perhaps, but what I wanted you to know is, I suspect there was also a touch of envy involved in my reaction to you. Envy for the kind of bond you obviously developed with your crew, something so strong it would lead Captain Scott to do what he did. I didn't realize it at the time, though. Or couldn't admit it to myself. In any event, when I first realized what Captain Scott was attempting, long before I first laid eyes on you, I was thinking things about you that I shouldn't have, and it showed through in my attitude toward you when we *did* finally meet. I had even found myself wondering how you felt about what Captain Scott had done. Were you appalled? Or gratified? I knew you would never—"

"To tell the truth, Picard—we are telling the truth, right? To tell the truth, I *was*—well, gratified isn't quite the right word, but flattered? Hell yes! A bit appalled, too, of course, knowing that he'd taken that kind of risk—and lost—just to save one person. And don't think I didn't tell him so."

"But it obviously didn't affect your relationship. Guinan told me what you did down in Ten-Forward, convincing Captain Scott to keep trying."

Kirk shrugged. "What can I tell you? We were together a long time. On the *Enterprise*." An almost dreamy looked seemed to swoop across Kirk's face like a shadow but was gone before Picard could be sure. "We were on that ship—those ships—a *long* time, went through a lot. It does something to you, the *Enterprise*. To everyone who serves on it, no matter what incarnation. Look at what Spock did for his first commander, Captain Pike. Risked court-martial and worse. Don't tell me you haven't felt it now and then."

He had, Picard realized, belatedly remembering the tremendous risks Riker, Data, and Worf had taken to rescue him after he had been assimilated by the Borg. But even then, as Locutus was purged from his body and mind, it hadn't been something he could have comfortably put into words, even to himself. And therefore he hadn't. Now, he nodded.

"I have," he said, resisting the compulsion to qualify his admission with a "perhaps" or an "it seemed."

"In any event," Picard continued abruptly, "I wanted you to know that, now, I have only the greatest admiration for you."

"Likewise, Captain. And under any other circumstances, I'd say it would be a privilege to work with you again someday." Kirk shrugged. "But who knows? No more than we know about the rules of time travel—or about the Vortex, for that matter—maybe we will. Or already have. But whatever happens," he added with another grin, "it's always nice to know that you made a difference."

Picard smiled. "You certainly did that."

"And so did you. Or should that be 'so *will* you'? Don't

forget, the Guardian not only wants *me* in the Vortex. It wants you—or Scotty, or *someone* on this ship, maybe several someones—*not* in the Vortex. That has to mean something. Have you asked your friend Guinan about *that?*"

Picard shook his head. "I don't think even she knows. Or if she does, she isn't talking."

"Time, Captain," Riker's voice came over Picard's combadge.

"Acknowledged, Number One."

After a moment's silence, Picard put his hand out. Kirk's eyebrows raised just slightly as he put his own hand out and the two captains shook firmly.

Despite his seemingly unruffled exterior, there was a lump in Picard's throat to match the butterflies in his stomach as he released Kirk's hand and watched him turn and, seemingly without a qualm, leave the ready room and head for the turbolift.

So, Kirk thought as the turbolift door opened on the corridor that led to the transporter room, *it's time.* No more guessing what the Vortex was or what the Guardian really wanted or even whose side the Guinan twins were really on.

It was time to find out. Time to start the process.

Time to be stored in the transporter's pattern buffer, where he would "wait" to be spat out when—if—the Vortex came within transporter range.

Not that he had any doubts . . .

Pulling in a breath, he stepped out into the corridor.

The Borg Queen was, once again, faced with the impossible.

The Picard creature's ship had disappeared.

It had not been destroyed. It had disappeared.

Nowhere in the teraquads of sensor data received from the hundreds of ships that had been closing in on the Picard creature was there anything to indicate what had happened to it.

Halfway to the Vortex, it had suddenly changed course in an obvious—and seemingly futile—attempt to elude the cluster of Borg ships that would have intercepted it within minutes.

But then it had entered one of the tiny but highly ionized nebulae that dotted this quadrant. And, unlike when it had ducked into that other, even smaller nebula, it had not come out.

A phalanx of Borg ships had swept through the entire nebula not once but twice and then a third time. There was no way the Picard creature's ship could have been missed, even with their ionization-limited sensors. Even if it had possessed its own version of the Alliance's "secret" weapon and used it to shift to a different level of reality, the inevitable and spectacular energy leakage would only have made it that much easier to detect.

Nor could it have exited from the nebula. Every cubic centimeter of surrounding space had been constantly monitored by at least two of the ships deployed around the nebula, all sensors of which were fully functional.

Could Picard have simply returned to wherever or whenever it had come from, she found herself wondering? According to data from the ships that had been monitoring the Vortex, the other, smaller interloper had literally appeared out of nowhere, just as the Narisian Balitor's information had claimed. And the smaller interloper had for some time now been stowed inside the larger. Who was to say that both could not then have returned to wherever or whenever they had come from?

But even if they had, were they no longer a threat? Or were they an even greater threat?

Unless she learned what had happened, she would never know the answer.

Until it was too late.

So completely connected to the cube that carried her that she had literally become a part of the ship, she began to reexamine the data, millisecond by millisecond, from each and every one of the more than a hundred cubes in and around the nebula.

Kirk stepped into the transporter circle.

Despite the suddenly churning stomach that had taken him by surprise as he stepped up onto the platform, he found himself grinning as he turned and looked down at Scotty and La Forge and the rest who had gathered to see him off. The only one that answered with even a subdued smile was Picard's odd friend, Guinan.

Earlier, before his final conversation with Picard, he had been filled with nervous uncertainty despite his calm but impatient exterior. Could he really trust the logic that told him that the Vortex was not synonymous with death? Should he trust Guinan's word that her twin had actually seen and spoken with the Guardian? And that this was indeed what the Guardian demanded?

But now, particularly after Picard's comment about "making a difference," Kirk's uneasiness had given way to a growing curiosity and excitement. It was, in a way, not unlike how he had felt the very first time he had been aboard a starship waiting for the warp drive to be engaged, waiting for energies he could barely comprehend to hurl him through dimensions and distances only mathematicians could describe.

Except that here no one—except possibly the Guinans?—had any idea where or when he was about to be hurled.

Which, now that the moment was almost here, just made him all the more curious, all the more excited.

This must be, he thought abruptly, *how Zefram Cochrane felt in the last few seconds before he took his life in his hands and engaged that very first, totally unproven, jury-rigged warp drive.*

Winking at Guinan, he pulled in a deep breath and stood up a little straighter as he turned to look at Scotty. "Let's get this show on the road, old friend, before whatever's controlling those cubes sees through your little miracle. If I don't see you again . . ." He shrugged lightly. Some thoughts didn't require voicing.

A moment later, the tingle of anticipation was replaced by the grip of the transporter energies.

The shimmering curtain enveloped him, obscuring the faces looking up at him.

With a sudden surge of almost boyish eagerness he hadn't felt since his retirement, he wondered what was going to happen next.

TWENTY-EIGHT

WITH PAINSTAKING deliberateness, the Borg Queen continued to re-examine the data, evaluating every aspect of every cube's sensor readings, not just those that the drones had been instructed to watch and act upon.

Finally, she found what she was looking for. Not Picard's ship, but a Borg cube—a cube that seemed, impossibly, to not be part of the armada she had just sent forth.

According to the data, it had first been sensed at the periphery of the stunted, overlapping sensor fields of two of the cubes sweeping the nebula and had then quickly taken up a position midway between the two. The interloper was not part of the phalanx performing the sweep and in fact was not itself producing a sensor scanning field of any detectable kind.

Sensor records of the cubes posted around the periphery of the nebula did not show the cube entering the nebula. They did, however, show it leaving. It had emerged from the nebula in company with the cubes performing the sweep. As the next sweep began, however, it had broken out of formation and headed away from the nebula on impulse power, moving in the general direction of the Vortex.

It took only seconds to confirm with a matrix-wide Link that all cubes were accounted for, not only those in the Terran armada but every single one she had constructed since the moment the time sphere had deposited her in the Terran system over two hundred years ago.

With growing uneasiness, she directed the sensors to focus on the projected path of the errant cube.

As she had expected, it had gone into warp drive minutes after leaving the nebula and was now only minutes from the Vortex and the cubes guarding it.

And it was still on a course that would take it within a few thousand kilometers of the Vortex.

Just as she had expected.

And feared.

"Time to transporter range, Mr. Data?" Picard asked, his eyes fixed on the image of the transporter room confined to the corner of the bridge viewscreen. Even as he spoke, Kirk, on one of the transporter pads, shimmered into nonexistence.

"Four minutes, thirty-seven seconds, Captain."

Even without the tweaking of the pattern buffer control circuits by La Forge and Scott, the matter stream that now contained all that currently existed of Captain James T. Kirk would be safe in the buffer for nearly seven minutes before the pattern began to degrade.

"Ready to complete transport, Mr. La Forge?" he asked redundantly.

"*Standing by, Captain. Transporters are operating on internal backup power.*"

Having Kirk already in the pattern buffer would essentially cut transport time—sitting-duck time—in half. Transferring to internal backup power in advance would avoid even momentary interruptions if they were hit and main power was lost. Even Picard's Locutus memories didn't tell him how much time would elapse between the moment he deactivated the deflectors and the moment the cubes, suddenly picking up the undisguised *Enterprise,* would begin firing. Every millisecond, however, could be critical.

On the viewscreen, the Vortex was already visible, even without sensor input. The image, derived from visual sub-systems only, was of course out of date by the several days it took light to travel the intervening distance through normal space. But it couldn't be helped. The Borg cube being simulated by the deflectors was sensor-opaque in both directions. Borg sensors couldn't see in and *Enterprise* sensors couldn't see out.

The two Borg cubes that had until hours ago been the only Borg ships in the vicinity of the Vortex appeared as tiny specks at approximately three and a half minutes out. The *Wisdom* and the Alliance observation platforms were of course still too small to be picked up. The new Borg cubes that had in reality positioned themselves around the Vortex several hours ago wouldn't be seen "arriving" until moments before the *Enterprise* dropped out of warp— within transporter range.

"Two minutes, Captain," Data said. "Chronometric radiation is increasing exponentially."

Picard's tension eased just slightly. Increased chronometric radiation was, according to unproven theory, indicative of increased instability. At some level, the timeline was already coming unraveled. The effects of whatever was about to happen were spreading in both directions through time, triggering the radiation just as their own "arrival" from the future had triggered a burst of radiation.

Whatever was about to happen . . .

Without warning, a half dozen Borg cubes appeared, not around the still-distant Vortex but around the *Enterprise* itself. Smoothly, effortlessly they matched its course.

Obviously the *Enterprise,* despite its "disguise," had been detected.

"Sixty seconds, Captain."

Before he could acknowledge Data's words, something closed around Picard's mind like an icy net, sending a new jolt of adrenaline through his body.

For a moment, he couldn't imagine what was happening to him, but as he tried instinctively to pull free, his Locutus memories recognized it:

A Borg Link.

Pausing only long enough to direct all the cubes surrounding the Vortex to "see" the approaching cube and to lock onto it as soon as it came within weapons range, the Borg Queen focused her mind on the approaching cube to the exclusion of all else.

And found herself Linked directly to the Picard creature!

Even though some part of her had been expecting precisely that, the reality was still a shock, momentarily freezing her thought processes as the "memories" of her own death at the creature's hands once more threatened to overwhelm her.

Recovering, she considered for another moment the possibility of using that Link to extract the information she wanted directly from Picard's mind, to find out where he had come from and how he had come to be here, but caution won out over curiosity. A Link might be precisely what the creature wanted. The Link would allow information to flow both ways, and she was at the point now where she feared that nothing was impossible in her dealings with this creature, whoever or whatever it really was, whenever and wherever it had come from.

Breaking the Link with Picard, she returned her full attention to the Link with the rest of the cubes. Their weapons systems, she noted with satisfaction, were already locking onto whatever it was that was carrying the Picard creature.

First one and then another fired, but the phaser blasts seemed to pass through the object with no effect.

After those two shots, before the other cubes could fire, all weapons locks were lost.

Impossibly, the object was gone!

In its place was not another ship, not even Picard's, but an irregular, pock-marked ovoid, apparently a small planetesimal traveling at warp speed.

A trick!

She had no idea how Picard had done it, but it *had* to be a trick of some kind, an illusion.

But it was an illusion that registered on Borg sensors and would prevent their weapons from even trying to regain their lock. The target they had been instructed to fire upon had vanished after two bursts of phaser fire. There was therefore no reason to fire again, no reason to lock onto this new and totally different object.

She couldn't take direct control of all weapons systems on all cubes quickly enough, but she was already in control of those in her own cube. Unlike the drones and the automated weapons systems, *she* was not limited to what was programmed into her. She could act independently.

And she did.

But even as she trained the weapons on the object and fired, it dropped out of warp.

And disappeared.

An instant later, the *Enterprise* appeared in its place, a tiny speck within the volume of space that had been occupied by the illusion. Her initial phaser blast shot through the area previously occupied by the vanished illusion but went harmlessly past the comparatively tiny ship offset several hundred meters from its center.

It took only seconds to redirect the phasers and fire a second salvo, followed by a series of photon torpedoes.

To her utter surprise, the ship's shields offered no resistance. It was as if they didn't exist.

Another trick? she wondered as one of the phaser blasts caught the ship solidly, sheering off one of the two linear extensions at the rear, sending the remains of the ship tumbling out of control.

Another illusion? she wondered as a substantial piece of the forward part of the saucer section was vaporized and a half dozen explosions erupted from other areas of the saucer.

And even as she continued to wonder, even as the remnants of the ship began to break up, the entire universe seemed to waver around her, as if *it* and not the ship being destroyed before her eyes was the illusion.

"Thirty seconds to transporter range," Data announced as a searing lance of phaser fire shot by only a few hundred meters away.

And another.

"Second image," Picard snapped.

An instant later, the holodeck computers switched from

the image of a Borg cube to that of an asteroid slightly larger than the cube had been. The visual subsystem images on the viewscreen shimmered for a split second but were otherwise unaffected by the reshaping of the deflector fields.

The Borg sensors, however, would see the asteroid, just as they had, until that moment, seen the cube. If Picard's Locutus memories were correct, the Borg ships would lose interest the moment the image changed—as long as they had not been programmed to deal with the new image. The Locutus memories had already been proven correct when the cubes had paid no attention to the sudden appearance of a new cube in their midst, so there was every reason to believe that this seemingly transparent subterfuge would also work. The Borg, at least at the drone level, did not deal well with the unexpected. Nor did they very often look out the window, so to speak, in order to see what was really happening.

All they needed was a few more seconds.

"Transporter range," Data announced.

Four things happened virtually simultaneously.

The *Enterprise* dropped out of warp drive.

Grimly, Worf disabled the deflectors, leaving the *Enterprise* both visible and defenseless.

Another bolt of phaser energy skimmed by, missing the *Enterprise* by less than a hundred meters.

And La Forge initiated the delayed second stage of Kirk's transport into the Vortex.

From the transporter room, Picard could hear—or at least imagined he could hear—the warble of the transporters as the matter stream that was Captain James Kirk was ejected from the pattern buffer and sent on its way to the heart of the Vortex more than ten thousand kilometers distant. Red warning lights were undoubtedly blinking wildly on the transporter console, indicating the destination was hazardous and unacceptable, but La Forge had already taken away the computer's ability to shut down the transmission and return the matter stream to the pattern buffer.

The ship shuddered as it was struck by the nearest cube's phaser fire. Lights flickered as emergency backup power came on line and what was left of the ship began to tumble helplessly.

A moment later, it shuddered again, even more violently from a second hit. Sparks erupted from every power bus as the viewscreen and all displays went dark for a moment, then briefly recovered.

"Hull breaches on all decks," the computer voice announced calmly in the moments before the last of the emergency power sources failed and the only light was the harsh glare of incoming fire.

In the transporter room, the last thing Geordi La Forge saw before everything went black was the barest flicker of the display indicating that transport was complete.

TWENTY-NINE

THE BORG QUEEN watched as the dispersing fragments of the Picard creature's ship seemed to melt and vanish into the now violently shifting background of stars while in the same instant the Borg ships that had destroyed it twisted into impossible shapes before they, too, vanished and the Borg Queen was enveloped in a terrible darkness that even her augmented senses could not penetrate.

For a few seconds or perhaps an eon, she drifted, feeling nothing, seeing nothing, until . . .

Suddenly, she was *living* the nightmarish memories of her own death. Picard's face loomed over her as his hands snapped in two the metallic spine that was all that remained of her body and let it fall to the floor . . .

And even as the rest of those memories blossomed and became real, even as they showed her dying mind how Picard had, in yet another timeline, pursued her back through time and defeated and then destroyed her . . .

. . . her consciousness faded and the final darkness enveloped her.

*　　*　　*

Captain Jean-Luc Picard's eyes snapped open, and for one terrifying moment he had no idea where he was. Fading memories of a dream—a nightmare—of the *Enterprise* disintegrating around him set his heart pounding even as his surroundings came into focus and he saw that he was in his quarters, in bed, his fingers in a claw-like grip on the crumpled sheet beneath his achingly rigid body.

Pulling in a breath, he released his grip, forced his body to relax, then sat up abruptly, taken with an intense desire to see the bridge and the crew—to see that the *Enterprise* was indeed still intact, still undamaged.

"Not that I don't appreciate what you were trying to do, Scotty, but there are no two ways about it. You screwed up royally."

Scotty came awake with a gasp, almost tipping over his chair as he jerked erect. Blinking away the startlingly vivid image of Jim Kirk, he tried to focus on the screen of the unfamiliar terminal before him.

For another instant he was still completely disoriented, unable to recognize his surroundings, but then the equations on the terminal screen came into sharp focus.

And he remembered.

He was in his guest quarters on board the *Enterprise*. The *new Enterprise*.

The equations were those that he had seen Spock use to slingshot the *Bounty* back through three centuries of time.

They were the equations *he* was going to use to take the *Bounty 2* back through time.

To save Jim Kirk.

His stomach knotted as he remembered Kirk's imagined words and realized that they were precisely what the captain *would* say if this mad scheme were to succeed.

And it *was* a mad scheme, the rational part of his mind told him harshly.

A mad scheme born not of common sense but of his own guilt, his own obsession.

A scheme that Kirk himself would certainly condemn—as he just had in that little scene that had apparently bubbled up from Scotty's own subconscious.

A subconscious which, he grudgingly admitted to himself, had a much better grip on reality than did his guilt-ridden conscious mind.

And the reality was that there were literally a million things that could go wrong on an ancient ship like the *Bounty 2,* no matter how well he took care of it. Even if everything worked perfectly, he would have to decloak a few seconds in order to use the transporters. Which meant that a Klingon bird-of-prey would appear, no matter how briefly, deep in Federation space at a time when the Khitomer Accords were less than a year old, at a time when Admiral Cartwright's treachery was common knowledge throughout both the Federation and the Klingon Empire.

Scotty shook his head. The precarious trust that had allowed the Accords to exist could be wiped out by a single incident, no matter how innocent.

And that was only one scenario. When you meddled in the past, the possibilities for disaster were infinite.

It would have been sheer insanity to take the kind of risk he had been planning to take just to save a single life, even if that life was that of his best friend. Kirk himself had taken risks all his life, but never anything as daft as this. Both the stakes and the odds were unacceptably high while the potential reward loomed large only on a personal level. Friendship was important, even sacred, but he couldn't allow it to totally blind him to the consequences of his actions.

True friendship meant knowing when to let go.

With one last, wistful look at the equations, Scotty cleared them away—and found himself confronted with a series of engineering specs scrolling across the screen.

For a moment he didn't recognize them, but then he remembered. In the weeks after he had first been brought on board this *Enterprise,* after he had been deservedly exiled from engineering itself, he had begun skimming through the engineering specs that described all the marvels of this new *Enterprise.* Surely, he had thought, the technology couldn't be totally beyond his understanding. Surely the basic rules still applied. Surely he could eventually prove he wasn't the technological dinosaur La Forge assumed he was.

In the end, however, all he had learned was that he *was* a technological dinosaur. And these were the very specs that had proven it: the specs for the holodeck and the computers that drove it. He had had some wild ideas about tying them in with the deflector system to produce a cloaking effect of sorts. But La Forge had shot him down, quickly and easily. That sort of thing just wasn't possible.

Except . . .

It *was* possible!

Somehow, without knowing how he knew, he *knew!*

For an instant, it was as if he was remembering having actually *done* it, as if he was remembering the elation he'd felt as the pieces of the puzzle had suddenly fallen into place.

But that was obviously impossible.

And yet . . .

But it doesn't make any bloody difference, he told himself sharply. Whatever the reason, he *knew* that his supposedly wild ideas would work. All he had to do was prove it!

And to do that . . .

To do that—and a thousand other things—he would have to do what he *should* have done right from the start: quit living in the past and start catching up with the present.

Suddenly, instead of being depressed at the thought of how much he had to learn in order to catch up, he felt just the opposite: exhilarated at the thought of how much he *could* learn, how much there *was* to learn. It was, he realized with an anticipatory shiver, much the same way he had felt when he first learned he had been accepted into the Academy.

Dinosaur I may be, but this is one dinosaur that won't be going extinct any time soon!

Blanking the screen, he stood up and headed for the bridge, hoping Picard's offer to arrange transportation to Earth and Starfleet Academy was still good.

Kirk looked around at the forest and the rustic cabin nestling in a clearing and wondered idly where he was and how he had gotten there.

He'd been in the guts of the *Enterprise*-B, he remembered, tearing something apart and putting it back together when the bulkhead had disappeared and he'd found himself looking out at a blinding wall of flame and lightning and being sucked out like a feather in a tornado, and—

Or had it been the *Enterprise*-D? No, that couldn't be. There wasn't any such ship, and besides—

Besides, he realized as he heard a horse whinnying somewhere in the distance, it didn't really matter, any of it.

Wherever he was, it was where he belonged.

At least for now . . .

* * *

Feelings of both satisfaction and sadness swept over Guinan as she turned from the viewscreen and saw Picard emerge from the turbolift and look slowly, almost reverently, around the bridge, as if seeing it for the first time.

As happened all too often, her feelings of satisfaction were as anonymous as their exasperating, even infuriating source, whoever or whatever it might be. They suggested only that—somewhere, somewhen—some unspecified words or actions dictated by past feelings had finally had the desired effect.

The source of the sadness, however, was disconcertingly specific: the death of her world at the hands of the Borg. She had lived with the sadness, gradually overcoming it, for over a century. She thought she had succeeded in at least containing it, but she obviously had not.

But then, as Picard's eyes met hers and the turbolift door slid open again, this time to reveal a happily grinning Captain Scott, the sadness was swept away in the most irrationally intense feeling of satisfaction, of "rightness" she had ever experienced.

For a moment—just a moment—she didn't even care that she had no idea what it was she had accomplished this time.

Epilogue

Somewhere in the Nexus

ALL WAS as it must be.

The Hive Mind would never reign supreme, stultifying life across billions of galaxies as it searched for its warped version of perfection.

The seed of its eventual destruction had been sown. Even the Guinan that existed here—the "echo" that always had and always would exist in this place that was both outside space and time and yet inside the minds of all who dwelt here—even that Guinan did not know how or when the Hive Mind would come to an end, only that it would.

There were many things, that among them, which she truly did not want to know. To know everything, she suspected, would be intolerable, dooming her to a Q-like tedium broken only by meaningless but deadly games of pretend.

To know that all was as it must be was enough.

For now . . .

Historian's Note

The Montgomery Scott Engineering Sciences Complex in the new Starfleet Academy was dedicated on the 200th anniversary of his birth. Professor Scott himself, sporting a trim white beard grown on a whim just for the occasion, cut the ribbon.

About the Author

Gene DeWeese, author of forty previous books including five and a half *Star Trek* novels, lives in Milwaukee with his retired-librarian wife and sundry cats.

STAR TREK

Sam Bellotto Jr.

ACROSS
1 Bajoran cell
5 Made for a colony of ex-Borg in "Unity" [VGR]
9 Justice Boonback
13 Use an energy containment cell
15 Kind of carnage in "Shadowplay" [DS9]
16 God-like computer in "The Apple" [TOS]
17 Arachnid with half-meter-long legs
19 Dax symbiont who succeeded Jadzia
20 Toor on Capella IV in "Friday's Child" [TOS]
21 Be a breadwinner
23 Spanish wave
24 2024 San Francisco problem
26 Science station Tango ____
29 PC alphanumeric abbr.
31 Soufflé
33 Taxi
34 Like 17 Across
36 Omicron ____ star system
39 Assault weapon
40 T'Lani government envoy in "Armageddon Game" [DS9]
43 Opposite of dep.
44 Whitewashed
46 ____ Twog (Klingon dishes)
48 Shogun capital
49 Bajoran poet Akorem in "Accession" [DS9]
50 Elevator inventor
51 Homeworld of two passengers sent to DS9 in "Babel"
53 Leader before Lenin
55 Altairian beverage served in Ten-Forward
60 Mass. motto word
56 ____ wing-slug
61 ____ caves of No'Mat
63 Lifeform indigenous to the Ocillian homeworld
66 Lt. Paris spent time here
67 Radiate
69 Female commander who offered Kirk tranya
69 Klaang escaped from one in "Broken Bow" [ENT]
70 Caps for Scotty
71 Söfjörð: Prefix

DOWN
1 Royal letters
2 Samoan friend of Jadzia Dax
3 Cheese trestle
4 Base where the Magellan crew put on a talent show
5 Natalie who played Drex
6 Used a travel pod
7 Restless
8 "Enterprise" supervising producer Howard
9 Brannon in "Violations" [TNG]
10 Tenkassian imaginary friend of Guinan as a child
11 McGivers who befriends Khan in "Space Seed" [TOS]
12 Saturn-ander
14 Actor Morales
16 ____ and Loser" [DS9]
22 Alpha-centura ____
25 Solvet
27 Superdome shout
35 Member of Klingon Intelligence in "Visionary" [DS9]
28 Regime on Ekos in "Patterns of Force" [TOS]
30 Danebian creature Korax compared to Kirk
32 Parent of P'Chan in "Survival Instinct" [VGR]
35 Modernized
37 Deanna on "Star Trek: The Next Generation"
38 Pound sounds
41 Warp core reactor output
42 Captain of the U.S.S. Equinox also in the Delta Quadrant
45 Author LeShan
47 Tactical officer on night shift in "Figurin's Hole" [TNG]
49 Bajoran grain-processing center
51 Kee is kidnapped to this planet in "Wasted" [VGR]
52 Tanandra Bay, for one
54 Show horse
55 Friendly robes
57 "Inter Arma ____ Silent Leges" [DS9]
58 Sect of the Kazon Collective
59 Miles O'Brien's coffee-cutoff hour
62 Of old
64 Gigatons: Abbr.
65 Fight finisher

STAR TREK CROSSWORD SERIES

---

50 ACROSS: Puzzles worked
on for amusement
CROSSWORDS
by New York Times
crossword puzzle
editor John M. Samson

Collect all four!
Available now wherever books are sold!

STCR.05

WARP INTO 2005...

STAR TREK

Wall calendars celebrating

STAR TREK

STAR TREK: ENTERPRISE

and

STAR TREK: SHIPS OF THE LINE

plus the

STAR TREK: STARDATE DAY-TO-DAY CALENDAR

Incorporating the entire Star Trek universe, with photos of all of your favorite characters and episodes!

NOW AVAILABLE

CLDR.01

STAR TREK

First in an all-new series!

Following the harrowing events of the
Errand of Vengeance trilogy, tensions
between the Federation and the Klingon
Empire are the highest they've been...

Errand of Fury:
Book One:
Seeds of Rage

by
Kevin Ryan

Available next month wherever books are sold!